Southern African Folktales

Southern African Folktales

Introduction by
Prof Enongene Mirabeau Sone

General Editor: Jake Jackson

**FLAME TREE
PUBLISHING**

This is a FLAME TREE Book

FLAME TREE PUBLISHING
6 Melbray Mews
Fulham, London SW6 3NS
United Kingdom
www.flametreepublishing.com

First published 2023
Copyright © 2023 Flame Tree Publishing Ltd

23 25 27 26 24
3 5 7 9 8 6 4 2

ISBN: 978-1-80417-582-8

The cover image is © copyright 2022 Flame Tree Publishing Ltd,
based on artwork courtesy of Shutterstock.com/Yuri Schmidt.

All inside images courtesy of Shutterstock.com and the
following: nadiia, Dervish45, Wiktoria Matynia, PO11.

The text in this book is selected and edited from the following original sources:
An expedition of discovery into the interior of Africa, by Sir James Edward
Alexander, 1838 (London: Henry Colburn); *Basutoland: Its Legends and Customs*
by Minnie Martin, 1903 (Nichols & Co.); *Folk-Tales Of Angola: Fifty Tales*, ed. Heli
Chatelain, 1894 (Houghton Mifflin and Co.); *Kaffir Folk-Lore* by Georg McCall Theal,
1886 (S. Sonnenschein, Le Bas & Lowrey); *Myths And Legends of the Bantu* by Alice
Werner, 1933; *Songs and Tales from the Dark Continent* by Natalie Curtis, recorded
from Madikane Cele, 1920 (G. Schirmer); *South-African Folk-Tales* by James A.
Honey, M.D., 1910 (The Baker & Taylor Co.); *Specimens of Bushman Folklore* by
W.H.I. Bleek and L.C. Lloyd, 1911 (George Allen & Co. Ltd); *The Grey Fairy Book*, ed.
Andrew Lang, 1905 (Longmans, Green & Co.); *The Ila-speaking peoples of Northern
Rhodesia* by Rev. Edwin W. Smith and Captain Andrew Murray Dale, 1920 (Macmillan
& Co.); *The Orange Fairy Book* by Andrew Lang, 1906 (Longmans, Green & Co.).

Printed and bound in China

Contents

Series Foreword

STRETCHING BACK to the oral traditions of thousands of years ago, tales of heroes and disaster, creation and conquest have been told by many different civilizations in many different ways. Their impact sits deep within our culture even though the detail in the tales themselves are a loose mix of historical record, transformed narrative and the distortions of hundreds of storytellers.

Today the language of mythology lives with us: our mood is jovial, our countenance is saturnine, we are narcissistic and our modern life is hermetically sealed from others. The nuances of myths and legends form part of our daily routines and help us navigate the world around us, with its half truths and biased reported facts.

The nature of a myth is that its story is already known by most of those who hear it, or read it. Every generation brings a new emphasis, but the fundamentals remain the same: a desire to understand and describe the events and relationships of the world. Many of the great stories are archetypes that help us find our own place, equipping us with tools for self-understanding, both individually and as part of a broader culture.

For Western societies it is Greek mythology that speaks to us most clearly. It greatly influenced the mythological heritage of the ancient Roman civilization and is the lens through which we still see the Celts, the Norse and many of the other great peoples and religions. The Greeks themselves learned much from their neighbours, the Egyptians, an older culture that became weak with age and incestuous leadership.

It is important to understand that what we perceive now as mythology had its own origins in perceptions of the divine and the rituals of the sacred. The earliest civilizations, in the crucible of the Middle East, in the Sumer of the third millennium BC, are the source to which many of the mythic archetypes can be traced. As humankind collected together in cities for the first time, developed writing and industrial scale agriculture, started to irrigate the rivers and attempted to control rather than be at the mercy of its environment, humanity began to write down its tentative explanations of natural events, of floods and plagues, of disease.

Early stories tell of Gods (or god-like animals in the case of tribal societies such as African, Native American or Aboriginal cultures) who are crafty and use their wits to survive, and it is reasonable to suggest that these were the first rulers of the gathering peoples of the earth, later elevated to god-like status with the distance of time. Such tales became more political as cities vied with each other for supremacy, creating new Gods, new hierarchies for their pantheons. The older Gods took on primordial roles and became the preserve of creation and destruction, leaving the new gods to deal with more current, everyday affairs. Empires rose and fell, with Babylon assuming the mantle from Sumeria in the 1800s BC, then in turn to be swept away by the Assyrians of the 1200s BC; then the Assyrians and the Egyptians were subjugated by the Greeks, the Greeks by the Romans and so on, leading to the spread and assimilation of common themes, ideas and stories throughout the world.

The survival of history is dependent on the telling of good tales, but each one must have the 'feeling' of truth, otherwise it will be ignored. Around the firesides, or embedded in a book or a computer, the myths and legends of the past are still the living materials of retold myth, not restricted to an exploration of origins. Now we have devices and global communications that give us unparalleled access to a diversity of traditions. We can find out about Native American, Indian, Chinese and tribal African mythology in a way that was denied to our ancestors, we can find connections, match the archaeology, religion and the mythologies of the world to build a comprehensive image of the human experience that is endlessly fascinating.

The stories in this book provide an introduction to the themes and concerns of the myths and legends of their respective cultures, with a short introduction to provide a linguistic, geographic and political context. This is where the myths have arrived today, but undoubtedly over the next millennia, they will transform again whilst retaining their essential truths and signs.

Jake Jackson
General Editor

Introduction to Southern African Folktales

Africa and the Art of Storytelling

'We all tell stories about our lives, both to ourselves and to others; and it is through such stories that we make sense of ourselves, of the world, and of our relationship to others. Stories, or narratives, are a means by which people make sense of, understand, and live their lives.'
Stephanie Lawler in *Mothering the Self: Mothers, Daughters, Subjects* (2000)

ONE OF THE MOST POPULAR traditions in Africa is storytelling. From the earliest times to the present, every society, culture and people have told stories that have passed from one generation to the next. These stories have maintained their presence for centuries, because they are amusing, interesting and instructive. In other words, stories let us express and shape ourselves, interpret the world and seek to influence others.

Irrespective of the modern phenomena of television and home videos, telling stories orally continues to be the main means of entertainment around the world. The most popular belief among Africans is that these stories, beyond their entertainment value, are also didactic instruments. Thus, storytelling in traditional Africa, as elsewhere, is an important event since it provides an occasion for storytellers to transmit a people's norms, values, ideas and thoughts through the narration of folktales, myths and legends. Although this age-long tradition has been neglected in recent years because of modernization and the advent technological developments, there is a need to restore interest in oral storytelling in our homes and schools, especially in primary and secondary schools, during the formative period of our children's lives. This would help to shape our children's values, condition their moral responsibilities and help them govern their emotions and appetites, as well as stimulate their creativity.

In Africa, traditional values form part of the intangible aspects of our cultures. However, these cultural values are under threat of erosion, especially among the youth, because of the forces of globalization and other forms of modern commercial entertainment that have already reached remote areas of the continent. Our folktales could be used as a tool to challenge these forces, because they hold much potential for inculcating traditional values in our children. As emphasized in the Convention for the Safeguarding of Intangible Cultural Heritage of UNESCO (2003), stories play an invaluable role, along with other cultural traditions, in bringing people together and 'ensuring exchange and understanding among them'. As globalization and social transformation demand renewed dialogue among communities, educators and artists are increasingly motivated to protect and promote oral traditions and related forms of cultural heritage. As a result, the art of storytelling enables us to integrate our consciousness, educate our minds, purify our souls and refine our sensibilities. The story speaks directly to the human heart, soul and mind, and engages our sympathy in a manner that straightforward ideas and logical arguments do not.

Introducing Southern Africa

Southern Africa is the southernmost region of Africa, south of the Democratic Republic of the Congo and Tanzania. The United Nations' scheme of geographic regions identifies the following five countries as making up southern Africa: Botswana, Namibia, Lesotho, Eswatini (Swaziland) and South Africa. However, many scholars argue that the U.N. definition of southern Africa is too limiting and does not properly express geographic and cultural ties in the region. These individuals support a broader definition of southern Africa that includes other countries in addition to those found in the U.N. definition. These countries are Angola (also included in central Africa), Mozambique and Madagascar (also included in eastern Africa), Malawi, Zambia and Zimbabwe (sometimes included in southern Africa and formerly of the Central African Federation), Comoros, Mauritius, Seychelles, Mayotte and Reunion (small island territories in the Indian Ocean, east of the African mainland).

In this book, the following countries will be considered as being part of southern Africa: Angola, Botswana, Eswatini, Lesotho, Malawi, Mozambique, Namibia, South Africa, Zambia and Zimbabwe. This is because these different countries in the region have similar cultures and traditions. The majority of the population groups of southern Africa are those that classify themselves as Black or indigenous people, but this grouping is not culturally or linguistically homogenous. The major ethnic groups are the Zulus, Xhosas, Bapedis (northern Sotho), Batswana, South Ndebele, Basotho (south Sotho), Venda, Tsonga and Swazis, all of which predominantly speak southern Bantu languages. It should be noted that many Black ethnic groups in South Africa are also found across neighbouring countries. For example, the Basotho are the majority ethnic group in Lesotho. The Tswana ethnic group constitute the majority of the population of Botswana. The Swazi ethnic group is the majority in Eswatini (Swaziland), and the Tsonga ethnic group is found in southern Mozambique, where they are also known as the Shangaan.

Notwithstanding the extraordinary tribal and ethnic diversity on the African continent, southern African traditional beliefs and worldviews are similar to beliefs and worldviews in other parts of Africa. As a result, most of the folktales in this book are similar to those from beyond the borders of southern Africa. In other words, what is true of the folktales (oral narratives) of the southern African region is also true, to a large extent, of the oral tales of other communities in Africa.

The Study of African Oral Narratives

The study of the oral narratives has always been a multidisciplinary pursuit. Sociologists, anthropologists and folklorists have collected a vast quantity of oral tales and also developed several seemingly irreconcilable approaches to the study of the folktale based on their disciplinary allegiances. The battles that have raged among proponents of the different approaches have been discussed in so much detail that it would be futile to repeat the exercise here. However, it is important to note that the clashes profoundly affected the direction of subsequent research. As historicist Robert A. Georges has stated in his article 'Toward an Understanding of Storytelling Events' (1969), 'They reinforced the notion that stories were surviving or traditional linguistic entities, and they motivated investigators to record additional story texts and to study the content of these texts in order to discover what information they might convey about the history and nature of man and culture. The first of these became the basic premise and the second the primary objective of twentieth-century story research.' Furthermore, the conclusions arrived at by scholars who assessed the controversies and contributions of the adversaries are important to the purpose of this collection of tales, so it is useful to outline some of them here.

Linguistic anthropologist Ruth Finnegan is of the opinion, in *Oral Literature in Africa* (1970), that many of the earlier approaches to the study of oral narratives in Africa have been inadequate in the sense that they have not only obscured certain points of interest, but have also given rise to several unexamined assumptions about the nature and role of the oral narratives. Sociolinguist P.N. Mbangwana, in his thesis *Cameroon Oral Tales in Ngemba: A Study in Language and Social Setting* (1982), emphasizes the point this way: '...though the inadequacies of the various perspectives have been suggested, one must be reminded that the assumptions resulting from these perspectives were formulated within a certain intellectual climate. Rooted in such a historical background, the assumptions might have been based, or probably not, on solid empirical evidence. Bearing this in mind, it has been shown how the different approaches popularised and perpetuated only certain aspects of the folk traditions, thus, narrowing its scope and growth.'

Nigerian classicist and scholar Isidore Okpewho maintains in his *Myth in Africa* (1983) that 'since the various approaches inevitably merge into one another, it is only logical that they should be seen as complementary rather than conflicting'. Robert A. Georges, for his part, opines:

> *...the study of the story texts amounts to nothing more than the study of written representations of one aspect of the messages of complex communicative events referred to as 'storytelling event'. If investigators expect to understand these events, they must conceive of them holistically rather than atomistically. This will only be possible when researchers recognize the fact that storytelling events are distinct events within a continuum of human communication and that they are unique social experiences for those individuals whose social interactions generate them.*

The above assessments of the story (oral narrative) research, when considered collectively, can be said to emphasize three points. First, they reveal that none of the multitude of approaches to the study of the oral narrative that are extant can be said to be adequate in themselves. Secondly, they call into question the basic premise of oral narrative research and the primary objectives of the study of stories (that the way to discover which information stories might convey about the history and nature of man and culture is to collect story texts and to study the content conveyed by linguistic coding). And, thirdly, they suggest the need for utilizing new or modified approaches to the study of the oral tale. Since none of the approaches is completely satisfactory, the researcher may have to choose an approach which is primarily eclectic.

This book shows that the oral narrative (tale) is a narrative discourse, because it relates events that have already taken place. The tale is usually told using the first- or third-person narrative point of view, and it has a plot which distinguishes it from other genres of discourse.

Previous Studies in Southern African Oral Narratives

Southern African tradition is not homogenous, but a blend of different traditions and cultures practiced by different ethnic groups in the region. The study of African oral narratives is beset by a number of problems, one of which is the dearth of appropriate texts. It is therefore a great delight to introduce *Southern African Folktales* in the Myths and Legends series.

In southern Africa, most of the pioneering works on folktales occurred within the context of colonization. For example, missionaries sought to understand their prospective converts, as well as the languages they spoke. Governors and magistrates wanted to find better ways to govern the people, and this led to their interest in folklore. As a result, the collection and documentation of southern African folktales during the colonial/apartheid period was done mostly from the perspective of colonial administration – and it is evident, as Professor of African Literature and Folklore E.M. Sone made clear in his PhD dissertation 'Symbolism of the Mountain in Bakossi-Cameroon Mythology' (2012), that not all aspects of oral literature were represented, because of the collecting, the collectors themselves or the manner of the collections. This was also because of the editorial requirements of the colonizers. Other collectors were more interested in translating and 'modernizing' the stories for Western consumption. A large number of collectors saw African oral narratives as the answer to literacy problems of Black people.

In post-colonial and/or post-apartheid southern Africa, apart from the few authors who have collected and published oral narratives about their respective cultures and countries, no collection of folktales has been published that includes the entire southern African region. This explains why the bringing together of this collection is a welcome initiative.

Classification of African Oral Narratives

In most cases, scholars have been unable to draw a convincing line of distinction between the different forms of oral narratives as myths, legends and folktales. One reason for this is the ambiguity and fluidity of the oral narratives as a whole. As American folklorist William Bascom has rightly remarked, in his article 'The Forms of Folklore: Prose Narratives' (1965), the different forms of oral narratives tend to overlap. 'In passing from one society to another through diffusion, a myth or legend may be accepted without being believed, thus becoming a folktale in the borrowing society; and the reverse may also happen,' Bascom states. 'It is entirely possible that the same tale might be a folktale in one society, a legend in a second and a myth in the third.

Bascom uses the element of belief to account for why a tale can pass as a myth in one community and as legend or folktale in another. While acknowledging the fact that there is considerable potential for an overlap between the three basic forms of oral narratives, the problem of categorizing them still remains. In an attempt to resolve the problem, I intend to emphasize the interplay of fact and fiction within a specific tale. That is, when a tale gets closer to true history or real life, but at the same time acquires a fictive colouration in the course of transmission, it can be termed a 'legend'. In other words, a legend is made up of a combination of fact and fiction. Where there is a greater tendency towards fact, it becomes a 'historical legend' and when the greater tendency is towards fiction, it becomes a 'romantic' or 'mythic' legend.

To put it differently, a legend is set in historical time. In simple terms, legends, like myths, are prose narratives regarded by their creators and users as true, but unlike myths, legends are generally secular and are set in a much more remote historical period in a conventional earthly locale. According to Kashim Tala, in *Orature in Africa* (1999), 'They tell us about people who really lived, their origins, genealogies, migrations, wars, exploits and political victories'. In short, legends tell us the history of the people. That is why legends are sometimes referred to as 'folk history', although the history is inevitably distorted by oral transmission. The people themselves believe that these tales are true or that they concern events which actually took place in the lives of people. That explains why the term 'belief tale' is applied to legends.

It is, however, interesting to note that most African tales like the ones in this collection do not belong to specific time schemes. Such an undetermined time scheme has been called the 'mythical time' because the narrative genius of the narrator is not fettered by the constraints of time. The folktales in this category can be divided into two kinds: aetiological tales and fables. Aetiological, or 'why' tales, are used to explain natural phenomena or the origin of societal customs, while fables are mainly told for entertainment, although they may also teach morals.

As the Nigerian oralist H. Chukwuma asserts in his essay 'The Igbo Mythic Schema' (1987):

> *The oral tale is the traditional folktale. Its characteristics are brevity and terseness, episodic plot and action, climatic heightening of a central conflict and the limitation of character. The folktale... portrays an aspect of life and reality through varied means. The final goal is to bring to man a knowledge and awareness of his nature and environment...The folktale is a child of tradition, almost always apocryphal, belonging to the whole community. It enjoys abundant freedom and identifies with anyone in the community who can articulate it creditably. Plagiarism makes no sense with regard to the folktale, and for its purposes, the important feature is the performer and not the coiner.*

Folklorist Peter Seitel, for his part, in *See So that We May See: Performances and Interpretations of Traditional Tales from Tanzania* (2008), defines the folktale as 'metaphors for aspects of social life'. He states that they are 'abstract, artistic statements that objectify and grant perspective on the culture they describe. They enable [a group] to hold aspects of their social world at arm's length, so to speak, to examine them, and to entertain themselves with those images of their own lives.'

From the above definitions, it can be said that the folktale, by its very nature, is short. It restricts its focus to a narrow bit of experience; it avoids digressions from its main intentions; it utilizes easily recognizable characters; and it emphasizes the moral lessons inherent in the outcome of the fictive characters' actions. In other words, the folktale focuses on the dynamics between the individual and society. That explains why folktale characters are deliberately underdeveloped and why almost anything can be a character in the folktale. In addition, the folktale is a unified artistic statement which may give pleasure and share knowledge. It is orally realized in face-to-face contact that involves the storyteller and an audience. It encompasses a great variety of narrative elements, and its actions can take place at any time and in any location.

From the point of view of a myth, the concept has prompted innumerable definitions, showing how rich and controversial the domain is. As Martin S. Day remarks, in *The Many Meanings of Myth* (1987), 'definers of myth are as varied and irreconcilable as delegates to the United Nations'. This plethora of definitions has emerged because of increased concerns attached to its study. Without going into the depth of many definitions of a myth, professors Egbe Ifie and Dapo Adelugba note the advantages of African mythologists over others. In *African Culture and Mythology* (1998), they intimate that 'African mythologists are far more able to appreciate the nature of myths as a kind of oral literature. We at once realise that myths are a type of oral literature – a traditional tale – they must possess some special characteristics, some enduring quality that separate them from other stories.'

It is from this premise that African scholars (especially Okpewho) are able to contextualize and define myths. Okpewho argues that a myth has creative elements. In *Myth in Africa*, he further defines a myth this way:

> *It is not really a particular type of a tale against another; it is neither the spoken counterpart of an antecedent ritual, nor is it a tale determined exclusively by binary schema of abstract ideas or*

sequential order of elements. It is simply that quality of fancy, which informs the creative or configurative powers of the human mind in varying degrees of intensity. In that case, we are free to call any narrative of oral tradition a myth so long as it gives due emphasis to fanciful play that provides one's solid structural link between several generations of the concept of myth, first on oral narratives and now as a fanciful idea.

The novelty of Okpewho's definition is that it puts emphasis on phantasmagoria. That is, Okpewho sees a myth as a special kind of literature and, therefore, a matter of aesthetic experience and imagination. In other words, a myth is not only a product of scientific or rational development, but also of collective imagination. Thus, a myth may portray the human condition with accuracy, but it is nonetheless a fantasy. From this standpoint, one is obliged to say that this definition ties in with the title of this book, because it deals with the recreation myths that move from fact to fanciful play.

Since we intend to present myth in this collection as literature which offers psychological insights into the human condition, it is only natural that we subscribe to a definition which sees a myth either as a fanciful idea or story which is rich, colourful and inventive. Thus, for the purposes of this book, we shall define myths as prose narratives used by our forefathers to explain anything they found difficult to understand in this world. Myths are used to explain the origin of this world, the relationship between God and man, man and his natural environment, the moon and the stars and the origin of different races. We also intend to adopt Okpewho's definition of a myth as 'that quality of fancy which informs the creative or configurative powers of the human mind in varying degrees of intensity'. The interest in this book will be centred mainly on the various levels of fictive or symbolic characters of myths.

For the sake of this book, it is important to note that African myths in general are not as highly elaborate or highly poetic as some Western classical myths. Their plots are not too complicated. As myths migrate from one place to the other, the names of some characters also change, depending on the nomenclature of the people. Nevertheless, the content does not ultimately change, though the form might vary. Some slight modifications might also result from the creative ability of the narrator.

It should be noted the word 'myth' is comfortably used among the many ethnic groups in southern Africa because the oral form exists, although the inhabitants in their local languages do not differentiate it from other forms of oral narratives, such as folktales and legends, as it is done in the West. The important thing is that this oral form has all the characteristics of myths, though it might appear the same in other societies. The stories that explain the meaning of life among the southern African communities in the past and the present will serve as a point of focus for this book. They are true stories about the lives and activities of people in their environments, which are usually blended with fancy. Thus, a myth on this note is seen as a fictive imagination of the creative mind, generating poetic ideas through symbols and images of fantasy that embody reality and serves as a vehicle for philosophical and psychological speculations.

Enongene Mirabeau Sone (Introduction) is Professor of English and African Literature as well as Folklore Studies at Walter Sisulu University in South Africa. Prof. Sone holds a BA, MA and MPhil in African literature from the University of Dschang in Cameroon and completed his PhD in African oral literature studies from the University of KwaZulu-Natal, South Africa. He has taught in many universities in Africa and has published extensively on various aspects of African oral literature and folklore in reputable academic journals across the globe. His collaboration with leading world and African folklorists led to the publication of two seminal books in oral literature and folklore studies: *The Challenge of Folklore to the Humanities* (2021) edited by Dan Ben-Amos, and *The Palgrave Handbook of African Oral Traditions and Folklore* (2021) edited by Akintunde Akinyemi and Toyin Falola. He is a C2 rated researcher by the South African National Research Foundation (NRF).

Origins, Death &
The Afterlife

THIS SECTION consists mainly of myths that deal with the theme of creation, death and the afterlife. Some of the stories in this section recount how the world came into being, who the various gods are and what powers they control, how the actions of these gods affect the world and men and the means by which men can propitiate these powers.

Some of these myths also reveal to man what is beneficial to him, such as the arts, sources of food, the use of fire and setting forth societal values to guide the individual toward the standards and goals of his culture. The stories indicate that Africans are the products of their beliefs about their origin and the origin of the natural phenomena. The theme of creation, death and afterlife explains man's connection to Earth and divinity. It reinforces the belief that Africans do not regard death as the ultimate end of human existence. They have persisted in believing that man returns to the physical world after death. For them, the end, which is called death, is only a means to a new beginning. In other words, to many Africans, life becomes a theatre with reincarnation as the unique entrance and death as the natural escape gate. Every living person is conceived as having been introduced into the drama of life through reincarnation and must quit the scene when the drama is over through the one and only exit, death.

The Origin of Death; Preceded by a Prayer Addressed to the Young Moon
(From the San people, southern Africa)

WE, WHEN THE MOON has newly returned alive, when another person has shown us the Moon, we look towards the place at which the other has shown us the Moon, and, when we look thither, we perceive the Moon, and when we perceive it, we shut our eyes with our hands, we exclaim: "Kabbi-a yonder! Take my face yonder! Thou shalt give me thy face yonder! Thou shalt take my face yonder! That which does not feel pleasant. Thou shalt give me thy face – (with) which thou, when thou hast died, thou dost again living return, when we did not perceive thee, thou dost again lying down come – that I may also resemble thee. For, the joy yonder, thou dost always possess it yonder, that is, that thou art wont again to return alive, when we did not perceive thee; while the hare told thee about it, that thou shouldst do thus. Thou didst formerly say, that we should also again return alive, when we died."

The hare was the one who thus did. He spoke, he said, that he would not be silent, for, his mother would not again living return; for his mother was altogether dead. Therefore, he would cry greatly for his mother.

The Moon replying, said to the hare about it that the hare should leave off crying; for, his mother was not altogether dead. For, his mother meant that she would again living return. The hare replying, said that he was not willing to be silent; for, he know that his mother would not again return alive. For, she was altogether dead.

And the Moon became angry about it, that the hare spoke thus, while he did not assent to him (the Moon). And he hit with his fist, cleaving the hare's mouth; and while he hit the hare's mouth with his fist, he exclaimed: "This person, his mouth which is here, his mouth shall altogether be like this, even when he is a hare; he shall always bear a scar on his mouth; he shall spring away, he shall do-doubling(?) come back. The dogs shall chase him; they shall, when they have caught him, they shall grasping tear him to pieces, he shall altogether die.

"And they who are men, they shall altogether dying go away, when they die. For, he was not willing to agree with me, when I told him about it, that he should not cry for his mother; for, his mother would again live; he said to me, that, his mother would not again living return. Therefore, he shall altogether become a hare. And the people, they shall altogether die. For, he was the one who said that his mother would not again living return. I said to him about it, that they (the people) should also be like me; that which I do; that I, when I am dead, I again living return. He contradicted me, when I had told him about it."

Therefore, our mothers said to me, that the hare was formerly a man; when he had acted in this manner, then it was that the Moon cursed him, that he should altogether become a hare. Our mothers told me, that, the hare has human flesh at his *katten-ttu*; therefore, we, when we have killed a hare, when we intend to eat the hare, we take out the "biltong flesh" yonder, which is human flesh, we leave it; while we feel that he who is the hare, his flesh it is not. For, flesh (belonging to) the time when he formerly was a man, it is.

Therefore, our mothers were not willing for us to eat that small piece of meat; while they felt that it is this piece of meat with which the hare was formerly a man. Our mothers said to us about it, did we not feel that our stomachs were uneasy if we ate that little piece of meat, while we felt that it was human flesh; it is not hare's flesh; for, flesh which is still in the hare it is; while it feels that the hare was formerly a man. Therefore, it is still in the hare; while the hare's doings are those on account of which the Moon cursed us; that we should altogether die. For, we should, when we died, we should have again living returned; the hare was the one who did not assent to the Moon, when the Moon was willing to talk to him about it; he contradicted the Moon.

Therefore, the Moon spoke, he said: "Ye who are people, ye shall, when ye die, altogether dying vanish away. For, I said, that, ye should, when ye died, ye should again arise, ye should not altogether die. For, I, when I am dead, I again living return. I had intended, that, ye who are men, ye should also resemble me (and) do the things that I do; that I do not altogether dying go away. Ye, who are men, are those who did this deed; therefore, I had thought that I (would) give you joy. The hare, when I intended to tell him about it – while I felt that I knew that the hare's mother had not really died, for, she slept – the hare was the one who said to me, that his mother did not sleep; for, his mother had altogether died. These were the things that I became angry about; while I had thought that the hare would say: 'Yes; my mother is asleep.'"

For, on account of these things, he (the Moon) became angry with the hare; that the hare should have spoken in this manner, while the hare did not say: "Yes, my mother lies sleeping; she will presently arise." If the hare had assented to the Moon, then, we who are people, we should have resembled the Moon; for, the Moon had formerly said, that we should not altogether die. The hare's doings were those on account of which the Moon cursed us, and we die altogether; on account of the story which the hare was the one who told him. That story is the one on account of which we altogether die (and) go away; on account of the hare's doings; when he was the one who did not assent to the Moon; when the Moon intended to tell him about it; he contradicted the Moon, when the Moon intended to tell him about it.

The Moon spoke, saying that he (the hare) should lie upon a bare place; vermin should be those who were biting him, at the place where he was lying; he should not inhabit the bushes; for, he should lie upon a bare place; while he did not lie under a tree. He should be lying upon a bare place. Therefore, the hare is used, when he springs up, he goes along shaking his head; while he shakes out, making to fall the vermin from his head, in which the vermin had been hanging; while he feels that the vermin hung abundantly in his head. Therefore, he shakes his head, so that the other vermin may fall out for him.

Death
(From the San people, southern Africa)

THE STAR DOES in this manner, at the time when our heart falls down, that is the time when the star also falls down; while the star feels that our heart falls over. Therefore, the star falls down on account of it. For the stars know the time at which we die. The star tells the other people who do not know that we have died.

Therefore, the people act thus, when they have seen a star, when a star has fallen down, they say: "Behold ye! Why is it that the star falls down? We shall bear news; for a star falls down. Something which is not good appears to have occurred at another place; for the star tells us, that a bad thing has happened at another place."

The hamerkop [bird] acts in this manner, when a star has fallen, it comes; when it flies over us, it cries. [*Yak!* or *Yaak!* is the bird's cry, which it repeats twice.] The people say: "Did ye not hear the hamerkop [a large, brownish, crested African wading bird] when the star fell? It came to tell us that our person is dead." The people speak, they say that the hammerkop is not a thing which deceives, for it would not come to our home, if it did not know; for, when it knows, then it comes to our home; because it intends to come and tell us about it, namely, that our person has died.

Therefore, mother and the others used – if they heard a hammerkop, when it flew, going over us – to say: "Do thou go (and) plunge in, for I know that which thou camest to tell me", while mother and the others said that the story, which it came to tell, should go into the Orange River's water, where the stars stand in the water. That is the place where its stories should go in. For mother and the others did not want to hear the story which it came to tell; for they knew that the hammerkop does in this manner at the time when a man dies, that is the time at which it comes to us, it tells us about it, that the man has died. For, mother and the others used to say, that the hammerkop is a thing which lives at that water in which we see all things. Therefore, it knows what has happened; while it is aware that it lives at the water which is like a pool, in which we see all things; the things which are in the sky we see in the water, while we stand by the water's edge. We see all things, the stars look like fires which burn.

When it is night, when another man walks across, we see him, as he walks passing the water. It seems as if it were noonday, when he walks by the water. We see him clearly. The place seems as if it were midday as we see him walking along. Therefore, mother and the others said, that, when the hammerkop has espied in the water a person who has died, even though it be at a distance, when it knows that (he) is our relative, it flies away from this water, it flies to us, because it intends to go to tell us about it, that our relative has died. (It) and the star are those who tell us about it when we have not heard the news; for they are those who tell us about it, and when we have heard the hammerkop, we also perceive the star, we afterwards hear the news, when we have just perceived them; and we hear the news, when they have acted in this manner towards us.

For, mother and the others used to tell us about it, that girls are those whom the Rain carries off; and the girls remain at that water, to which the Rain had taken them, girls with whom the Rain is angry. The Rain lightens, killing them; they become stars, while their appearance has been changed. They become stars. For, mother and the others used to tell us about it, that a girl, when the Rain has carried her off, becomes like a flower which grows in the water.

We who do not know are apt(?) to do thus when we perceive them, as they stand in the water, when we see that they are so beautiful; we think, "I will go (and) take the flowers which are standing in the water. For they are not a little beautiful." Mother and the others said to us about it, that the flower – when it saw that we went towards it – would disappear in the water. We should think, "The flowers which were standing here, where are they? Why is it that I do not perceive them at the place where they stood, here?" It would disappear in the water, when it saw that we went towards it; we should not perceive it, for it would go into the water.

Therefore, mother and the others said to – as about it, that we ought not to go to the flowers which we see standing in the water, even if we see their beauty. For, they are girls whom the Rain has taken away, they resemble flowers; for (they) are the water's wives, and we look at them, leaving them alone. For we (should) also be like them (in) what they do.

Therefore, mother and the others do in this manner with regard to their Bushman women, they are not willing to allow them to walk about, when the Rain comes; for they are afraid that the Rain also intends, lightening, to kill them. For the Rain is a thing which does in this manner when it rains here, it smells our scent, it lightens out of the place where it rains. It lightens, killing us at this place; therefore, mother and the others told us about it, that when the Rain falls upon us (and) we walk passing through the Rain, if we see that the Rain lightens in the sky we must quickly look towards the place where the Rain lightens; the Rain, which intended to kill us by stealth. It will do in this manner, even if its thunderbolts have come near us, (if) we look towards (the place where it has lightened), we look, making its thunderbolts turn back from us; for our eye also shines like its thunderbolts. Therefore, it also appears to fear our eye, when it feels that we quickly look towards it. Therefore, it passes over us on account of it; while it feels that it respects our eye which shines upon it. Therefore, it goes over us; it goes to sit on the ground yonder, while it does not kill us.

The Relations of Wind, Moon and Cloud to Human Beings After Death
(From the San people, southern Africa)

THE WIND DOES thus when we die, our (own) wind blows; for we, who are human beings, we possess wind; we make clouds, when we die. Therefore, the wind does thus when we die, the wind makes dust, because it intends to blow, taking away our footprints, with which we had walked about while we still had nothing the matter with us; and our footprints, which the wind intends to blow away, would (otherwise still) lie plainly visible. For, the thing would seem as if we still lived. Therefore, the wind intends to blow, taking away our footprints.

And, our gall, when we die, sits in the sky; it sits green in the sky, when we are dead.

Therefore, mother was wont to do thus when the moon lying down came, (when) the moon stood hollow. Mother spoke, she said: "The moon is carrying people who are dead. For, ye are those who see that it lies in this manner; and it lies hollow, because it is killing itself (by) carrying people who are dead. This is why it lies hollow. It is not a *k'auru*; for, it is a moon of badness(?). Ye may (expect to) hear something, when the moon lies in this manner. A person is the one who has died, he whom the moon carries. Therefore, ye may (expect to) hear what has happened, when the moon is like this."

The hair of our head will resemble clouds, when we die, when we in this manner make clouds. These things are those which resemble clouds; and

ORIGINS, DEATH & THE AFTERLIFE

we think that (they) are clouds. We, who do not know, we are those who think in this manner, that (they) are clouds. We, who know, when we see that they are like this, we know that (they) are a person's clouds; (that they) are the hair of his head. We, who know, we are those who think thus, while we feel that we seeing recognize the clouds, how the clouds do in this manner form themselves.

Concerning Two Apparitions
(From the San people, southern Africa)

WE BURIED MY WIFE in the afternoon. When we had finished burying her, we returned to the home of my sister, Whai-ttu, and the other people, whence they had come forth. They had come to bury my wife with me; and we went away, crossing over the salt pan.

And we perceived a thing, which looked like a little child, as it sat upon the salt pan, seeming as if it sat with its legs crossed over each other.

And my sister, Whai-ttu, spoke, she questioned us: "Look ye! What thing sits yonder upon the salt pan? It is like a little child." And Kweiten-ta-ken [another sister] spoke, she asked us: "Look ye! Why is it that this thing is truly like a person? It seems as if it had on the cap which Ddiakwain's wife used to wear." And my sister, Whai-ttu, spoke, she answered: "Yes, O my younger sister! The thing truly resembles that which brother's wife was like." It did thus as we went along, it seemed as if it sat looking (towards) the place from which we came out.

And Ku-ang spoke, she said: The old people used to tell me, that the angry people were wont to act thus, at the time when they took a person away, they used to allow the person to be in front of us, (so that) we might see it. Ye know that she really had a very little child, therefore, ye should allow us to look at the thing which sits upon this salt pan; it strongly resembles a person, its head is there, like a person." And I spoke, I said: "Wait! I will do thus, as I return to my home, I will see, whether I shall again perceive it, as it sits."

And we went to their home. And we talked there, for a little while. And I spoke, I said to them that they appeared to think that I did not wish to return (home); for the sun was setting. And I returned on account of it. I thought that I would go in the same manner as we had come; that I might, going along, look whether I should again perceive it, as it sat. Going along I looked at the place, where it had sat; because of thought that it might have been a bush. I saw that I did not perceive it, at the place where it had sat. And I agreed that it must have been a different kind of thing.

For my mothers used to tell me that, when the sorcerers are those who take us away, at the time when they intend to take us quite away, that is the time when our friend is in front of us, while he desires that we may perceive him, because he feels that he still thinks of us. Therefore, his outer skin still looks at us, because he feels that he does not want to go away (and) leave us; for he insists upon coming to us. Therefore, we still perceive him on account of it.

My sister's husband, Mansse, told us about it, that it had happened to him, when he was hunting about, as he was going along, he espied a little child, peeping at him by the side of a bush. And he thought: "Can it be my child who seems to have run after me? It seems to have lost its way, while it seems to have followed me." And Mansse thought: "Allow me to walk nearer, that I may look at this child (to see) what child (it) be."

And Mansse saw that the child acted in this manner, when the child saw that he was going up to it, that he might see what child it was, he saw that the child appeared as if it feared him. The child sat behind the bush; the child looked from side to side; it seemed as if it wanted to run away. And he walked, going near to it; and the child arose, on account of it. It walked away, looking from side to side; it seemed as if it wanted to run away.

And Mansse looked (to see) why it was that the child did not wish him to come to it; and the child seemed to be afraid of him. And he examined the child; as the child stood looking at him. He saw that it was a little girl; he saw that the child was like a person. In other parts (of it) it was not like a person; be thought that he would let the child alone. For a child who was afraid of him was here. And he walked on, while the child stood looking from side to side. And (as) the child saw that he went away from it, it came forward (near the bush), it sat down.

The Girl of the Early Race,
Who Made Stars
(From the San people, southern Africa)

M Y MOTHER WAS THE ONE WHO TOLD ME that the girl arose; she put her hands into the wood ashes; she threw up the wood ashes into the sky. She said to the wood ashes: "The wood ashes which are here, they must altogether become the Milky Way. They must white lie along in the sky, that the stars may stand outside of the Milky Way, while the Milky Way is the Milky Way, while it used to be wood ashes." They (the ashes) altogether become the Milky Way. The Milky Way must go round with the stars; while the Milky Way feels that, the Milky Way lies going round; while the stars sail along; therefore, the Milky Way, lying, goes along with the stars. The Milky Way, when the Milky Way stands upon the earth, the Milky Way turns across in front, while the Milky Way means to wait(?), While the Milky Way feels that the Stars are turning back; while the Stars feel that the Sun is the one who has turned back; he is upon his path; the Stars turn back; while they go to fetch the daybreak; that they may lie nicely, while the Milky Way lies nicely. The Stars shall also stand nicely around.

They shall sail along upon their footprints, which they, always sailing along, are following. While they feel that, they are the Stars which descend.

The Milky Way lying comes to its place, to which the girl threw up the wood ashes, that it may descend nicely; it had lying gone along, while it felt that it lay upon the sky. It had lying gone round, while it felt that the Stars also turned round. They turning round passed over the sky. The sky lies (still); the Stars are those which go along; while they feel that they sail. They had been setting; they had, again, been coming out; they had, sailing along, been following their footprints. They become white, when the Sun comes out. The Sun sets, they stand around above; while they feel that they did turning follow the Sun.

The darkness comes out; they (the Stars) wax red, while they had at first been white. They feel that they stand brightly around; that they may sail along; while they feel that it is night. Then, the people go by night; while they feel that the ground is made light. While they feel that the Stars shine a little. Darkness is upon the ground. The Milky Way gently glows; while it feels that it is wood ashes. Therefore, it gently glows. While it feels that the girl was the one who said that the Milky Way should give a little light for the people, that they might return home by night, in the middle of the night. For, the earth would not have been a little light, had not the Milky Way been there. It and the Stars.

The girl thought that she would throw up (into the air) roots of the *huing* (a scented root eaten by some Bushmen), in order that the *huing* roots should become Stars; therefore, the Stars are red; while they feel that (they) are *huing* roots.

She first gently threw up wood ashes into the sky, that she might presently throw up *huing* roots; while she felt that she was angry with her mother, because her mother had not given her many *huing* roots, that she might eat abundantly; for, she was in the hut. She did not herself go out to seek food; that she might get(?) *huing* for herself; that she might be bringing it (home) for herself; that she might eat; for, she was hungry; while she lay ill in the hut. Her mothers were those who went out. They were those who sought for food. They were bringing home *huing*, that they might eat. She lay in her little hut, which her mother had made for her. Her stick stood there; because she did not yet dig out food. And, she was still in the hut. Her mother was the one who was bringing her food. That she might be eating, lying in the little hut; while her mother thought that she (the girl) did not eat the young men's game (i.e. game killed by them). For, she ate the game of her father, who was an old man. While she thought that the hands of the young men would become cool. Then, the arrow would become cool. The arrow head which is at the top, it would be cold; while the arrow head felt that the bow was cold; while the bow felt that his (the young man's) hands were cold. While the girl thought of her saliva, which, eating, she had put into the springbok meat; this saliva would go into the bow, the inside of the bow would become cool; she, in this manner, thought. Therefore, she feared the young men's game. Her father was the one from whom she alone ate (game). While she felt that she had worked (i.e. treated) her father's hands: she had worked, taking away her saliva (from them).

How the Mason Wasp Fetched Fire from God
(From the Ila people, Zambia)

VULTURE, Fish-eagle and Crow were without fire, for there was no fire on earth. So, needing fire, all the birds assembled together and asked: "Whence shall we find fire?" Some of the birds said: "Perhaps from God." Thereupon Mason Wasp volunteered, saying: "Who will go with me to God?" Vulture answered and said: "We will go with you, I and Fish-eagle and Crow."

So on the morrow they took leave of all the other birds, saying: "We are going to see whether we can get fire from God." Then they flew off. After they had spent ten days on the road, there fell to earth some small bones that was Vulture; later, there also fell to earth some other small bones that was Fish-eagle; Mason Wasp and Crow were left to go on alone. When the second ten days were ended, there fell other small bones to earth that was Crow. Mason Wasp was left to go on by himself. When the third ten days were over, he was going along, reposing upon the clouds. Nevertheless he never reached the summit of the sky.

As soon as God heard of it, He came to where Mason Wasp was, and answering His question Mason Wasp said: "No, Chief, I am not going anywhere particular, I have only come to beg some fire. All my companions have stopped short; but, nevertheless, I have persevered in coming, for I had set my heart upon arriving to where the Chief is." Thereupon God answered him, saying: "Mason Wasp, since you have reached Me, you shall be chief over all the birds and reptiles on earth. You, now, I give a blessing. You shall not have to beget children. When you desire a child, go and look into a grain stalk and you will find an insect whose name is Ngongwa. When you have found him, take and carry him into a house. When you arrive in the house, look out for the fireplace where men cook, and build there a dwelling for your child Ngongwa. When you have finished building, put him in and let him remain there. When many days have elapsed, just go and have a look at him; and one day you will find he has changed and become just as you are yourself."

So it is today: Mason Wasp builds a house, looking for the fireplace, just as he was commanded by God.

The Story of the Blue Jay
Who Married the Daughter of God
(From the Ila people, Zambia)

ONG AGO Blue Jay had a wife. After a time he went to God; he went to seek the Daughter of God as his wife. God replied: "Since you ask for her, you must not take her to the earth, you must stay just here in the sky. Because, if you take her to the earth, she may not eat meat of Zebra or Gnu or Kudu; of any large animal she may not eat. If you desire to carry her to earth, let her eat only of the smaller animals." Blue Jay answered: "It is well, Chief."

So Blue Jay was allowed to bring the Daughter of God to earth. Upon his arrival on earth he told these things to his earthly wife, saying: "I was told by God that His child may not eat of Zebra or Gnu or Kudu; she may not eat of any large animal." These things he told his wife and mother; when they heard them, his mother said: "It is well, my child." Nevertheless his wife was terribly jealous.

One day Blue Jay went off hunting. He went and killed a Zebra and a young Duiker. When he returned to his first wife, he ordered her, saying: "You must on no account give my wife the meat of the Zebra. Let her eat only of the young Duiker." His wife replied: "It is well."

Another day while Blue Jay was out walking, the old wife deceived her fellow, the Daughter of God, giving her zebra meat and saying: "Eat, it is young Duiker." But she was simply deceiving her. As soon as the Daughter of God ate it, she died. Then Blue Jay returned; on his arrival he asked: "My wife! What has she died of?" The old wife replied: "I don't know."

Nevertheless God had seen her from the sky. Said He: "It is that one yonder who killed My child."

Thereupon Blue Jay returned to the sky; on arrival he went to tell the news, saying: "My wife is dead, Chief." God answered, saying: "You forgot the orders I gave you that My child must not eat of Zebra or Gnu or Kudu; nevertheless, there on earth you went and gave her it. She ate and died." Then Blue Jay replied: "It may be so, Chief." God answered: "Return."

When thirty days had passed, God gathered together a small cloud. Then He opened wide His mouth and thundered. After a time He descended and swept open the grave in which His child was buried; He took her out and carried her to the sky. Nevertheless, Blue Jay did not survive; He took him away also. When He arrived midway He thrust him down to earth; but he never arrived: only some small bones reached the ground. He died just there midway. To this very day this is what Blue Jay does: when he flies he goes up into the air with a loud cry; on the point of descending he dies.

How God First Gave Men Grain and Fruits
(From the Ila people, Zambia)

ONG AGO when God caused men to descend to earth, He gave them grain, and said: "Take good care of the grain." On their arrival, they cultivated the grain and got a fine harvest.

When they had gathered it, they put it into their temporary bins. Having put it into their temporary bins, they ate; they ate bread, but (extravagant people) they ate during the day. Having eaten all day, they said: "This great quantity of meal will never get finished, whereas we are altogether satisfied." So as they were filled, they said: "Let us burn the grain." And they rose up with firebrands and burnt the grain. After they had burnt all the grain, famine came upon them. However, he alone who had come as their leader, did not burn his. Thereupon all the people flocked out of the village and went to gather fruit. And God gave them fruits, saying: "Here are fruits, you foolish people; I gave you great quantities of grain, and when you had eaten of it you burnt the rest. Now, as you have burnt it, you will have to eat only mantembe and mankolongwa and busala."

And so, truly, since He said that, to this day the people have found it so. To this day, people act in this manner. They destroy the grain, they waste it; some brew beer, others follow their own inclinations. When the grain is finished, they have to go after mankolongwa and mantembe and busala. To this day they eat those roots.

Why Men Became Babboons
(From the Ila people, Zambia)

LONG AGO Baboons were men; their clan was the Bankontwe. In the years of long ago they were just as men are. They got their living on earth by stealing.

After a time they said: "As we have become lazy, let us go into the veld." They went off to live in the veld. When they reached the veld they ate wild fruits.

After a time they said: "We cannot live well on these fruits, and as for returning to the village we cannot return, so let us just steal from the fields." To this day, as soon as they see a man's field they send their servant to spy out the land. When he arrives, he looks round and climbs a tree; if he finds that the owner is not there, he goes back to tell them and takes them some maize.

On his arrival he says: "Here is some maize; there are no people." Then they come. When they reach the field, they break off all the maize and steal. When they have finished stealing they go away.

To look at their hands and feet they are human, all but the hair and overhanging forehead.

The Explanation of the Origin of Murder
(From the Ila people, Zambia)

A WOMAN had a child. One day she went to work in the fields. When she was going to her work the child cried. When it stopped crying she suckled it, and when she had finished suckling it she laid it down in the shade. Then she went on hoeing. Once again the child cried, and a bird came, an Eagle, and sat upon it. It soothed the child with its wings. Then the child which was crying became silent. When she saw this the woman was greatly alarmed; said she:

"Dear me! I am amazed; the Eagle is eating my child." When she went towards it the Eagle flew away, and she suckled her child. When she had done suckling it she put it upon her back. When she had finished hoeing, she left off work and returned to the village.

On her arrival there, she did not tell her husband the marvel she had seen but kept it to herself. Next morning, once again the woman went to work in the field with her child. The same thing happened; once again she laid the child to sleep in the shade. After a time the child cried. Then she beheld the Eagle come on to the child and quieten it. The woman was again amazed, and said: "What is that Eagle doing? It is sitting upon my child, but it neither bites nor scratches it no, and then the child is quiet. Truly an astounding thing!" Once again the woman went to her child. When the Eagle saw her coming, it flew off and went to sit on a tree. The woman took her child and was greatly alarmed.

She returned to the village, and on her arrival told her husband about it, saying: "A great marvel!" Her husband answered, saying: "What about?" The woman said: "Today is the second day I have seen the thing there where I hoe. This did I: I put my child to sleep in the shade, and as soon as it cried an Eagle came, and on its arrival stooped over its body and soothed it with its wings. Today is the second day that I have seen that bird act thus. Its name is Eagle." Thereupon the husband refused to believe, saying: "No, you are lying; there never was such a thing." The wife said no more.

In the afternoon she took her hoe and went late to work in the field. On her arrival she laid her child in the shade. The child cried. Thereupon the woman thought: "Now I will go and call my husband, who disputed my word and said I lied." So the woman ran. When she arrived where her husband was, she said: "Come on! It is you who disputed, saying there never was such a thing. Let us go and see now."

The man took his bow and three arrows. On his arrival the woman told him, saying: "Sit here, I will put the child to sleep in the shade yonder, and then, when you see the bird coming, hide yourself." The woman left the child and went away some distance, and the man hid himself there. Then the child cried very loudly. As he was watching, he saw the Eagle come and sit upon the child. Then the man was greatly alarmed, and charged his bow with two arrows that he might pierce the Eagle sitting on his child. Then he shot; but at the moment of shooting the Eagle dodged, and both arrows pierced his child.

Now that is the explanation of the origin of murder. The Eagle was a kind person, nevertheless the father of the child wished to kill it. Then the Eagle cursed him, saying: "Now is kindness among men at an end; because you killed your child, beginning with you and going on to all people, you shall kill each other." To this day people kill each other.

The Daughter of the Sun and Moon
(From the Bantu-speaking
peoples, Angola)

KIMANAWEZE'S SON, when the time came for him to choose a wife, declared that he would not "marry a woman of the earth," but must have the daughter of the Sun and Moon. He wrote "a letter of marriage" (a modern touch, no doubt added by the narrator) and cast about for a messenger to take it up to the sky. The little duiker (*mbambt*) refused, so did the larger antelope, known as *soko*, the hawk, and the vulture. At last a frog came and offered to carry the letter. The son of Kimanaweze, doubtful of his ability to do this, said, "Begone! Where people of life, who have wings, gave it up dost thou say, 'I will go there'?" But the frog persisted, and was at last sent off, with the threat of a thrashing if he should be unsuccessful. It appears that the Sun and Moon were in the habit of sending their handmaidens down to the earth to draw water, descending and ascending by means of a spider's web. The frog went and hid himself in the well to which they came, and when the first one filled her jar he got into it without being seen, having first placed the letter in his mouth. The girls went up to heaven, carried their water jars into the room, and set them down. When they had gone away he came out, produced the letter, laid it on a table, and hid.

After a while "Lord Sun" (Kumbi Mwene) came in, found the letter, and read it. Not knowing what to make of it, he put it away, and said nothing about it. The frog got into an empty water jar, and was carried down again when the girls went for a fresh supply. The son of Kimanaweze, getting no answer, refused at first to believe that the frog had executed his commission; but, after waiting for some days, he wrote another letter and sent him again. The frog carried it in the same way as before, and the Sun, after reading it, wrote that he would consent, if the suitor came himself, bringing his 'first present' (the usual gift for opening marriage negotiations). On receiving this the young man wrote another letter, saying that he must wait till told the amount of the 'wooing present', or bride-price (*kilembu*). He gave this to the frog, along with a sum of money, and it was conveyed as before. This time the Sun consulted his wife, who was quite ready to welcome the mysterious son-in-law.

She solved the question of providing refreshments for the invisible messenger by saying, "We will cook a meal anyhow, and put it on the table where he leaves the letters." This was done, and the frog, when left alone, came out and ate. The letter, which was left along with the food, stated the amount of the bride-price to be "a sack of money." He carried the letter back to the son of Kimanaweze, who spent six days in collecting the necessary amount, and then sent it by the frog with this message: "Soon I shall find a day to bring home my wife." This, however, was more easily said than done, for when his messenger had once more returned he waited twelve days, and then told the frog that he could not find people to fetch the bride. But the frog was equal to the occasion. Again he had himself carried up to the Sun's palace, and, getting out of the water jar, hid in a corner of the room till after dark, when he came out and went through the house till he found the princess's bedchamber. Seeing that she was fast asleep, he took out one of her eyes without waking her, and then the other. He tied up the eyes in a handkerchief, and went back to his corner in the room where the water jars were kept. In the morning, when the girl did not appear, her parents came to inquire the reason, and found that she was blind. In their distress they sent two men to consult the diviner, who, after casting lots, said (not having heard from them the reason of their coming), "Disease has brought you; the one who is sick is a woman; the sickness that ails her the eyes. You have come, being sent; you have not come of your own will. I have spoken." The Sun's messengers replied,

"Truth. Look now what caused the ailment." He told them that a certain suitor had cast a spell over her, and she would die unless she were sent to him. Therefore they had best hasten on the marriage. The men brought back word to the Sun, who said, "All right. Let us sleep. Tomorrow they shall take her down to the earth." Next day, accordingly, he gave orders for the spider to "weave a large cobweb" for sending his daughter down. Meanwhile the frog had gone down as usual in the water jar and hidden himself in the bottom of the well. When the water carriers had gone up again he came out and went to the village of the bridegroom and told him that his bride would arrive that day. The young man would not believe him, but he solemnly promised to bring her in the evening, and returned to the well.

After sunset the attendants brought the princess down by way of the stronger cobweb and left her by the well. The frog came out, and told her that he would take her to her husband's house; at the same time he handed back her eyes. They started, and came to the son of Kimanaweze, and the marriage took place. And they lived happy ever after – on earth, for, as the narrator said, "They had all given up going to heaven; who could do it was Mainu the frog."

The Story of the Hero Makóma
(From the Senna people, Zimbabwe)

ONCE UPON A TIME, at the town of Senna on the banks of the Zambesi, was born a child. He was not like other children, for he was very tall and strong; over his shoulder he carried a big sack, and in his hand an iron hammer. He could also speak like a grown man, but usually he was very silent.

One day his mother said to him: "My child, by what name shall we know you?"

And he answered: "Call all the head men of Senna here to the river's bank." And his mother called the head men of the town, and when they had come he led them down to a deep black pool in the river where all the fierce crocodiles lived.

"O great men!" he said, while they all listened, "which of you will leap into the pool and overcome the crocodiles?" But no one would come forward. So he turned and sprang into the water and disappeared.

The people held their breath, for they thought: "Surely the boy is bewitched and throws away his life, for the crocodiles will eat him!" Then suddenly the ground trembled, and the pool, heaving and swirling, became red with blood, and presently the boy rising to the surface swam on shore.

But he was no longer just a boy! He was stronger than any man and very tall and handsome, so that the people shouted with gladness when they saw him.

"Now, O my people!" he cried waving his hand, "you know my name – I am Makóma, 'the Greater'; for have I not slain the crocodiles in the pool where none would venture?"

Then he said to his mother: "Rest gently, my mother, for I go to make a home for myself and become a hero." Then, entering his hut, he took Nu-éndo, his iron hammer, and throwing the sack over his shoulder, he went away.

Makóma crossed the Zambesi, and for many moons he wandered towards the north and west until he came to a very hilly country where, one day, he met a huge giant making mountains.

"Greeting," shouted Makóma, "who are you?"

"I am Chi-éswa-mapíri, who makes the mountains," answered the giant, "and who are you?"

"I am Makóma, which signifies 'greater'," answered he.

"Greater than who?" asked the giant.

"Greater than you!" answered Makóma.

The giant gave a roar and rushed upon him. Makóma said nothing, but swinging his great hammer, Nu-éndo, he struck the giant upon the head.

He struck him so hard a blow that the giant shrank into quite a little man, who fell upon his knees saying: "You are indeed greater than I, O Makóma; take me with you to be your slave!" So Makóma picked him up and dropped him into the sack that he carried upon his back.

He was greater than ever now, for all the giant's strength had gone into him; and he resumed his journey, carrying his burden with as little difficulty as an eagle might carry a hare.

Before long he came to a country broken up with huge stones and immense clods of earth. Looking over one of the heaps he saw a giant wrapped in dust dragging out the very earth and hurling it in handfuls on either side of him.

"Who are you," cried Makóma, "that pulls up the earth in this way?"

"I am Chi-dúbula-táka," said he, "and I am making the riverbeds."

"Do you know who I am?" said Makóma. "I am he that is called 'greater'!"

"Greater than who?" thundered the giant.

"Greater than you!" answered Makóma.

With a shout, Chi-dúbula-táka seized a great clod of earth and launched it at Makóma. But the hero had his sack held over his left arm and the stones and earth fell harmlessly upon it, and, tightly gripping his iron hammer, he rushed in and struck the giant to the ground. Chi-dúbula-táka grovelled before him, all the while growing smaller and smaller; and when he had become a convenient size Makóma picked him up and put him into the sack beside Chi-éswa-mapíri.

He went on his way even greater than before, as all the river-maker's power had become his; and at last he came to a forest of baobabs and thorn trees. He was astonished at their size, for everyone was full grown and larger than any trees he had ever seen, and close by he saw Chi-gwísa-míti, the giant who was planting the forest.

Chi-gwísa-míti was taller than either of his brothers, but Makóma was not afraid and called out to him: "Who are you, O Big One?"

"I," said the giant, "am Chi-gwísa-míti, and I am planting these baobabs and thorns as food for my children the elephants."

"Leave off!" shouted the hero, "for I am Makóma, and would like to exchange a blow with thee!"

The giant, plucking up a monster baobab by the roots, struck heavily at Makóma; but the hero sprang aside, and as the weapon sank deep into the soft earth, whirled Nu-éndo the hammer round his head and felled the giant with one blow.

So terrible was the stroke that Chi-gwísa-míti shrivelled up as the other giants had done; and when he had got back his breath he begged Makóma to take him as his servant. "For," said he, "it is honourable to serve a man so great as thou."

Makóma, after placing him in his sack, proceeded upon his journey, and travelling for many days he at last reached a country so barren and rocky that not a single living thing grew upon it – everywhere reigned grim desolation. And in the midst of this dead region he found a man eating fire.

"What are you doing?" demanded Makóma.

"I am eating fire," answered the man, laughing; "and my name is Chi-ídea-móto, for I am the flame-spirit, and can waste and destroy what I like."

"You are wrong," said Makóma; "for I am Makóma, who is 'greater' than you – and you cannot destroy me!"

The fire-eater laughed again, and blew a flame at Makóma. But the hero sprang behind a rock – just in time, for the ground upon which he had been standing was turned to molten glass, like an overbaked pot, by the heat of the flame-spirit's breath.

Then the hero flung his iron hammer at Chi-ídea-móto, and, striking him, it knocked him helpless; so Makóma placed him in the sack, Woro-nówu, with the other great men that he had overcome.

And now, truly, Makóma was a very great hero; for he had the strength to make hills, the industry to lead rivers over dry wastes, foresight and wisdom in planting trees, and the power of producing fire when he wished.

Wandering on he arrived one day at a great plain, well-watered and full of game; and in the very middle of it, close to a large river, was a grassy spot, very pleasant to make a home upon.

Makóma was so delighted with the little meadow that he sat down under a large tree, and removing the sack from his shoulder, took out all the giants and set them before him. "My friends," said he, "I have travelled far and am weary. Is not this such a place as would suit a hero for his home? Let us then go, tomorrow, to bring in timber to make a kraal [a pen for cattle or sheep]."

So the next day Makóma and the giants set out to get poles to build the kraal, leaving only Chi-éswa-mapíri to look after the place and cook some venison which they had killed. In the evening, when they returned, they found the giant helpless and tied to a tree by one enormous hair!

"How is it," said Makóma, astonished, "that we find you thus bound and helpless?"

"O Chief," answered Chi-éswa-mapíri, "at midday a man came out of the river; he was of immense stature, and his grey moustaches were of such length that I could not see where they ended! He demanded of me 'Who is thy master?' And I answered: 'Makóma, the greatest of heroes.' Then the man seized me, and pulling a hair from his moustache, tied me to this tree – even as you see me."

Makóma was very wroth, but he said nothing, and drawing his fingernail across the hair (which was as thick and strong as palm rope) cut it, and set free the mountain-maker.

The three following days exactly the same thing happened, only each time with a different one of the party; and on the fourth day Makóma stayed in camp when the others went to cut poles, saying that he would see for himself what sort of man this was that lived in the river and whose moustaches were so long that they extended beyond men's sight.

So when the giants had gone he swept and tidied the camp and put some venison on the fire to roast. At midday, when the sun was right overhead, he heard a rumbling noise from the river, and looking up he saw the head and shoulders of an enormous man emerging from it. And behold! right down the riverbed and up the riverbed, till they faded into the blue distance, stretched the giant's grey moustaches!

"Who are you?" bellowed the giant, as soon as he was out of the water.

"I am he that is called Makóma," answered the hero; "and, before I slay thee, tell me also what is thy name and what thou doest in the river?"

"My name is Chin-débou Máu-giri," said the giant. "My home is in the river, for my moustache is the grey fever-mist that hangs above the water, and with which I bind all those that come unto me so that they die."

"You cannot bind me!" shouted Makóma, rushing upon him and striking with his hammer. But the river giant was so slimy that the blow slid harmlessly off his green chest, and as Makóma stumbled and tried to regain his balance, the giant swung one of his long hairs around him and tripped him up.

For a moment Makóma was helpless, but remembering the power of the flame-spirit which had entered into him, he breathed a fiery breath upon the giant's hair and cut himself free.

As Chin-débou Máu-giri leaned forward to seize him the hero flung his sack Woro-nówu over the giant's slippery head, and gripping his iron hammer, struck him again; this time the blow alighted upon the dry sack and Chin-débou Máu-giri fell dead.

When the four giants returned at sunset with the poles they rejoiced to find that Makóma had overcome the fever-spirit, and they feasted on the roast venison till far into the night; but in the morning, when they awoke, Makóma was already warming his hands at the fire, and his face was gloomy.

"In the darkness of the night, O my friends," he said presently, "the white spirits of my fathers came unto me and spoke, saying: 'Get thee hence, Makóma, for thou shalt have no rest until thou hast found and fought with Sákatirína, who has five heads, and is very great and strong; so take leave of thy friends, for thou must go alone."'

Then the giants were very sad, and bewailed the loss of their hero; but Makóma comforted them, and gave back to each the gifts he had taken from them. Then bidding them "Farewell," he went on his way.

Makóma travelled far towards the west; over rough mountains and waterlogged morasses, fording deep rivers, and tramping for days across dry deserts where most men would have died, until at length he arrived at a hut standing near some large peaks, and inside the hut were two beautiful women.

"Greeting!" said the hero. "Is this the country of Sákatirína of five heads, whom I am seeking?"

"We greet you, O Great One!" answered the women. "We are the wives of Sákatirína; your search is at an end, for there stands he whom you seek!" And they pointed to what Makóma had thought were two tall mountain peaks. "Those are his legs," they said; "his body you cannot see, for it is hidden in the clouds."

Makóma was astonished when he beheld how tall was the giant; but, nothing daunted, he went forward until he reached one of Sákatirína's legs, which he struck heavily with Nu-éndo. Nothing happened, so he hit again and then again until, presently, he heard a tired, faraway voice saying: "Who is it that scratches my feet?"

And Makóma shouted as loud as he could, answering: "It is I, Makóma, who is called 'Greater'!" And he listened, but there was no answer.

Then Makóma collected all the dead brushwood and trees that he could find, and making an enormous pile round the giant's legs, set a light to it.

This time the giant spoke; his voice was very terrible, for it was the rumble of thunder in the clouds. "Who is it," he said, "making that fire smoulder around my feet?"

"It is I, Makóma!" shouted the hero. "And I have come from far away to see thee, O Sákatirína, for the spirits of my fathers bade me go seek and fight with thee, lest I should grow fat, and weary of myself."

There was silence for a while, and then the giant spoke softly: "It is good, O Makóma!" he said. "For I too have grown weary. There is no man so great as I, therefore I am all alone. Guard thyself!" And bending suddenly he seized the hero in his hands and dashed him upon the ground. And lo! instead of death, Makóma had found life, for he sprang to his feet mightier in strength and stature than before, and rushing in he gripped the giant by the waist and wrestled with him.

Hour by hour they fought, and mountains rolled beneath their feet like pebbles in a flood; now Makóma would break away, and summoning up his strength, strike the giant with Nu-éndo his iron hammer, and Sákatiríña would pluck up the mountains and hurl them upon the hero, but neither one could slay the other. At last, upon the second day, they grappled so strongly that they could not break away; but their strength was failing, and, just as the sun was sinking, they fell together to the ground, insensible.

In the morning when they awoke, Mulímo the Great Spirit was standing by them; and he said: "O Makóma and Sákatiríña! Ye are heroes so great that no man may come against you. Therefore ye will leave the world and take up your home with me in the clouds." And as he spake the heroes became invisible to the people of the Earth, and were no more seen among them.

Creation Story: The Eternal One
(From the Zulu people, South Africa)

ON A BEAUTIFUL DAY Umuve'li Ngqa'nge, the Eternal One, creator of the world, went up into the hills. There were many reeds growing by the river, and he spoke to a reed and said, "Bring forth male creatures!" Then he put all the males together in one place and spoke again to the reed and said, "Bring forth female creatures!" Then he went home. And he said to himself, "These that I have made shall live forever and never die."

He called Unwa'ba, the Chameleon, one of the creatures that he had created, and said to him, "Go up to the hilltop where I stood when I spoke to the reed, and cry aloud to the people and tell them that they shall live forever and never die."

So the Chameleon started. After he had been gone a long time the Creator changed his mind and said to himself, "I will have people live a long time until they are old, and then die." So he called Intu'lo, the Lizard, to him and said, "Go and stand where I stood when I was creating the people, and tell them that I say: 'You shall live until you are old and then die!'"

The Lizard went quickly and reached the hilltop before the Chameleon, who had been stopping all along the wayside, enjoying himself eating red berries. When the Lizard came to the place where the Creator had stood, he cried out and said, "The Creator says you shall all live until you row old and then die." Then the Lizard went back.

Long, long after came the Chameleon and cried aloud to the people, and said, "The Creator says that you shall live always and never die." But the people answered: "The Creator has sent us his word by the Lizard, who told us that we shall live until we are old and then die. So we believe the Lizard. You can go back; to you we will not reply."

And so the Zulus believe that no one should die in youth. When a young person dies, it is not as it should be, but because he has been conjured or bewitched.

Thus does the belief in witchcraft have its place even in the very story of creation – a belief that underlies the spiritual life and the instinctive thought of all black Africa.

Huveane Produces a Child
(From the Pedi and Venda peoples, South Africa)

OF THIS LEGEND there are various versions, none apparently complete, but they can be used to supplement each other. One begins in a way which recalls the story of Murile. Only whereas Murile cherishes a *Colocasia* tuber, which magically develops into an infant, Huveane is quite baldly stated to have "had a baby". The narrator seems to see nothing improbable in this (though Huveane's

parents and their neighbours did), and no explanation is given of this extraordinary proceeding; but there is a story resembling this in which the result is produced by the boy having swallowed some medicine intended for his mother. Another version has it that Huveane modelled a baby in clay and breathed life into it. This may possibly have some vague connection with the idea of his having originated the human race; it may, on the other hand, be due to some echo of missionary teaching.

Huveane kept his child in a hollow tree, and stole out early every morning to feed it with milk before it was time for him to begin herding the sheep and goats. His parents noticed that he used to take the milk, and could not make out what he did with it; so one day his father followed him stealthily, saw him feeding the child, hid till Huveane had one away, and carried the baby to his wife. They then placed it among the firewood and other things stacked up under the eaves of the hut. When Huveane brought the flock home he went straight to his tree and found no baby there. He went into the courtyard, sat down by the fire, where his parents were seated, and did not speak, only looking miserable. His mother asked him what was the matter, and he said the smoke was hurting his eyes. "Then you had better go out and sit somewhere else." He did so, but remained gloomy. At last his mother told him to go and fetch a piece of wood from the pile, which he did, and found the baby wrapped in a sheepskin and quite safe. His parents, relieved to find that he had recovered his spirits, let him have his way, and he went on caring for the child, whom he called Sememerwane sa Matedi a Telele ('One who causes much trouble').

Huveane Plays Tricks with the Stock

His parents continued, however, to be uneasy; they could not understand how the child had been produced, and the neighbours, when the story leaked out, began to talk of witchcraft. Huveane did not trouble himself, but went on herding his father's stock and devising practical jokes to play upon him. When a ewe or goat had twins, which not infrequently happened, he took one of the lambs or kids and shut it up in a hollow ant-heap. In this way he gradually collected a whole flock. Someone, who had noticed that the ewes, when driven out in the morning, always collected round the ant-heaps, told Huveane's father, and the latter followed his son to the pasture, heard the bleating of the lambs and kids inside the ant-heaps, took away the stones which blocked the entrance, and seized the lambs to take them to their mothers. But as he did not know to which mother each belonged the result was confusion worse confounded. Huveane, exasperated beyond endurance, struck his father with the switch he had in his hand. No doubt this helped to bring matters to a crisis, but for the moment the old man was too much impressed with the sudden increase of the flock to be very angry. In the evening, when the villagers saw the full number being driven home, they were filled with envy, and asked him where he had got all those animals. He told the whole story, which gave rise to endless discussions.

Plans for Huveane's Destruction

It was certain that Huveane could be up to no good; he must have produced those sheep and goats by magic – and how came he to have a child and no mother for it? He certainly ought to be got rid of. They put it to his father that the boy would end by bewitching the whole village. They handed him some poison, and in the evening, when Huveane was squatting by the fire, his mother brought him a bowl of milk. He took it, but, instead of drinking, poured it out on the ground. The neighbours took counsel, and suggested to the father that he should dig a pit close to the fireplace, where Huveane was in the habit of sitting, and cover it over. But Huveane, instead of sitting down in his usual place, forced himself in between his brothers, who were seated by the fire, and in the struggle for a place one of them fell into the pit. Next they dug another pit in the gateway of his father's enclosure, where he would have to pass when he came home with the flocks in the evening. He jumped over the pitfall, and all his sheep and goats did likewise.

This having failed, someone suggested that a man with a spear should be tied up in a bundle of grass, a device adopted, as we have seen, by Kachirambe's mother. This was done, and Huveane's father sent him to fetch the bundle. He took his spear with him – to his father's surprise – and, when near enough, threw it with unerring aim. The man inside jumped up and ran away. Huveane returned to his father, saying, "Father, I went to do as you told me, but the grass has run away."

Huveane's Practical Jokes

The villagers were driven to the conclusion that it was quite impossible to compass Huveane's destruction by any stratagem, however cunning, and they were fain to let him be. He knew that he was a match for them, and thenceforth set himself to fool them by pretended stupidity. Whatever tricks he played on them he knew that he was safe.

One day he found a dead zebra, and sat down on it while watching his flock. In the evening, when he returned and was asked where he had been herding that day, he said, "By the striped hill." Three or four days running he gave the same answer, and, his relatives' curiosity being roused, some of them followed him and found the zebra – by this time badly decomposed. They told him, "Why, this is game; if you find an animal like this you should heap branches over it, to keep the hyenas away, and come and call the people from the village to fetch the meat." Next day Huveane found a very small bird lying dead; he heaped branches over it and ran home with the news. Half the village turned out, carrying large baskets; their feelings on beholding the 'game' may be imagined. One of the men informed him that this kind of game should be hung round one's neck; he did this next day, and was set down as a hopeless idiot. Several other tricks of the same kind are told of him; at last, one day, his father, thinking he should no longer be left to himself, went herding with him. When the sun was high he became very thirsty; Huveane showed him a high rock, on the top of which was a pool of water, and knocked in a number of pegs, so that he could climb up. They both went up and drank; then Huveane came down, took away the pegs, one by one, and ran home, where his mother had prepared the evening meal. Huveane ate all that was ready; then he took the empty pots, filled them with cow dung, and ran off to drive in the pegs and let his father come down. The old man came home and sat down to the supper, which, as his graceless son now informed him, had been magically changed, so as to be entirely uneatable. After this the parents and neighbours alike seem to have felt that there was nothing to be done with Huveane, except to put up with him as best they could. We hear nothing more about the child in the hollow tree.

It almost seems as if the trick played by Huveane on his father were a kind of inverted echo of one tradition about the High God, whom some call Huveane. "His abode is in the sky. He created the sky and the earth. He came down from the sky to make the earth and men. When he had finished he returned to the sky. They say he climbed up by pegs, and after he had gone up one step he took away the peg below him, and so on, till he had drawn them all out and disappeared into the sky."

Some say that all the incidents detailed above belong, not to Huveane (whom the narrators call the Great God, Modimo o Moholo), but to his son Hutswane, who, it is believed, will one day come again, bringing happiness and prosperity to mankind – a somewhat unexpected conclusion after all that we have heard about him.

Animal Fables & Stories

THIS SECTION deals with stories mainly about animals, plants or forces of nature which are anthropomorphised (given human qualities). These stories originate from oral historical traditions of the southern African societies. They are rooted in the region's landscape, with animals – and the animal kingdom – playing a dominant role.

Most of the animal characters are predominantly heroic. The heroic tales are characterised by the protagonists, who by nature, are heroic, and are capable of improving or debasing existing situations. Trickster characters feature prominently in this class. The characters in trickster tales differ according to the different geographical and cultural areas in which the stories were collected. In some of the tales, it is the jackal. For others, it is the tortoise, hare, wolf or snake. No matter what names they assume, these animal tricksters have several things in common. They are usually small and weak, but they are also shrewd, conniving, greedy, exhibitionistic and unpredictable. Their main preoccupation seems to be to make up for their physical lack of ability with a very high degree of intelligence, which they inevitably misuse in a cunning way. As a result, they are always engaged in trying to outwit their more powerful, but less intelligent, animal counterparts (the elephant, lion, tiger, baboon, etc.). In other words, most tricksters are social deviants who manage to survive mainly by their wit and cunning. Although they create disorder wherever they go, they are tolerated by the other animals because of their wisdom. In most of the tales in this section, the animals are used to explore man's follies or weaknesses in order to instil valuable ethical and moral lessons in their listeners or readers.

The Man Who Found a Lion in a Cave
(From the San people, southern Africa)

MY GRANDFATHER, XUGEN-DDI, formerly told me, that a man long ago did thus: when the rain fell he thought that he would go (and) sleep in a cave; when a lion had been the one who had made rain for him, so that he should not know the place at which (his) home seemed to be, that he might pass (it) by (in the darkness), so that he might go to a different place, that the lion might get hold of him.

The place was not a little dark, for, he continued to go into the bushes; he did not see the place along which he was walking. He did not know the place at which (his) home seemed to be. And he thought, "I must go along in the darkness seeking for a cave, that I may go to sleep in it, if I find it; I can afterwards in the morning return home; for, the rain does not a little fall upon me."

And the lion had come first to the cave; it came to wait for the man in the cave.

And it felt that it was also wet; when it had sat (for a little while) inside the cave, it became warm, and it slept, when it had become warm; while it had thought that it would sit watching for the man, that it might do thus, if the man came in; while the man thought he would look for a place where he could lay down his things; it might catch hold of the man. It had thought so; (but) it fell fast asleep.

And the man came, while it sat asleep. And the man, when he had entered the cave, heard a thing which seemed to breathe; and the man thought: "Can people have come to the cave? Do they wait at the cave, those who breathe here?" And he thought, "How is it that the people do not talk, if people (they) be? Can the people have fallen fast asleep, that the people do not speak to me?" And he thought: "I will not call out to the people, for I do not know, whether they are people; for, I will first feel gently about (with my hands), that I may feel whether real people (they) be. For, I should, if it were a different thing, I should call awakening it."

And he felt about; and he felt that a thing which seemed to have hair was there. And he gently approached a little nearer to it; and he felt well about, and he felt that a lion was the one which slept sitting inside the cave. And he gently stepped backwards (and) turned round; and he went out on tiptoe.

And, when he had gone to a little distance, he ran swiftly, because he thought that the lion would smell his scent (where) he had gone to feel about for the lion; the lion would run to seek him.

And when he had gone to a little distance, when a little time had passed, he heard the lion, because the lion had smelt his scent, while the lion slept. And as the lion had in this manner sat sleeping, the man's scent had entered its nose, and, because of the man's scent, which seemed as if the man were standing beside it, it had growling arisen; because the man's scent which it smelt, seemed as if the man were standing beside it; that was why it snatched, it the place at which the man seemed to be.

And the man heard it; and the man exclaimed: "It sounds as if it had perceived my scent; for thou (addressing himself) art the one who hearest that the cave sounds thus; for the lion sounds as if (it) had been startled awake by my scent; for it sounds as if (it) were biting about, seeking for me in the cave." And the man thought, that he would not go home; for, he would run to a different place; for, he knew that the lion would find his spoor; he would afterwards do as follows, when the day had broken – if the lion had not killed him, he would afterwards look seeking for (his) home in the morning.

And the day broke, while the man was (still) running, because he had heard the lion, namely, the noise that the lion made, while the lion sought to get him. And, as he ran along, he espied the fire of some other people, which they kindled to warm themselves. And he thought: "I will run to the fire which stands yonder(?), that I may go to the people who are making fire there, that I may go to sleep (among) them." And he thought: "Dost thou not think (that) our fathers also said to me, that the lion's eye can also sometimes resemble a fire by night? I will look whether it be a real fire which burns there." And he ran nearer to the fire; he looked, and he saw that people were lying round(?) in front of the fire. And he thought: "I will go to the people; for the thing seems as if they are people."

And he went to the people. And he told the people about it: "Do ye think, that I have not walked into death this night? It happened to me that the lion slept; therefore ye see me! For, ye would not have seen me, had the lion not slept; because it slept, hence it is that the thing seems that ye see me; I have come to you. For, I had thought that I would go to wait there (in) the cave, but, the lion had come to wait for me in the cave. I did not know that the lion was sitting inside the cave; I thought that I would feel about, seeking for a place which was dry, that I might lay down my things there. Then, when I walked into the cave, I heard a thing which sounded as if it breathed; and I thought that people seemed also to be waiting there (in) the cave. I heard that the breathing of the thing did not sound like a man; I thought that I would first feel about, while I did not lay down my things. I felt about, while I (still) had my things; and I felt gently about. I felt that I was touching hair; and I became aware that (it) must be a lion which slept, sitting in (the cave). I turned softly back, when I became aware that it was a lion."

He told the other people about it: Did not the other people hear its seeking? Therefore, the other people must watch for the lion; for the lion would come, when the lion had found his spoor. And they heard the lion, as the lion questioned, seeking to get him. The lion asked, where was the man who had come to it – because it smelt that the scent of the man's spoor had ceased at this house? The thing seemed, as if he were at this house; it wanted the man to become visible, that it might get hold of the man.

Day broke, while the lion was (still) threatening them. When the day broke, then it was, that the lion went away, leaving the people; because the sun was rising; therefore, it went away, leaving the people, while it felt that the sun rose. For (otherwise), the people would perceive it; for the lion is a thing which is not willing to come to us, when the sun stands (in the sky).

The Young Man of the Ancient Race, Who Was Carried off by a Lion, When Asleep in the Field
(From the San people, southern Africa)

A YOUNG MAN WAS THE ONE WHO, formerly hunting, ascended a hill; he became sleepy; while he sat looking around (for game), he became sleepy. And he thought that he would first lie down; for he was not a little sleepy. For what could have happened to him today? Because he had not previously felt like this.

And he lay down on account of it; and he slept, while a lion came; it went to the water, because the noonday (heat) had 'killed' it; it was thirsty; and it espied the man lying asleep; and it took up the man.

And the man awoke startled; and he saw that it was a lion which had taken him up. And he thought that he would not stir; for the lion would biting kill him, if he stirred; he would first see what the lion intended to do; for the lion appeared to think that he was dead.

And the lion carried him to a zwart-storm tree; and the lion laid him in. it. And the lion thought that it would (continue to) be thirsty if it ate the man; it would first go to the water, that it might go to drink; it would come afterwards to eat, when it had drunk; for, it would (continue to) be thirsty if it ate.

And it trod, (pressing) in the man's head between the stems of the zwart-storm tree; and it went back. And the man turned his head a little. And the lion looked back on account of it; namely, why had the man's head moved? when it had first thought that it had trodden, firmly fixing the man's head. And the lion thought that it did not seem to have laid the man nicely; for, the man fell over. And it again trod, pressing the man's head into the middle (of the stems) of the zwart-storm tree. And it licked the man's eyes' tears. And the man wept; hence it licked the man's eyes. And the man felt that a stick did not a little pierce the hollow at the back of his head; and the man turned his head a little, while he looked steadfastly at the lion, he turned his head a little. And the lion looked (to see) why it was that the thing seemed as if the man had moved. And it licked the man's eyes' tears.

And the lion thought it would tread, thoroughly pressing down the man's head, that it might really see whether it had been the one who had not laid the man down nicely. For, the thing seemed as if the man had stirred. And the man saw that the thing seemed as if the lion suspected that he was alive; and he did not stir, although the stick was piercing him. And the lion saw that the thing appeared as if it had laid the man down nicely; for the man did not stir; and it went a few steps away, and it looked towards the man, while the man drew up his eyes; he looked through his eyelashes; he saw what the lion was doing.

And the lion went away, ascending the hill; and the lion descended (the hill on the other side), while the man gently turned his head because he wanted to see whether the lion had really gone away. And he saw that the lion appeared to have descended (the hill on the other side); and he perceived that the lion again (raising its head) stood peeping behind the top of the hill; because the lion thought that the thing had seemed as if the man were alive; therefore, it first wanted again to look thoroughly. For, it seemed as if the man had intended to arise; for, it had thought that the man had been feigning death. And it saw that the man was still lying down; and it thought that it would quickly run to the water, that it might go to drink, that it might again quickly come out (from the water), that it might come to eat. For, it was hungry; it was one who was not a little thirsty; therefore, it first intended to go to drink, that it might come afterwards to eat, when it had drunk.

The man lay looking at it, at that which it did; and the man saw that its head's turning away (and disappearing), with which it turned away (and disappeared), seemed as if it had altogether gone. And the man thought that he would first lie still, that he might see whether the lion would not again come peeping. For, it is a thing which is cunning; it would intend to deceive him, that the thing might seem (as if) it had really gone away; while it thought that he would arise; for, he had seemed as if he stirred. For, it did not know why the man had, when it thought that it had laid the man down nicely, the man had been falling over. Therefore, it thought that it would quickly run, that it might quickly come, that it might come to look whether the man still lay.

And the man saw that a long time had passed since it again came to peep (at him); and the thing seemed as if it had altogether gone. And the man thought that he would first wait a little; for, he would (otherwise) startle the lion, if the lion were still at this place. And the man saw that a little time had now passed, and he had not perceived it (the lion); and the thing seemed as if it had really gone away.

And he did nicely at the place yonder where he lay; he did not arise (and) go; for, he arose, be first sprang to a different place, while he wished that the lion should not know the place to which he seemed to have gone. He, when he had done in this manner, ran in a zigzag direction, while he desired that the lion should not smell out his footsteps, that the lion should not know the place to which he seemed to have gone; that the lion, when it came, should come to seek about for him (there). Therefore, he thought that he would run in a zigzag direction, so that the lion might not smell out his footsteps; that he might go home; for, the lion, when it came, would come to seek for him. Therefore, he would not run straight into the house; for, the lion, when it came (and) missed him, would intend to find his footprints, that the lion might, following his spoor, seek for him, that the lion might see whether it could not get hold of him.

Therefore, when he came out at the top of the hill, he called out to the people at home about it, that he had just been 'lifted up' while the sun stood high, he had been 'lifted up'; therefore, they must look out many hartebeest skins, that they might roll him up in them; for, he had just been 'lifted up', while the sun was high. Therefore, he thought that the lion would – when it came out from the place to which it had gone – it would come (and) miss him; it would resolve to seek (and) track him out. Therefore, he wanted the people to roll him up in many hartebeest skins, so that the Lion should not come (and) get him. For, they were those who knew that the lion is a thing which acts thus to the thing which it has killed, it does not leave it, when it has not eaten it. Therefore, the people must do thus with the hartebeest skins, the people must roll him up in them; and also (in) mats; these (are) things which the people must roll him up in, (in order) that the lion should not get him.

And the people did so; the people rolled him up in mats, and also (in) hartebeest skins, which they rolled together with the mats. For, the man was the one who had spoken thus to them about it; therefore it was that they rolled him up in hartebeest skins, while they felt that their hearts' young man (he) was, whom they did not wish the lion to eat. Therefore, they intended to hide him well, that the lion should not get hold of him. For, a young man whom they did not a little love he was. Therefore, they did not wish the lion to eat him; and they said that they would cover over the young man with the hut's sheltering bushes, so that the lion, when it came, should come seeking about for the young man it should not get hold of the young man, when it came; it should come seeking about for him.

And the people went out to seek for *kui-sse* (an edible root); and they dug out *kui-sse*; and they brought (home) *kui-sse*, at noon, and they baked *kui-sse*. And an old Bushman, as he went along getting wood for his wife, in order that his wife might make a fire above the *kui-sse,* espied the lion, as the lion came over (the top of the hill), at the place which the young man had come over. And he told the house folk about it; and he spoke, he said:

"Ye are those who see the hill yonder, its top, the place yonder (where) that young man came over, what it looks like!"

And the young man's mother spoke, she said:

"Ye must not allow the lion to come into the huts; ye must shoot it dead, when it has not (yet) come to the huts."

And the people slung on their quivers; and they went to meet the lion; and they were shooting at the lion; the lion would not die, although the people were shooting at it.

And another old woman spoke, she said: "Ye must give to the lion a child, (in order) that the lion may go away from us." The lion answered, it said that it did not want a child; for, it wanted the person whose eyes' tears it had licked; he was the one whom it wanted.

And the (other) people speaking, said: "In what manner were ye shooting at the lion that ye could not manage to kill the lion?" And another old man spoke, he said: "Can ye not see that (it) must be a sorcerer? It will not die when we are shooting at it; for, it insists upon (having) the man whom it carried off."

The people threw children to the lion; the lion did not want the children which the people threw to it; for, it, looking, left them alone.

The people were shooting at it, while it sought for the man – that it might get hold of the man – the people were shooting at it. The people said: "Ye must bring for us assegais, we must kill the lion." The people were shooting at it; it did not seem as if the people were shooting at it; they were stabbing it with assegais, while they intended to stab it to death. It did not seem as if the people were stabbing it; for, it continued to seek for the young man; it said that it wanted the young man whose tears it had licked; he was the one whom it wanted.

It scratched asunder, breaking to pieces for the people the huts, while it scratched asunder, seeking for the young man. And the people speaking, said: "Can ye not see that the lion will not eat the children whom we have given to it?" And the people speaking, said: "Can ye not see that a sorcerer (it) must be?" And the people speaking, said: "Ye must give a girl to the lion, that we may see whether the lion will not eat her, that it may go away." The lion did not want the girl; for, the lion only wanted the man whom it had carried off; he was the one whom it wanted.

And the people spoke, they said, they did not know in what manner they should act towards the lion; for, it had been morning when they shot at the lion; the lion would not die; for, it had, when the people were shooting at it, it had been walking about. "Therefore, we do not know in what manner we shall act towards the lion. For, the children whom we gave to the lion, the lion has refused, on account of the man whom it had carried off."

And the people speaking, said: "Say ye to the young man's mother about it, that she must, although she loves the young man, she must take out the young man, she must give the young man to the lion, even if he be the child of her heart. For, she is the one who sees that the sun is about to set, while the lion is threatening us; the lion will not go (and) leave us; for, it insists upon (having) the young man."

And the young man's mother spoke, she said:

"Ye may give my child to the lion; ye shall not allow the lion to eat my child; that the lion may go walking about; for, ye shall killing lay it upon my child; that it may die, like my child; that it may die, lying upon my child."

And the people, when the young man's mother had thus spoken, the people took the young man out from the hartebeest skins in which they had rolled him up, they gave the young man to the lion. And the lion bit the young man to death; the people, when it was biting at the young man, were shooting at it; the people were stabbing it; and it bit the young man to death.

And the lion spoke, it said to the people about it, that this time was the one at which it would die; for, it had got hold of the man for whom it had been seeking; it had got hold of him!

And it died, while the man also lay dead; it also lay dead, with the man.

The Mantis Assumes the Form of a Hartebeest
(From the San people, southern Africa)

THE MANTIS IS ONE WHO CHEATED the children, by becoming a hartebeest, by resembling a dead hartebeest. He, feigning death, lay in front of the children, when the children went to seek gambroo (*kui*, a sort of cucumber); because he thought (wished) that the children should cut him up with a stone knife, as these children did not possess metal knives.

The children perceived him, when he had laid himself stretched out, while his horns were turned backwards. The children then said to each other: "It is a hartebeest that yonder lies; it is dead." The children jumped for joy (saying): "Our hartebeest! we shall eat great meat." They broke off stone knives by striking (one stone against another), they skinned the Mantis. The skin of the Mantis snatched itself quickly out of the children's hands. They say to each other: "Hold thou strongly fast for me the hartebeest skin!" Another child said: "The hartebeest skin pulled at me."

Her elder sister said: "It does seem that the hartebeest has not a wound from the people who shot it; for, the hartebeest appears to have died of itself. Although the hartebeest is fat, (yet) the hartebeest has no shooting wound."

Her elder sister cut off a shoulder of the hartebeest, and put it down (on a bush). The hartebeest's shoulder arose by itself, it sat down nicely (on the other side of the bush), while it placed itself nicely. She (then) cut off a thigh of the hartebeest, and put it down (on a bush); it placed itself nicely on the bush. She cut off another shoulder of the hartebeest, and put it upon (another) bush. It arose, and sat upon a soft (portion of the) bush; as it felt that the bush (upon which the child had laid it) pricked it.

Another elder sister cut off the other thigh of the hartebeest. They spoke thus: "This hartebeest's flesh does move; that must be why it shrinks away."

They arrange their burdens; one says to the other: "Cut and break off the hartebeest's neck, so that (thy) younger sister may carry the hartebeest's head, for, (thy) yonder sitting elder sister, she shall carry the hartebeest's back, she who is a big girl. For, we must carrying return (home); for, we came (and) cut up this hartebeest. Its flesh moves; its flesh snatches itself out of our hand. *Atta* it of itself places itself nicely."

They take up the flesh of the Mantis; they say to the child: "Carry the hartebeest's head, that father may put it to roast for you." The child slung on the hartebeest's head, she called to her sisters "Taking hold help me up; this hartebeest's head is not light." Her sisters taking hold of her help her up.

They go away, they return (home). The hartebeest's head slips downwards, because the Mantis's head wishes to stand on the ground. The child lifts it up (with her shoulders), the hartebeest's head (by turning a little) removes the thong from the hartebeest's eye. The hartebeest's head was whispering, it whispering said to the child: "O child! the thong is standing in front of my eye.

Take away for me the thong; the thong is shutting my eye." The child looked behind her; the Mantis winked at the child. The child whimpered; her elder sister looked back at her. Her elder sister called to her: "Come forward quickly; we return (home)."

The child exclaimed: "This hartebeest's head is able to speak." Her elder sister scolded her: "Lying come forward; we go. Art thou not coming deceiving (us) about the hartebeest's head?"

The child said to her elder sister: "The hartebeest has winked at me with the hartebeest's eye; the hartebeest desired that I should take away the thong from his eye. Thus it was that the hartebeest's head lay looking behind my back."

The child looked back at the hartebeest's head, the hartebeest opened and shut its eyes. The child said to her elder sister: "The hartebeest's head must be alive, for it is opening and shutting its eyes."

The child, walking on, unloosened the thong; the child let fall the hartebeest's head. The Mantis scolded the child, he complained about his head. He scolded the child: "Oh! oh! my head! Oh! bad little person! hurting me in my head."

Her sisters let fall the flesh of the Mantis. The flesh of the Mantis sprang together, it quickly joined itself to the lower part of the Mantis's back. The head of the Mantis quickly joined (itself) upon the top of the neck of the Mantis. The neck of the Mantis quickly joined (itself) upon the upper part of the Mantis's spine. The upper part of the Mantis's spine joined itself to the Mantis's back. The thigh of the Mantis sprang forward, it joined itself to the Mantis's back. His other thigh ran forward, racing it joined itself to the other side of the Mantis's back. The chest of the Mantis ran forward, it joined itself to the front side of the upper part of the Mantis's spine. The shoulder blade of the Mantis ran forward, it joined itself on to the ribs of the Mantis.

The other shoulder blade of the Mantis ran forward, while it felt that the ribs of the Mantis had joined themselves on, when they raced.

The children still ran on; he (the Mantis, arose from the ground and) ran, while be chased the children – he being whole, his head being round – while he felt that he was a man. Therefore, he was stepping along with (his) shoes, while he jogged with his shoulder blade.

He saw that the children had reached home; he quickly turned about, be, jogging with his shoulder blade, descended to the river. He went along the riverbed, making a noise as he stepped in the soft sand; he yonder went quickly out of the river bed. He returned, coming out at a different side of the house (i.e., his own house) he returned, passing in front of the house.

The children said: "We have been (and) seen a hartebeest which was dead. That hartebeest, it was the one which we cut up with stone knives; its flesh quivered. The hartebeest's flesh quickly snatched itself out of our hands. It by itself was placing itself nicely upon bushes which were comfortable; while the hartebeest felt that the hartebeest's head would go along whispering. While the child who sits (there) carried it, it talking stood behind the child's back."

The child said to her father "O papa! Dost thou seem to think that the hartebeest's head did not talk to me? For the hartebeest's head felt that it would be looking at my hole above the nape of the neck, as I went along; and then it was that the hartebeest's head told me that I should take away for him the thong from his eye. For, the thong lay in front of his eye."

Her father said to them: "Have you been and cut up the old man, the Mantis, while he lay pretending to be dead in front of you?"

The children said: "We thought that the hartebeest's horns were there, the hartebeest had hair. The hartebeest was one which had not an arrow's wound; while the hartebeest felt that the hartebeest would talk. Therefore, the hartebeest came and chased us, when we had put down the hartebeest's flesh. The hartebeest's flesh jumped together, while it springing gathered (itself) together, that it might mend, that it might mending hold together to the hartebeest's back. The hartebeest's back also joined on.

"Therefore, the hartebeest ran forward, while his body was red, when he had no hair (that coat of hair in which he had been lying down), as he ran, swinging his arm like a man.

"And when he saw that we reached the house, he whisked round, He ran, kicking up his heels (showing the white soles of his shoes), while running went before the wind, while the sun shone upon his feet's face (soles), while he ran with all his might into the little river (bed), that he might pass behind the back of the hill lying yonder."

Their parents said to the children: "You are those who went and cut up the old man 'Tinderbox Owner'. He, there behind, was one who gently came out from the place there behind."

The children said to their fathers: "He has gone round, he ran fast. He always seems as if he would come over the little hill lying yonder when he sees that we are just reaching home. While this little daughter, she was the one to whom the hartebeest's head, going along, talked; and then she told us. Therefore, we let fall the hartebeest's flesh; we laid our karosses on our shoulders, that we might run very fast.

"While its flesh running came together on its back, it finished mending itself. He arose and ran forward, he, quickly moving his arms, chased us. Therefore, we did thus, we became tired from it, on account of the running with which he had chased us, while he did verily move his arms fast.

"Then he descended into the small river, while he thought that he would, moving his arms fast, run along the small river. Then he thus did, he, picking up wood, came out; while we sat, feeling the fatigue, because he had been deceiving. While he felt that all the people saw him, when we came carrying his thighs, when he went to die lying in front of us; while he wished that we should feel this fatigue, while this child here, it carried his head, he looked up with fixed eyes. He was as if he was dead; he was (afterwards) opening and shutting his eyes; he afar lay talking (while the children were running off). He talked while he mended his body; his head talked, while he mended his body. His head talking reached his back; it came to join upon the top (of his neck).

"He ran forward; he yonder will sit deceiving (at home), while we did cut him up with stone knives (splinters). *A-tta*, he went feigning death to lie in front of us, that we might do so, we run.

"This fatigue, it is that which we are feeling; and our hearts burnt on account of it. Therefore, we shall not hunt (for food), for we shall altogether remain at home."

Gaunu-tsaxau, the Baboons and the Mantis
(From the San people, southern Africa)

GAUNU-TSAXAU (SON OF THE MANTIS) formerly went to fetch for his father sticks, that his father might take aim at the people who sit upon (their) heels. Fetching, he went up to them (the baboons)

as they were going along feeding. Therefore, a baboon who feeding went past him – he who was an older baboon – he was the one to whom *Gaunu-tsaxau* came. Then he questioned *Gaunu-tsaxau*. And *Gaunu-tsaxau* told him about it, that he must fetch for his father sticks, that his father might take aim at the people who sit upon (their) heels. Therefore, he (the baboon) exclaimed "Hie! Come to listen to this child." And the other one said:

> *"First going*
> *I listen,*
> *To the child yonder.*
> *First going*
> *I listen,*
> *To the child yonder."*

And he reached them. He said: "What does this child say?" And the child said: "I must fetch for my father sticks (bushes?), that my father may take aim at the people who sit upon (their) heels." Then the baboon said: "Tell the old man yonder that he must come to hear this child." Then the baboon called out: "Hie! Come to hear this child." Then the other one said:

> *"First going*
> *I listen,*
> *To the child yonder."*

And he came up (to them); he exclaimed: "What does this child say?" And the other one answered: "This child, he wishes, he says, to fetch sticks for his father, that his father may take aim at the people who sit upon (their) heels." And this baboon said: "Tell the old man yonder that he must come to hear this child." Then this (other) baboon called out: "O person passing across in front! come to listen to this child." Therefore, the other one said:

> *"First going*
> *I listen,*
> *To the child yonder."*

And he came up (to them). He said: "What does this child say?" And the other one answered: "This child wants, he says, to fetch sticks for his father, that his father may take aim at the people who sit upon (their) heels." Therefore, this baboon exclaimed It is ourselves! Thou shalt tell the old man yonder that he shall come to listen to this child." Therefore, this other baboon called out: "Ho! come to listen to this child." Then the other one said:

> *"First going*
> *I listen,*
> *To the child yonder."*

He came up to the other people on account of it. He said: "What does this child say?" And the other one answered: "This child, he wants, he says, to fetch sticks for his father, that his father may take aim at the people who sit upon (their) heels." Therefore, this baboon exclaimed (with a sneering kind of laugh): "O ho! It is ourselves! Thou shalt quietly go to tell the old man yonder, that he may come to listen to this child." And the other one called out: "O person passing across in front! come to listen to this child." And the other said:

> *"First going*
> *I listen,*
> *To the child yonder."*

And he went up to the other people; he said: "What does this child say?" And the other one answered: "This child, he wants, he says, to fetch sticks for his father, that his father may take aim at the people who sit upon their heels."

Then that baboon – he felt that he was an old baboon – therefore, he said, when the other one had said, "This child wanted, he said, to fetch sticks for his father," therefore the other one (the old baboon) exclaimed: "What? It is we ourselves; ourselves it is! Ye shall strike the child with your fists."

Therefore, they were striking *Gaunu-tsaxau* with their fists on account of it; they hit with their fists, breaking (his) head. And another struck with his fist, knocking out *Gaunu-tsaxau*'s eye, the and the child's eye in this manner sprang (or rolled) away. Then this baboon exclaimed: "My ball! my ball!"

Therefore, they began to play a game at ball, while the child died; the child lay still. They said (sang):

> *"And I want it,*
> *Whose ball is it?*
> *And I want it,*
> *Whose ball is it?*
> *And I want it."*

The other people said, while they were playing at ball there with the child's eye:

> *"My companion's ball it is,*
> *And I want it,*
> *My companion's ball it is,*
> *And I want it,"*

The Mantis was waiting for the child. Therefore, the Mantis lay down at noon. Therefore, the Mantis was dreaming about the child, that the baboons were those who had killed the child; that they had made a ball of the child's eye; that he went to the baboons, while the baboons played at ball there with the child's eye.

Therefore, he arose; he took up the quiver, he slung on the quiver; he said, "Rattling along, rattling along," while he felt that he used formerly to do so, he used to say, "Rattling along." Then, when he came into sight, he perceived the baboons' dust, while the baboons were playing at ball there with the child's eye. Then the Mantis cried on account of it, because the baboons appeared really to have killed the child. Therefore, they were playing at ball there with the child's eye. Therefore, when he came into sight, he perceived the baboons' dust, while the baboons were playing at ball there with the child's eye. Therefore he cried about it. And he quickly shut his mouth; he thoroughly dried the tears from his eyes, while he desired that the baboons should not perceive tears in his eyes; that he appeared to have come crying, hence tears were in his eyes; so that he might go to play at ball with the baboons, while his eyes had no tears in them.

Then he, running, came up to the baboons, while the baboons stared at him, because they were startled at him. Then, while the baboons were still staring at him, he came running to a place where he laid down the quiver; he took off (his) kaross (i.e. skin cloak), he put down the kaross, he, grasping, drew out the feather brush which he had put into the bag, he shook out the brush, he played with(?) the ball. He called out to the baboons, why was it that the baboons were staring at him, while the baboons did not play with(?) the ball, that the baboons might throw it to him.

Then the baboons looked at one another, because they suspected why he spoke thus. Then he caught hold of the ball, when the ball had merely flown to another baboon, when this (the first) baboon had thrown the ball to the other. Then the child's eye, because the child's eye felt that it was startled(?), on account of his father's scent, it went playing about; the baboons trying to get it, missed it. Then one baboon, he was the one who caught hold of it, he threw it towards another. Then the Mantis merely sprang out from this place, the Mantis caught hold of the child's eye, the Mantis, snatching, took the child's eye. Then the Mantis whirled around the child's eye; he anointed the child's eye with (the perspiration of) his armpits. Then he threw the child's eye towards the baboons, the child's eye ascended, the child's eye went about in the sky; the baboons beheld it above, as it played about above in the sky. And the child's eye went to stand yonder opposite to the quiver; it appeared as if it sprang over the quiver, while it stood inside the quiver's bag.

Then the baboons went to seek for it. The Mantis also sought for it, while the baboons sought for it. Then all the baboons were altogether seeking for the child's eye. They said: "Give my companion the ball." The baboon whose ball it was, he said: "Give me the ball." The Mantis said: "Behold ye! I have not got the ball." The baboons said: "Give my companion the ball." The baboon whose ball it was, he said: "Give me the ball." Then the baboons said that the Mantis must shake the bag, for the ball seemed to be inside the bag. And the Mantis exclaimed: "Behold ye! Behold ye! the ball is not inside the bag. Behold ye!" while he grasped the child's eye, he shook, turning the bag inside out. He said: "Behold ye! Behold ye! the ball cannot be inside the bag."

Then this baboon exclaimed: "Hit the old man with (your) fists." Then the other one exclaimed: "Give my companion the ball!" while he struck the head of the Mantis. Then the Mantis exclaimed: "I have not got the ball," while he struck the baboon's head. Therefore, they were all striking the Mantis with their fists; the Mantis was striking them with his fist. Then the Mantis got the worst of it; the Mantis exclaimed: "Ow! Hartebeest's Children! ye must go, *kau Yerriggu*, ye must go!" ('Hartebeest's Children' may refer to a bag made from the skin of young hartebeests, which the Mantis had with him.) while the baboons watched him ascend; as he flew up, as he flew to the water. Then he popped into the water on account of it; while he exclaimed: "*I ke, tten khwaiten khwaiten, kui ha i ka!*" Then he walked out of the water; he sat down; he felt inside (his) bag; he took out the child's eye; he walked on as he held it; he walked, coming up to the grass at the top of the water's bank; he sat down. He exclaimed: "*Oh wwi ho!*" as he put the child's eye into the water.

"Thou must grow out, that thou mayest become like that which thou hast been." Then he walked on; he went to take up (his) kaross, he threw it over his shoulder; be took up the quiver, he slung on the quiver; and, in this manner, he returning went, while he returning arrived at home.

Then the young Ichneumon exclaimed: "Who can have done thus to my grandfather, the Mantis, that the Mantis is covered with wounds?" Then the Mantis replied: "The baboons were those who killed grandson, *Gaunu-tsaxau*; I went [the Mantis speaks very sadly and slowly here], as they were playing at ball there with grandson's eye; I went to play at ball with them. Then grandson's eye vanished. Therefore, the baboons said (that) I was the one who had it; the baboons were fighting me; therefore, I was fighting them; and I thus did, I flying came."

Then *kuammang-a* said: "I desire thee to say to grandfather, Why is it that grandfather continues to go among strangers?" Then the Mantis answered: "Thou dost appear to think that yearning was not that on account of which I went among the baboons;" while he did not tell *kuammang-a* and the others that he came (and) put the child's eye into the water.

Then he remained there (i.e., at home), while he did not go to the water. Then he went there, while he went to look at the place where he had put in the child's eye. And he approached gently, while he wished that he might not make a rustling noise. Therefore, he gently came. And the child heard him, because he had not come gently when afar off; and the child jumped up, it splashed into the water. Then the Mantis was laughing about it, while his heart yearned (for the child). And he returned; altogether returned.

Then the child grew; it became like that which it had (formerly) been. Then the Mantis came; while he came to look; and be in this manner walking came. While he came walking and looking, he espied the child, as the child was sitting in the sun. Then the child heard him, as he came rustling (along); the child sprang up, the child entered the water. And he looking stood, he went back, he went; he went to make for the child a front kaross (or apron), that and a *koroko*. He put the things aside; then he put the front kaross (into a bag), that and the *koroko*; he in this manner went; he in this manner came he approached gently. And, as he approached gently, he espied the child lying in the sun, as the child lay yonder, in the sun, opposite the water. Therefore, he gently came up to the child. And the child heard him, as his father gently came. And the Mantis, when the child intended to get up, the Mantis sprang forward, he caught hold of the child. And he anointed the child with his scent; he anointed the child; he said: "Why art thou afraid of me? I am thy father; I who am the Mantis, I am here; thou art my son, thou art *Gaunu-tsaxau*; I am the Mantis, I whose son thou art; the father is myself." And the child sat down, on account of it; and he took out the front kaross, he took out the *koroko*. He put the front kaross on to the child; he put the *koroko* on to the child; he put the front kaross on to the child. Then he took the child with him; they, in this manner, returning went; they returning arrived at home.

Then the young Ichneumon exclaimed: "What person can it be who comes with the Mantis?" And *kuammang-a* replied: "Hast thou not just(?) heard that grandfather said he had gone to the baboons, while they were playing at ball there with the child's eye? while grandfather must have been playing before us; his son comes yonder with him!" And they returned, reaching the house. Then the young Ichneumon spoke; he said: "Why did my grandfather, the Mantis, first say that the baboons were those who killed the child, while the child is here?" Then the Mantis said: "Hast thou not seen (that) he is not strong? while he feels that I came to put his eye into the water; while I wished that I might see whether the thing would not accomplish itself for me; therefore, I came to put his eye into the water. He came out of the water; therefore, thou seest (that) he is not strong. Therefore, I wished that I might wait, taking care of him; that I may see whether he will not become strong."

The Mason Wasp and His Wife
(From the San people, southern Africa)

THE MASON WASP FORMERLY did thus as he walked along, while (his) wife walked behind him, the wife said: "O my husband! Shoot for me that hare!" And the Mason Wasp laid down his quiver; the Mason Wasp said: "Where is the hare?" And (his) wife said: "The hare lies there."

And the Mason Wasp took out an arrow; the Mason Wasp in this manner went stooping along. And the wife said: "Put down (thy) kaross! Why is it that thou art not willing to put down (thy) kaross?" Therefore, the Mason Wasp, walking along, unloosened the strings of the kaross; he put down the kaross. Therefore the wife said: "Canst thou be like this? This must have been why thou wert not willing to lay down the kaross." (She mocked the man on account of the middle of his body, which was slender.)

Therefore, the Mason Wasp walked, turning to one side; he aimed at (his) wife, he shot, hitting the (head of) the arrow on (his) wife's breast (bone).

And (his) wife fell down dead on account of it. Then he exclaimed: "*Yi ii hihi!* O my wife *hi*!" (crying) as if he had not been the one to shoot (his) wife. He cried, that he should have done thus, have shot his wife; his wife died.

The Vultures, Their Elder Sister and Her Husband
(From the San people, southern Africa)

THE VULTURES FORMERLY MADE their elder sister of a person; they lived with her.

They, when their elder sister's husband brought (home) a springbok, they ate up the springbok. And their elder sister's husband cursed them, he scolded at them.

And their elder sister took up the skin of the springbok, she singed it. Their elder sister boiled the skin of the springbok, their elder sister took it out (of the pot).

And they were taking hold of the pieces of skin, they swallowed them down. Their elder sister's husband scolded them, because they again, they ate with their elder sister, of the springbok's skin, when they had just eaten the body of the springbok, they again, they ate with their elder sister of the springbok's skin.

And they were afraid of their elder sister's husband, they went away, they went in all directions, they, in this manner, sat down. And they looked at their elder sister's husband, they were looking furtively at their elder sister's husband.

Their elder sister's husband went hunting. He again, he went (and) killed a springbok; he brought the springbok home, slung upon his back. They again, they came (and) ate up the springbok. Their elder sister's husband scolded them. And they moved away, they sat down.

Their elder sister singed the springbok's skin she boiled the springbok's skin. Their elder sister was giving to them pieces of the skin, they were swallowing them down.

Therefore, on the morrow, their elder sister's husband said that his wife must go with him; she should altogether eat on the hunting ground; for, his younger sisters-in-law were in the habit of eating up the springbok. Therefore, the wife should go with him. Then, the wife went with him.

Therefore, they, when their elder sister had gone, they went out of the house, they sat down opposite to the house, and they conspired together about it. They said, this other one said: "Thou shalt ascend, and then thou must come to tell us what the place seems to be like." And another said: "Little sister shall be the one to try; and then, she must tell us." And then, a Vulture who was a little Vulture girl, she arose, she ascended.

They said: "Allow us, that we may see what little sister will do." Then, she went, disappearing in the sky, they no longer perceived her.

They sat; they were awaiting the time at which their younger sister should descend. Then, their younger sister descended (lit. fell) from above out of the sky, she (came and) sat in the midst of them.

And they exclaimed "Ah! What is the place like?" And their younger sister said: "Our mate (the elder sister) who is here shall ascend, that she may look. For, the place seems as if we should perceive a thing, when we are above there."

Then, her elder sister who was a grownup girl, she arose, she ascended, she went, disappearing in the sky. She descended from above, she sat in the midst of the other people.

And the other people said: "What is the place like?" And she said: "There is nothing the matter with the place; for, the place is clear. The place is very beautiful; for, I do behold the whole place; the stems of the trees, I do behold them; the place seems as if we should perceive a springbok, if a springbok were lying under a tree; for the place is very beautiful."

Then, they altogether arose, all of them, they ascended into the sky, while they wished that their elder sister should eat; for, their elder sister's husband scolded them.

Therefore, they used, when they espied their elder sister's husband coming, they ate in great haste. They said: "Ye must eat! ye must eat! ye must eat in great haste! for, that accursed man who comes yonder, he could not endure us." And, they finished the springbok, they flew away, flew heavily away, they thus, they yonder alighted; while their elder sister's husband came to pick up the bones.

They, when they perceived a springbok, they descended, and their elder sister perceived them, their elder sister followed them up. They ate, (they) ate, they were looking around; they said: "Ye must eat; ye should look around; ye shall leave some meat for (our) elder sister; ye shall leave for (our) elder sister the undercut, when ye see that (our) elder sister is the one who comes." And they perceived their older sister coming, they exclaimed: "Elder sister really seems to be coming yonder, ye must leave the meat which is in the springbok's skin." And, they left (it). And, when they beheld that their elder sister drew near to them, they went away, they went in all directions.

Their elder sister said: "Fie! how can ye act in this manner towards me? as if I had been the one who scolded you!"

And their elder sister came up to the springbok, she took up the springbok, she returned home; while the Vultures went forward(?), they went to fly about, while they sought for another springbok, which they intended again to eat.

The Animals and the Well
(From the Bantu-speaking peoples, central and southern Africa)

ONCE UPON A TIME there was a terrible drought over all the country. No rain had fallen for many months, and the animals were like to die of thirst. All the pools and watercourses were dried up. So the lion called the beasts together to the dry bed of a river, and suggested that they should all stamp on the sand and see whether they could not bring out some water. The elephant began, and stamped his hardest, but produced no result, except a choking cloud of dust. Then the rhinoceros tried, with no better success; then the buffalo; then the rest in turn – still nothing but dust, dust! At the beginning of the proceedings the elephant had sent to call the hare, but he said, "I don't want to come."

Now there was no one left but the tortoise, whom they all had overlooked on account of his insignificance. He came forward and began to stamp; the onlookers laughed and jeered. But, behold! before long there appeared a damp spot in the riverbed. And the rhinoceros, enraged that a little thing like that should succeed where he had failed, tossed him up and dashed him against a rock, so that his shell was broken into 100 pieces. While he sat, picking up the fragments and painfully sticking them together, the rhinoceros went on stamping, but the damp sand quickly disappeared, and clouds of dust rose, as before. The others repeated their vain efforts, till at last the elephant said, "Let the tortoise come and try." Before he had been at work more than a few minutes the water gushed out and filled the well, which had gradually been excavated by their combined efforts.

The animals then passed a unanimous resolution that the hare, who had refused to share in the work, should not be allowed to take any of the water. Knowing his character, they assumed that he would try to do so, and agreed to take turns in keeping watch over the well.

The hyena took the first watch, and after an hour or two saw the hare coming along with two calabashes, one empty and one full of honey. He called

74

out a greeting to the hyena, was answered, and asked him what he was doing there. The hyena replied, "I am guarding the well because of you, that you may not drink water here." "Oh," said the hare, "I don't want any of your water; it is muddy and bitter. I have much nicer water here." The hyena, his curiosity roused, asked to taste the wonderful water, and Sungura handed him a stalk of grass which he had dipped in the honey. "Oh, indeed, it is sweet! Just let me have some more!" "I can't do that unless you let me tie you up to the tree; this water is strong enough to knock you over if you are not tied." The hyena had so great a longing for the sweet drink that he readily consented; the hare tied him up so tightly that he could not move, went on to the well, and filled his calabash; then he jumped in, splashed about to his heart's content, and finally departed laughing.

In the morning the animals came and found the hyena tied to the tree. "Why, Hyena, who has done this to you?" "A great host of strong men came in the middle of the night, seized me, and tied me up." The lion said, "No such thing! Of course it was the hare, all by himself." The lion took his turn at watching that night; but, strange to say, he fell a victim to the same trick. Unable to resist the lure of the honey, he was ignominiously tied to the tree.

There they found him next morning, and the hyena, true to his currish nature, sneered: "So it was many men who tied you up, Lion? "The lion replied, with quiet dignity: "You need not talk; he would be too much for any of us."

The elephant then volunteered to keep watch, but with no better success; then the rest of the animals, each in his turn, only to be defeated by one trick or another.

At last the tortoise came forward, saying, "I am going to catch that one who is in the habit of binding people!" The others began to jeer: "Nonsense! Seeing how he has outwitted us, the elders, what can you do – a little one like you?" But the elephant took his part, and said that he should be allowed to try.

The Tortoise Is Too Sharp for the Hare

The tortoise then smeared his shell all over with birdlime, plunged into the well, and sat quite still at the bottom. When the hare came along that night and saw no watcher he sang out, "Hallo! Hallo! the well! Is there no one here?" Receiving no answer, he said, "They're afraid of me! I've beaten them all! Now for the water!"

75

He sat down beside the well, ate his honey, and filled both his gourds, before starting to bathe. Then he stepped into the water and found both his feet caught. He cried out, "Who are you? I don't want your water; mine is sweet. Let me go, and you can try it." But there was no answer. He struggled; he put down one hand to free himself; he put down the other; he was caught fast. There was no help for it: there he had to stay till the animals came in the morning. And when they saw him they said, "Now, indeed, the hare has been shown up!" So they carried him to the *bwalo* for judgment, and the lion said, "Why did you first disobey and afterwards steal the water?" The hare made no attempt to plead his cause, but said, "Just tie me up, and I shall die!" The lion ordered him to be bound, but the hare made one more suggestion. "Don't tie me with coconut rope, but with green banana fibre; then if you throw me out in the sun I shall die very quickly."

They did so, and after a while, when they heard the banana bast cracking as it dried up in the heat, they began to get suspicious, and someone said to the lion that the hare would surely break his bonds. The hare heard him and groaned out, as though at his last gasp, "Let me alone. I'm just going to die!" So he lay still for another hour, and then suddenly stretched himself; the banana fibre gave way, and he was off before they could recover from their astonishment. They started in pursuit, but he outran them all, and they were nearly giving up in despair when they saw him on the top of a distant anthill, apparently waiting for them to come up. When they got within earshot he called out, "I'm off! You're fools, all of you!" and disappeared into a hole in the side of the anthill. The animals hastened up and formed a circle round the hill, while the elephant came forward and thrust his trunk into the hole. After groping about for a while he seized the hare by the ear, and the hare cried, "That's a leaf you've got hold of. You've not caught me!" The elephant let go and tried again, this time seizing the hare's leg. "*O-O-O-O-O!* He's got hold of a root." Again the elephant let go, and Sungura slipped out of his reach into the depths of the burrow.

The animals grew tired of waiting, and, leaving the elephant to watch the anthill, went to fetch hoes, so that they might dig out the hare. While they were gone the hare, disguising his voice, called out to the elephant, "You who are watching the burrow open your eyes wide and keep them fixed on this hole, so that the hare may not get past without your seeing him! "The elephant unsuspectingly obeyed, and Sungura, sitting just inside the entrance, kicked up a cloud of sand into his eyes and dashed out past him. The elephant, blinded and in pain, was quite unaware of his escape, and kept on watching the hole till the other animals came back. They asked if Sungura was still there. "He may be, but he has thrown sand into my eyes." They fell to digging, and, of course, found nothing.

The Hare's Disguises

Meanwhile the hare had gone away into the bush, plaited his hair in the latest fashion, plastered it with wax taken from a wild bees' nest, and whitened his face with clay, so that he was quite unrecognizable. Then he strolled casually past the place where the animals were at work, asked what they were doing, and offered to help. He was given a hoe, which he used with such vigour that it soon came off the handle. He asked the giraffe for the loan of his leg, used it as the handle of his hoe, and speedily broke it, whereupon he shouted, "I'm the hare!" and fled, taking refuge in another anthill, which had more than one entrance. They started to dig; he escaped through the second hole, which they had not noticed, disguised himself afresh, and came back as before. This time, when his hoe came off the handle, he asked the elephant to let him hammer it in on his head; and he did it with such goodwill that he soon killed him. He ran away once more, shouting insults as he went, and the animals, having lost their two principal leaders, returned home, weary and discouraged.

The Hare Nurses the Lioness's Cubs

The hare then went on his way quite happily, till, sometime later, he met a lioness, who seized him and was about to kill him. But he pleaded so eloquently for his life, assuring her that he could make himself very useful if she would let him be her servant, that at last she relented and took him home to her den. Next day, when she went out to hunt, she left him in charge of her ten cubs. While she was gone Sungura took the cubs down to the stream to play, and suggested that they should wrestle. He wrestled with one of them, threw it, and twisted its neck as they lay on the ground. Returning to the cave with the others, he skinned and ate the dead one at the first convenient opportunity. In the evening the mother came home and, staying outside the cave, told the hare to bring the children out for her to nurse. He brought one, and when she told him to bring the rest he objected, saying it was better to bring them out one by one. Having suckled the first, she handed it back, and he brought her the remaining eight, taking the last twice over.

Next day he did the same, bringing out the last cub three times, and so deceived the mother into thinking she had suckled the whole ten. This went on until he had eaten all but one, which he brought out ten times; when it came to the tenth time the lioness noticed that the cub refused to suck. The hare explained that it had not been well all day, and the lioness was satisfied, and only told him to take good care of it.

The Hare and the Baboons

As soon as she was gone next day he killed, skinned and ate the last cub, and, taking the other skins from the place where he had hidden them, set out on his travels. Towards evening he came to the village of the baboons, and found the 'men' playing with teetotums in the 'forum'. He went and sat down in the usual place for strangers, and when some of them came to greet him said, "I have brought beautiful skins to sell. Does anyone want to buy them?" The baboons crowded round, admiring the skins, and all ten were soon disposed of. They then returned to their game, and the hare sat watching them. Presently he said, "You are not playing right. Shall I show you how?" They handed him a teetotum, and he began to spin it, singing all the time:

"We have eaten the lion's children on the quiet!"

They listened attentively, and then said, "Let us learn this song"; so he taught them the words, and they practised for the rest of the evening. After which he shared their meal, and was given a hut to sleep in.

In the morning he was off before it was light, and made his way back to the lions' den, where he found the lioness distractedly searching for her missing cubs. On the way he had been careful to roll in the mud and get himself well scratched by the thorny bushes, so that he presented a most disorderly appearance. On seeing her he set up a dismal wail. "Oh! Oh! Some wild beasts came yesterday and carried off your children. They were too much for me; I could do nothing. See how they knocked me about and wounded me! But I followed them, and I can show you where they live. If you come with me you will be able to kill them all. But you had better let me tie you up in a bundle of grass and put some beans just inside, and I will carry you and tell them that I have brought a load of beans. They have the skins of your children, whom I saw them eating." The lioness agreed, and, having tied her up, the hare started with his load. Arriving at the village, he laid it down in the place for strangers.

The baboons were so intent on their game that they hardly noticed him at first, and the lioness could hear them singing with all their might:

"We have eaten the lion's children on the quiet!"

After a while they came up and greeted Sungura, and he said that he had brought them a load of beans in return for their hospitality of the day before. He loosened one end of the bundle, to show them the beans, and then eagerly accepted their invitation to join in the game. By the time it was once more in full swing the lioness had worked herself free, and sprang on the nearest baboon, bearing him to the ground. The others tried to escape, but the hare had run round to the gate of the enclosure, closed it, and fastened the bar. Then began a murder grim and great; not one of the baboons was left alive, and when the hare had brought out the skins of the poor cubs and laid them before the lioness she knew for a certainty that she had but done justice, and was duly grateful to the hare. He, however, thought it just as well not to remain in her neighbourhood, so took his leave and resumed his wanderings.

The Hare, the Hyena and the Pot of Beans
(From the Bantu-speaking peoples, central and southern Africa)

ONE DAY, THE HARE AND THE HYENA, being in want of food, they went to the chief of a certain village and offered to cultivate his garden. He agreed, and gave them a pot of beans as their food supply for the day.

When they reached the garden they made a fire and put the beans on to boil. By the time they knocked off for the midday rest the beans were done, and the hyena, saying that he wanted to wash before eating, went to the stream and left the hare to watch the pot. No sooner was he out of sight than he stripped off his skin and ran back. The hare, thinking this was some strange and terrible beast, lost his head and ran away; the hyena sat down by the fire, finished the whole pot full of beans, returned to the stream, resumed his skin and came back at his leisure.

The hare, as all seemed quiet, ventured back, found the pot empty and the hyena clamorously demanding his food. The hare explained that he had been frightened away by an unknown monster, which had evidently eaten up the beans. The hyena refused to accept this excuse, and accused the hare of having eaten the beans himself. The unfortunate hare had to go hungry; but, finding denial useless, contented himself with remarking that if that beast came again he meant to shoot it; so he set to work making a bow.

The hyena watched him till the bow was finished, and then said. "You have not made it right. Give it here!" And, taking it from him, he pretended to trim it into shape, but all the while he was cutting away the wood so as to weaken it in one spot. The hare so far suspected nothing, and kept his bow handy against the lunch hour on the following day. When the 'wild beast' appeared, he fitted an arrow to the string and bent the bow, but it broke in his hand, and once more he fled.

By this time his suspicions were awakened, and when he had made himself a new bow he hid it in the grass when the hyena was not looking. On the next occasion when the hyena appeared he shot at him and wounded him, but not seriously, so that he ran back to get into his skin and returned to find the hare calmly eating beans.

The Hare, the Hyena
and the Roasted Guinea Fowl
(From the Bantu-speaking peoples, central and southern Africa)

THE HARE AND THE HYENA went into the bush together after game. They found a guinea fowl's nest full of eggs, and soon after trapped a guinea fowl. They carried their spoils home, and the

hare said to his friend, "You roast the fowl and the eggs. I'm tired; I want to go to sleep."

The hyena made up the fire, spitted the bird on a stick, and put the eggs into the hot ashes. When the savoury steam filled the hut, his mouth began to water, and when he had made sure that the guinea fowl was done he ate it up, all but the legs, which he put into the fire. He then ate the eggs, carefully cleaned the shell of one and put it aside, together with one quill, threw the rest of the feathers into the fire, and lay down to sleep.

The smell of the burning feathers awakened Sungura, who started up, called the hyena, and then noticed that the guinea fowl was missing. When asked where it was the hyena said he had fallen asleep while it was roasting, and it had got burned. The hare suspected the truth, but said nothing at the time. A little later he suggested that they should go to their respective relations and get some food; so they separated. The hyena went a little way, and as soon as he was out of sight lay down in the grass and slept. The hare, too, did not go far, but hid himself and waited awhile; then he gathered some banana leaves and stealthily followed his partner. He tied him up and gave him a good beating, which effectually wakened him, so that he cried for mercy, though he could not see who was attacking him. The hare then went away, and a little later pretended to come upon his victim unexpectedly, kicked the supposedly unknown object in his path, and said, "What's this?"

"I'm here, your friend!"

"What's the matter?"

"Some man came along and tied me up and beat me."

"Do you know who it was?"

"No, I don't."

The hare condoled with the hyena, and they remained quiet for a few days, when the hyena heard that there was to be a dance at his village, and invited the hare to go with him. The hare accepted, but said he wanted to go home first: he would come in the afternoon.

The hyena went and had a bath, got himself up in his best clothes, complete with beads, for the dance, and, as a finishing touch, put the eggshell on his head and stuck the feather into it. When the hare arrived he welcomed him warmly, asked him to sit down, and thereupon took his *zomari* (a kind of clarinet) and played:

"The guinea fowl and all! Put the blame on the fire! ti! ti! ti!"

These are 'riddling words' (*maneno ya fumbo*). They mean: "I've eaten up the guinea fowl and all, though I pretended it had got burned!" The hare understood them well enough; he sprang up, seized a big drum and fell to beating it and singing:

"I took him and bound him with banana leaves and beat him! pu! pu! pu!"

Then ensued a free fight, which, strange to say, did not dissolve the partnership.

The Hyena Kills the Hare's Mother
(From the Bantu-speaking peoples, central and southern Africa)

IN A TIME OF FAMINE, having exhausted every possible food supply, the hyena proposed that he should kill and eat his mother, and the hare should do the same. The hare agreed, but kept his reflections to himself. The hyena went away, killed his mother, and ate her; the hare went, ostensibly for the same purpose, but hid his mother in a cave which could be reached only by climbing up the face of the cliff, and left with her a supply of wild herbs and roots, having first agreed on a signal to make his presence known. Next day, when the hyena had departed on his own business, the hare went to the cave and uttered the password. On hearing his mother's answer he called out to her to let down a rope, by which he climbed up into the cave. She had cooked sufficient food for herself and him, and after a hearty meal he returned to the place where he had left his friend. And this he did day by day.

The hyena, in the meantime, had finished his meat by the second day, and could not make out why the hare never seemed in want of food. So one day he followed him, and, hiding in the bushes, heard him give the password and the mother answer, and saw him drawn up into the cave. Next day he watched his opportunity, went to the cave, and called out the word, but there was no answer, the hare having warned his mother to take no notice should anyone else come. He saw that the hare had deceived him, and went away nursing his grievance, but at a loss what to do about it. He decided to consult the leopard, but got no help from him, only the suggestion that he had better go to the anteater.

The anteater, on hearing his story, said that there was no hope for him unless he could imitate the hare's voice so skilfully as to deceive his mother; and to make this possible he advised him to go to a nest of soldier ants and put his tongue in among them; if he got it well stung his voice would be softened. He did this, but was unable to endure the pain for more than a short time. He returned to the anteater, who desired him to try his voice, and found that it was not much improved. The anteater said, "My friend, you're a coward. If you want to eat the hare's mother you will have to go back and let the ants bite your tongue till it is half its present size!"

The hyena's greed and resentment were stronger than his dread of pain, so he went back and let the ants work their will on him till the desired result was obtained. In fact, when he went back to the cave the hare's mother was completely taken in and let down the rope at once – to her undoing.

The Hare's Revenge

When the hare went as usual on the following day he got no answer to his call, and, looking round, saw traces of blood on the grass. Then he guessed what had happened, and thought how he might be revenged. When he met the hyena again he said nothing, but went away and made his preparations.

He came forth in the evening most splendidly adorned (the details, of course, vary locally, from a wealth of brass and copper chains, pendants, rings and ear ornaments to the white shirt, embroidered coat, silver-mounted sword and jewelled dagger of the coast men). Having thoroughly excited the hyena's admiration and envy, he showed him a mark on the top of his head, and told him that he had had a red-hot nail driven in there, and that if he, the hyena, would submit to the same operation he might be similarly adorned. The foolish beast was quite willing – the hare had the red-hot iron ready – and that, of course, was the end of Hyena.

The Hare Overcomes
Both Rhino and Hippo
(From the Bantu-speaking peoples, central and southern Africa)

THE HARE CHALLENGED THE HIPPOPOTAMUS and the rhinoceros to a trial of strength, going to each in turn and saying, "Take hold of this rope, and let us pull against each other. I am going to the bank yonder." He then disappeared into the bushes, carrying what purported to be his end of the rope, and calling out as he went, "Wait till you feel me pull at my end, and then begin."

He had stationed the two on opposite sides of a bush-covered island, and when he reached a point midway between them he pulled the rope in both directions. Rhino and hippo both pulled with all their might; their strength being about equal, neither gave way to any extent, though the former, after a while, was dragged forward a little, and when he recovered himself went back with such a rush that he dragged the hippo out on to the bank, whereat they both ejaculated, "Stupendous!" and Hippo called, "Hare! hare!" but without receiving any answer. They went on pulling till they were both exhausted, and the rhino said, "I will go and see that man who is pulling me," and just then the hippo put his head out of the water, and said, "Who is that pulling me?" And Chipembele (the rhino) said, "Why, Shinakambeza (one of Hippo's 'praise names'), is it you pulling me?" "It is I. Why, who was he that brought you the rope, Chipembele?" "It was the hare. Was it he who gave it to you, Hippo?" "Yes, it was he."

It seems that these two had previously been at enmity, and the rhino had vowed never to set foot in the river. But the fact that both had equally been made fools of disposed them more favourably towards each other.

Thus they became reconciled, and that is why Rhinoceros drinks water today. Rhinoceros and Hippopotamus, when they do not see each other in the flesh, Rhinoceros will drink water in the river where Hippo lives, and Hippopotamus comes out to go grazing where Rhinoceros has his home.

The Hare's End
(From the Bantu-speaking peoples, central and southern Africa)

THE HARE WENT ONE DAY to call on his friend the cock, and found him asleep, with his head under his wing. The hare had never seen him in this position before, and never thought of doubting the hens' word when they informed him (as previously instructed) that their husband was in the habit of taking off his head and giving it to the herd boys to carry with them to the pasture. "Since you were born have you ever seen a man have his head cut off and for it to go to pasture, while the man himself stayed at home in the village?" And the hare said, "Never! But when those herd boys come, will he get up again?" And those women said, "Just wait and see!" At last, when the herd boys arrived, their mother said, "Just rouse your father there where he is sleeping." The cock, when aroused, welcomed his guest, and they sat talking till dinner was ready, and still conversed during the meal. The hare was anxious to know how it was done, and the cock told him, "It is quite easy, if you think you would like to do it." The hare confidently accepted the explanation, and they parted, having agreed that the cock should return the visit next day.

He was so greatly excited that he began to talk of his wonderful experience as soon as he reached his home. "That person the fowl is a clever fellow; he has

85

just shown me his clever device of cutting off the head till, on your being hit, you see, you become alive again. Well, tomorrow I intend to show you all this device!"

Next morning he told his boys what to do. They hesitated, but he insisted, and when they were ready to go out with the cattle they cut off his head, bored the ears and put a string through them, to carry it more conveniently. The women picked up the body and laid it on the bed, trusting, in spite of appearances, to his assurance that he was not dead.

By and by his friend arrived, and, not seeing him, inquired for him; the women showed him the body lying on the bed. He was struck with consternation, and, let us hope, with remorse. "But my friend is a simpleton indeed!" They said, "Is not this device derived from you?" but he turned a deaf ear to this hint, and only insisted that the hare was a simpleton. He thought, however, he would wait and see whether, after all, he did get up. The boys came home when the sun declined; they struck their father, as he had told them, but he did not get up. And the children burst out crying. And the mothers of the family cried. And folks sat mourning. And all the people that heard of it were amazed at his death: "Such a clever man! And for him to have met with his death through such a trifling thing!"

That was 'Harey's' epitaph.

The Name of the Tree
(From the Lamba people, southern Africa)

IN A TIME OF FAMINE all the animals gathered near a tree full of wonderful fruit, which could not be gathered unless the right name of the tree was mentioned, and built their huts there. When the fruit ripened Wakalulu ('Mr Little Hare') went to the chief of the tree and asked him its name. The chief answered, "When you arrive just stand still and say *Uwungelema.*" The hare started on his way back, but when he had reached the outskirts of his village he tripped, and the name went out of his head.

Trying to recover it, he kept saying to himself, *"Uwungelenyense, Uwuntuluntumba*, Uwu-what?"

When he arrived the animals asked, "What is the name, Little Hare, of these things?" But he could only stammer the wrong words, and not a fruit fell. Next morning two buffaloes arose and tried their luck – it seems to have been considered safer to send two – but on their return both tripped and forgot the word. In answer to their eager questioners they said, "He said, *Uwumbilakanwa, Uwuntu-luntumba,* or what?" – which, of course, could not help matters.

Then two elands were sent, with the same result.

Then the lion went, and, though he took care to repeat the word· over and over again on the way home, he too tripped against the obstacle and forgot it. Then all the animals, the roans and the sables, and the mongooses, all came to an end going there. They all just returned in vain.

Then the tortoise went to the chief and asked for the name. He had it repeated more than once, to make sure, and then set out on his slow and cautious journey.

He travelled a great distance and then said, *"Uwungelema."* Again he reached the outskirts of the village, again he said, *"Uwungelema."* Then he arrived in the village and reached his house and had a smoke. When he had finished smoking, the people arrived and said, "What is it, Tortoise?" Mr Tortoise went out and said, *"Uwungelema!"* The fruit pelted down. The people just covered the place, all the animals picking up. They sat down again: in the morning they said, "Go to Mr Tortoise." And Mr Tortoise came out and said, *"Uwungelema!"* Again numberless fruits pelted down. Then they began praising Mr Tortoise, saying, "Mr Tortoise is chief, because he knows the name of these fruits."

This happened again and again, till the fruit came to an end, and the animals dispersed, to seek subsistence elsewhere.

So in the Benga country the grateful beasts proclaimed Kudu, the tortoise, as their second chief, the python, Mbama, having been their sole ruler hitherto. "We shall have two kings, Kudu and Mbama, each at his end of the country. For the one, with his wisdom, told what was fit to be eaten, and the other, with his skill, brought the news."

How Isuro the Rabbit Tricked Gudu
(From the Mashona people, Zimbabwe)

FAR AWAY IN A HOT COUNTRY, where the forests are very thick and dark, and the rivers very swift and strong, there once lived a strange pair of friends. Now one of the friends was a big white rabbit named Isuro, and the other was a tall baboon called Gudu, and so fond were they of each other that they were seldom seen apart.

One day, when the sun was hotter even than usual, the rabbit awoke from his midday sleep, and saw Gudu the baboon standing beside him.

"Get up," said Gudu; "I am going courting, and you must come with me. So put some food in a bag, and sling it round your neck, for we may not be able to find anything to eat for a long while."

Then the rabbit rubbed his eyes, and gathered a store of fresh green things from under the bushes, and told Gudu that he was ready for the journey.

They went on quite happily for some distance, and at last they came to a river with rocks scattered here and there across the stream.

"We can never jump those wide spaces if we are burdened with food," said Gudu, "we must throw it into the river, unless we wish to fall in ourselves." And stooping down, unseen by Isuro, who was in front of him, Gudu picked up a big stone, and threw it into the water with a loud splash.

"It is your turn now," he cried to Isuro. And with a heavy sigh, the rabbit unfastened his bag of food, which fell into the river.

The road on the other side led down an avenue of trees, and before they had gone very far Gudu opened the bag that lay hidden in the thick hair about his neck, and began to eat some delicious-looking fruit.

"Where did you get that from?" asked Isuro enviously.

"Oh, I found after all that I could get across the rocks quite easily, so it seemed a pity not to keep my bag," answered Gudu.

"Well, as you tricked me into throwing away mine, you ought to let me share with you," said Isuro. But Gudu pretended not to hear him, and strode along the path.

By-and-by they entered a wood, and right in front of them was a tree so laden with fruit that its branches swept the ground. And some of the fruit was still green, and some yellow. The rabbit hopped forward with joy, for he was very hungry; but Gudu said to him: "Pluck the green fruit, you will find it much the best. I will leave it all for you, as you have had no dinner, and take the yellow for myself." So the rabbit took one of the green oranges and began to bite it, but its skin was so hard that he could hardly get his teeth through the rind.

"It does not taste at all nice," he cried, screwing up his face; "I would rather have one of the yellow ones."

"No! no! I really could not allow that," answered Gudu. "They would only make you ill. Be content with the green fruit." And as they were all he could get, Isuro was forced to put up with them.

After this had happened two or three times, Isuro at last had his eyes opened, and made up his mind that, whatever Gudu told him, he would do exactly the opposite. However, by this time they had reached the village where dwelt Gudu's future wife, and as they entered Gudu pointed to a clump of bushes, and said to Isuro: "Whenever I am eating, and you hear me call out that my food has burnt me, run as fast as you can and gather some of those leaves that they may heal my mouth."

The rabbit would have liked to ask him why he ate food that he knew would burn him, only he was afraid, and just nodded in reply; but when they had gone on a little further, he said to Gudu:

"I have dropped my needle; wait here a moment while I go and fetch it."

"Be quick then," answered Gudu, climbing into a tree. And the rabbit hastened back to the bushes, and gathered a quantity of the leaves, which he hid among his fur, "for," thought he, "if I get them now I shall save myself the trouble of a walk by-and-by."

When he had plucked as many as he wanted he returned to Gudu, and they went on together.

The sun was almost setting by the time they reached their journey's end, and being very tired they gladly sat down by a well. Then Gudu's betrothed, who had been watching for him, brought out a pitcher of water – which she poured over them to wash off the dust of the road – and two portions of food. But once again the rabbit's hopes were dashed to the ground, for Gudu said hastily:

"The custom of the village forbids you to eat till I have finished." And Isuro did not know that Gudu was lying, and that he only wanted more food. So he sat hungrily looking on, waiting till his friend had had enough.

In a little while Gudu screamed loudly: "I am burnt! I am burnt!" though he was not burnt at all. Now, though Isuro had the leaves about him, he did not dare to produce them at the last moment lest the baboon should guess why he had stayed behind. So he just went round a corner for a short time, and then came hopping back in a great hurry. But, quick though he was, Gudu had been quicker still, and nothing remained but some drops of water.

"How unlucky you are," said Gudu, snatching the leaves; "no sooner had you gone than ever so many people arrived, and washed their hands, as you see, and ate your portion." But, though Isuro knew better than to believe him, he said nothing, and went to bed hungrier than he had ever been in his life.

Early next morning they started for another village, and passed on the way a large garden where people were very busy gathering monkey nuts.

"You can have a good breakfast at last," said Gudu, pointing to a heap of empty shells; never doubting but that Isuro would meekly take the portion shown him, and leave the real nuts for himself. But what was his surprise when Isuro answered:

"Thank you; I think I should prefer these." And, turning to the kernels, never stopped as long as there was one left. And the worst of it was that, with so many people about, Gudu could not take the nuts from him.

It was night when they reached the village where dwelt the mother of Gudu's betrothed, who laid meat and millet porridge before them.

"I think you told me you were fond of porridge," said Gudu; but Isuro answered: "You are mistaking me for somebody else, as I always eat meat when I can get it." And again Gudu was forced to be content with the porridge, which he hated.

While he was eating it, however, a sudden thought darted into his mind, and he managed to knock over a great pot of water which was hanging in front of the fire, and put it quite out.

"*Now*," said the cunning creature to himself, "I shall be able in the dark to steal his meat!" But the rabbit had grown as cunning as he, and standing in a corner hid the meat behind him, so that the baboon could not find it.

"O Gudu!" he cried, laughing aloud, "it is you who have taught me how to be clever." And calling to the people of the house, he bade them kindle the fire, for Gudu would sleep by it, but that he would pass the night with some friends in another hut.

It was still quite dark when Isuro heard his name called very softly, and, on opening his eyes, beheld Gudu standing by him. Laying his finger on his nose, in token of silence, he signed to Isuro to get up and follow him, and it was not until they were some distance from the hut that Gudu spoke.

"I am hungry and want something to eat better than that nasty porridge that I had for supper. So I am going to kill one of those goats, and as you are a good cook you must boil the flesh for me." The rabbit nodded, and Gudu disappeared behind a rock, but soon returned dragging the dead goat with him. The two then set about skinning it, after which they stuffed the skin with dried leaves, so that no one would have guessed it was not alive, and set it up in the middle of a clump of bushes, which kept it firm on its feet. While he was doing this, Isuro collected sticks for a fire, and when it was kindled, Gudu hastened to another hut to steal a pot which he filled with water from the river, and, planting two branches in the ground, they hung the pot with the meat in it over the fire.

"It will not be fit to eat for two hours at least," said Gudu, "so we can both have a nap." And he stretched himself out on the ground, and pretended to fall fast asleep, but, in reality, he was only waiting till it was safe to take all the meat for himself. "Surely I hear him snore," he thought; and he stole to the place where Isuro was lying on a pile of wood, but the rabbit's eyes were wide open.

"How tiresome," muttered Gudu, as he went back to his place; and after waiting a little longer he got up, and peeped again, but still the rabbit's pink eyes stared widely. If Gudu had only known, Isuro was asleep all the time; but this he never guessed, and by-and-by he grew so tired with watching that he went to sleep himself. Soon after, Isuro woke up, and he too felt hungry, so he crept softly to the pot and ate all the meat, while he tied the bones together and hung them in Gudu's fur. After that he went back to the woodpile and slept again.

In the morning the mother of Gudu's betrothed came out to milk her goats, and on going to the bushes where the largest one seemed entangled, she found out the trick. She made such lament that the people of the village came running, and Gudu and Isuro jumped up also, and pretended to be as surprised and interested as the rest. But they must have looked guilty after all, for suddenly an old man pointed to them, and cried:

"Those are the thieves." And at the sound of his voice the big Gudu trembled all over.

"How dare you say such things? I defy you to prove it," answered Isuro boldly. And he danced forward, and turned head over heels, and shook himself before them all.

"I spoke hastily; you are innocent," said the old man; "but now let the baboon do likewise." And when Gudu began to jump the goat's bones rattled, and the people cried: "It is Gudu who is the goat slayer!" But Gudu answered:

"Nay, I did not kill your goat; it was Isuro, and he ate the meat, and hung the bones round my neck. So it is he who should die!" And the people looked at each other, for they knew not what to believe. At length one man said:

"Let them both die, but they may choose their own deaths."

Then Isuro answered:

"If we must die, put us in the place where the wood is cut, and heap it up all round us, so that we cannot escape, and set fire to the wood; and if one is burned and the other is not, then he that is burned is the goat slayer."

And the people did as Isuro had said. But Isuro knew of a hole under the woodpile, and when the fire was kindled he ran into the hole, but Gudu died there.

When the fire had burned itself out, and only ashes were left where the wood had been, Isuro came out of his hole, and said to the people:

"Lo! did I not speak well? He who killed your goat is among those ashes."

The Jackal and the Spring
(From Lesotho, southern Africa)

ONCE UPON A TIME all the streams and rivers ran so dry that the animals did not know how to get water. After a very long search, which had been quite in vain, they found a tiny spring, which only wanted to be dug deeper so as to yield plenty of water. So the

beasts said to each other, "Let us dig a well, and then we shall not fear to die of thirst;" and they all consented except the jackal, who hated work of any kind, and generally got somebody to do it for him.

When they had finished their well, they held a council as to who should be made the guardian of the well, so that the jackal might not come near it, for, they said, "he would not work, therefore he shall not drink."

After some talk it was decided that the rabbit should be left in charge; then all the other beasts went back to their homes.

When they were out of sight the jackal arrived. "Good morning! Good morning, rabbit!" and the rabbit politely said, "Good morning!" Then the jackal unfastened the little bag that hung at his side, and pulled out of it a piece of honeycomb which he began to eat, and turning to the rabbit he remarked:

"As you see, rabbit, I am not thirsty in the least, and this is nicer than any water."

"Give me a bit," asked the rabbit. So the jackal handed him a very little morsel.

"Oh, how good it is!" cried the rabbit; "give me a little more, dear friend!"

But the jackal answered, "If you really want me to give you some more, you must have your paws tied behind you, and lie on your back, so that I can pour it into your mouth."

The rabbit did as he was bid, and when he was tied tight and popped on his back, the jackal ran to the spring and drank as much as he wanted. When he had quite finished he returned to his den.

In the evening the animals all came back, and when they saw the rabbit lying with his paws tied, they said to him: "Rabbit, how did you let yourself be taken in like this?"

"It was all the fault of the jackal," replied the rabbit; "he tied me up like this, and told me he would give me something nice to eat. It was all a trick just to get at our water."

"Rabbit, you are no better than an idiot to have let the jackal drink our water when he would not help to find it. Who shall be our next watchman? We must have somebody a little sharper than you!" and the little hare called out, "I will be the watchman."

The following morning the animals all went their various ways, leaving the little hare to guard the spring. When they were out of sight the jackal came back. "Good morning! good morning, little hare," and the little hare politely said, "Good morning."

"Can you give me a pinch of snuff?" said the jackal.

"I am so sorry, but I have none," answered the little hare.

The jackal then came and sat down by the little hare, and unfastened his little bag, pulling out of it a piece of honeycomb. He licked his lips and exclaimed, "Oh, little hare, if you only knew how good it is!"

"What is it?" asked the little hare.

"It is something that moistens my throat so deliciously," answered the jackal, "that after I have eaten it I don't feel thirsty anymore, while I am sure that all you other beasts are forever wanting water."

"Give me a bit, dear friend," asked the little hare.

"Not so fast," replied the jackal. "If you really wish to enjoy what you are eating, you must have your paws tied behind you, and lie on your back, so that I can pour it into your mouth."

"You can tie them, only be quick," said the little hare, and when he was tied tight and popped on his back, the jackal went quietly down to the well, and drank as much as he wanted. When he had quite finished he returned to his den.

In the evening the animals all came back; and when they saw the little hare with his paws tied, they said to him: "Little hare, how did you let yourself be taken in like this? Didn't you boast you were very sharp? You undertook to guard our water; now show us how much is left for us to drink!"

"It is all the fault of the jackal," replied the little hare, "He told me he would give me something nice to eat if I would just let him tie my hands behind my back."

Then the animals said, "Who can we trust to mount guard now?" And the panther answered, "Let it be the tortoise."

The following morning the animals all went their various ways, leaving the tortoise to guard the spring. When they were out of sight the jackal came back. "Good morning, tortoise; good morning."

But the tortoise took no notice.

"Good morning, tortoise; good morning." But still the tortoise pretended not to hear.

Then the jackal said to himself, "Well, today I have only got to manage a bigger idiot than before. I shall just kick him on one side, and then go and have a drink." So he went up to the tortoise and said to him in a soft voice, "Tortoise! tortoise!" but the tortoise took no notice. Then the jackal kicked him out of the way, and went to the well and began to drink, but scarcely had he touched the water, than the tortoise seized him by the leg. The jackal shrieked out: "Oh, you will break my leg!" but the tortoise only held on the tighter. The jackal then took his bag and tried to make the tortoise smell the honeycomb he had inside; but the tortoise turned away his head and smelt nothing. At last the jackal said to the tortoise, "I should like to give you my bag and everything in it," but the only answer the tortoise made was to grasp the jackal's leg tighter still.

So matters stood when the other animals came back. The moment he saw them, the jackal gave a violent tug, and managed to free his leg, and then took to his heels as fast as he could. And the animals all said to the tortoise:

"Well done, tortoise, you have proved your courage; now we can drink from our well in peace, as you have got the better of that thieving jackal!"

Morongoe the Snake
(From Lesotho, southern Africa)

MOKETE WAS A CHIEF'S DAUGHTER, but she was also beautiful beyond all the daughters of her father's house, and Morongoe the brave and Tau the lion both desired to possess her, but Tau found not favour in the eyes of her parents, neither desired she to be his wife, whereas Morongoe was rich and the son of a great chief, and upon him was Mokete bestowed in marriage.

But Tau swore by all the evil spirits that their happiness should not long continue, and he called to his aid the old witch doctor, whose power was greater than the tongue of man could tell; and one day Morongoe walked down to the water and was seen no more. Mokete wept and mourned for her brave young husband, to whom she had been wedded but ten short moons, but Tau rejoiced greatly.

When two more moons had waned, a son was born to Mokete, to whom she gave the name of Tsietse (sadness). The child grew and throve, and the years passed by, but brought no news of Morongoe.

One day, when Tsietse was nearly seven years old, he cried unto his mother, saying, "Mother, how is it that I have never seen my father? My companions see and know their fathers, and love them, but I alone know not the face of my father, I alone have not a father's protecting love."

"My son," replied his mother, "a father you have never known, for the evil spirits carried him from amongst us before ever you were born." She then related to him all that had happened.

From that day Tsietse played no more with the other boys, but wandered about from one pool of water to another, asking the frogs to tell him of his father.

Now the custom of the Basuto, when anyone falls into the water and is not found, is to drive cattle into the place where the person is supposed to have fallen, as they will bring him out. Many cattle had been driven into the different pools of water near Morongoe's village, but as they had failed to bring his father, Tsietse knew it was not much use looking near home. Accordingly, one day he went to a large pond a long distance off, and there he asked the frogs to help him in his search. One old frog hopped close to the child, and said, "You will find your father, my son, when you have walked to the edge of the world and taken a leap into the waters beneath; but he is no longer as you are, nor does he know of your existence."

This, at last, was the information Tsietse had longed for, now he could begin his search in real earnest. For many days he walked on, and ever on. At length, one day, just as the sun was setting, he saw before him a large sea of water of many beautiful colours. Stepping into it, he began to ask the same question; but at every word he uttered, the sea rose up, until at length it covered his head, and he began falling, falling through the deep sea. Suddenly he found himself upon dry ground, and upon looking round he saw flocks and herds, flowers and fruit, on every side. At first he was too much astonished to speak, but after a little while he went up to one of the herd boys and asked him if he had ever seen his (Tsietse's) father. The herd boy told him many strangers visited that place, and he had better see the chief, who would be able to answer his question.

When Tsietse had told his story to the chief, the old man knew at once that the great snake which dwelt in their midst must be the child's father; so, bidding the boy remain and rest, he went off to consult with the snake as to how they should tell Tsietse the truth without frightening him; but as they talked, Tsietse ran up to them, and, seeing the snake, at once embraced it, for he knew it was his father.

Then there was great joy in the heart of Morongoe, for he knew that by his son's aid he should be able to overcome his enemy, and return at length to his wife and home. So he told Tsietse how Tau had persuaded the old witch doctor to turn him into a snake, and banish him to this world below the earth. Soon afterwards Tsietse returned to his home, but he was no longer a child, but a noble youth, with a brave, straight look that made the wicked afraid. Very gently he told his mother all that had happened to him, and how eager his father was to return to his home. Mokete consulted an old doctor who lived in the mountain alone, and who told her she must get Tsietse to bring his father to the village in the brightness of the daytime, but that he must be so surrounded by his followers from the land beyond that none of his own people would be able to see him.

Quickly the news spread through the village that Morongoe had been found by his son and was returning to his people.

At length Tsietse was seen approaching with a great crowd of followers, while behind them came all the cattle which had been driven into the pools to seek Morongoe. As they approached Mokete's house the door opened and the old doctor stood upon the threshold.

Making a sign to command silence, he said: "My children, many years ago your chief received a grievous wrong at the hand of his enemy, and was turned into a snake, but by the love and faithfulness of his son he is restored to you this day, and the wiles of his enemy are made of no account. Cover, then, your eyes, my children, lest the Evil Eye afflict you."

He then bade the snake, which was in the centre of the crowd, enter the hut, upon which he shut the door, and set fire to the hut. The people, when they saw the flames, cried out in horror, but the old doctor bade them be still, for that no harm would come to their chief, but rather a great good. When everything was completely burnt, the doctor took from the middle of the ruins a large burnt ball; this he threw into the pool nearby, and lo! from the water up rose Morongoe, clad in a kaross, the beauty of which was beyond all words, and carrying in his hand a stick of shining black, like none seen on this earth before, in beauty, or colour, or shape. Thus was the spell broken through the devotion of a true son, and peace and happiness restored, not only to Mokete's heart, but to the whole village.

The Maid and Her Snake-lover
(From Lesotho, southern Africa)

WHEN OUR FATHERS' FATHERS were children, there lived in the valley of the rivers two chiefs, who governed their people wisely and with great kindness. The name of the one was Mopeli, and of the other Khosi.

Now Mopeli had a son whom he loved as his own heart, a youth, tall and brave, and fearless as the young lion. To him was given the name of Tsiu. When Tsiu was able to stand alone, and to play on the mat in front of his father's dwelling, a daughter was born unto the chief Khosi, to whom was given the name of Tebogo. The years passed, and Tsiu and Tebogo grew and thrived. Often the youth drove his father's cattle down towards the lands where Tebogo and her father's maidens worked, and many happy days were spent, while the love each bore the other grew and strengthened, even as they themselves grew older.

When the time came for Tsiu to take a wife, he went to his father and asked that Tebogo might be given him, for none other could he wed. Gladly the parents consented, and preparations were made for the wedding.

Now Tebogo had another lover, upon whom she looked with scorn, but who had vowed that never, never should she be the bride of Tsiu; so he consulted a witch doctor, who promised to aid him. Imagine then his joy when, ere the wedding feast had begun, he heard that Tsiu had disappeared. "Now," thought he, "Tebogo shall be mine;" but the maiden turned from him in anger, nor would her parents listen to his suit.

Meanwhile desolation hung over the home of the chief Mopeli. "My son, my son," cried the unhappy father; but no voice replied, no son came back to rejoice his father's heart.

When the moon had once more grown great in the heavens, an old man came to the village of Mopeli, and called the chief to him. Long they talked, and greatly the people wondered. At length they arose, and, saluting each other, parted at the door of the chief's dwelling. Mopeli then departed for the village of Chief

Khosi, where he remained all night. The next day he returned to his own village, and bade his people prepare a great feast.

In the village of the Chief Khosi, also, much wonder filled the people's minds, for they, likewise, were commanded to make ready a marriage feast, for the chief's daughter, the lovely Tebogo, was about to be married, but none knew to whom.

Calling his daughter to him, Khosi said, "My child, your lover Tsiu has been taken from you, so it is my wish that you should marry one who has found favour in my eyes."

"Tell me, my father," replied Tebogo, "who is the man you have chosen for me? Let me at least know his name."

"Nay, my child, that I cannot do," answered Khosi, and with this the maiden was obliged to be content. Behold then her horror when she was brought forth to meet her bridegroom, to find not a man, but a snake. All the people cried "shame" upon the parents who could be so cruel as to wed their daughter to a reptile.

With cries and tears Tebogo implored her parents to spare her; in vain were her entreaties. She was told to take her reptile husband home to the new hut which had been built for them, near the large pool where the cattle drank. Tremblingly she obeyed, followed by her maidens, the snake crawling by her side. When she entered the hut, she tried to shut out the snake, but it darted half its body through the door, and so terrified her that she ran to the other end of the hut.

The snake followed, and began lashing her with its tail, till she ran out of the hut down to the clump of willows which grew by the side of the pool. Here she found an old doctor sitting, and to him she told her trouble. "My daughter," he said, "return to your hut. Do not let the snake see you, but close the door very softly from the outside, and set fire to the hut. When it is all burnt down, you will find the ashes of the snake lying in a little heap in the centre of the hut. Bring them here, and cast them into the water."

Tebogo did as the old doctor directed her, and while the hut was burning, many people ran from both the villages to see what had happened; but Tebogo called to them to keep away, as she was burning the snake. When all was destroyed, she went up, took the ashes of the snake, which she found in the middle of the ruins, and, putting them into a pitcher, ran with them down to the pool and threw them in. No sooner had she done so, than from the water arose, not a snake, but her lover Tsiu. With a joyful cry, she flung herself into his arms, and a great shout went up from all the people gathered there.

As the lightning darts across the heaven, so the news of Tsiu's return spread from hut to hut, and great was the people's wonderment. The story of how he had been turned into a snake, and banished to the pool, until he could find a maiden whose parents would bestow her upon him in marriage, and of how the good old doctor Intō had revealed the secret to Mopeli, was soon told. For many days there was feasting and merry making in the homes of Mopeli the chief and of Khosi, while in the hearts of Tsiu and his bride Tebogo there dwelt a great content; but the wicked lover fled to the mountains, where he cherished a bitter hatred in his heart against Tebogo and her husband, and longed for the time when he could be revenged.

Elephant and Tortoise
(From South Africa)

TWO POWERS, ELEPHANT AND RAIN, had a dispute. Elephant said, "If you say that you nourish me, in what way is it that you say so?" Rain answered, "If you say that I do not nourish you, when I go away, will you not die?" And Rain then departed.

Elephant said, "Vulture! cast lots to make rain for me."

Vulture said, "I will not cast lots."

Then Elephant said to Crow, "Cast lots!" who answered, "Give the things with which I may cast lots." Crow cast lots and rain fell. It rained at the lagoons, but they dried up, and only one lagoon remained.

Elephant went a-hunting. There was, however, Tortoise, to whom Elephant said, "Tortoise, remain at the water!" Thus Tortoise was left behind when Elephant went a-hunting.

There came Giraffe, and said to Tortoise, "Give me water!" Tortoise answered, "The water belongs to Elephant."

There came Zebra, who said to Tortoise, "Give me water!" Tortoise answered, "The water belongs to Elephant."

There came Gemsbok, and said to Tortoise, "Give me water!" Tortoise answered, "The water belongs to Elephant."

There came Wildebeest, and said, "Give me water!" Tortoise said, "The water belongs to Elephant."

There came Roodebok, and said to Tortoise, "Give me water!" Tortoise answered, "The water belongs to Elephant."

There came Springbok, and said to Tortoise, "Give me water!" Tortoise said, "The water belongs to Elephant."

There came Jackal, and said to Tortoise, "Give me water!" Tortoise said, "The water belongs to Elephant."

There came Lion, and said, "Little Tortoise, give me water!" When little Tortoise was about to say something, Lion got hold of him and beat him; Lion drank of the water, and since then the animals drink water.

When Elephant came back from the hunting, he said, "Little Tortoise, is there water?" Tortoise answered, "The animals have drunk the water." Elephant asked, "Little Tortoise, shall I chew you or swallow you down?" Little Tortoise said, "Swallow me, if you please!" and Elephant swallowed him whole.

After Elephant had swallowed Little Tortoise, and he had entered his body, he tore off his liver, heart and kidneys. Elephant said, "Little Tortoise, you kill me."

So Elephant died; but little Tortoise came out of his dead body, and went wherever he liked.

The White Man and Snake
(From South Africa)

A WHITE MAN, IT IS SAID, met Snake upon whom a large stone had fallen and covered her so that she could not rise. The White Man lifted the stone off Snake, but when he had done so, she wanted to bite him. The White Man said, "Stop! let us both go first to some wise people." They went to Hyena, and the White Man asked him, "Is it right that Snake should want to bite me, when I helped her as she lay under a stone and could not rise?"

Hyena (who thought he would get his share of the White Man's body) said, "If you were bitten what would it matter?"

Then Snake wanted to bite him, but the White Man said again, "Wait a little, and let us go to other wise people, that I may hear whether this is right."

They went and met Jackal. The White Man said to Jackal, "Is it right for Snake to want to bite me, when I lifted up the stone which lay upon her?"

Jackal replied, "I do not believe that Snake could be covered by a stone so she could not rise. Unless I saw it with my two eyes, I would not believe it. Therefore, come let us go and see the place where you say it happened whether it can be true."

They went, and arrived at the place where it had happened. Jackal said, "Snake, lie down, and let thyself be covered."

Snake did so, and the White Man covered her with the stone; but although she exerted herself very much, she could not rise. Then the White Man wanted again to release Snake, but Jackal interfered, and said, "Do not lift the stone. She wanted to bite you, therefore she may rise by herself."

Then they both went away and left Snake under the stone.

The Tiger, the Ram and the Jackal
(From South Africa)

TIGER (LEOPARD) WAS RETURNING HOME from hunting on one occasion, when he lighted on the kraal of Ram. Now, Tiger had never seen Ram before, and accordingly, approaching submissively, he said, "Good day, friend! What may your name be?"

The other in his gruff voice, and striking his breast with his forefoot, said, "I am Ram. Who are you?"

"Tiger," answered the other, more dead than alive, and then, taking leave of Ram, he ran home as fast as he could.

Jackal lived at the same place as Tiger did, and the latter going to him, said, "Friend Jackal, I am quite out of breath, and am half dead with fright, for I have just seen a terrible looking fellow, with a large and thick head, and on my asking him what his name was, he answered, 'I am Ram.'"

"What a foolish fellow you are," cried Jackal, "to let such a nice piece of flesh stand! Why did you do so? But we shall go tomorrow and eat it together."

Next day the two set off for the kraal of Ram, and as they appeared over a hill, Ram, who had turned out to look about him, and was calculating where he should that day crop a tender salad, saw them, and he immediately went to his wife and said, "I fear this is our last day, for Jackal and Tiger are both coming against us. What shall we do?"

"Don't be afraid," said the wife, "but take up the child in your arms, go out with it, and pinch it to make it cry as if it were hungry." Ram did so as the confederates came on.

No sooner did Tiger cast his eyes on Ram than fear again took possession of him, and he wished to turn back. Jackal had provided against this, and made Tiger fast to himself with a leathern thong, and said, "Come on," when Ram cried in a loud voice, and pinching his child at the same time, "You have done well, Friend Jackal, to have brought us Tiger to eat, for you hear how my child is crying for food."

On these dreadful words Tiger, notwithstanding the entreaties of Jackal to let him go, to let him loose, set off in the greatest alarm, dragged Jackal after him over hill and valley, through bushes and over rocks, and never stopped to look behind him till he brought back himself and half-dead Jackal to his place again. And so Ram escaped.

The Lion, the Jackal and the Man
(From South Africa)

IT SO HAPPENED ONE DAY that Lion and Jackal came together to converse on affairs of land and state. Jackal, let me say, was the most important adviser to the king of the forest, and after they had spoken about these matters for quite a while, the conversation took a more personal turn.

Lion began to boast and talk big about his strength. Jackal had, perhaps, given him cause for it, because by nature he was a flatterer. But now that Lion began to assume so many airs, said he, "See here, Lion, I will show you an animal that is still more powerful than you are."

They walked along, Jackal leading the way, and met first a little boy.

"Is this the strong man?" asked Lion.

"No," answered Jackal, "he must still become a man, O king."

After a while they found an old man walking with bowed head and supporting his bent figure with a stick.

"Is this the wonderful strong man?" asked Lion.

"Not yet, O king," was Jackal's answer, "he has been a man."

Continuing their walk a short distance farther, they came across a young hunter, in the prime of youth, and accompanied by some of his dogs.

"There you have him now, O king," said Jackal. "Pit your strength against his, and if you win, then truly you are the strength of the earth."

Then Jackal made tracks to one side toward a little rocky kopje from which he would be able to see the meeting.

Growling, growling, Lion strode forward to meet the man, but when he came close the dogs beset him. He, however, paid but little attention to the dogs, pushed and separated them on all sides with a few sweeps of his front paws. They howled aloud, beating a hasty retreat toward the man.

Thereupon the man fired a charge of shot, hitting him behind the shoulder, but even to this Lion paid but little attention. Thereupon the hunter pulled out his steel knife, and gave him a few good jabs. Lion retreated, followed by the flying bullets of the hunter.

"Well, are you strongest now?" was Jackal's first question when Lion arrived at his side.

"No, Jackal," answered Lion, "let that fellow there keep the name and welcome. Such as he I have never before seen. In the first place he had about ten of his bodyguard storm me. I really did not bother myself much about them, but when I attempted to turn him to chaff, he spat and blew fire at me, mostly into my face, that burned just a little but not very badly. And when I again endeavoured to pull him to the ground he jerked out from his body one of his ribs with which he gave me some very ugly wounds, so bad that I had to make chips fly, and as a parting he sent some warm bullets after me. No, Jackal, give him the name."

The Lion and Jackal
(From South Africa)

LION HAD NOW CAUGHT a large eland which lay dead on the top of a high bank. Lion was thirsty and wanted to go and drink water. "Jackal, look after my eland, I am going to get a drink. Don't you eat any."

"Very well, Uncle Lion."

Lion went to the river and Jackal quietly removed a stone on which Lion had to step to reach the bank on his return. After that Jackal and his wife ate heartily of the eland. Lion returned, but could not scale the bank. "Jackal, help me," he shouted.

"Yes, Uncle Lion, I will let down a rope and then you can climb up."

Jackal whispered to his wife, "Give me one of the old, thin hide ropes." And then aloud he added, "Wife, give me one of the strong, buffalo ropes, so Uncle Lion won't fall."

His wife gave him an old rotten rope. Jackal and his wife first ate ravenously of the meat, then gradually let the rope down. Lion seized it and struggled up. When he neared the brink Jackal gave the rope a jerk. It broke and down Lion began to roll – rolled the whole way down, and finally lay at the foot near the river.

Jackal began to beat a dry hide that lay there as he howled, cried, and shouted: "Wife, why did you give me such a bad rope that caused Uncle Lion to fall?"

Lion heard the row and roared, "Jackal, stop beating your wife. I will hurt you if you don't cease. Help me to climb up."

"Uncle Lion, I will give you a rope." Whispering again to his wife, "Give me one of the old, thin hide ropes," and shouting aloud again, "Give me a strong, buffalo rope, wife, that will not break again with Lion."

Jackal gave out the rope, and when Lion had nearly reached the top, he cut the rope through. Snap! and Lion began to roll to the bottom. Jackal again beat on the hide and shouted, "Wife, why did you give me such a rotten rope? Didn't I tell you to give me a strong one?" Lion roared, "Jackal, stop beating your wife at once. Help me instantly or you will be sorry."

"Wife," Jackal said aloud, "give me now the strongest rope you have," and aside to her, "Give me the worst rope of the lot."

Jackal again let down a rope, but just as Lion reached the top, Jackal gave a strong tug and broke the rope. Poor old Lion rolled down the side of the hill and lay there roaring from pain. He had been fatally hurt.

Jackal inquired, "Uncle Lion, have you hurt yourself? Have you much pain? Wait a while, I am coming directly to help you." Jackal and his wife slowly walked away.

The Hunt of Lion and Jackal
(From South Africa)

LION AND JACKAL, IT IS SAID, were one day lying in wait for Eland. Lion shot (with a bow) and missed, but Jackal hit and sang out, "Hah! hah!"

Lion said, "No, you did not shoot anything. It was I who hit."

Jackal answered, "Yea, my father, thou hast hit."

Then they went home in order to return when the eland was dead, and cut it up. Jackal, however, turned back, unknown to Lion, hit his nose so that the blood ran on the spoor of the eland, and followed their track thus, in order to cheat Lion. When he had gone some distance, he returned by another way to the dead eland, and creeping into its carcass, cut out all the fat.

Meanwhile Lion followed the blood-stained spoor of Jackal, thinking that it was eland blood, and only when he had gone some distance did he find out that he had been deceived. He then returned on Jackal's spoor, and reached the dead eland, where, finding Jackal in its carcass, he seized him by his tail and drew him out with a swing.

Lion upbraided Jackal with these words: "Why do you cheat me?"

Jackal answered: "No, my father, I do not cheat you; you may know it, I think. I prepared this fat for you, father."

Lion said: "Then take the fat and carry it to your mother" (the lioness); and he gave him the lungs to take to his own wife and children.

When Jackal arrived, he did not give the fat to Lion's wife, but to his own wife and children; he gave, however, the lungs to Lion's wife, and he pelted Lion's little children with the lungs, saying:

> *"You children of the big-pawed one!*
> *You big-pawed ones!"*

He said to Lioness, "I go to help my father" (the lion); but he went far away with his wife and children.

Jackal and Monkey
(From South Africa)

EVERY EVENING JACKAL WENT to the Boer's kraal. He crept through the sliding door and stole a fat young lamb. This, clever Jackal did several times in succession. Boer set a wip [A Dutch word for a spring trap in which the tripping of a stick causes a noose to snare an animal and lift it into the air] for him at the door. Jackal went again and zip – there he was caught around the body by the noose. He swung and swayed high in the air and couldn't touch ground. The day began to dawn and Jackal became uneasy.

On a stone kopje, Monkey sat. When it became light he could see the whole affair, and descended hastily for the purpose of mocking Jackal. He went and sat on the wall. "Ha, ha, good morning. So there you are hanging now, eventually caught."

"What? I caught? I am simply swinging for my pleasure; it is enjoyable."

"You fibber. You are caught in the wip."

"If you but realized how nice it was to swing and sway like this, you wouldn't hesitate. Come, try it a little. You feel so healthy and strong for the day, and you never tire afterwards."

"No, I won't. You are caught."

After a while Jackal convinced Monkey. He sprang from the kraal wall, and freeing Jackal, adjusted the noose around his own body. Jackal quickly let go and began to laugh, as Monkey was now swinging high in the air.

"Ha, ha, ha," he laughed. "Now Monkey is in the wip."

"Jackal, free me," he screamed.

"There, Boer is coming," shouted Jackal.

"Jackal, free me of this, or I'll break your playthings."

"No, there Boer is coming with his gun; you rest a while in the noose."

"Jackal, quickly make me free."

"No, here's Boer already, and he's got his gun. Good morning." And with these parting words he ran away as fast as he could. Boer came and saw Monkey in the wip.

"So, so, Monkey, now you are caught. You are the fellow who has been stealing my lambs, hey?"

"No, Boer, no," screamed Monkey, "not I, but Jackal."

"No, I know you; you aren't too good for that."

"No, Boer, no, not I, but Jackal," Monkey stammered.

"Oh, I know you. Just wait a little," and Boer, raising his gun, aimed and shot poor Monkey dead.

Jackal's Bride
(From South Africa)

JACKAL, IT IS SAID, MARRIED HYENA, and carried off a cow belonging to the ants, to slaughter her for the wedding; and when he had slaughtered her, he put the cowskin over his bride; and when he had fixed a pole (on which to hang the flesh), he placed on the top of the pole (which was forked) the hearth for the cooking, in order to cook upon it all sorts of delicious food.

There came also Lion, and wished to go up. Jackal, therefore, asked his little daughter for a thong with which he could pull Lion up; and he began to pull him up; and when his face came near to the cooking pot, he cut the thong in two, so that Lion tumbled down. Then Jackal upbraided his little daughter with these words: "Why do you give me such an old thong?" And he added, "Give me a fresh thong."

She gave him a new thong, and he pulled Lion up again, and when his face came near the pot, which stood on the fire, he said, "open your mouth." Then he put into his mouth a hot piece of quartz which had been boiled together with the fat, and the stone went down, burning his throat. Thus died Lion.

There came also the ants running after the cow, and when Jackal saw them he fled. Then they beat the bride in her brookaross dress. Hyena, believing that it was Jackal, said:

"You tawny rogue! have you not played at beating long enough? Have you no more loving game than this?"

But when she had bitten a hole through the cowskin, she saw that they were other people; then she fled, falling here and there, yet made her escape.

The Story of Hare
(From South Africa)

ONCE UPON A TIME the animals made a kraal and put some fat in it. They agreed that one of their number should remain to be the keeper of the gate. The first one that was appointed was the coney (imbila). He agreed to take charge, and all the others went away. In a short time the coney fell asleep, when the inkalimeva (a fabulous animal) went in and ate all the fat. After doing this, he threw a little stone at the coney.

The coney started up and cried out: "The fat belonging to all the animals has been eaten by the inkalimeva."

It repeated this cry several times, calling out very loudly. The animals at a distance heard it, they ran to the kraal, and when they saw that the fat was gone they killed the coney.

They put fat in the kraal a second time, and appointed the muishond (ingaga; a weasel) to keep the gate. The muishond consented, and the animals went away as before. After a little time the inkalimeva came to the kraal, bringing some honey with it. It invited the keeper of the gate to eat honey, and while the muishond was enjoying himself the inkalimeva went in and stole all the fat. It threw a stone at the muishond, which caused him to look up.

The muishond cried out: "The fat belonging to all the animals has been eaten by the inkalimeva."

As soon as the animals heard the cry, they ran to the kraal and killed the muishond.

They put fat in the kraal a third time, and appointed the duiker (impunzi) to be the keeper of the gate. The duiker agreed, and the others went away. In a short time the inkalimeva made its appearance. It proposed to the duiker that they should play hide and look for. The duiker agreed to this. Then the inkalimeva hid itself, and the duiker looked for it till he was so tired that he lay down and went to sleep. When the duiker was asleep, the inkalimeva ate up all the fat.

Then it threw a stone at the duiker, which caused him to jump up and cry out: "The fat belonging to all the animals has been eaten by the inkalimeva."

The animals, when they heard the cry, ran to the kraal and killed the duiker.

They put fat in the kraal the fourth time, and appointed the bluebuck (inputi) to be the keeper of the gate. When the animals went away, the inkalimeva came as before.

It said: "What are you doing by yourself?"

The bluebuck answered: "I am watching the fat belonging to all the animals."

The inkalimeva said: "I will be your companion. Come, let us scratch each other's heads."

The bluebuck agreed to this. The inkalimeva sat down and scratched the head of the other till he went to sleep. Then it arose and ate all the fat. When it had finished, it threw a stone at the bluebuck and awakened him.

The bluebuck saw what had happened and cried out: "The fat belonging to all the animals has been eaten by the inkalimeva."

Then the animals ran up and killed the bluebuck also.

They put fat in the kraal the fifth time, and appointed the porcupine (incanda) to be the keeper of the gate. The animals went away, and the inkalimeva came as before.

It said to the porcupine, "Let us run a race against each other."

It let the porcupine beat in this race.

Then it said, "I did not think you could run so fast, but let us try again." They ran again, and it allowed the porcupine to beat the second time. They ran till the porcupine was so tired that he said, "Let us rest now."

They sat down to rest, and the porcupine went to sleep. Then the inkalimeva rose up and ate all the fat. When it had finished eating, it threw a stone at the porcupine, which caused him to jump up.

He called out with a loud voice, "The fat belonging to all the animals has been eaten by the inkalimeva."

Then the animals came running up and put the porcupine to death.

They put fat in the kraal the sixth time, and selected the hare (umvundla) to be the keeper of the gate. At first the hare would not consent.

He said, "The coney is dead, and the muishond is dead, and the duiker is dead, and the bluebuck is dead, and the porcupine is dead and you will kill me also."

They promised him that they would not kill him, and after a good deal of persuasion he at last agreed to keep the gate. When the animals were gone he laid himself down, but he only pretended to be asleep.

In a short time the inkalimeva went in, and was just going to take the fat when the hare cried out: "Let the fat alone."

The inkalimeva said, "Please let me have this little bit only."

The hare answered, mocking, "Please let me have this little bit only."

After that they became companions. The hare proposed that they should fasten each other's tail, and the inkalimeva agreed. The inkalimeva fastened the tail of the hare first.

The hare said, "Don't tie my tail so tight."

Then the hare fastened the tail of the inkalimeva.

The inkalimeva said, "Don't tie my tail so tight," but the hare made no answer. After tying the tail of the inkalimeva very fast, the hare took his club and killed it. The hare took the tail of the inkalimeva and ate it, all except a little piece which he hid in the fence.

Then he called out, "The fat belonging to all the animals has been eaten by the inkalimeva."

The animals came running back, and when they saw that the inkalimeva was dead they rejoiced greatly. They asked the hare for the tail, which should be kept for the chief.

The hare replied, "The one I killed had no tail."

They said, "How can an inkalimeva be without a tail?"

They began to search, and at length they found a piece of the tail in the fence. They told the chief that the hare had eaten the tail.

He said, "Bring him to me!"

All the animals ran after the hare, but he fled, and they could not catch him. The hare ran into a hole, at the mouth of which the animals set a snare, and then went away. The hare remained in the hole for many days, but at length he managed to get out without being caught.

He went to a place where he found a bushbuck (imbabala) building a hut. There was a pot with meat in it on the fire.

He said to the bushbuck, "Can I take this little piece of meat?"

The bushbuck answered, "You must not do it."

But he took the meat and ate it all. Afterwards he whistled in a particular manner, and there fell a storm of hail which killed the bushbuck. Then he took the skin of the bushbuck, and made for himself a mantle.

After this the hare went into the forest to procure some weapons to fight with. While he was cutting a stick the monkeys threw leaves upon him. He called to them to come down and beat him. They came down, but he killed them all with his weapons.

Lion's Illness
(From South Africa)

LION, IT IS SAID, WAS ILL, and they all went to see him in his suffering. But Jackal did not go, because the traces of the people who went to see him did not turn back. Thereupon, he was accused by Hyena, who said, "Though I go to look, yet Jackal does not want to come and look at the man's sufferings."

Then Lion let Hyena go, in order that she might catch Jackal; and she did so, and brought him.

Lion asked Jackal: "Why did you not come here to see me?"

Jackal said, "Oh, no! when I heard that my uncle was so very ill, I went to the witch (doctor) to consult him, whether and what medicine would be good for my uncle against the pain. The doctor said to me, 'Go and tell your uncle to take hold of Hyena and draw off her skin, and put it on while it is still warm. Then he will recover.' Hyena is one who does not care for my uncle's sufferings."

Lion followed his advice, got hold of Hyena, drew the skin over her ears, whilst she howled with all her might, and put it on.

Jackal, Dove and Heron
(From South Africa)

J ACKAL, IT IS SAID, CAME ONCE TO DOVE, who lived on the top of a rock, and said, "Give me one of your little ones."

Dove answered, "I shall not do anything of the kind."

Jackal said, "Give me it at once! Otherwise, I shall fly up to you." Then she threw one down to him.

He came back another day and demanded another little one, and she gave it to him. After Jackal had gone, Heron came, and asked, "Dove, why do you cry?"

Dove answered him, "Jackal has taken away my little ones; it is for this that I cry." He asked her, "In what manner did he take them?" She answered him, "When he asked me I refused him; but when he said, 'I shall at once fly up, therefore give me it,' I threw it down to him."

Heron said, "Are you such a fool as to give your young ones to Jackal, who cannot fly?" Then, with the admonition to give no more, he went away.

Jackal came again, and said, "Dove, give me a little one." Dove refused, and told him that Heron had told her that he could not fly up. Jackal said, "I shall catch him."

So when Heron came to the banks of the water, Jackal asked him: "Brother Heron, when the wind comes from this side, how will you stand?" He turned his neck towards him and said, "I stand thus, bending my neck on one side." Jackal asked him again, "When a storm comes and when it rains, how do you stand?" He said to him: "I stand thus, indeed, bending my neck down."

Then Jackal beat him on his neck, and broke his neck in the middle.

Since that day Heron's neck is bent.

The World's Reward
(From South Africa)

ONCE THERE WAS A MAN that had an old dog, so old that the man desired to put him aside. The dog had served him very faithfully when he was still young, but ingratitude is the world's reward, and the man now wanted to dispose of him. The old dumb creature, however, ferreted out the plan of his master, and so at once resolved to go away of his own accord.

After he had walked quite a way he met an old bull in the veldt.

"Don't you want to go with me?" asked the dog.

"Where?" was the reply.

"To the land of the aged," said the dog, "where troubles don't disturb you and thanklessness does not deface the deeds of man."

"Good," said the bull, "I am your companion."

The two now walked on and found a ram.

The dog laid the plan before him, and all moved off together, until they afterwards came successively upon a donkey, a cat, a cock and a goose.

These joined their company, and the seven set out on their journey.

Late one night they came to a house and through the open door they saw a table spread with all kinds of nice food, of which some robbers were having their fill. It would help nothing to ask for admittance, and seeing that they were hungry, they must think of something else.

Therefore the donkey climbed up on the bull, the ram on the donkey, the dog on the ram, the cat on the dog, the goose on the cat and the cock on the goose, and with one accord they all let out terrible (threatening) noises (cryings).

The bull began to bellow, the donkey to bray, the dog to bark, the ram to bleat, the cat to mew, the goose to giggle gaggle and the cock to crow, all without cessation.

The people in the house were frightened perfectly limp; they glanced out through the front door, and there they stared on the strange sight. Some of them took to the ropes over the back lower door, some disappeared through the window, and in a few counts the house was empty.

Then the seven old animals climbed down from one another, stepped into the house, and satisfied themselves with the delicious food.

But when they had finished, there still remained a great deal of food, too much to take with them on their remaining journey, and so together they contrived a plan to hold their position until the next day after breakfast.

The dog said, "See here, I am accustomed to watch at the front door of my master's house," and thereupon flopped himself down to sleep; the bull said, "I go behind the door," and there he took his position; the ram said, "I will go up on to the loft"; the donkey, "I at the middle door"; the cat, "I in the fireplace"; the goose, "I in the back door"; and the cock said, "I am going to sleep on the bed."

The captain of the robbers after a while sent one of his men back to see if these creatures had yet left the house.

The man came very cautiously into the neighbourhood, listened and listened, but he heard nothing; he peeped through the window, and saw in the grate just two coals still glimmering, and thereupon started to walk through the front door.

There the old dog seized him by the leg. He jumped into the house, but the bull was ready, swept him up with his horns, and tossed him on to the loft. Here the ram received him and pushed him off the loft again. Reaching ground, he made for the middle door, but the donkey set up a terrible braying and at the same time gave him a kick that landed him in the fireplace, where the cat flew at him and scratched him nearly to pieces. He then jumped out through the back door, and here the goose got him by the trousers. When he was some distance away the cock crowed. He thereupon ran so that you could hear the stones rattle in the dark.

Purple and crimson and out of breath, he came back to his companions.

"Frightful, frightful!" was all that they could get from him at first, but after a while he told them.

"When I looked through the window I saw in the fireplace two bright coals shining, and when I wanted to go through the front door to go and look, I stepped into an iron trap. I jumped into the house, and there someone seized me with a fork and pitched me up on to the loft, there again someone was ready, and threw me down on all fours. I wanted to fly through the middle door, but there someone blew on a trumpet, and smote me with a sledgehammer so that I did not know where I landed; but coming to very quickly, I found I was in the fireplace, and there another flew at me and scratched the eyes almost out of my head. I thereupon fled out of the back door, and lastly I was attacked on the leg by the sixth with a pair of fire tongs, and when I was still running away, someone shouted out of the house, 'Stop him, stop h – i – m!'"

Lion and Baboon
(From South Africa)

BABOON, IT IS SAID, once worked bamboos, sitting on the edge of a precipice, and Lion stole upon him. Baboon, however, had fixed some round, glistening, eye-like plates on the back of his head.

When, therefore, Lion crept upon him, he thought, when Baboon was looking at him, that he sat with his back towards him, and crept with all his might upon him. When, however, Baboon turned his back towards him, Lion thought that he was seen, and hid himself. Thus, when Baboon looked at him, he crept upon him.

When he was near him Baboon looked up, and Lion continued to creep upon him. Baboon said (aside), "Whilst I am looking at him he steals upon me, whilst my hollow eyes are on him."

When at last Lion sprung at him, he lay (quickly) down upon his face, and Lion jumped over him, falling down the precipice, and was dashed to pieces.

Lion Who Thought Himself Wiser than His Mother
(From South Africa)

IT IS SAID THAT WHEN Lion and Gurikhoisip (the Only man), together with Baboon, Buffalo and other friends, were playing one day at a certain game, there was a thunderstorm and rain at Aroxaams. Lion and Gurikhoisip began to quarrel. "I shall run to the rain field," said Lion. Gurikhoisip said also, "I shall run to the rain field." As neither would concede this to the other, they separated (angrily). After they had parted, Lion went to tell his Mother those things which they had both said.

His Mother said to him, "My son! that Man whose head is in a line with his shoulders and breast, who has pinching weapons, who keeps white dogs, who goes about wearing the tuft of a tiger's tail, beware of him!" Lion, however, said, "Why need I be on my guard against those whom I know?" Lioness answered, "My Son, take care of him who has pinching weapons!"

But Lion would not follow his Mother's advice, and the same morning, when it was still pitch dark, he went to Aroxaams, and laid himself in ambush. Gurikhoisip went also that morning to the same place. When he had arrived he let his dogs drink, and then bathe. After they had finished they wallowed. Then also Man drank; and, when he had done drinking, Lion came out of the bush.

Dogs surrounded him as his Mother had foretold, and he was speared by Gurikhoisip. Just as he became aware that he was speared, the Dogs drew him down again. In this manner he grew faint. While he was in this state, Gurikhoisip said to the Dogs, "Let him alone now, that he may go and be taught by his Mother." So the Dogs let him go. They left him, and went home as he lay there.

The same night he walked towards home, but whilst he was on the way his strength failed him, and he lamented:

"Mother! take me up!
Grandmother! take me up! Oh me! Alas!"

At the dawn of day his Mother heard his wailing, and said –

"My Son, this is the thing which I have told thee:
'Beware of the one who has pinching weapons,
Who wears a tuft of tiger's tail,
Of him who has white dogs!
Alas! thou son of her who is short-eared,
Thou, my short-eared child!
Son of her who eats raw flesh,
Thou flesh-devourer;
Son of her whose nostrils are red from the prey,
Thou with blood-stained nostrils!
Son of her who drinks pit-water,
Thou water-drinker!'"

Lion Who Took a Woman's Shape
(From South Africa)

SOME WOMEN, IT IS SAID, went out to seek roots and herbs and other wild food. On their way home they sat down and said, "Let us taste the food of the field."

Now they found that the food picked by one of them was sweet, while that of the others was bitter. The latter said to each other, "Look here! this Woman's herbs are sweet." Then they said to the owner of the sweet food, "Throw it away and seek for other." So she threw away the food, and went to gather more.

When she had collected a sufficient supply, she returned to join the other Women, but could not find them. She went therefore down to the river, where Hare sat lading water, and said to him, "Hare, give me some water that I may drink." But he replied, "This is the cup out of which my uncle (Lion) and I alone may drink."

She asked again: "Hare, draw water for me that I may drink." But Hare made the same reply. Then she snatched the cup from him and drank, but he ran home to tell his uncle of the outrage which had been committed.

The Woman meanwhile replaced the cup and went away. After she had departed Lion came down, and, seeing her in the distance, pursued her on the road. When she turned round and saw him coming, she sang in the following manner:

> *"My mother, she would not let me seek herbs,*
> *Herbs of the field, food from the field. Hoo!"*

When Lion at last came up with the Woman, they hunted each other round a shrub. She wore many beads and arm rings, and Lion said, "Let me put them on!" So she lent them to him, but he afterwards refused to return them to her.

They then hunted each other again round the shrub, till Lion fell down, and the Woman jumped upon him, and kept him there. Lion (uttering a form of conjuration) said:

> *"My Aunt! it is morning, and time to rise;*
> *Pray, rise from me!"*

She then rose from him, and they hunted again after each other round the shrub, till the Woman fell down, and Lion jumped upon her. She then addressed him:

> *"My Uncle! it is morning, and time to rise;*
> *Pray, rise from me!"*

He rose, of course, and they hunted each other again, till Lion fell a second time. When she jumped upon him he said:

> *"My Aunt! it is morning, and time to rise;*
> *Pray, rise from me!"*

They rose again and hunted after each other. The Woman at last fell down. But this time when she repeated the above conjuration, Lion said:

"Hè Kha! Is it morning, and time to rise?"

He then ate her, taking care, however, to leave her skin whole, which he put on, together with her dress and ornaments, so that he looked quite like a woman, and then went home to her kraal.

When this counterfeit woman arrived, her little sister, crying, said, "My sister, pour some milk out for me." She answered, "I shall not pour you out any." Then the Child addressed their Mother: "Mama, do pour out some for me." The Mother of the kraal said, "Go to your sister, and let her give it to you!" The little Child said again to her sister, "Please, pour out for me!" She, however, repeated her refusal, saying, "I will not do it." Then the Mother of the kraal said to the little One, "I refused to let her (the elder sister) seek herbs in the field, and I do not know what may have happened; go therefore to Hare, and ask him to pour out for you."

So then Hare gave her some milk; but her elder sister said, "Come and share it with me." The little Child then went to her sister with her bamboo (cup), and they both sucked the milk out of it. Whilst they were doing this, some milk was spilt on the little one's hand, and the elder sister licked it up with her tongue, the roughness of which drew blood; this, too, the Woman licked up.

The little Child complained to her Mother: "Mama, sister pricks holes in me and sucks the blood." The Mother said, "With what Lion's nature your sister went the way that I forbade her, and returned, I do not know."

Now the Cows arrived, and the elder sister cleansed the pails in order to milk them. But when she approached the Cows with a thong (in order to tie their forelegs), they all refused to be milked by her.

Hare said, "Why do not you stand before the Cow?" She replied, "Hare, call your brother, and do you two stand before the Cow." Her husband said, "What has come over her that the Cows refuse her? These are the same Cows she always milks." The Mother (of the kraal) said, "What has happened this evening? These are Cows which she always milks without assistance. What can have affected her that she comes home as a woman with a Lion's nature?"

The elder daughter then said to her Mother, "I shall not milk the Cows." With these words she sat down. The Mother said therefore to Hare, "Bring me the bamboos, that I may milk. I do not know what has come over the girl."

So the Mother herself milked the cows, and when she had done so, Hare brought the bamboos to the young wife's house, where her husband was, but she (the wife) did not give him (her husband) anything to eat. But when at nighttime she fell asleep, they saw some of the Lion's hair, which was hanging out where he had slipped on the Woman's skin, and they cried, "Verily! this is quite another being. It is for this reason that the Cows refused to be milked."

Then the people of the kraal began to break up the hut in which Lion lay asleep. When they took off the mats, they said (conjuring them), "If thou art favourably inclined to me, O Mat, give the sound 'sawa' (meaning, making no noise).

To the poles (on which the hut rested) they said, "If thou art favourably inclined to me, O Pole, thou must give the sound 'gara.'"

They addressed also the bamboos and the bed skins in a similar manner.

Thus gradually and noiselessly they removed the hut and all its contents. Then they took bunches of grass, put them over the Lion, and lighting them, said, "If thou art favourably inclined to me, O Fire, thou must flare up, 'boo boo,' before thou comest to the heart."

So the Fire flared up when it came towards the heart, and the heart of the Woman jumped upon the ground. The Mother (of the kraal) picked it up, and put it into a calabash.

Lion, from his place in the fire, said to the Mother (of the kraal), "How nicely I have eaten your daughter." The Woman answered, "You have also now a comfortable place!"

Now the Woman took the first milk of as many Cows as had calves, and put it into the calabash where her daughter's heart was; the calabash increased in size, and in proportion to this the girl grew again inside it.

One day, when the Mother (of the kraal) went out to fetch wood, she said to Hare, "By the time that I come back you must have everything nice and clean." But during her Mother's absence, the girl crept out of the calabash, and put the hut in good order, as she had been used to do in former days, and said to Hare, "When Mother comes back and asks, 'Who has done these things?' you must say, 'I, Hare, did them.'" After she had done all, she hid herself on the stage.

When the Mother of the kraal came home, she said, "Hare, who has done these things? They look just as they used when my daughter did them." Hare said, "I did the things." But the Mother would not believe it, and looked at the calabash. Seeing it was empty, she searched the stage and found her daughter. Then she embraced and kissed her, and from that day the girl stayed with her Mother, and did everything as she was wont in former times; but she now remained unmarried.

The Dance for Water
or Rabbit's Triumph
(From South Africa)

THERE WAS A FRIGHTFUL DROUGHT. The rivers after a while dried up and even the springs gave no water.

The animals wandered around seeking drink, but to no avail. Nowhere was water to be found.

A great gathering of animals was held: Lion, Tiger, Wolf, Jackal, Elephant, all of them came together. What was to be done? That was the question. One had this plan, and another had that; but no plan seemed of value.

Finally one of them suggested: "Come, let all of us go to the dry river bed and dance; in that way we can tread out the water."

Good! Everyone was satisfied and ready to begin instantly, excepting Rabbit, who said, "I will not go and dance. All of you are mad to attempt to get water from the ground by dancing."

The other animals danced and danced, and ultimately danced the water to the surface. How glad they were. Everyone drank as much as he could, but Rabbit did not dance with them. So it was decided that Rabbit should have no water.

He laughed at them: "I will nevertheless drink some of your water."

That evening he proceeded leisurely to the riverbed where the dance had been, and drank as much as he wanted. The following morning the animals saw the footprints of Rabbit in the ground, and Rabbit shouted to them: "Aha! I did have some of the water, and it was most refreshing and tasted fine."

Quickly all the animals were called together. What were they to do? How were they to get Rabbit in their hands? All had some means to propose; the one suggested this, and the other that.

Finally old Tortoise moved slowly forward, foot by foot: "I will catch Rabbit."

"You? How? What do you think of yourself?" shouted the others in unison.

"Rub my shell with pitch [black beeswax], and I will go to the edge of the water and lie down. I will then resemble a stone, so that when Rabbit steps on me his feet will stick fast."

"Yes! Yes! That's good."

And in a one, two, three, Tortoise's shell was covered with pitch, and foot by foot he moved away to the river. At the edge, close to the water, he lay down and drew his head into his shell.

Rabbit during the evening came to get a drink. "Ha!" he chuckled sarcastically," they are, after all, quite decent. Here they have placed a stone, so now I need not unnecessarily wet my feet."

Rabbit trod with his left foot on the stone, and there it stuck. Tortoise then put his head out. "Ha! old Tortoise! And it's you, is it, that's holding me? But here I still have another foot. I'll give you a good clout." Rabbit gave Tortoise what he said he would with his right fore foot, hard and straight; and there his foot remained.

"I have yet a hind foot, and with it I'll kick you." Rabbit drove his hind foot down. This also rested on Tortoise where it struck.

"But still another foot remains, and now I'll tread you." He stamped his foot down, but it stuck like the others.

He used his head to hammer Tortoise, and his tail as a whip, but both met the same fate as his feet, so there he was tight and fast down to the pitch.

Tortoise now slowly turned himself round and foot by foot started for the other animals, with Rabbit on his back.

"Ha! ha! ha! Rabbit! How does it look now? Insolence does not pay after all," shouted the animals.

Now advice was sought. What should they do with Rabbit? He certainly must die. But how? One said, "Behead him"; another, "Some severe penalty."

"Rabbit, how are we to kill you?"

"It does not affect me," Rabbit said. "Only a shameful death please do not pronounce."

"And what is that?" they all shouted.

"To take me by my tail and dash my head against a stone; that I pray and beseech you don't do."

"No, but just so you'll die. That is decided."

It was decided Rabbit should die by taking him by his tail and dashing his head to pieces against some stone. But who is to do it?

Lion, because he is the most powerful one.

Good! Lion should do it. He stood up, walked to the front, and poor Rabbit was brought to him. Rabbit pleaded and beseeched that he couldn't die such a miserable death.

Lion took Rabbit firmly by the tail and swung him around. The white skin slipped off from Rabbit, and there Lion stood with the white bit of skin and hair in his paw. Rabbit was free.

When Lion Could Fly
(From South Africa)

ION, IT IS SAID, used once to fly, and at that time nothing could live before him. As he was unwilling that the bones of what he caught should be broken into pieces, he made a pair of White Crows watch the bones, leaving them behind at the kraal whilst he went a-hunting. But one day Great Frog came there, broke the bones in pieces, and said, "Why can men and animals live no longer?" And he added these words, "When he comes, tell him that I live at yonder pool; if he wishes to see me, he must come there."

Lion, lying in wait (for game), wanted to fly up, but found he could not fly. Then he got angry, thinking that at the kraal something was wrong, and returned home. When he arrived, he asked, "What have you done that I cannot fly?" Then they answered and said, "Someone came here, broke the bones into pieces, and said, 'If he wants me, he may look for me at yonder pool!'" Lion went, and arrived while Frog was sitting at the water's edge, and he tried to creep stealthily upon him. When he was about to get hold of him, Frog said, "Ho!" and, diving, went to the other side of the pool, and sat there. Lion pursued him; but as he could not catch him he returned home.

From that day, it is said, Lion walked on his feet, and also began to creep upon (his game); and the White Crows became entirely dumb since the day that they said, "Nothing can be said of that matter."

Human Folly & Adventure

FIN THE LAST section of this collection, most of the stories focus on the fundamental and recurrent problems of social relations and tend to instruct on social behaviour, while satirizing weaknesses and foibles of human society which cause the story to unfold. Among the faults which are severely castigated or made a mockery of are greed and gluttony, jealousy, the stubbornness of sons and daughters, stupidity, witchcraft, the nature of disobedience, the ethics of choice and stress conditions such as drinking alcohol too much or too often, or gambling. These stories deal with everyday problems. In appearance, they are the most fanciful and sometimes even the most ridiculous tales.

Also, tales with humans as heroes form the majority in this section. Here, man's love, his hatred, cleverness and stupidity are pitted against other men and the sociopolitical environment. In the tales with animals as characters, the animals speak reason and behave like human beings. In other words, the animals in the tales are used as examples for humans to follow or avoid in fables that serve as standards of moral didacticism, they represent various human and godly attributes, they are used to teach moral and religious lessons, and satirically, they are used as mirrors that serve to ridicule human foibles and political corruption.

Kachirambe of the Anyanja
(From the Nyanja/Chewa people, southern Africa)

SOME LITTLE GIRLS had gone out into the bush to gather herbs. While they were thus busied one of them found a hyena's egg and put it into her basket. Apparently, none of the others saw it; she told them, somewhat to their surprise, that she had now picked enough, and hastened home. After she was gone the hyena came and asked them, "Who has taken my egg?" They said they did not know, but perhaps their companion who had gone home had carried it off.

Meanwhile the girl's mother, on finding the egg in her basket, had put it on the fire. The hyena arrived and demanded the egg; the woman said it was burnt, but offered to give him the next child she had to eat. Apparently this callous suggestion was quite spontaneous on her part; but as there was no child in prospect just then she probably thought that the promise was quite a safe one, and that by the time its fulfilment became possible some way out could be found. The hyena, however, left her no peace, waylaid her every day when she went to the stream for water, and kept asking her when the child was to be produced. At last he said, "If you do not have that child quickly I will eat you yourself."

She went home in great trouble, and soon after noticed a boil on her shinbone, which swelled and swelled, till it burst, and out came a child. He was fully armed, with bow, arrows and quiver, had his little gourd of charms slung round his neck, and was followed by his dogs! He announced himself in these words: "I, Kachirambe, have come forth, the child of the shinbone!" The mother was struck with astonishment, but it does not seem to have occurred to her to go back on her promise.

When next she went to draw water and the hyena met her with the usual question she replied, "Yes, I have borne a child, but he is very clever; you will never be able to catch him, but I myself will beguile him for you. I will tie you up in a bundle of grass, and tell Kachirambe to go and fetch it." So she tied up the hyena in a bundle of the long grass used for thatching, and left it lying beside the path. Kachirambe, when sent to fetch it, stood still a little way off, and said, "You, bundle, get up, that I may lift you the better!" And the bundle of grass rose up of itself. Kachirambe said, "What sort of bundle is this that gets up by itself? I have never seen the like, and I am not going to lift it, not I!" So he went home.

The hyena, after releasing himself from the grass, came back and said to the woman, "Yes, truly, that youngster of yours is a sharp one!" She told him to go in the evening and wait in a certain place; then she called Kachirambe and said, "I want you to set a trap in such and such a place for the rats; they have been destroying all my baskets." Kachirambe went and chose out a large, flat stone; then he cut a forked stick, and whittled the crosspiece and the little stick for the catch, and twisted some bark string, and made a falling trap, of the kind called *diwa*, and set and baited it.

In the evening his mother said to him, "The trap has fallen. Go and see what it has caught!" He said, "You, trap, fall again, so that I may know whether you have caught a rat!" The hyena, waiting beside the trap, heard him, lifted up the stone, and let it fall with a bang. Kachirambe said, "What sort of trap is it that falls twice? I have never seen such a one."

Next the mother told the hyena that she would send Kachirambe to pick beans. The boy took the basket and went to the field, but then he turned himself into a fly, and the hyena waited in vain. Kachirambe returned home with a full basket, to his mother's astonishment. She was nearly at her wits' end, but thought of one last expedient; she sent him into the bush to cut wood.

The night before he had a dream, which warned him that he was in great danger, so he took with him his bow, and his quiver full of arrows, and his medicine gourd, as well as a large knife. He climbed up into a tree which had dead branches, and began to cut. Presently he saw the hyena below, who said, "You are dead today; you shall not escape. Come down quickly, and I will eat you!" He answered, "I am coming down, but just open your mouth wide!" The hyena, with his usual stupidity, did as he was told, and Kachirambe threw down a sharp stick which he had just cut – it entered the hyena's mouth and killed him.

Kachirambe then came down and went home; when drawing near the house he shot an arrow towards it, to frighten his mother, and said, "What have I done to you, that you should send wild beasts after me to eat me?" She, thoroughly scared, begged his pardon.

The Woman Who Married a Fish
(From the Ila people, Zambia)

THERE WAS A WOMAN who had no husband, and she said: "I wish I had a man to marry me." Then they told her: "As you want a husband, cut some small sticks and weave a fish trap. When you have finished weaving it, go to the river. When you arrive, set your trap in the river. Then you will kill a barbel. When you have killed it, bring it to the village. Then look for a large water jar, put it in and cover it up. When you uncover it, you will find it has become a human being, and so you will get a husband."

The woman went off to catch a barbel. When she saw that the people had gone out of the village she went to uncover the pot, and looking into it saw that the barbel had become a man.

Said he: "Do not cook me; I am a man. And as you have no husband, marry me. And as for my food, I do not eat grain, I eat baboon's fruit. If you eat it also I shall go back to the water and you won't see me again." The woman agreed; after a time she stole some of his fruit.

When the man returned he examined his food and said: "My fruit is not all here. The woman has stolen some." Then he grew angry, saying: "As you have taken my food, I am going back into the water."

Now next morning the woman took her hoe and left her husband in the village. When the woman came back from hoeing, on her arrival she uncovered the pot where her husband lived, and found that he had gone out of the pot. He said: "I am going back to my home as you ate my food."

The woman said: "We will go together." When they arrived at the water the man went in. Said he: "I am going back. You, oh woman, will find other men." So he went alone into the water to his home.

The woman watched and watched, but she never saw him again.

The Little Old Woman
Who Changed into a Maiden
(From the Ila people, Zambia)

🦁

THERE WAS A LITTLE OLD WOMAN who lived away among the fields. Long ago when the people had cattle they sent their children, saying: "Take the cattle into the plain, let them graze, and build yourselves a house." So they built a village.

The people at that cattle post were in the act of playing when that little old woman entered the house and stole out of Mbwalu's churn. Then when the cattle-post men returned and came to look about they found there that little old woman. In her malice that little old woman, after stealing out of the churn, put into it a whole lot of fleas.

When they arrived the cattle-post men said: "Who has done this?" Others said: "It's yon little old woman." When the little old woman heard that she came back, and on arrival said: "Mbwalu has married me." Mbwalu said: "I am still a youngster, I cannot marry." But the little old woman stuck to it, saying: "You have married me." Then Mbwalu said: "No, I will not marry you because you purposely stole out of my churn."

Wherever Mbwalu sat the little old woman followed him, saying: "You have married me." Then his comrades laughed at Mbwalu, saying: "You fool! If you cry about it, shall we not kill the little old woman?" Then they went off to the fields, to the elders their fathers. And the same little old woman went also to the village. They inquired: "What is the matter?" Mbwalu answered, saying: "I shall kill that little old woman who sticks to me."

So when the sun went down, Mbwalu went into one of the huts and the little old woman followed him. Next day the elders said: "Just marry the little old woman as she keeps on at it." So afterwards Mbwalu consented, and he went off crying into one of the huts.

At night, when it was about to dawn, she that had been a little old woman was found to have changed into a pretty maiden. And after it dawned all the village came in some alarm, saying: "Is not that the little old woman who cried after you?" Mbwalu answered, saying: "It is she." His comrades were confounded then who had laughed at Mbwalu, saying: "You have married a little old woman."

The Little Old Woman
Who Killed a Child
(From the Ila people, Zambia)

THERE WAS A LITTLE OLD WOMAN who nursed a child. When the mother got up early to go to hoe, that little old woman said: "Bring your child and I will nurse it for you." The woman answered: "Take it and nurse it for me so that I can hoe easily." When the woman left off work, she called the little old woman, saying: "Little old woman, my child!" The woman came quickly and said to the mother: "Tomorrow you can bring your child again and I will nurse it for you."

The woman went back to her home and slept. Next morning she rose early and on arrival called: "Little old woman!" The little old woman answered: "Hallo!" When she arrived she gave her the child. On arrival at her village the little old woman passed through to where the melons were; she went to get a melon. After getting the melon, she throttled the child, killed it, and having killed it put it into a pot. The arms of the child, which she had cut off, she attached to the melon, and she also fastened on the head to the melon.

When the mother left off work she called, saying: "Little old woman!" Said she, "Hallo! Come here, here is your child." The child's mother declined, saying: "Bring me here my child, I want to go." The little old woman refused, saying: "Come here." So the mother went to the little old woman.

On arrival there she said: "Now sit down in there." Then the little old woman took a basin and went to dish up; she put a leg into the dish and took it to the mother. The woman took and ate, and asked: "This meat, what is it?" The little old woman answered: "It is a young warthog. My husband killed it." Then she went back and fetched another leg. The mother did not refuse, but ate. When she had finished eating, she said: "Now bring my child, and let us go." Then the little old woman said: "Turn round, so that I can give you the child on your back." When the little old woman was putting it on the mother's back, the mother saw the melon fall down. The woman cried and said: "Little old woman, you have killed my child." Then the little old woman answered: "You ate my meat, we both ate it."

Then the woman went off weeping to the village. On her arrival at the village the people laughed at her, saying: "You are a fool to go and give your child to a little old woman, and now you see she has eaten your child." Then they began to weep.

The Fool Who Hunted for His Axe
(From the Ila people, Zambia)

HE PUT HIS AXE on his shoulder. Nevertheless when he thought of his axe, he began to search for it; beginning early in the morning he sought it. One day went by, and then his thoughts told him: "My axe is lost." He went seeking it everywhere where he had been walking about. All the time the axe was on his shoulder. When the people saw him they said: "What is that person looking for?" He could not ask he was so busy searching. Next day one asked him: "What are you looking for? Yonder where we were gathering fruit we saw you looking about."

Then he said: "I am in great trouble." One answered: "What's troubling you?" Said he: "My axe is lost." One said: "Have you two axes?" He said: "No, only one." Then they said: "What about the one on your shoulder, whose is that?" He was greatly astonished and said: "I am a fool."

And to this day it is put on record. When a person looks for a thing he has got, they say: "You are like yon man who looked for the axe that was on his shoulder."

The Fool Who Chopped Himself
(From the Ila people, Zambia)

SOME MEN WENT HUNTING. While they were going about hunting the sun went down, and when it set they said: "Let us build a shelter." So they built a shelter, and having done so went to gather firewood. When it was dark they went to sleep.

As they were sleeping, in the night one man got up and made a fire. When he had done making the fire, he went back to sleep.

Another was lying asleep on his back with his knees sticking up in the air; he slept very soundly. After a time he woke up, and when he looked he saw his knees and was very much alarmed. Said he: "Oh dear! oh dear! that lion is going to bite me!" Presently his thoughts said: "Take your axe, which you put near your head, and wound that lion before it bites you."

So he reached out his hand towards the axe very carefully, on feeling about he found the axe, and then taking it in both hands he brought it down with all his force and chopped into his knee, and split it all to pieces. Then he set up a loud yell. One of his companions got up and asked him: "What's bitten you?" He was astounded to see the axe fixed in his knee and he asked: "What have you done?" Said he: "My thoughts are of foolishness. I saw the knee sticking up and I thought it was a lion, and now I have killed myself."

And to this day if a man hurts himself or wounds himself with an axe or a spear, they say: "In your foolishness you are like yon man who wounded himself with an axe in the knee."

The Fool Who Lay Down and Slept in the Road
(From the Ila people, Zambia)

A TRAVELLER WAS PASSING to another district. When he reached a certain village he inquired, saying: "Where does this road lead to?" They answered: "It goes there to the village." "Is it there where my relations come from?" The others answered: "Yes." "And is the road one only?" They said: "No, there are two. You will go along some way, and when you reach the dividing of the road, take the one to the left; turn aside, and take that one."

He went on and when he arrived at the dividing of the roads, he lay down and slept. As he was sleeping and sleeping, next day some people passed by and found him asleep, and they said: "Is this man dead or alive, or what's the matter with him?" Then they roused him and found that on one side of him the termites had been building. They asked him: "Why do you sleep in the road?" Said he: "I slept because they said: when you get to the dividing of the road, take the one to the left, lie down, and leave the one to the right." Then those wise people asked him: "Which is the right and which is the left?" He answered, saying: "I do not know the roads." Then they told him: "This is the one to the right and this the one to the left." Then they said: "Come on, let us go."

When they reached the village, to the people, they said to them: "This fool of a man whom you told the road, when he got to the dividing of the roads lay down to sleep as you said to him, when you reach the dividing of the roads turn aside." Now to this day they do not forget that man. Youngsters and children and adults say: "That man was a fool." His fame went abroad in all the land: "That person was truly a fool. A fool who was told, 'When you reach the dividing of the roads turn aside (pinuka) and take the left,' and when he reached there he lay down (pinuka) and slept until the termites built on him. Foolishness indeed!"

How Two Men Had a Dispute
(From the Ila people, Zambia)

TWO MEN STARTED OFF, one with a dog and the other with a pot. When they got into the veld he who had the dog killed an animal. He with the pot said: "Let us cook and eat." When they had done cooking they ate.

Then the dog got into the pot to lick it out, and when he wanted to withdraw his head he stuck fast. The owner of the pot said: "Friend, my pot will be broken. Your dog is stuck fast in my pot. Come and take him out." The owner of the dog said: "I cannot manage the dog." "Well, as you cannot manage the dog, let us cut off his head so that it may come out of the pot."

Said he: "You, my friend, which is more valuable, the dog or the pot?" Said he in answer: "My pot is the more valuable." Said he: "All right, cut away." So the owner of the pot took an axe and cut the dog's head off. When he had cut off his head, he took his pot and found it was not broken, so he brought water and washed out the blood. When he had done washing it, he brought some string, tied it, put it on his shoulder, and went off to the village. And the owner of the dog went also to the village.

When he arrived at the village, the owner of the dog found his child sick, and he thought: "Yon person who has the pot, his child took my brass bracelet." So he ran quickly and went where he was. On arrival he said: "My friend, give me my bracelet." They called the girl, but the bracelet refused to come off her arm, for it had been put on long ago while she was yet a child, and now she was grown into a maiden.

Said he: "As it refuses to come off let us cut off the hand." Said he: "My friend, don't cut off the hand, let us rather give you another bracelet." That man said: "I don't want another; this is my bracelet."

"Which is of more consequence, the bracelet or the hand of the child?"

That man refused, saying: "As for me it is my bracelet that I want." So the father of the child said: "Take an axe and cut off the hand." He cut it off and the bracelet came away.

He took his bracelet, saying: "This is the hand of your child, join it up, and let us see how you will join it. You cut my dog's head off." He took the bracelet and went to divine for his child who was sick. When he reached the diviner, the oracle said: "Dig up some medicine and your child will recover." He came back and dug the medicine, gave it to her, and she recovered.

The Man and the Mushrooms
(From the Ila people, Zambia)

THERE WAS ONCE A GREAT FAMINE in the land and many people were dying with hunger. A certain woman found some mushrooms and filled her pot with them and water.

The husband was looking on and noticed that the pot was quite full when it was put on the fire to boil. He went out, and on his return shortly after the woman took the pot off the fire and set it between his legs. Now the man said: "The pot is not full. Where are the rest?" So he began to hint that she had helped herself to them in his absence. "I saw the pot full," said he, "now it is half empty."

The woman said: "But, my husband, don't mushrooms shrink when cooked?" But he wouldn't have it. "You're lying," he said.

"Well," she went on, "if they haven't shrunk, where are they?"

"You have eaten them," said he.

His wife replied: "No, my husband, I couldn't eat the food in your absence." But the man got very angry and said to her: "You are a bad woman. You stole the mushrooms while I was away."

The woman denied, saying: "I did not steal. They shrank in the boiling," but he took a stick and beat her to death. Then he told the people that his wife had died of starvation.

As he had no other wife, he had to fend for himself. One day he brought home some mushrooms and filled that same pot his dead wife had used. He sat there and watched it boil, and when he took it off the fire saw that the mushrooms had so shrunk that there was hardly anything left at the bottom of the pot that pot which had been full to overflowing.

The man was greatly startled. He began to tremble and cry: "Oh dear! oh dear! This pot which I filled with mushrooms and now they have shrunk away! I killed my wife without reason. She did not steal; the mushrooms did shrink as she said. Dear! oh dear! I am the child of a foreigner!"

Since that day they have put him on record as an example. Do not be in a hurry to accuse people of stealing.

The Child Who Wanted to Sleep in the Middle
(From the Ila people, Zambia)

A MAN TOOK HIS CHILD with him hunting in the veld. There the boy set four traps by the side of a pool while his father looked for game. They were by themselves those two, no third.

The boy presently caught a guinea fowl in one of his traps and went off to the shelter he and his father had built in the veld. He found there his father, who had returned unsuccessful, and was therefore glad to see the guinea fowl brought by his son. The boy said: "Father!" The man replied: "What do you say, namesake of my father?"

"I say, cook this guinea fowl and eat it alone; I won't eat it, no, no. And tonight when we sleep put me in the middle." The father answered nothing: he thought the boy was only playing by talking about being put in the middle.

When the fowl was cooked the man called the boy and said: "Namesake of my father, come and let us eat the guinea fowl you killed, it's already cooked." But the boy said: "Eat it alone, father, as I told you before. But when we sleep put me in the middle, because I do not wish to sleep on the outside for fear of being bitten by some wild beast in the night." So the father ate the guinea fowl by himself.

Presently the boy said: "Father, have you done eating?" "Yes, namesake of my father, I have done." Said the child: "As you have done eating, let us sleep."

The father replied: "Right, namesake of my father, let us sleep." They went into the shelter and the man lay down first. Then his child asked him: "Where am I to lie, Dad?" "Wherever you please, namesake of my father." "Where I like," said the child, "is in the middle." "How can I put you in the middle?" replied the man, "I am only one person." But the child began to cry, sitting on the ground.

Presently his father got up and tied a bundle of grass and laid it on one side of the bed, then took hold of the child's hand and said: "Come sleep here in the middle as you wished." The child lay down, but as he was falling asleep he touched the thing by his side and found it was not a person but only grass. He got up and began to cry. His father was fast asleep. Then the boy took his father's spear – it was an iyonga, with a blade, broad and long and sharp – a spear that a man takes to tackle a warthog. He sharpened it on a stone and then lifting it in two hands he brought the point down with all his strength upon his father's stomach, cutting him open. He did not think of his father dying, but he died. And the child died too: he died of fright.

The Girl Who Married a Lion
(From the Lamba people, southern Africa)

A LION WENT TO A VILLAGE of human beings and married. And the people thought that maybe it was but a man and not a wild creature.

In due course the couple had a child. Sometime after this the husband proposed that they should visit his parents, and they set out, accompanied by the wife's brother. [In several parallel stories a younger brother or sister of the bride desires to go with her, and when she refuses follows the party by stealth, but there is no indication of this here.]

At the end of the first day's journey they all camped in the forest, and the husband cut down thorn bushes and made a kraal (*mutanda*), after which he went away, saying that he was going to catch some fish in the river. When he was gone the brother said to his sister, "He has built this kraal very badly," and he took his axe and cut down many branches, with which to strengthen the weak places.

Meanwhile the husband had gone to seek out his lion relations, and when they asked him, "How many animals have you killed?" he replied, "Two and a young one." When darkness fell he had become a huge male lion, and led the whole clan (with a contingent of hyenas) to attack his camp. Those inside heard the stealthy footfalls and sat listening. The lions hurled themselves on the barrier, trying to break through, but it was too strong, and they fell back, wounded with the thorns. He who by day had been the husband growled: "M...," and the baby inside the kraal responded: "M...". Then the mother sang:

> *"The child has bothered me with crying; watch the dance!*
> *Walk with a stoop; watch the dance!"*

The were-lion's father, quite disgusted, said, "You have brought us to a man who has built a strong kraal; we cannot eat him." And as day was beginning to break they all retired to the forest.

When it was light the husband came back with his fish, and said that he had been detained, adding, "You were nearly eaten," meaning that his absence had left them exposed to danger. It seems to be implied that the others were taken in by his excuses, but the brother, at any rate, must have had his suspicions. When the husband had gone off again, ostensibly to fish, he said, "See, it was that husband of yours who wanted to eat us last night." So he went and walked about, thinking over the position.

Presently he saw the head of a gnome (*akachekulu*) projecting from a deft in a tree; it asked him why he had come, and, on being told, said, "You are already done for; your brother-in-law is an ogre that has finished off all the people in this district." The creature then asked him to sweep out the midden inside his house – and after he had done so told him to cut down the tree, which it then hollowed out and made into a drum, stretching two prepared skins over the ends. It then slung the drum round the man's waist, and said, "Do as if you were going to do this" – that is, raise himself from the ground. And, behold, he found himself rising into the air, and he reached the top of a tree.

The gnome told him to jump down, and he did so quite easily. Then it said, "Put your sister in the drum and go home." So he called her, and, having stowed her in it, with the baby, rose up and sat in the treetop, where he began to beat the drum. The lion, hearing the sound, followed it, and when he saw the young man in the tree said, "Brother-in-law, just beat a little"; so the man beat the drum and sang:

> "Boom, boom sounds the little drum
> Of the sounding drum, sounds the little drum!
> Ogre, dance, sounds the little drum
> Of the sounding drum, sounds the little drum!"

The lion began to dance, and the skins he was wearing fell off and were blown away by the wind, and he had to go back and pick them up. Meanwhile the drum carried the fugitives on, and the lion pursued them as soon as he had recovered his skins. Having overtaken them, he called up into the tree, "Brother-in-law, show me my child!" and the following dialogue took place:

"What, you lion, am I going to show you a relation of mine?"

"Would I eat my child?" conveniently ignoring the fact that he had himself announced the killing of the young one.

"How about the night you came? You would have eaten us!"

Again the brother-in-law beat the drum, and the lion danced (apparently unable to help himself), and as before lost his skins, stopped to pick them up, and began the chase again, while the man went springing along the treetops like a monkey. At last he reached his own village, and his mother saw as it were a swallow settle in the courtyard of his home. She said, "Well, I never! Greeting, my child!" and asked where his sister was. He frightened her at first by telling her that she had been eaten by her husband, who was really a lion, but afterwards relented and told her to open the drum. Her daughter came out with the baby, safe and sound, and the mother said, praising her son, "You have grown up; you have saved your sister!" She gave him five slave girls.

The lion had kept up the pursuit, and reached the outskirts of the village, but, finding that his intended victims were safe within the stockade, he gave up and returned to the forest.

The Magic Mirror
(From the Senna people, Zimbabwe)

A LONG, LONG WHILE AGO, before ever the white men were seen in Senna, there lived a man called Gopani-Kufa.

One day, as he was out hunting, he came upon a strange sight. An enormous python had caught an antelope and coiled itself around it; the antelope, striking out in despair with its horns, had pinned the python's neck to a tree, and so deeply had its horns sunk in the soft wood that neither creature could get away.

"Help!" cried the antelope, "for I was doing no harm, yet I have been caught, and would have been eaten, had I not defended myself."

"Help me," said the python, "for I am Insato, King of all the Reptiles, and will reward you well!"

Gopani-Kufa considered for a moment, then stabbing the antelope with his assegai, he set the python free.

"I thank you," said the python; "come back here with the new moon, when I shall have eaten the antelope, and I will reward you as I promised."

"Yes," said the dying antelope, "he will reward you, and lo! your reward shall be your own undoing!"

Gopani-Kufa went back to his kraal, and with the new moon he returned again to the spot where he had saved the python.

Insato was lying upon the ground, still sleepy from the effects of his huge meal, and when he saw the man he thanked him again, and said: "Come with me now to Pita, which is my own country, and I will give you what you will of all my possessions."

Gopani-Kufa at first was afraid, thinking of what the antelope had said, but finally he consented and followed Insato into the forest.

For several days they travelled, and at last they came to a hole leading deep into the earth. It was not very wide, but large enough to admit a man. "Hold on to my tail," said Insato, "and I will go down first, drawing you after me." The man did so, and Insato entered.

Down, down, down they went for days, all the while getting deeper and deeper into the earth, until at last the darkness ended and they dropped into a beautiful country; around them grew short green grass, on which browsed herds of cattle and sheep and goats. In the distance Gopani-Kufa saw a great collection of houses all square, built of stone and very tall, and their roofs were shining with gold and burnished iron.

Gopani-Kufa turned to Insato, but found, in the place of the python, a man, strong and handsome, with the great snake's skin wrapped round him for covering; and on his arms and neck were rings of pure gold.

The man smiled. "I am Insato," said he, "but in my own country I take man's shape – even as you see me – for this is Pita, the land over which I am king." He then took Gopani-Kufa by the hand and led him towards the town.

On the way they passed rivers in which men and women were bathing and fishing and boating; and farther on they came to gardens covered with heavy crops of rice and maize, and many other grains which Gopani-Kufa did not even know the name of. And as they passed, the people who were singing at their work in the fields, abandoned their labours and saluted Insato with delight, bringing also palm wine and green coconuts for refreshment, as to one returned from a long journey.

"These are my children!" said Insato, waving his hand towards the people. Gopani-Kufa was much astonished at all that he saw, but he said nothing. Presently they came to the town; everything here, too, was beautiful, and everything that a man might desire he could obtain. Even the grains of dust in the streets were of gold and silver.

Insato conducted Gopani-Kufa to the palace, and showing him his rooms, and the maidens who would wait upon him, told him that they would have a great feast that night, and on the morrow he might name his choice of the riches of Pita and it should be given him. Then he was away.

Now Gopani-Kufa had a wasp called Zengi-mizi. Zengi-mizi was not an ordinary wasp, for the spirit of the father of Gopani-Kufa had entered it, so that it was exceedingly wise. In times of doubt Gopani-Kufa always consulted the wasp as to what had better be done, so on this occasion he took it out of the little rush basket in which he carried it, saying: "Zengi-mizi, what gift shall I ask of Insato tomorrow when he would know the reward he shall bestow on me for saving his life?"

"Biz-z-z," hummed Zengi-mizi, "ask him for Sipao the Mirror." And it flew back into its basket.

Gopani-Kufa was astonished at this answer; but knowing that the words of Zengi-mizi were true words, he determined to make the request. So that night they feasted, and on the morrow Insato came to Gopani-Kufa and, giving him greeting joyfully, he said:

"Now, O my friend, name your choice amongst my possessions and you shall have it!"

"O king!" answered Gopani-Kufa, "out of all your possessions I will have the Mirror, Sipao."

The king started. "O friend, Gopani-Kufa," he said, "ask anything but that! I did not think that you would request that which is most precious to me."

"Let me think over it again then, O king," said Gopani-Kufa, "and tomorrow I will let you know if I change my mind."

But the king was still much troubled, fearing the loss of Sipao, for the mirror had magic powers, so that he who owned it had but to ask and his wish would be fulfilled; to it Insato owed all that he possessed.

As soon as the king left him, Gopani-Kufa again took Zengi-mizi, out of his basket. "Zengi-mizi," he said, "the king seems loth to grant my request for the Mirror – is there not some other thing of equal value for which I might ask?"

And the wasp answered: "There is nothing in the world, O Gopani-Kufa, which is of such value as this Mirror, for it is a Wishing Mirror, and accomplishes the desires of him who owns it. If the king hesitates, go to him the next day, and the day after, and in the end he will bestow the Mirror upon you, for you saved his life."

And it was even so. For three days Gopani-Kufa returned the same answer to the king, and, at last, with tears in his eyes, Insato gave him the Mirror, which was of polished iron, saying: "Take Sipao, then, O Gopani-Kufa, and may thy wishes come true. Go back now to thine own country; Sipao will show you the way."

Gopani-Kufa was greatly rejoiced, and, taking farewell of the king, said to the Mirror:

"Sipao, Sipao, I wish to be back upon the Earth again!"

Instantly he found himself standing upon the upper earth; but, not knowing the spot, he said again to the Mirror:

"Sipao, Sipao, I want the path to my own kraal!"

And behold! right before him lay the path!

When he arrived home he found his wife and daughter mourning for him, for they thought that he had been eaten by lions; but he comforted them, saying that while following a wounded antelope he had missed his way and had wandered for a long time before he had found the path again.

That night he asked Zengi-mizi, in whom sat the spirit of his father, what he had better ask Sipao for next?

"Biz-z-z," said the wasp, "would you not like to be as great a chief as Insato?"

And Gopani-Kufa smiled, and took the Mirror and said to it:

"Sipao, Sipao, I want a town as great as that of Insato, the King of Pita; and I wish to be chief over it!"

Then all along the banks of the Zambesi river, which flowed nearby, sprang up streets of stone buildings, and their roofs shone with gold and burnished iron like those in Pita; and in the streets men and women were walking, and young boys were driving out the sheep and cattle to pasture; and from the river came shouts and laughter from the young men and maidens who had launched their canoes and were fishing. And when the people of the new town beheld Gopani-Kufa they rejoiced greatly and hailed him as chief.

Gopani-Kufa was now as powerful as Insato the King of the Reptiles had been, and he and his family moved into the palace that stood high above the other buildings right in the middle of the town. His wife was too astonished at all these wonders to ask any questions, but his daughter Shasasa kept begging him to tell her how he had suddenly become so great; so at last he revealed the whole secret, and even entrusted Sipao the Mirror to her care, saying:

"It will be safer with you, my daughter, for you dwell apart; whereas men come to consult me on affairs of state, and the Mirror might be stolen."

Then Shasasa took the Magic Mirror and hid it beneath her pillow, and after that for many years Gopani-Kufa ruled his people both well and wisely, so that all men loved him, and never once did he need to ask Sipao to grant him a wish.

Now it happened that, after many years, when the hair of Gopani-Kufa was turning grey with age, there came white men to that country. Up the Zambesi they came, and they fought long and fiercely with Gopani-Kufa; but, because of the power of the Magic Mirror, he beat them, and they fled to the sea coast. Chief among them was one Rei, a man of much cunning, who sought to

HUMAN FOLLY & ADVENTURE

discover whence sprang Gopani-Kufa's power. So one day he called to him a trusty servant named Butou, and said: "Go you to the town and find out for me what is the secret of its greatness."

And Butou, dressing himself in rags, set out, and when he came to Gopani-Kufa's town he asked for the chief; and the people took him into the presence of Gopani-Kufa. When the white man saw him he humbled himself, and said: "O Chief! take pity on me, for I have no home! When Rei marched against you I alone stood apart, for I knew that all the strength of the Zambesi lay in your hands, and because I would not fight against you he turned me forth into the forest to starve!"

And Gopani-Kufa believed the white man's story, and he took him in and feasted him, and gave him a house.

In this way the end came. For the heart of Shasasa, the daughter of Gopani-Kufa, went forth to Butou the traitor, and from her he learnt the secret of the Magic Mirror. One night, when all the town slept, he felt beneath her pillow and, finding the Mirror, he stole it and fled back with it to Rei, the chief of the white men.

So it befell that, one day, as Gopani-Kufa was gazing up at the river from a window of the palace he again saw the war canoes of the white men; and at the sight his spirit misgave him.

"Shasasa! my daughter!" he cried wildly, "go fetch me the mirror, for the white men are at hand."

"Woe is me, my father!" she sobbed. "The Mirror is gone! For I loved Butou the traitor, and he has stolen Sipao from me!"

Then Gopani-Kufa calmed himself, and drew out Zengi-mizi from its rush basket.

"O spirit of my father!" he said, "what now shall I do?"

"O Gopani-Kufa!" hummed the wasp, "there is nothing now that can be done, for the words of the antelope which you slew are being fulfilled."

"Alas! I am an old man – I had forgotten!" cried the chief. "The words of the antelope were true words – my reward shall be my undoing – they are being fulfilled!"

Then the white men fell upon the people of Gopani-Kufa and slew them together with the chief and his daughter Shasasa; and since then all the power of the Earth has rested in the hands of the white men, for they have in their possession Sipao, the Magic Mirror.

Sudika-Mbambi the Invincible
(From the Bantu-speaking people, Angola)

SUDIKA-MBAMBI WAS THE SON of Nzua dia Kimanaweze, who married the daughter of the Sun and Moon. The young couple were living with Nzua's parents, when one day Kimanaweze sent his son away to Loanda to trade. The son demurred, but the father insisted, so he went. While he was gone certain cannibal monsters, called *makishi*, descended on the village and sacked it – all the people who were not killed fled. Nzua, when he returned, found no houses and no people; searching over the cultivated ground, he at last came across his wife, but she was so changed that he did not recognize her at first. "The *makishi* have destroyed us," was her explanation of what had happened.

They seem to have camped and cultivated as best they could; and in due course Sudika-Mbambi ('the Thunderbolt') was born. He was a wonder child, who spoke before his entrance into the world, and came forth equipped with knife, stick and his *kilembe* (a 'mythic plant', explained as 'life tree'), which he requested his mother to plant at the back of the house. Scarcely had he made his appearance when another voice was heard, and his twin brother Kabundungulu was born. The first thing they did was to cut down poles and build a house for their parents. Soon after this, Sudika-Mbambi announced that he was going to fight the *makishi*. He told Kabundungulu to stay at home and to keep an eye on the *kilembe*: if it withered he would know that his brother was dead; he then set out. On his way he was joined by four beings who called themselves *kipalendes* and boasted various accomplishments – building a house on the bare rock (a sheer impossibility under local conditions), carving ten clubs a day, and other more recondite operations, none of which, however, as the event proved, they could accomplish successfully. When they had gone a certain distance through the bush Sudika-Mbambi directed them to halt and build a house, in order to fight the *makishi*. As soon as he had cut one pole all the others needed cut themselves. He ordered the *kipalende* who had said he could erect a house on a rock to begin building, but as fast as a pole was set up it fell down again. The leader then took the work in hand, and it was speedily finished.

Next day he set out to fight the *makishi*, with three *kipalendes*, leaving the fourth in the house. To him soon after appeared an old woman, who told him that he might marry her granddaughter if he would fight her (the grandmother) and overcome her. They wrestled, but the old woman soon threw the *kipalende*, placed a large stone on top of him as he lay on the ground, and left him there, unable to move.

Sudika-Mbambi, who had the gift of second sight, at once knew what had happened, returned with the other three, and released the *kipalende*. He told his story, and the others derided him for being beaten by a woman. Next day he accompanied the rest, the second *kipalende* remaining in the house. No details are given of the fighting with the *makishi*, beyond the statement that "they are firing." The second *kipalende* met with the same fate as his brother, and again Sudika-Mbambi was immediately aware of it. The incident was repeated on the third and on the fourth day. On the fifth Sudika-Mbambi sent the *kipalendes* to the war, and stayed behind himself. The old woman challenged him; he fought her and killed her – she seems to have been a peculiarly malignant kind of witch, who had kept her granddaughter shut up in a stone house, presumably as a lure for unwary strangers. It is not stated what she intended to do with the captives whom she secured under heavy stones, but, judging from what takes place in other stories of this kind, one may conclude that they were kept to be eaten in due course.

Sudika-Mbambi married the old witch's granddaughter, and they settled down in the stone house. The *kipalendes* returned with the news that the *makishi* were completely defeated, and all went well for a time.

Treachery of the Kipalendes

The *kipalendes*, however, became envious of their leader's good fortune, and plotted to kill him. They dug a hole in the place where he usually rested and covered it with mats; when he came in tired they pressed him to sit down, which he did, and immediately fell into the hole. They covered it up, and thought they had made an end of him. His younger brother, at home, went to look at the 'life tree', and found that it had withered. Thinking that, perhaps, there was still some hope, he poured water on it, and it grew green again.

Sudika-Mbambi was not killed by the fall; when he reached the bottom of the pit he looked round and saw an opening. Entering this, he found himself in a road – the road, in fact, which leads to the country of the dead. When he had gone some distance he came upon an old woman, or, rather, the upper half of one [half-beings are very common in African folklore, but they are usually split lengthways, having one eye, one arm, one leg and so on], hoeing her garden by the wayside. He greeted her, and she returned his greeting. He then asked her to show him the way, and she said she would do so if he would hoe a little for her, which he did. She set him on the road, and told him to take the narrow path, not the broad one, and before arriving at Kalunga-ngombe's house he must carry a jug of red pepper and a jug of wisdom. It is not explained how he was to procure these, though it is evident from the sequel that he did so, nor how they were to be used, except that Kalunga-ngombe makes it a condition that anyone who wants to marry his daughter must bring them with him. We have not previously been told that this was Sudika-Mbambi's intention. On arriving at the house a fierce dog barked at him; he scolded it, and it let him pass. He entered, and was courteously welcomed by people who showed him into the guest house and spread a mat for him. He then announced that he had come to marry the daughter of Kalunga-ngombe. Kalunga answered that he consented if Sudika-Mbambi had fulfilled the conditions. He then retired for the night, and a meal was sent in to him – a live cock and a bowl of the local porridge (*Junji*). He ate the porridge, with some meat which he had brought with him; instead of killing the cock he kept him under his bed. Evidently it was thought he would assume that the fowl was meant for him to eat [perhaps we have here a remnant of the belief, not known to or not understood by the narrator of the story, that the living must not eat of the food of the dead], and a trick was intended, to prevent his return to the upper world. In the middle of the night he heard people inquiring who had killed Kalunga's cock; but the cock crowed from under the bed, and Sudika-Mbambi was not trapped. Next morning, when he reminded Kalunga of his promise, he was told that the daughter had been carried off by the huge serpent called Kinyoka kya Tumba, and that if he wanted to marry her he must rescue her.

Sudika-Mbambi started for Kinyoka's abode, and asked for him. Kinyoka's wife said, "He has gone shooting." Sudika-Mbambi waited awhile, and presently saw driver ants approaching – the dreaded ants which would consume any living thing left helpless in their path. He stood his ground and beat them off; they were followed by red ants, these by a swarm of bees, and these by wasps, but none of them harmed him. Then Kinyoka's five heads appeared, one after the other. Sudika-Mbambi cut off each as it came, and when the fifth fell the snake was dead. He went into the house, found Kalunga's daughter there, and took her home to her father.

But Kalunga was not yet satisfied. There was a giant fish, Kimbiji, which kept catching his goats and pigs. Sudika-Mbambi baited a large hook with a sucking-pig and caught Kimbiji, but even he was not strong enough to pull the monster to land. He fell into the water, and Kimbiji swallowed him.

Kabundungulu, far away at their home, saw that his brother's life tree had withered once more, and set out to find him. He reached the house where the *kipalendes* were keeping Sudika-Mbambi's wife captive, and asked where he was. They denied all knowledge of him, but he felt certain there had been foul play. "You have killed him. Uncover the grave." They opened up the pit, and Kabundungulu descended into it. He met with the old woman, and was directed to Kalunga-ngombe's dwelling. On inquiring for his brother he was told, "Kimbiji has swallowed him." Kabundungulu asked for a pig, baited his hook, and called the people to his help. Between them they landed the fish, and Kabundungulu cut it open. He found his brother's bones inside it, and took them out. Then he said, "My elder, arise!" and the bones came to life. Sudika-Mbambi married Kalunga-ngombe's daughter, and set out for home with her and his brother. They reached the pit, which had been filled in, and the ground cracked and they got out. They drove away the four *kipalendes* and, having got rid of them, settled down to a happy life.

Kabundungulu felt that he was being unfairly treated, since his brother had two wives, while he had none, and asked for one of them to be handed over to him. Sudika-Mbambi pointed out that this was impossible, as he was already married to both of them, and no more was said for the time being. But sometime later, when Sudika-Mbambi returned from hunting, his wife complained to him that Kabundungulu was persecuting them both with his attentions. This led to a desperate quarrel between the brothers, and they fought with swords, but could not kill each other. Both were endowed with some magical power, so that

theswords would not cut, and neither could be wounded. At last they got tired
of fighting and separated, the elder going east and the younger west.

The Woman Who Longed for Fish
(From the Ambundu people, Angola)

I WILL TELL OF ngana Kimalauezu kia Tumb' a Ndala, who was
staying with his wife, a long time back; and they lived. His wife
then came to conceive. She ate no meat; she longed only for fish.

The man, when he went fishing, brought a lot of fish; the fishes then fled to
another river. One day the man tells the woman, saying: "Prepare me food,
that I go fishing." And the woman prepared the food. The man then went to
the river, where the fish had fled; and he made there his camping hut, and ate.

When he finished, he said: "I will go to fish," and he cast the net. The first
time he caught nothing; the second time the same. The third time he feels it
is heavy. Under the water then it says: "Wait, please; because thy friend is the
father of a child." When he finished waiting, then he hears again there saying:
"Pull now!" He then pulled (out) a big fish, very large; and he put it into (his)
basket, and began to walk. But the fishes all were following this big fish; the
man heard always in the grass only: ualalá! ualalá!

When he was already about to arrive at home, his woman went to meet him
with her neighbours. When they arrived at home, the man then gave the fish
to be scaled. The woman, however, then told the man, saying: "Thou, scale it!"
The man said: "I won't." The woman then began to scale it. But the fish was (all
the time) singing, saying:

> "When thou me scalest, scale me well!
> When thou me scalest, scale me well!"

When she had finished, then she put it in the pot; but the fish was still
singing. When the fish was done, the woman then prepared five plates, and

invited the man with her neighbours. But they refused. She then ate alone by herself.

When she had finished, then she took her pipe and the mat; and she spread it in the open. When she was seated, then she heard in her belly, saying: "Where shall I get out?" The woman said: "Get out by the soles of (my) feet." The fish answered her: "By thy feet, wherewith thou art wont to tread on dirt, there shall I get out?" The woman said: "Get out by the mouth." "By (thy) mouth, where thou didst swallow me, there shall I get out?" The woman said: "Seek wherever thou wishest." The fish said: "Then I get out here!" and the woman burst in the middle. The fish then went away.

Two Men, One Woman
(From the Ambundu people, Angola)

AN ELDERLY MAN had one daughter; her name (was) nga Samba. This daughter, a number of men wanted her. Her father would not give her. When there comes a man, her father demands of him a living deer. The men, each and all, who wanted his daughter, then they refuse, saying: "The living deer, we cannot get it."

One day, there appear two men, saying: "We have come to the old man who owns a daughter, nga Samba." The man then comes out, and they greet each other. He asks them, saying: "What is it you wish?" One of them says to him: "I have come to ask for thy daughter, whom I want." He turns to the other; he asks him also what brought him. The other tells him, saying: "I have come to ask for thy daughter; I want her, (that) she be my consort."

Then her father says: "The girl is one. You have come to ask her, two of you. I now am possessor of one daughter (only); I have not two children. He, who brings me the living deer; the same, I will give him my daughter." And they go away.

On the road, on which they were walking, one speaks, saying: "Tomorrow, I will seek the living deer in the forest." Then the other: "I too, tomorrow I will go to seek the deer. Where shall we meet tomorrow, to go and seek the deer?" The other then says to him: "Tomorrow we will meet at the muxixi tree, outside (the forest)." And they go, each one to his home. And they sleep.

In early morning, they rise, dress, with their machetes; and they go to meet for seeking the living deer. When they found each other, then they go until (they are) in the forest.

They come across a deer; they begin to pursue it. One pursued, got tired; he cannot run any more. Says: "That woman will destroy my life. Shall I suffer distress because of a woman? If I bring her home, if she dies, would I seek another? I will not run again to catch a living deer. I never saw it, (that) a girl was wooed (with) a living deer. I will await my comrade, whether he gives up, that we may go."

When he had spent a while, he sees the other, who comes with a deer bound. When he had completed approaching, he says: "Friend, the deer, didst thou catch it indeed?" Then the other: "I caught it. That girl delights me much. Rather I would sleep in the forest, than to fail to catch it."

And they go to the man, who begat the young woman. They bring him the deer. Then the old man: "The deer, keep ye it; eat, please. Directly we will talk the matter over." And he orders to cook the food for them.

When they had done eating, this old man, who begat his daughter, then calls four old men, and says to them, saying: "I have one daughter; I did not beget a son. I need a good son-in-law, gentle of heart. Therefore I always demand a living deer. These gentlemen came yesterday, two of them, to ask for my daughter, and I told them saying "I am possessor of one daughter; he who wants her let him bring me a living deer." Today these have come with it. They two came to ask for the girl; one only brought the deer. The other, what has moved him, that he did not come with a deer? You, aged men and neighbours, to you indeed I have given my daughter. Choose ye our son-in-law among these two."

The aged men, they ask these two gentlemen, saying: "Yesterday you came to ask for the girl, two of you; today, one came with the deer; the other, what has caused him not to come with it?"

Then these two gentlemen said: "We went into the forest to seek deer, both of us, and we saw them. My comrade pursued and gave up; I, your daughter charmed me much, even to the heart, and I pursued the deer till it gave in.

And I caught it; I bound it; and joined my comrade where he got tired. My comrade, he came only to accompany me."

Then the aged men say: "Thou, sir, who gavest up the deer, what crime caused thee to get tired of catching the deer, if thou didst want our daughter?"

"I never saw, that they wooed a girl (with) a deer. I went with my comrade to seek a deer, perhaps I might catch it. When I saw the great running, I said "No, that woman will cost my life. Women are plentiful." And I sat down to await my comrade, (to see) whether he would give up chasing the deer, and come, so that we might go. I saw my companion coming with the deer bound. I have only come to accompany him. I have not come again to your daughter."

Then the aged men: "Thou, who gavest up catching the deer, thou art our son-in-law. This gentleman, who caught the deer, he may go with it; he may eat it or may sell it; for he is a man of great heart. If he wants to kill, he kills at once; he does not listen to one who scolds him, or gives him advice. Our daughter, if we gave her to him, and she did wrong, when he would beat her, he would not hear (one) who entreats for her. We do not want him; let him go. This gentleman, who gave up the deer, he (is) our son-in-law; because, our daughter, when she does wrong, when we come to pacify him, he will listen to us. Although he were in great anger, when he sees us, his anger will cease. He is our good son-in-law, whom we have chosen."

The Young Man and the Skull
(From the Ambundu people, Angola)

A YOUNG MAN STARTED ON A JOURNEY; he arrived in middle of the path. He finds a skull of the head of a person. They all used to pass it by there. But he, when he arrived there, he struck it (with) staff, saying: "Thou, foolishness has killed thee." The skull said: "I, foolishness has killed me; thou, soon smartness shall kill thee." The young man said: "I have met an omen; where I was to go, I will (not go, but) return hence at once. The head of a person has spoken to me!"

And he returned; arrived at home. He finds others, old men, says: "You, gentlemen, I have met an ominous wonder." The old men said: "What omen?" He says: "The head of a person has spoken to me." The people say: "O man, thou hast told a lie. We all of us, at same place we are wont to pass by the head. We never yet heard it speak; how has the head spoken to thee?" He said: "Let us go. When I beat it (with) staff, if it does not speak, I, cut off my head." They say: "All right."

The crowd starts with him; they arrive at the place; they found it. The young man beat it (with) his staff: "Foolishness has killed thee." The head kept silent. He beat it again, the second time, saying: "Foolishness has killed thee." The head kept silent. The crowd say: "O man! thou didst tell a lie." They cut off his head. When they finished cutting it off, the skull said: "I, foolishness has killed me; thou, smartness has killed thee." The people said: "Why, we killed him unjustly; the head of a person has spoken."

The young man found the head of a person, and he beat it, saying: "Foolishness has killed thee." The head of the person said: "Thou, soon smartness shall kill thee." Wits and foolishness, all are equal. The young man, his wits killed him.

The Four Uouas
(From the Ambundu people, Angola)

WE WILL TELL OF THE FOUR UOUAS, of the elder two, and the younger two. Na Kimanaueze kia Tumb' a Ndala, favourite of friends, built, lived. He begat his four children; all females. There came no male child. They all (had) one mother.

The eldest, when she came to name herself, said: "I (am) Uoua." Her younger, who followed her behind, also said: "I (am) Uoua." Their sister, the third, says: "I (am) Uoua." The youngest, the fourth, says: "I (am) Uoua." The other people say: "The name is one, that you called yourselves, in your sistership of four. How shall they call you?"

They grew up; have come to the age of marrying.

There came a man to woo, to Uoua the eldest. They (were in) one house, of virginity. They placed him in the guest house. The sun died. They cooked food for him; he ate. The night came; the man went out; he went to the house of the girls.

He says: "Evening, you, ladies." The girls accept it, saying: "This is evening." They spread for him a mat on the ground; he sits down. The girls entertain him; saying: "Thou spentest (the day) how, young man?" He says:

> *"I spent the day as an elephant spends it.*
> *I played, as a player of backgammon.*
> *The elephant is lame, (because) they shot him.*
> *The path is worn down, (because) they walked it.*
> *A nice bottle of bird seed, (is) food of birds.*
> *The wild fig tree and the Mubangu tree (are) ornaments of a home.*
> *In the East, we are children of the hippo;*
> *In the West, we are children of the Governor.*
> *The young man, when he covers himself,*
> *(Casts) the mantle over the left (shoulder).*
> *Staff, staff; sword, sword:*
> *Staff, we took it for ornament;*
> *The sword, we took it for sergeantship.*
> *The tobacco slept at head of bed;*
> *The palm wine slept in the glass;*
> *Tobacco, (is) the cause of spitting;*
> *Palm wine, (is) the cause of talking.*
> *There is where his heart went. This is the end, ladies."*

They say: "We accept." They say: "Let us pass time. The sun is down, the evening dark. That thou thoughtest, saying, "I will go to give them (good) evening," we praise it, that thou didst so. The end." He answered, saying: "(Is) of God." They continue their conversation. He says: "I came (because of) thee, thou, na Uoua the eldest."

Na Uoua says: "Very well. Thou shalt marry me, (if) thou marriest us all, the four of us. If thou thinkest, that (thou wilt have) me alone, the eldest, thou canst not marry me. It must be that we marry our one man, the four of us in the fourhood (of) one mother." The man assents, saying: "I can marry you." He gives them tobacco; he goes to his guest house; sleeps.

At daybreak, he goes to na Kimanaueze, saying: "I have come to have a talk; I want to marry with thy daughters." Na Kimanaueze says: "Very well. If thou canst afford the four of them, bring me the price." The man agrees to, saying: "I can. All right."

He returns to his home. He finds his father; says: "Where I went they accepted me. They asked me for the wooing presents of four girls." His father took up four mothers of cows; he gave them to him, saying: "Go and woo." He slept.

In the morning, he starts. He arrives at his parents-in-law; he hands the cows. They accept. The bridegroom says: "I give you four days. The fifth day I shall come to fetch the brides." They cook him a mother of goat.

Morning comes; he returns to his home. He slept four days. The fifth day having come, the man took the companions. They go to fetch the brides; they arrive. They spent the day. They cooked them a goat and mush. The evening came; they gave them the brides.

They come with them. They introduce them into their houses. The eldest has her house; the younger has her house; the third has her house; the youngest has her house. They kill them a goat. They eat in the houses of brideship. The two days are over. The band of the companions scatters.

The man will not come into the houses of the brides. All days he is sleeping in the house of bachelorship. One day his father scolded him, saying: "Thou, na Nzuá, the girls strangers, since thou hast brought them home, in their houses thou refusest to enter, why?" He replied to his father, saying: "Father, shame has held me, because since I brought them home, they not yet ate nice food. Tomorrow I will go to the bush to hunt; perhaps I may there kill a deer for them to eat." He slept.

When shone the morning, he took up his gun, and his knife, and his dog and his boy. He says: "Let us go to hunt." They start; they arrive in bush. They build a hut; they get in. They sleep.

Morning shines. Na Nzuá goes to set traps for rats. He comes away; comes to his hut. He slept. They went to look at the traps. They loosened the rats; forty rats. They return to the grass hut.

Na Nzuá tells his boy, saying: "Cut green leaves." The boy cuts leaves. He says: "Bind four bundles of the rats." He says: "Boy, I will send thee directly home.

Thou shalt arrive at night; do not arrive by day. These four bundles, carry them to my wives."

The boy went. He begins with Uoua the eldest. He enters into the house, says: "This bundle (is) that which the master sends thee, saying, "The bundle, which the wise bound, let a fool untie it. I remain here, I cannot yet go." He, the master, told me, saying, this bundle, go, give it na Uoua the eldest; do not mention it to her sisters." The boy went out.

He went again to Uoua the second; she opened to him. The boy said: "The bundle here, master says, 'The bundle, which the wise bound, let a fool untie it. Thou alone, I sent thee the bundle; thy sisters, do not mention it to them. I still remain.'" The boy went out.

He went again to Uoua the third; she opened to him. He entered: "Master says, 'the bundle, that the wise bound, let a fool untie it. Thou only, I send thee this bundle; thy sisters, do not mention it to them.'" The boy went out.

He went further to Uoua the youngest; she opened to him. The boy said: "Master says, 'This bundle, thou only I sent it to thee; thy sisters, do not mention it to them. The bundle, which the wise bound, let a fool untie it.'" The boy says: "I am going now. Tomorrow do not mention me to thy sisters."

The boy went in the night. He arrived at his master's in the bush. His master asks him: "Didst thou do as I ordered thee?" The boy says: "I did do so."

The women at home, to whom the bundles were sent, Uoua the first kept the bundle in the box. Uoua the second kept it in the box. Uoua the third also, she kept it in the box. Uoua the fourth thought, saying: "The bundle, that he sent me, saying, 'Let her open it,' I will open it, that I see what is in it."

She opened it; she sees the rats, that are in. She cleans them out; she shaves them. She puts them in pot; she cooks them. She sticks them on a spit; she sticks it in roof. She kept quiet. They live on some days; ten days.

Na Nzuá, who had gone hunting, comes; he is in the house of Uoua the eldest, saying: "Bring the bundle that I sent thee." She opens the box; takes out the bundle; she unties it. The rats are all rotten; they have become maggots.

The man goes out; he goes to Uoua the second: "Bring the bundle that I sent thee." The woman opens the box; she takes it out; she unties it. In it are all maggots.

The man goes out; goes to Uoua the third. Says: "Bring the bundle that I sent thee." The woman opens the box; she takes out the bundle; she unties it. In it are maggots only.

The man goes out; goes to Uoua the youngest: "Bring the bundle that I sent thee." The woman stands up; she takes off the spit from the roof. The rats are dried.

The man laughs. He goes outside; he calls the crowd of the people of the village. He says: "You, gentlemen, I went a-hunting. I tied four bundles; I sent them to my wives, saying, "The bundle which the wise tied, let the fool untie it." I made ten days. in the bush. Today I have come home, saying, "You, wives, bring the bundles, that I sent you." They take out the bundles; those of the elder three are rotten; the bundle of the fourth, of the youngest, is dried. Her rats are these. The elder three are fools; they are not intelligent. I will marry the youngest." The elder three went away.

Mr Carry-Me-Not
and Mr Tell-Me-Not
(From the Ambundu people, Angola)

MR CARRY-ME-NOT and Mr Tell-me-not bound their merchandise; they are going to Loanda to make trade, with their carriers.

They made trade in the city of Loanda; they bind their baskets; they lift (them). They go as far as Kifuangondo. Then Mr Tell-me-not: "Friend, let us go now!" Says: "Let me sleep first!" They rest. They reach the evening: "How? friend, thou hast rested how?" Says: "I rested not." They sleep.

(He) arrives in morning: "Let us go, friend!" Says: "I cannot walk." Then his friend: "Let us rest. You, carriers, go ye home. When you reach home, tell them, the old people at Ambaca, saying: 'Mr Carry-me-not is sick. We left them at Kifuangondo, both Mr Tell-me-not and Mr Carry-me-not. Mr Carry-me-not is sick; the other remained, to look after him, until the sickness is over.'" The carriers have gone. They, who stayed behind, spend the day; they sleep.

Arriving in the morning, then Mr Tell-me-not says: "My friend, the sickness is much. Let me carry thee that we may go." "They do not carry me." "Lies thine." Says: "Friend, I spoke the truth. I, they do not carry me." (The other) says: "I will carry thee indeed; I am telling thee so! "He says: " I, they do not carry me at all; it is a law of my family."

(The first) says: "Thy lies! I will carry thee anyhow. "He puts him on (his) back. They start…as far as on Bengo River at Palma's. "Friend, get down!" "I shall not get down. I have been telling thee: I, they carry me not.' The day of today, thou hast carried me, I cannot get down. "He sleeps with him on (his) back until day breaks. They set out.

Halting on the road, Mr Tell-me-not wants to do something, says: "Friend, get down, that I may do something." "I have told thee already; me, they carry me not. The day of today, thou art carrying me; I can no more get down. "Mr Tell-me-not did it standing.

They start…as far as Pulungo. Then Mr Tell-me-not: "Get down, friend, that I may rest." He says: "My friend, I shall not get down anymore.

Mr Tell-me-not eats nothing, drinks no water. drinks no water, eats no food. They start. Mr Carry-me-not They halt on the road; Mr Tell-me-not falls on the ground. Their fathers sent a hammock. They put them in the hammock…as far as home. Mr Tell-me-not, Mr Carry-me-not, they made eight days. Mr Tell-me-not died, Mr Carry-me-not died. The one, Mr Carry-me-not, died on the back of the other. They buried them, (one) man in his grave, (the other) man in his grave.

If there is left, on the face of earth, somebody who hears that another says: "Thou, friend, do not do this; it will bring thee trouble," if he says: "It will not do me any harm," he is wrong.

On the face of the earth, one listens to another; thou, too, shalt listen to thy companion when he speaks. Thou, who dost not listen to anyone, art a beast of the forest; thou shalt find only what will kill thee, what thee will report thou shalt not find.

Mutelembe and Ngunga
(From the Ambundu people, Angola)

WE WILL TELL of Mutelembe and Ngunga. Two men, elder and younger, say: "Let us go a-hunting!" The younger, he has his two dogs; this one, his name (is) Mutelembe, this one, his

name (is) Ngunga. They start; they arrive in game ground. They build a hut; they go in; they stay on.

The younger is (always) shooting the game, the elder none. They spent a month, the younger says: "Elder, let us go home now!"

They start. The elder thinks, saying: "We came a-hunting. The child, he killed the game; I, the elder, not. When I arrive at home, shame will take me." He killed his younger. He took out the bowels of his younger; he gave them to Mutelembe. Mutelembe smelled them; he refused. He gave them to the other dog, Ngunga; he refused. He lifted the basket of meat. The dogs looked at their master (who was) killed; they begin to sing:

> "Ndala the elder
> And Ndala the younger,
> They went into the world
> To destroy others.
> We praise
> Mutelembe and Ngunga,
> To whom were thrown the bowels;
> They refused to them eat."

Ndala the elder set down the basket of meat on ground; he killed one dog. Says: "They will report me at home, saying, 'He killed his younger.'" He took up the basket; he goes ahead. The dog that he killed, here it comes again, singing:

> "Ndala the elder
> And Ndala the younger,
> Went into the world
> To destroy others.
> We praise Mutelembe and Ngunga;
> They threw them the bowels;
> They refused to them eat."

He set down again the basket of meat on the ground; he killed them both. He dug a grave; he covered them up.

He lifts up; goes on. The dogs, here they come again, singing:

> *"Ndala the elder*
> *And Ndala the younger,*
> *Went into the world*
> *To kill others.*
> *We praise Mutelembe and Ngunga;*
> *They threw them the bowels;*
> *They refused to them eat."*

He arrives in vicinity of the village. He dresses; lifts up; enters into the house. They ask him: "You went two; thy companion, where is he?" He said: "He went to his country." He finishes speaking, (and) the dogs arrive; they enter the house of their master; they begin to sing again. The people say: "Hear the dogs are singing! Thou, Ndala the elder, thy younger thou wentest with him, thou hast killed him! His dogs, they told us!" They wailed the mourning.

The Son of Kimanaueze and the Daughter of Sun and Moon
(From the Ambundu people, Angola)

I OFTEN TELL OF na Kimanaueze, who begat a male child. The child grew up; he came to the age of marrying. His father said: "Marry." He said: "I will not marry a woman of the earth." His father said: "Then where wilt thou marry?" He said: "I, it must be, (that) I marry the daughter of Lord Sun and Moon." The people said: "Who can go to heaven, where is the daughter of Lord Sun and Moon?" He said: "I indeed, I want her; if on earth, I will not marry here."

He wrote a letter of marriage; he gives it to Deer. Deer says: "I cannot go to heaven." He gives it again to Antelope. Antelope says: "I cannot go to heaven." He gives it to Hawk. Hawk says: "I cannot go to heaven." He gives it to Vulture.

Vulture says: "I reach halfway; to heaven I cannot arrive." The young man said: "How shall I do?" He laid it aside in (his) box; he kept quiet.

The people at Lord Sun and Moon's used to come to get water on earth. Frog comes; he finds the son of Kimanaueze, says: "Young master, give me the letter, that I go with it." He, the young master, said: "Begone; where people of life, who have wings, gave it up, dost thou say: 'I will go there?' How canst thou get there?" Frog said: "Young master, I am equal to it." He gave him the letter, saying: "If thou canst not go there, and thou return. with it, I will give thee a thrashing."

Frog started; he goes to the well, where are wont to come the people of Lord Sun and Moon to get water. He puts in his mouth the letter; he gets into the well; he keeps quiet. A while, the people of Lord Sun and Moon come to get water. They put a jug into the well; Frog enters into the jug. They have got the water; they lift up. They don't know that Frog has entered into the jug. They arrive in heaven; they set down the jugs in their place; they go thence. Frog gets out of the jug. In that room where they were keeping the jugs of water, they kept also a table. Frog spat out the letter; he set it on the top of the table. He went; he hid in the corner of the room.

A while, Lord Sun himself comes into the room of the water; he looks on the table; a letter is on (it). He takes it, asks, saying: "Whence comes this letter?" They say: "Lord, we don't know." Lord Sun opens it; he reads it. Who wrote it says: "I, son of na Kimanaueze kia Tumb' a Ndala, on earth, I want to marry with the daughter of Lord Sun and Moon." Lord Sun thinks, saying in his heart: "Na Kimanaueze lives on earth; I am a man that lives in heaven; he who came with the letter, who is he?" He put away the letter into the box; he kept quiet.

Lord Sun, when he finished reading the letter, Frog got into the jug. A while, the water is out of the jugs; the water girls lift the jugs; they go down on earth. They arrive at the well; they put the jugs in the water. Frog gets out; goes underwater; hides himself. The girls have finished bailing out; they go.

Frog comes out of the water; he goes to his village; he keeps quiet. When many days had passed, the son of na Kimanaueze asks Frog: "O fellow, where thou wentest with the letter, how?" Frog said: "Master, the letter, I delivered it; they have not yet returned (an) answer." The son of na Kimanaueze said: "O man, thou toldest a lie; thou didst not go there." Frog said: "Master, that same (place) where I went, thou shalt see."

They spent six days; the son of na Kimanaueze wrote again a letter to ask about the former letter, saying: "I wrote to you, you Lord Sun and (Lady) Moon. My letter went; not at all did you return me an answer, saying, 'We accept thee,' or 'We refuse thee.'" He finished writing it; he closed it. He called Frog; he gave it to him. Frog starts; he arrives at the well. He takes in his mouth the letter; he gets into the water; he squats on the bottom of the well.

A while, (and) the girls, the water carriers, come down; they arrive at the well. They put the jugs into the water; Frog gets into a jug. They finish filling; they lift up. They go up by the cobweb, which Spider had woven. They arrive in heaven; they enter the house. They set down the jugs; they go. Frog comes out of the jug; he spits out the letter. He lays it on the table; he hides in the corner.

A while, (and) Lord Sun passes through the room of the water. He looks on the table; a letter is on it. He uncovers it; he reads it. The letter says: "I, son of na Kimanaueze kia Tumb' a Ndala, I ask thee, Lord Sun, (about) my letter, that went before. Not at all didst thou return me an answer." Lord Sun said: "You, girls, who always go to fetch water, (are) you always carrying letters?" The girls said: "We, master, no. " Lord Sun, doubt possessed him; he laid the letter into the box. He writes to the son of na Kimanaueze, saying: "Thou, who art sending me letters about marrying my daughter, I agree; on condition that thou in person, the man, comest with thy first present; that I too may know thee." He finished writing; he folded the letter. He laid it on the table; he went away. Frog comes out of the corner; he takes the letter. He puts it in his mouth; he enters into the jug; keeps quiet.

A while, the water is out in the jugs; the girls come; they lift the jugs. Now (they go) to the cord of Spider; they get down on earth. They arrive at the well; they put the jugs into the water. Frog gets out of the jug; goes to the bottom of the well. The girls have done filling; they go up. Frog goes ashore; he arrives in their village; he keeps quiet.

The evening come, he said: "Now I will take the letter." He spat it out; he arrived at the house of the son of na Kimanaueze. He knocks at the door; the son of na Kimanaueze asks, saying: "Who?" Frog says: "I am Mainu the Frog." The son of na Kimanaueze got up from bed, where he had reclined, saying: " Come in." Frog went in; he delivered him the letter; he went out. The son of na Kimanaueze he uncovers it; he reads it. What Lord Sun announces, it pleases him; says: "Frog, why, (it was) his truth he told me, saying, 'Thou shalt see where I went.'" He paused; slept.

Morning, he took forty macutas; wrote a letter, saying: "You, Lord Sun and Moon, the first present is coming here; I remain to seek for the wooing present. You there, ye send me the amount of the wooing present." He finished the letter; called Mainu the Frog. He came; he gave him the letter and the money, saying: "Carry."

The Frog starts, he arrives at the well. He enters under the well; he keeps quiet. A while, (and) the girls come down; they put the jugs in the water; Frog enters into a jug. The girls have finished filling; they take up. They go up by the cobweb; they arrive in the room of the water. They set down the jugs; they go.

Frog gets out of the jug; he puts down the letter on the table with the money. He went; hid in the corner. A while, (and) Lord Sun comes into the room of the water; he finds the letter on the table. He takes it with the money; he reads it. He tells his wife the news that came from the son-in-law; his wife assents.

Lord Sun says: "Who is coming with the letters, I do not know him; his food, how shall it be cooked?" His wife said: "We will cook it anyhow, and put (it) on the table, where are usually the letters." Lord Sun said: "Very well." They kill a mother hen; they cook it. Evening comes; they cook the mush. They set the eatables on the table; they shut (the door). Frog comes to the table; he eats the victuals. He goes to the corner; he keeps quiet.

Lord Sun writes a letter, saying: "Thou, son-in-law (of) mine, the first present, which thou hast sent me, I have received. The amount of the wooing present, thou shalt give me a sack of money." He finished the letter; he laid it on the table; went. Frog came out of the corner; took the letter. He entered the jug; slept.

Morning, (and) the girls take the jugs; they go down to the earth. They arrive at the well; they put the jugs into the water. Frog got out of the jug. The girls finished filling; they went up.

Frog went out from the water; he arrived in their village. He enters into his house; he waits. The sun is gone; evening has come down; he says: "I will now bring the letter." He started; arrived at the house of the son of na Kimanaueze. He knocks at the door; the son of na Kimanaueze says: "Who?" Frog says: "I am Mainu the Frog." Says he: "Come in." Frog went in; he gave the letter; he went out. The son of na Kimanaueze uncovers the letter; he reads it; now he sets it aside.

He spent six days; he has completed the sack of money. He called Frog; Frog came. The son of na Kimanaueze wrote a letter, saying: "You, my parents-in-law, the wooing present comes here; soon I myself, I shall find a day to bring home my wife." The letter, he gave it to the Frog, with the money.

Frog started; he arrived at the well. He went in underwater; he hid. A while, (and) the water carriers came down; they arrived at the well. They put the jugs into the water; Frog entered into a jug. They finished filling; they take up. They go up by the cobweb of Spider; they arrive in heaven. They set down the jugs in the room of the water; they go out. Frog gets out of the jug; he lays down the letter on the table with the money. He goes into the corner; he hides.

Lord Sun comes into the house of the water; he finds the letter and the money. He takes them; he shows the money to his wife, Lady Moon. Lady Moon says: "Very well." They take a young hog; they kill it. They have cooked the food; they set (it) down on table; shut (the door). Frog came to eat; he ate. He finished; entered into the jug; slept.

Morning, (and) the water carriers take up the jugs; they get down on earth. They arrive at the well; they dip the jugs into the water. Frog gets out of the jug; he hides. They finish filling; go up to heaven. Frog went ashore; he arrived in their village. He entered his house; kept quiet; slept.

Morning, he tells the son of na Kimanaueze, saying: "Young master, where I went, I gave them the wooing present; they received it. They cooked me a young hog; I ate. Now, thou thyself shalt choose the day of going to bring her home." The son of na Kimanaueze said: "Very well." They lived on; ten days and two.

The son of na Kimanaueze said: "I need people, to go to bring home the bride for me; I find them not. They say, 'We cannot go to heaven.' Now, how shall I do, thou, Frog?" Frog said: "My young master, be quiet; I am equal to it, to go and bring her home." The son of na Kimanaueze said: "Thou canst not. Thou couldst indeed carry the letters, but bring her home thou canst not." Frog said again: "Young master, be quiet; be not troubled for naught. I indeed am able to go and bring her home; do not despise me." The son of na Kimanaueze said: "Let me try thee." He took victuals; he gave to Frog.

Frog starts; he arrives at the well. He gets into the well; he hides. A while, the water carriers come down; they arrive at the well. They dip in the jugs; Frog enters. They have filled; they go to heaven. They arrive in the room of the water; they set down the jugs; they go. Frog gets out of the jug; he hides in the corner. The sun set; in the evening of the night, Frog went out of the room of the water; he went seeking in the room where slept the daughter of Lord Sun. He finds her asleep here. He takes out one of her eyes; he takes out again the other. He tied them up in a handkerchief; he came in the room of the water, in his corner. slept. He hid; slept.

Morning, all people got up. The daughter of Lord Sun cannot get up. They ask her: "Dost thou not get up?" She says: "(My) eyes are closed; I cannot see." Her father and mother say: "What may cause this? Yesterday, she did not complain."

Lord Sun takes up two messengers, saying: "Go to Ngombo, to divine (about) my child, who is sick as to the eyes." They start; they arrive at the Ngombo-man's. They spread for them; the Ngombo-man takes out the paraphernalia. The divining people, (they) do not let know the disease; they say only: "We have come to be divined." The Ngombo-man looks into the paraphernalia, says: "Disease has brought you; the one who is sick is a woman; the sickness that ails her, the eyes. You have come, being sent; you have not come of your own will. I have spoken." The divining people said: "Truth. Look now what caused the ailment." The Ngombo-man looks again; says: "She, the woman, who is sick, is not yet married; she is chosen only. Her master, who bespake her, he sent the spell, saying, 'My wife, let her come; if she does not come, she shall die.' You, who came to divine, go, bring her to her husband, that she may escape. I have spoken." The divining men assented; they got up. They find Lord Sun; they report him the words of Ngombo. Lord Sun said: "All right. Let us sleep; tomorrow they shall take her down to the earth." Frog being in his corner, he hears all that they are saying. They slept.

(At) morning, Frog got into the jug; the water carriers come; they take up the jugs. They descend to the earth; they arrive at the well. They put the jugs into the water; Frog came out of the jug. He hid under the well. The water carriers went up.

Lord Sun tells Spider, saying: "Weave a large cobweb, down to the earth; for today is the taking down of my daughter to the earth." Spider wove; finished. They are passing time.

Frog got out of the well; he goes to their village. He finds the son of na Kimanaueze, says: "O young master! thy bride, today she comes." The son of na Kimanaueze says: "Begone, man, thou art a liar." Frog says: "Master, truth itself. I will bring her to thee in the evening of the night." They kept quiet.

Frog returned to the well; he got into the water; he was silent. The sun set; the daughter of Lord Sun, they take her down to the earth. They leave her at the well; they go up.

Frog gets out of the well; he tells the young woman, saying: "I myself am thy guide; let us go that I bring thee to your master." Frog returned to her her eyes; they started. They enter the house of the son of na Kimanaueze. Frog says: "O young master! thy bride (is) here." The son of na Kimanaueze said: "Welcome! Mainu the Frog."

The son of na Kimanaueze married with the daughter of Lord Sun and (Lady) Moon; they lived on. They all had given up going to heaven; who could (do) it (was) Mainu the Frog.

Kingungu a Njila and Ngundu a Ndala
(From the Ambundu people, Angola)

KINGUNGU A NJILA TOOK UP (HIS) GUN, saying: "I will go a-shooting." He arrived in forest; he is stalking the elephants. He approached them; he shot one elephant; it fell on ground.

Ngundu a Ndala heard the gun of Kingungu a Njila. He is looking, "Who has shot here?" He arrives where is the elephant of Kingungu a Njila. He too shot (it) again, saying: "The elephant (is) mine."

Kingungu a Njila came; said: "This (is) my elephant; thou foundest me with it. Thou, why speakest thou, saying 'The elephant is mine'?" Then they begin a quarrel about the elephant. They say: "Let us go home; there let us plead!"

Kingungu a Njila went to So and So; he accused. They call Ngundu a Ndala; they say: "Plead ye." Kingungu a Njila explained how he killed the elephant. Ngundu a Ndala pleaded too. So and So said: "The case, how shall I judge it? There is no witness who saw which one spoke the truth and which one spoke untruth." Says: "Go ye home. The case, tomorrow I shall decide it; because my wife is not here." They separate; the sun goes down.

Kingungu a Njila went to his elephant; Ngundu a Ndala came too. Kingungu a Njila begins to cry, saying: "This, this elephant (is) my elephant!" Ngungu a

Ndala too begins to cry, saying: "This elephant (is) my elephant! This elephant (is) my elephant!" He cried one hour. He went away.

Kingungu a Njila still kept on crying: "This elephant (is) my elephant! This elephant (is) my elephant!" He laid (all night) there crying.

The morning shone. They call them: "Come now to plead." Kingungu a Njila pleaded the same as he pleaded yesterday. Ngundu a Ndala pleaded falsely. So and So asks the messengers, saying: "You, who stayed overnight with Kingungu a Njila and Ngundu a Ndala, now who laid all night crying until dawn?" The messengers said: "Kingungu a Njila, he laid all night crying. Ngundu a Ndala yesterday cried one hour."

So and So says: "Kingungu a Njila is going to win." They have come to decide the case. So and So says: "Thou, Kingungu a Njila art right; thou, Ngundu a Ndala art wrong. The other wanted to take wrongly his elephant."

Thus far, that we have heard it. The end.

A Story of Witchcraft
(From the Nama people, South Africa, Namibia and Botswana)

ONCE ON A TIME a certain Namaqua was travelling in company with a Boschwoman carrying a child on her back. They had proceeded some distance on their journey, when a troop of wild horses appeared, and the man said to the woman, "I am hungry; and as I know you can turn yourself into a lion, do so now, and catch us a wild horse, that we may eat."

The woman answered, "You'll be afraid."

"No, no," said the man; "I am afraid of dying of hunger, but not of you."

Whilst he was yet speaking, hair began to appear at the back of the woman's neck, her nails began to assume the appearance of claws, and her features altered. She set down the child.

The man alarmed at the change, climbed a tree close by, the woman glared at him fearfully, and going to one side she threw off her skin petticoat, when a perfect lion rushed out into the plain; it bounded and crept among the bushes towards the wild horses, and springing on one of them, it fell, and the lion lapped its blood. The lion then came back to where the child was crying, and the man called from the tree, "Enough! Enough! Don't hurt me. Put off your lion's shape, I'll never ask to see this again."

The lion looked at him and growled. "I'll remain here till I die," said the man, "if you don't become a woman again." The mane and tail then began to disappear, the lion went towards the bush where the skin petticoat lay; it was slipped on, and the woman in her proper shape took up the child. The man descended, partook of the horse's flesh, but never again asked the woman to catch game for him.

Hlakanyana's Precocious Development and Mischievous Pranks
(From the Pedi and Venda peoples, South Africa)

THEY SAID THAT "Uhlakanyana is a very cunning man; he is also very small, of the size of a weasel", "it is as though he really was of that genus; he resembles it in all respects" – hence his other name *icakide*.

Hlakanyana was a chief's son. Like Ryangombe, he spoke before he was born; in fact, he repeatedly declared his impatience to enter the world. No sooner had he made his appearance than he walked out to the cattle kraal, where his father had just slaughtered some oxen, and the men were sitting round, ready for a feast of meat. Scared by this portent – for they had been waiting for the birth to be announced – they all ran away, and Hlakanyana sat down by the fire and began to eat a strip of meat which was roasting there. They came back, and asked the mother whether this was really the expected baby. She answered, "It is he"; whereupon they said, "Oh, we thank you, our queen. You have brought forth for us a child who is wise as soon as he is born. We never saw a child like this child. This child is fit to be the great one among all the king's children, for he has made us wonder by his wisdom."

But Hlakanyana, thinking that his father did not take this view, but looked upon him as a mere infant, asked him to take a leg of beef and throw it downhill, over the kraal fence (the gateway being on the upper side). All the boys and men present were to race for it, and "he shall be the man who gets the leg."

They all rushed to the higher opening, but Hlakanyana wormed his way between the stakes at the lower end of the kraal, picked up the leg, and carried it in triumph to meet the others, who were coming round from the farther side. He handed it over to his mother, and then returned to the kraal, where his father was distributing the rest of the meat. He offered to carry each man's share to his hut for him, which he did, smeared some blood on the mat (on which meat is laid to be cut up), and then carried the joint to his mother. He did this to each one in turn, so that by the evening no house had any meat except that of the chief's wife, which was overstocked. No wonder that the women cried out, "What is this that has been born today? He is a prodigy, a real prodigy!"

His next feat was to take out all the birds which had been caught in the traps set by the boys, and bring them home, telling his mother to cook them and cover the pots, fastening down the lids. He then went off to sleep in the boys' house (*ilau*), which he would not ordinarily have entered for several years to come, and overbore their objections, saying, "Since you say this I shall sleep here, just to show you!"

He rose early in the morning, went to his mother's house, got in without waking her, opened the pots, and ate all the birds, leaving only the heads, which he put back, after filling the lower half of the pots with cow dung, and fastened down the lids. Then he went away for a time, and came back to play Huveane's trick on his mother. He pretended to have come in for the first time, and told her that the sun had risen, and that she had slept too long – for if the birds were not taken out of the pot before the sun was up they would turn into dung. So he washed himself and sat down to his breakfast, and when he opened the pots it was even as he had said, and his mother believed him.

He finished up the heads, saying that, as she had spoilt his food she should not have even these, and then announced that he did not consider himself her child at all, and that his father was a mere man, one of the people and nothing more. He would not stay with them, but would go on his travels. So he picked up his stick and walked out, still grumbling about the loss of his birds.

He Goes on His Travels

When he had gone some distance and was beginning to get hungry he came upon some traps with birds in them and, beginning to take them out, found himself stuck fast. The owner of the traps was a 'cannibal' – or, rather, an ogre – who, finding that birds had more than once disappeared from his traps, had put sticks smeared with birdlime in front of them. Now he came along to look at them, and found Hlakanyana, who, quite undisturbed, addressed him thus: "Don't beat me, and I will tell you. Take me out and cleanse me from the birdlime and take me home with you. Have you a mother?" The ogre said he had. Hlakanyana, evidently assuming that he was to be eaten, said that if he were beaten and killed at once his flesh would be ruined for the pot. "I shall not be nice; I shall be bitter. Cleanse me and take me home with you, that you may put me in your house, that I may be cooked by your mother. And do you go away and just leave me at your home. I cannot be cooked if you are there; I shall be bad; I cannot be nice."

The ogre, a credulous person, like most of his kind, did as he was asked, and handed Hlakanyana over to his mother, to be cooked next morning.

When the ogre and his younger brother were safely out of the way, Hlakanyana proposed to the old woman that they should "play at boiling each other." He got her to put on a large pot of water, made up the fire under it, and when it was beginning to get warm he said, "Let us begin with me." She put him in and covered the pot. Presently he asked to be taken out, and then, saying that the fire was not hot enough, made it up to a blaze and began, very rudely, to unfasten the old woman's skin petticoat. When she objected he said: "What does it matter if I have unfastened your dress, I who am mere game, which is about to be eaten by your sons and you?"

He thrust her in and put on the lid. No sooner had he done so than she shrieked that she was being scalded; but he told her that could not be, or she would not be able to cry out. He kept the lid on till the poor creature's cries ceased, and then put on her clothes and lay down in her sleeping place. When the sons came home he told them to take their 'game' and eat; he had already eaten, and did not mean to get up. While they were eating he slipped out at the door, threw off the clothes, and ran away as fast as he could. When he had reached a safe distance he called out to them, "You are eating your mother, you cannibals!" They pursued him hot-foot; he came to a swollen river and changed himself into a piece of wood. They came up, saw his footprints on the ground, and, as he was nowhere in sight, concluded he had crossed the river and flung the piece of wood after him. Safe on the other bank, he resumed his own shape and jeered at the ogres, who gave up the pursuit and turned back.

He Kills a Hare, Gets a Whistle and Is Robbed of It

Hlakanyana went on his way, and before very long he spied a hare. Being hungry, he tried to entice it within reach by offering to tell a tale, but the hare would not be beguiled. At last, however (this part of the story is not very clear, and the hare must have been a different creature from the usual Bantu hare!), he caught it, killed it and roasted it, and, after eating the flesh, made one of the bones into a whistle. He went on, playing his whistle and singing:

> "I met Hloya's mother,
> And we cooked each other.
> I did not burn;
> She was done to a turn."

In time he came to a large tree on the bank of a river, overhanging a deep pool. On a branch of the tree lay an iguana, who greeted him, and Hlakanyana responded politely. The iguana said, "Lend me your whistle, so that I can hear if it will sound." Hlakanyana refused, but the iguana insisted, promising to give it back. Hlakanyana said, "Come away from the pool, then, and come out here on to the open ground; I am afraid near a pool. I say you might run into the pool with my whistle, for you are a person that lives in deep water." The iguana came down from his tree, and when Hlakanyana thought that he was at a safe distance from the river he handed him the whistle. The iguana tried the whistle, approved the sound, and wanted to take it away with him. Hlakanyana would not hear of this, and laid hold of the iguana as he was trying to make off, but received such a blow from the powerful tail that he had to let go, and the iguana dived into the river, carrying the whistle with him.

Hlakanyana again went on till he came to a place where a certain old man had hidden some bread. He ran off with it, but not before the owner had seen him; the old man evidently knew him, for he called out, "Put down my bread, Hlakanyana." Hlakanyana only ran the faster, the old man after him, till, finding that the latter was gaining on him, he crawled into a snake's hole. The old man put in his hand and caught him by the leg. Hlakanyana cried, laughing, "*He! He!* you've caught hold of a root!" So the old man let go, and, feeling about for the leg, caught a root, at which Hlakanyana yelled, "Oh! oh! you're killing me!" The old man kept pulling at the root till he was tired out and went away. Hlakanyana ate the bread in comfort, and then crawled out and went on his way once more.

He Nurses the Leopard's Cubs

In the course of his wanderings he came upon a leopard's den, where he found four cubs and sat down beside them till the mother leopard came home, carrying a buck with which to feed her little ones. She was very angry when she saw Hlakanyana, and was about to attack him, but he disarmed her by his flattering tongue, and finally persuaded her to let him stay and take care of the cubs, while she went out to hunt. "I will take care of them, and I will build a beautiful house, that you may lie here at the foot of the rock with your children." He also told her he could cook – a somewhat unnecessary accomplishment, one would think, in this case; but it would seem that he had his reasons. The leopard having agreed, Hlakanyana brought the cubs, one by one, for her to suckle. She objected, wanting them all brought at once, but the little cunning fellow persisted and got his way. When they had all been fed she called on him to make good his promise and skin the buck and cook it, which he did. So they both ate, and all went to sleep. In the morning, when the leopard had gone to hunt, Hlakanyana set to work building the house. He made the usual round Zulu hut, but with a very small doorway; then, inside, he dug a burrow, leading to the back of the hut, with an opening a long way off. Then he took four assagais which he had carried with him on his travels, broke them off short to rather less than the width of the doorway, and hid them in a convenient place. Having finished, he ate one of the cubs. When the mother came home he brought them out as before, one by one, taking the third twice, so that she never missed any of them. He did the same the next day, and the next.

On the fourth day he brought out the last cub four times, and at length it refused to drink. The mother was naturally surprised at this, but Hlakanyana said he thought it was not well. She said, "Take care of it, then," and when he had carried it into the house called him to prepare supper. When she had eaten Hlakanyana went into the house, and the leopard called out that she was coming in to look after the child. Hlakanyana said, "Come in, then," knowing that she would take some time squeezing herself through the narrow entrance, and at once made his escape through the burrow. Meanwhile she had got in, found only one cub, concluded that he must have eaten the rest, and followed him into the burrow. By this time Hlakanyana was out at the other end; he ran round to the front of the house, took his assagais from the hiding place, and fixed them in the ground at the doorway, the points sloping inward. The leopard found she could not get very far in the burrow, so she came back into the hut, and, squeezing through the doorway to pursue Hlakanyana into the open, was pierced by the assagais and killed.

Hlakanyana and the Ogre

Hlakanyana now sat down and ate the cub; then he skinned the leopard, and gradually – for he remained on the spot for some time – ate most of the flesh, keeping, however, one leg, with which he set out once more on his travels, "for he was a man who did not stay long in one place." Soon after he met a hungry ogre, with whom he easily made friends by giving him some meat, and they went on together. They came across two cows, which the *izimu* said belonged to him. Hlakanyana suggested that they should build a hut, so that they could slaughter the cows and eat them in peace and comfort. The ogre agreed; they killed the cows and started to build. As rain was threatening Hlakanyana said they had better get on with the thatching.

This is done by two people, one inside the hut and the other on the roof, passing the string with which the grass is tied backward and forward between them, pushing it through by means of a pointed stick. Hlakanyana went inside, while the ogre climbed on the roof. The latter had very long hair (a distinguishing feature of the *amazimu*), and Hlakanyana managed to knit it, lock by lock, into the thatch, so firmly that he would not be able to get off. He then sat down and ate the beef which was boiling on the fire. A hailstorm came on, Hlakanyana went into the house with his joint, and the ogre (who seems to have been a harmless creature enough) was left to perish. "He was struck with the hailstones, and died there on the house" – as anyone who has seen an African hailstorm can readily believe.

Having caused the death of another *izimu* in a way which need not be related here, Hlakanyana took up his abode for a time with yet another, who seems to have had no reason to complain of him. As usual, when no ill fortune befell him he became restless, and took the road once more, directing his steps towards the place on the river where the iguana had robbed him of his whistle. He found the iguana on his tree, called him down, killed him, and recovered the whistle. Then he went back to the ogre's hut, but the owner had gone away, and the hut was burned down. So he said, "I will now go back to my mother, for, behold, I am in trouble."

He Goes Home

But his return was by no means in the spirit of the Prodigal Son, for he professed to have come back purely out of affection for her, saying, "Oh, now I have returned, my mother, for I remembered you!" and calmly omitting all mention of his exploits during his absence. She believed this, being only too ready to welcome him back, and he seems to have behaved himself for a time. Nothing is said of his father's attitude, or of that of the clansmen.

The day after his return home Hlakanyana went to a wedding, and as he came over a hill on the way back he found some *umdiandiane* – a kind of edible tuber, of which he was very fond. He dug it up and took it home to his mother, asking her to cook it for him, as he was now going to milk the cow. She did so, and, tasting one to see if it was done, liked it so much that she ate the whole. When he asked for it she said, "I have eaten it, my child," and he answered, "Give me my *umdiandiane*, for I dug it up on a very little knoll, as I was coming from a wedding." His mother gave him a milk pail by way of compensation, and he went off. Soon he came upon some boys herding sheep, who were milking the ewes into old, broken potsherds. He said, "Why are you milking into potsherds? You had better use my milk pail, but you must give me a drink out of it." They used his milk pail, but the last boy who had it broke it. Hlakanyana said, "Give me my milk pail, my milk pail my mother gave me, my mother having eaten my *umdiandiane*" and so on, as before. The boys gave him an assagai, which he lent to some other boys, who were trying to cut slices of liver with splinters of sugar cane. They broke his assagai, and gave him an axe instead. Then he met some old women gathering firewood, who had nothing to cut it with, so he offered them the use of his axe, which again got broken. They gave him a blanket, and he went on his way till nightfall, when he found two young men sleeping out on the hillside, with nothing to cover them. He said, "Ah, friends, do you sleep without covering? Have you no blanket?" They said, "No." He said, "Take this of mine," which they did, but it was rather small for two, and as each one kept dragging it from the other it soon got torn. Then he demanded it back. "Give me my blanket, my blanket which the women gave me," and so on. The young men gave him a shield. Then he came upon some men fighting with a leopard, who had no shields. He questioned them as he had done the other people, and lent one of them his shield. It must have been efficient as a protection, for they killed the leopard, but the hand loop by which the man was holding it broke, and of course it was rendered useless. So Hlakanyana said:

> *"Give me my shield, my shield the young men gave me,*
> *The young men having torn my blanket,*
> *My blanket the women gave me,*
> *The women having broken my axe,*
> *My axe the boys gave me,*
> *The boys having broken my assagai,*
> *My assagai the boys gave me,*
> *The boys having broken my milk pail,*
> *My milk pail my mother gave me,*
> *My mother having eaten my* umdiandiane,
> *My* umdiandiane *I dug up on a very little knoll,*
> *As I was coming from a wedding."*

They gave him a war assagai (*isinkemba*). What he did with that perhaps I may tell you on another occasion.

The Village Maiden
and the Cannibal
(From Lesotho, southern Africa)

THE VILLAGE WAS STARVING, there was no running away from the fact; the men's eyes were big and hungry looking, and even the plumpest girl was thin. What was to be done?

The maidens must go out to find roots. Perhaps the spirits would take pity on their starved looks and guide them to where the roots grew; so early in the morning all the maidens, led by the chiefs two daughters, left the village to seek for food; they walked two by two, a maid and a little girl, side by side. Long they journeyed, and weary were their feet, yet they found nothing, and darkness was creeping over the land. So they laid themselves down to rest under the Great Above, with no shelter or covering over them, to wait for the coming dawn. Next day as they journeyed, behold one of the children espied a root, another, and yet another, until all were busy digging up the precious food. Now a strange thing happened, for, while the maidens only found long thin roots, the children gathered only thick large ones. At length enough had been found to last the village for a time, so the girls set off to return home. As they came near the river they saw it was terribly flooded, and an old, old woman sat crooning upon the bank.

As they approached they began to distinguish the words she was chanting:

> *"The Water Spirit loves not the thin roots,*
> *They are the food of swine –*
> *There is no safety for them.*
> *But the large root, how good it is –*
> *It is the food of spirits, even of the*
> *Great Water Spirit.*
> *Safety and strength are in it;*
> *The water flows on, flows on."*

"Mother," said the elder of the chief's daughters, approaching the old woman, "tell us of your wisdom how we shall cross this swollen river, for we are in haste to reach our home."

Without lifting her eyes from the water, the dame replied, "To the swollen river a swollen root; in each maid's right hand a root that is large, then cross and fear not."

Accordingly the girls chose their largest root, which they threw upon the water, and then each child of her store of fat roots chose two; one she gave to one of the elder maidens, the other she held in her own right hand, then two by two they stepped into the river and in safety gained the opposite bank. But when it came to the turn of the chiefs two daughters, the child refused to give her sister one of her large roots, nor were threats or entreaties of any avail. The night was fast approaching, their companions were almost out of sight, and the river rolled at their feet, dark, swift and deep.

At length the child relented, and soon the two girls were speeding after their friends; but it was too dark to see, and they missed their road and wandered far in the darkness. When midnight was fast approaching they saw a light shining near, and upon going up to it, found themselves at the door of a hut, over which a mat hung. "Let us ask for shelter for the night," said the elder girl, and shook the mat.

"Get up! get up! son of mine, and see if people are at the door; for I am hungry and would eat meat." The voice was that of a man, who was seated in front of some red-hot cinders in the middle of the hut.

The little boy ran to the door, and, upon seeing the two girls standing there, implored them to run away at once, as his father was a cannibal and would eat them up; but before they had time to do so, the old man appeared and dragged them into the hut.

Early the next morning the old cannibal left the hut to call two of his friends to share his feast. Before he left he securely fastened the two girls together, and told his son to watch them carefully.

Now, as soon as he was out of sight, there appeared at the door the old woman who yesterday had been sitting on the river bank. She at once set the girls free, but told them she must cut off all their hair. When this was done, she took a little and buried it under the floor of the hut, another bunch she buried under the refuse heap outside, another near the spring, and yet another half way up the hill. She then returned to the hut and burnt the remaining hair.

"Now, my children," said she, "you must fly to your home. I shall follow you under the ground, but your guide shall be a bee. Follow where it leads, and you will be safe." So saying, she led them to the door and drew down the mat.

"Run!" said the boy; "make haste! There is the bee grandmother told you of. Follow quickly, lest my father find you and kill you."

Seeing a bee hovering near, the girls followed where it led. Presently they met two men, who stopped them, and asked, "Who are you? Are you not the two girls our friend has told us of? Did you not stay last night in a hut with an old man and a boy?"

"We know not of whom you speak," replied the girls. "We have seen no old man, nor little boy."

"Ho, ho! is that true? But yes, we see it is true. He told us his victims had plenty of hair, but you have none. No, no; these are not they; these are only people." So saying, they allowed the girls to continue their journey.

Now when the old man and his friends found the girls had escaped, they were very angry; but the little boy said he did not think they could be very far away. The old man went out and began calling, but, as he called, there answered him a voice from the hair under the hut, another voice from the hair by the spring, another from the mountain, and so on from each spot where the old woman had buried the hair, until he became mad with rage and disappointment; then, guessing that witchcraft had been used, and that the two girls his friends had spoken to were indeed his intended victims, he set off in pursuit; but when he caught sight of them, they were almost at their father's village, and a large swarm of bees was between him and them, which, when he tried to overtake the girls, stung him so terribly that he howled with agony, and dared not approach any nearer. Thus the girls escaped, and returned to bring the light of day to their parents' eyes.

Morena-y-a-Letsatsi, or the Sun Chief
(From Lesotho, southern Africa)

IN THE TIME OF THE GREAT FAMINE, when our fathers' fathers were young, there lived across the mountains, many days' journey, a great chief, who bore upon his breast the signs of the sun, the

moon, and eleven stars. Greatly was he beloved, and marvellous was his power. When all around were starving, his people had plenty, and many journeyed to his village to implore his protection. Amongst others came two young girls, the daughters of one mother. Tall and lovely as a deep still river was the elder, gentle and timid as the wild deer, and her they called Siloane (the teardrop.)

Of a different mould was her sister Mokete. Plump and round were her limbs, bright as the stars her eyes, like running water was the music of her voice, and she feared not man nor spirit. When the chief asked what they could do to repay him for helping them in their need, Mokete replied, "Lord, I can cook, I can grind corn, I can make 'leting' [A mild beer], I can do all a woman's work."

Gravely the chief turned to Siloane – "And you," he asked, "what can you do?"

"Alas, lord!" Siloane replied, "what can I say, seeing that my sister has taken all words out of my mouth."

"It is enough," said the chief, "you shall be my wife. As for Mokete, since she is so clever, let her be your servant."

Now the heart of Mokete burned with black hate against her sister, and she vowed to humble her to the dust; but no one must see into her heart, so with a smiling face she embraced Siloane.

The next day the marriage feast took place, amidst great rejoicing, and continued for many days, as befitted the great Sun Chief. Many braves came from far to dance at the feast, and to delight the people with tales of the great deeds they had done in battle. Beautiful maidens were there, but none so beautiful as Siloane. How happy she was, how beloved! In the gladness of her heart she sang a song of praise to her lord: "Great is the sun in the heavens, and great are the moon and stars, but greater and more beautiful in the eyes of his handmaiden is my lord. Upon his breast are the signs of his greatness, and by their power I swear to love him with a love so strong, so true, that his son shall be in his image, and shall bear upon his breast the same tokens of the favour of the heavens."

Many moons came and went, and all was peace and joy in the hearts of the Sun Chief and his bride; but Mokete smiled darkly in her heart, for the time of her revenge approached. At length came the day, when Siloane should fulfil her vow, when the son should be born. The chief ordered that the child should be brought to him at once, that he might rejoice in the fulfilment of Siloane's vow. In the dark hut the young mother lay with great content, for had not Mokete assured her the child was his father's image, and upon his breast were the signs of the sun, the moon and eleven stars?

Why then this angry frown on the chief's face, this look of triumph in the eyes of Mokete? What is this which she is holding covered with a skin? She turns back the covering, and, with a wicked laugh of triumph, shows the chief, not the beautiful son he had looked for, but an ugly, deformed child with the face of a baboon. "Here, my lord," she said, "is the long-desired son. See how well Siloane loves you, see how well she has kept her vow! Shall I tell her of your heart's content?"

"Woman," roared the disappointed chief, "speak not thus to me. Take from my sight both mother and child, and tell my headman it is my will that they be destroyed ere the sun hide his head in yonder mountains."

Sore at heart, angry and unhappy, the chief strode away into the lands, while Mokete hastened to the headman to bid him carry out his master's orders; but ere they could be obeyed, a messenger came from the chief to say the child alone was to be destroyed, but Siloane should become a servant, and on the morrow should witness his marriage to Mokete.

Bitter tears rolled down Siloane's cheeks. What evil thing had befallen her, that the babe she had borne, and whom she had felt in her arms, strong and straight, should have been so changed ere the eyes of his father had rested upon him? Not once did she doubt Mokete. Was she not her own sister? What reason would she have for casting the "Evil Eye" upon the child? It was hard to lose her child, hard indeed to lose the love of her lord; but he had not banished her altogether from his sight, and perhaps someday the spirits might be willing that she should once again find favour in his sight, and should bear him a child in his own image.

Meanwhile Mokete had taken the real baby to the pigs, hoping they would devour him, for each time she tried to kill him some unseen power held her hand; but the pigs took the babe and nourished him, and many weeks went by – weeks of triumph for Mokete, but of bitter sorrow for Siloane.

At length Mokete bethought her of the child, and wondered if the pigs had left any trace of him. When she reached the kraal, she started back in terror, for there, fat, healthy and happy, lay the babe, while the young pigs played around him. What should she do? Had Siloane seen him? No, she hardly thought so, for the child was in every way the image of the chief. Siloane would at once have known who he was.

Hurriedly returning to her husband, Mokete begged him to get rid of all the pigs, and have their kraal burnt, as they were all ill of a terrible disease. So the chief gave orders to do as Mokete desired; but the spirits took the child to the elephant which lived in the great bush, and told it to guard him.

After this Mokete was at peace for many months, but no child came to gladden the heart of her lord, and to take away her reproach. In her anger and bitterness she longed to kill Siloane, but she was afraid.

One day she wandered far into the bush, and there she beheld the child, grown more beautiful than ever, playing with the elephant. Mad with rage, she returned home, and gave her lord no rest until he consented to burn the bush, which she told him was full of terrible wild beasts, which would one day devour the whole village if they were not destroyed. But the spirits took the child and gave him to the fishes in the great river, bidding them guard him safely.

Many moons passed, many crops were reaped and Mokete had almost forgotten about the child, when one day, as she walked by the river bank, she saw him, a beautiful youth, playing with the fishes. This was terrible. Would nothing kill him? In her rage she tore great rocks from their beds and rolled them into the water; but the spirits carried the youth to a mountain, where they gave him a wand. "This wand," said they, "will keep you safe. If danger threatens you from above, strike once with the wand upon the ground, and a path will be opened to you to the country beneath. If you wish to return to this upper world, strike twice with the wand, and the path will reopen."

So again they left him, and the youth, fearing the vengeance of his stepmother, struck once upon the ground with his wand. The earth opened, showing a long narrow passage. Down this the youth went, and, upon reaching the other end, found himself at the entrance to a large and very beautiful village. As he walked along, the people stood to gaze at him, and all, when they saw the signs upon his breast, fell down and worshipped him, saying, "Greetings, lord!" At length, he was informed that for many years these people had had no chief, but the spirits had told them that at the proper time a chief would appear who should bear strange signs upon his breast; him the people were to receive and to obey, for he would be the chosen one, and his name should be Tsepitso, or the promise.

From that day the youth bore the name of Tsepitso, and ruled over that land; but he never forgot his mother, and often wandered to the world above, to find how she fared and to watch over her. On these journeys he always clothed himself in old skins, and covered up his breast that none might behold the signs. One day, as he wandered, he found himself in a strange village, and as he passed the well, a maiden greeted him, saying, "Stranger, you look weary. Will you not rest and drink of this fountain?"

Tsepitso gazed into her eyes, and knew what love meant. Here, he felt, was the wife the spirits intended him to wed. He must not let her depart, so he sat down by the well and drank of the cool, delicious water, while he questioned the maid. She told him her name was Ma Thabo (mother of joy), and that her father was chief of that part of the country. Tsepitso told her he was a poor youth looking for work, whereupon she took him to her father, who consented to employ him.

One stipulation Tsepitso made, which was that for one hour every day before sunset he should be free from his duties. This was agreed to, and for several moons he worked for the old chief, and grew more and more in favour, both with him and with his daughter. The hour before sunset each day he spent amongst his own people, attending to their wants and giving judgment. At length he told Ma Thabo of his love, and read her answering love in her beautiful eyes. Together they sought the old chief, to whom Tsepitso told his story, and revealed his true self. The marriage was soon after celebrated, with much rejoicing, and Tsepitso bore his bride in triumph to his beautiful home in the world beneath, where she was received with every joy.

But amidst all his happiness Tsepitso did not forget his mother, and after the feasting and rejoicing were ended, he took Ma Thabo with him, for the time had at length come when he might free his mother forever from the power of Mokete.

When they approached his father's house, Mokete saw them, and, recognising Tsepitso, knew that her time had come. With a scream she fled to the hut, but Tsepitso followed her, and sternly demanded his mother. Mokete only moaned as she knelt at her lord's feet. The old chief arose, and said, "Young man, I know not who you are, nor who your mother is; but this woman is my wife, and I pray you speak to her not thus rudely."

Tsepitso replied, "Lord, I am thy son."

"Nay now, thou art a liar," said the old man sadly, "I have no son."

"Indeed, my father, I am thy son, and Siloane is my mother. Dost need proof of the truth of my words? Then look," and turning to the light, Tsepitso revealed to his father the signs upon his breast, and the old chief, with a great cry, threw himself upon his son's neck and wept. Siloane was soon called, and knew that indeed she had fulfilled her vow, that here before her stood in very truth the son she had borne, and a great content filled her heart. Tsepitso and Ma Thabo soon persuaded her to return with them, knowing full well that her life would no longer be safe were she to remain near Mokete; so, when the old chief was absent, in the dusk of the evening they departed to their own home.

When the Sun Chief discovered their flight, he determined to follow, and restore his beloved Siloane to her rightful place; but Mokete followed him, though many times he ordered her to return to the village, for that never again would she be wife of his, and that if she continued to follow him, he would kill her. At length he thought, "If I cut off her feet she will not be able to walk," so, turning round suddenly, he seized Mokete, and cut off her feet. "Now, wilt thou leave me in peace, woman? Take care nothing worse befall thee." So saying, he left her, and continued his journey.

But Mokete continued to follow him, till the sun was high in the heavens. Each time he saw her close behind him, he stopped and cut off more of her legs, till only her body was left; even then she was not conquered, but continued to roll after him. Thoroughly enraged, the Sun Chief seized her, and called down fire from the heavens to consume her, and a wind from the edge of the world to scatter her ashes.

When this was done, he went on his way rejoicing, for surely now she would trouble him no more. Then as he journeyed, a voice rose in the evening air, "I follow, I follow, to the edge of the world, yea, even beyond, shall I follow thee."

Placing his hands over his ears to shut out the voice, the Sun Chief ran with the fleetness of a young brave, until, at the hour when the spirits visit the abodes of men, he overtook Tsepitso and the two women, and with them entered the kingdom of his son.

How he won pardon from Siloane, and gained his son's love, and how it was arranged that he and Siloane should again be married, are old tales now in the country of Tsepitso. When the marriage feast was begun, a cloud of ashes dashed against the Sun Chief, and an angry voice was heard from the midst of the cloud, saying, "Nay, thou shalt not wed Siloane, for I have found thee, and I shall claim thee forever." Hastily the witch doctor was called to free the Sun Chief from the power of Mokete. As the old man approached the cloud, chanting a hymn to the gods, everyone gazed in silence. Raising his wand, the wizard made some mystic signs, the cloud vanished, and only a handful of ashes lay upon the ground.

Thus was the Evil Eye of Mokete stilled for evermore, and peace reigned in the hearts of the Sun Chief and his wife Siloane.

Khodumodumo, or Kammapa, the Swallowing Monster
(From Lesotho, southern Africa)

ONCE UPON A TIME there appeared in our country a huge, shapeless thing called Khodumodumo (but some people call it Kammapa). It swallowed every living creature that came in its way. At last it came through a pass in the mountains into a valley where there were several villages; it went to one after another, and swallowed the people, the cattle, the goats, the dogs and the fowls. In the last village was a woman who had just happened to sit down on the ash heap. She saw the monster coming, smeared herself all over with ashes, and ran into the calves' pen, where she crouched on the ground. Khodumodumo, having finished all the people and animals, came and looked into the place, but could see nothing moving, for, the woman being smeared with ashes and keeping quite still, it took her for a stone. It then turned and went away, but when it reached the narrow pass (or *nek*) at the entrance to the valley it had swelled to such a size that it could not get through, and was forced to stay where it was.

Meanwhile the woman in the calves' pen, who had been expecting a baby shortly, gave birth to a boy. She laid him down on the ground and left him for a minute or two, while she looked for something to make a bed for him. When she came back she found a grown man sitting there, with two or three spears in his hand and a string of divining bones (*ditaola*) round his neck. She said, "Hallo, man! Where is my child?" and he answered, "It is I, Mother!" Then he asked what had become of the people, and the cattle and the dogs, and she told him.

"Where is this thing, Mother?"

"Come out and see, my child."

So they both went out and climbed to the top of the wall surrounding the calves' kraal, and she pointed to the pass, saying, "That object which is filling the *nek*, as big as a mountain, that is Khodumodumo."

Ditaolane got down from the wall, fetched his spears, sharpened them on a stone, and set off to the end of the valley, where Khodumodumo lay. The beast saw him, and opened its mouth to swallow him, but he dodged and went round its side – it was too unwieldy to turn and seize him – and drove one of his spears into it. Then he stabbed it again with his second spear, and it sank down and died.

He took his knife, and had already begun to cut it open, when he heard a man's voice crying out, "Do not cut me!" So he tried in another place, and another man cried out, but the knife had already slashed his leg. Ditaolane then began cutting in a third place, and a cow lowed, and someone called out, "Don't stab the cow!" Then he heard a goat bleat, a dog bark and a hen cackle, but he managed to avoid them all, as he went on cutting, and so, in time, released all the inhabitants of the valley.

There was great rejoicing as the people collected their belongings, and all returned to their several villages praising their young deliverer, and saying, "This young man must be our chief." They brought him gifts of cattle, so that, between one and another, he soon had a large herd, and he had his choice of wives among their daughters. So he built himself a fine kraal and married and settled down, and all went well for a time.

But the unintentionally wounded man never forgot his grudge, and long after his leg was healed began, when he noticed signs of discontent among the people, to drop a cunning word here and there and encourage those who were secretly envious of Ditaolane's good fortune, as well as those who suspected him because, as they said, he could not be a normal human being, to give voice to their feelings.

So before long they were making plans to get rid of their chief. They dug a pit and covered it with dry grass – just as the Bapedi did in order to trap Huveane – but he avoided it. They kindled a great fire in the courtyard, intending to throw him into it, but a kind of madness seized them; they began to struggle with each other, and at last threw in one of their own party. The same thing happened when they tried to push him over a precipice; in this case he restored to life the man who was thrown over and killed.

Next they got up a big hunt, which meant an absence of several days from the village. One night when the party were sleeping in a cave they induced the chief to take the place farthest from the entrance, and when they thought he was asleep stole out and built a great fire in the cave mouth. But when they looked round they saw him standing among them.

After this, feeling that nothing would soften their inveterate hatred, he grew weary of defeating their stratagems, and allowed them to kill him without offering any resistance. Some of the Basuto, when relating this story, add, "It is said that his heart went out and escaped and became a bird."

Untombinde and the Squatting Monster
(From the Zulu people, southern Africa)

A CHIEF'S DAUGHTER, Untombinde, goes, with a number of other girls, to bathe in the Ilulange, against the warnings of her parents: "To the Ilulange nothing goes and returns again; it goes there forever." The girls found, on coming out of the water, that the clothes and ornaments they had left on the bank had disappeared; they knew that the *isiququmadevu* must have taken them, and one after another petitioned politely for their return. Untombinde, however, said, "I will never beseech the *isiququmadevu*," and was immediately seized by the monster and dragged down into the water.

Her companions went home and reported what had happened. The chief, though he evidently despaired of recovering her ("Behold, she goes there forever!"), sent a troop of young men to fetch the *isiququmadevu*, which has killed Untombinde. The warriors found the monster squatting on the river bank, and were swallowed up, everyone, before they could attack her. She then went on to the chiefs kraal, swallowed up all the inhabitants, with their dogs and their cattle, as well as all the people in the surrounding country.

Among the victims were two beautiful children, much beloved. Their father, however, escaped, took his two clubs and his large spear, and went his way, saying, "It is I who will kill the *isiququmadevu*."

By this time the monster had left the neighbourhood, and the man went on seeking her till he met with some buffaloes, whom he asked, "Whither has Usiququmadevu gone? She has gone away with my children!" The buffaloes directed him on his way, and he then came across some leopards, of whom he asked the same question, and who also told him to go forward. He next met an elephant, who likewise sent him on, and so at last he came upon the monster herself, and announced, "I am seeking Usiququmadevu, who is taking away my children!" Apparently she hoped to escape recognition, for she directed him, like the rest, to go forward. But the man was not to be deceived by so transparent a device: he came and stabbed the lump, and so the *isiququmadevu* died."

Then all the people, cattle and dogs, and, lastly, Untombinde herself, came out unharmed, and she returned to her father.

The Magic Flight
(From the Zulu people, southern Africa)

ONE DAY A NUMBER OF MEN seated by the fence of the chief's cattle fold saw several birds of a kind they had never seen before perched on a tree not far off. The chief's son, Sikulumi, said, "These are indeed beautiful birds. I want to catch one and make a plume for my head [*isidhodhlo*] of his feathers."

So he and some friends set off in pursuit of the birds, which had already flown away while they were seizing their knobkerries. They followed them across country for a long time, and at last succeeded in knocking down several. By this time the sun had set, and they were far from home; but as darkness fell they perceived the glimmer of a distant fire, and made for it straightway. When they came up with it they found it was burning in an empty hut, which, though they could not know it, belonged to some *amazimu*. They went in and made themselves at home, plucked their birds, roasted and ate them, after cutting off the heads, which Sikulumi arranged all round the ledge of the hut. Then they made plumes out of the feathers, and when they had done so went to sleep – all but Sikulumi.

In the middle of the night an ogre arrived, having left his fellows at a distance, and Sikulumi heard him muttering to himself, "Something smells very good here in my house!" He looked at the sleepers, one by one – Sikulumi, of course, pretending to be asleep – and said, "I will begin with this one, I will eat that one next, and then that one, and finish up with him whose little feet are white from walking through the sand!" He then caught sight of the birds' heads, crunched them up, and swallowed them, before starting off to call the other ogres to the feast.

Sikulumi at once roused his friends and told them what had happened, and they, picking up their plumes and their sticks, set off for home, running for all they were worth. They had gone quite a long way when Sikulumi remembered suddenly that he had left his plume behind. His friends said, "Don't go back. Take one of ours. Why should you go where cannibals are?" But he persisted. He took his stick, rubbed it with 'medicine', and planted it upright in the ground, saying, "If this stick falls over without rising again you will know that I am dead, and you must tell my father when you get home. As long as it stands firm I am safe; if it shakes you will know that I am running for my life."

Meanwhile the ogre had come back with his friends, and when they found no one in the hut they were furious with him for cheating them, so they killed and ate him.

On his way back to the hut Sikulumi saw an old woman sitting by a big stone beside the path. She asked him where he was going, and he told her. She gave him some fat, and said, "If the ogres come after you put some of this on a stone." He reached the hut, and found a whole party seated round the fire, passing his plume from hand to hand. On the fire a large pot was boiling, in which they were cooking toads. Sikulumi sprang in among them, snatched his plume from an old hag who happened to be holding it at that moment, and at the same time shattered the pot with a blow of his knobkerrie, scattering the toads all over the floor. While the ogres were occupied in picking them up he made his escape. They were not long, however, in following him, and when he saw them he did as the friendly old woman had told him and threw some of the fat on a stone. When the ogres came up to this stone they began (it is not explained why) to fight for the possession of it. One of them swallowed it, whereupon the others killed and ate him. Sikulumi thus gained some advantage, but soon they had nearly come up with him again. He threw some more fat on a stone, and the same thing happened as before. Again they started after him, and this time he threw down his skin cloak, which began to run off by itself. The ogres ran after it, and were so long catching it that he was able to rejoin his friends, and they all made their way home.

The Story of the Bird that Made Milk
(From the Xhosa people, South Africa)

Version I

THERE WAS ONCE upon a time a poor man living with his wife in a certain village. They had three children, two boys and a girl. They used to get milk from a tree. That milk of the tree was got by squeezing. It was not nice as that of a cow, and the people that drank it were always thin. For this reason, those people were never glossy like those who are fat.

One day the woman went to cultivate a garden. She began by cutting the grass with a pick, and then putting it in a big heap. That was the work of the first day, and when the sun was just about to set she went home. When she left, there came a bird to that place, and sang this song:

"Weeds of this garden,
Weeds of this garden,
Spring up, spring up;
Work of this garden,
Work of this garden,
Disappear, disappear."

It was so.

The next morning, when she returned and saw that, she wondered greatly. She again put it in order on that day, and put some sticks in the ground to mark the place.

In the evening she went home and told that she had found the grass which she had cut growing just as it was before.

Her husband said: "How can such a thing be? You were lazy and didn't work, and now tell me this falsehood. just get out of my sight, or I'll beat you."

On the third day she went to her work with a sorrowful heart, remembering the words spoken by her husband. She reached the place and found the grass growing as before. The sticks that she stuck in the ground were there still, but she saw nothing else of her labour. She wondered greatly.

She said in her heart, "I will not cut the grass off again, I will just hoe the ground as it is."

She commenced. Then the bird came and perched on one of the sticks.

It sang:

"Citi, citi, who is this cultivating the ground of my father?
Pick, come off;
Pick handle, break;
Sods, go back to your places!"

All these things happened.

The woman went home and told her husband what the bird had done. Then they made a plan. They dug a deep hole in the ground, and covered it with sticks and grass. The man hid himself in the hole, and put up one of his hands. The woman commenced to hoe the ground again. Then the bird came and perched on the hand of the man, and sang:

"This is the ground of my father.
Who are you, digging my father's ground?
Pick, break into small pieces
Sods, return to your places."

It was so.

Then the man tightened his fingers and caught the bird. He came up out of the place of concealment.

He said to the bird: "As for you who spoil the work of this garden, you will not see the sun anymore. With this sharp stone I will cut off your head!"

Then the bird said to him: "I am not a bird that should be killed. I am a bird that can make milk."

The man said: "Make some, then."

The bird made some milk in his hand. The man tasted it. It was very nice milk.

The man said: "Make some more milk, my bird."

The bird did so. The man sent his wife for a milk basket. When she brought it, the bird filled it with milk.

The man was very much pleased. He said: "This pretty bird of mine is better than a cow."

He took it home and put it in a jar. After that he used to rise even in the night and tell the bird to make milk for him. Only he and his wife drank of it. The children continued to drink of the milk of the tree. The names of the children were Gingci, the first-born son; Lonci, his brother; and Dumangashe, his sister. That man then got very fat indeed, so that his skin became shining.

The girl said to her brother Gingci: "Why does father get fat and we remain so thin?"

He replied: "I do not know. Perhaps he eats in the night."

They made a plan to watch. They saw him rise in the middle of the night. He went to the big jar and took an eating mat off it. He said: "Make milk, my bird." He drank much. Again he said: "Make milk, my bird," and again he drank till he was very full. Then he lay down and went to sleep.

The next day the woman went to work in her garden, and the man went to visit his friend. The children remained at home, but not in the house. Their father fastened the door of the house, and told them not to enter it on any account till his return.

Gingci said: "Today we will drink of the milk that makes father fat and shining; we will not drink of the milk of the euphorbia today."

The girl said: "As for me, I also say let us drink of father's milk today."

They entered the house. Gingci removed the eating mat from the jar, and said to the bird: "My father's bird, make milk for me."

The bird said: "If I am your father's bird, put me by the fireplace, and I will make milk."

The boy did so. The bird made just a little milk.

The boy drank, and said: "My father's bird, make more milk."

The bird said: "If I am your father's bird, put me by the door, then I will make milk."

The boy did this. Then the bird made just a little milk, which the boy drank.

The girl said: "My father's bird, make milk for me."

The bird said: "If I am your father's bird, just put me in the sunlight, and I will make milk."

The girl did so. Then the bird made a jar full of milk.

After that the bird sang:

> *"The father of Dumangashe came, he came,*
> *He came unnoticed by me.*
> *He found great fault with me.*
> *The little fellows have met together.*
> *Gingci the brother of Lonci.*
> *The Umkomanzi cannot be crossed,*
> *It is crossed by swallows*
> *Whose wings are long."*

When it finished its song it lifted up its wings and flew away. But the girl was still drinking milk.

The children called it, and said: "Return, bird of our father," but it did not come back. They said, "We shall be killed today."

They followed the bird. They came to a tree where there were many birds.

The boy caught one, and said to it: "My father's bird, make milk."

It bled. They said, "This is not our father's bird."

This bird bled very much; the blood ran like a river. Then the boy released it, and it flew away. The children were seized with fear.

They said to themselves: "If our father finds us, he will kill us today."

In the evening the man came home. When he was yet far off, he saw that the door had been opened.

He said: "I did not shut the door that way."

He called his children, but only Lonci replied. He asked for the others.

Lonci said: "I went to the river to drink; when I returned they were gone."

He searched for them, and found the girl under the ashes and the boy behind a stone. He inquired at once about his bird. They were compelled to tell the truth concerning it.

Then the man took a riem [a strip of hide which has been treated to preserve it before making it into leather] and hung those two children on a tree that projected over the river. He went away, leaving them there. Their mother besought their father, saying that they should be released; but the man refused. After he was gone, the boy tried to escape. He climbed up the riem and held on to the tree; then he went up and loosened the riem that was tied to his sister. After that they climbed up the tree, and then went away from their home. They slept three times on the road.

They came to a big rock. The boy said: "We have no father and no mother; rock, be our house."

The rock opened, and they went inside. After that they lived there in that place. They obtained food by hunting animals, they were hunted by the boy.

When they were already in that place a long time, the girl grew to be big. There were no people in that place. A bird came one day with a child, and left it there by their house.

The bird said: "So have I done to all the people."

After that a crocodile came to that place. The boy was just going to kill it, but it said: "I am a crocodile; I am not to be killed; I am your friend."

Then the boy went with the crocodile to the house of the crocodile, in a deep hole under the water.

The crocodile had many cattle and [much] millet. He gave the boy ten cows and ten baskets of millet.

The crocodile said to the boy: "You must send your sister for the purpose of being married to me."

The boy made a fold to keep his cattle in; his sister made a garden and planted millet. The crocodile sent more cattle. The boy made a very big fold, and it was full of cattle.

At this time there came a bird.

The bird said: "Your sister has performed the custom, and as for you, you should enter manhood."

The crocodile gave one of his daughters to be the wife of the young man. The young woman went to the village of the crocodile, she went to be a bride.

They said to her: "Whom do you choose to be your husband?"

The girl replied: "I choose Crocodile."

Her husband said to her: "Lick my face."

She did so. The crocodile cast off its skin, and arose a man of great strength and fine appearance.

He said: "The enemies of my father's house did that; you, my wife, are stronger than they."

After this there was a great famine, and the mother of those people came to their village. She did not recognize her children, but they knew her and gave her food. She went away, and then their father came. He did not recognize them either, but they knew him. They asked him what he wanted. He told them that his village was devoured by famine. They gave him food, and he went away.

He returned again.

The young man said: "You thought we would die when you hung us in the tree."

He was astonished, and said: "Are you indeed my child?"

Crocodile then gave them [the parents] three baskets of corn, and told them to go and build on the mountains. He [the man] did so and died there on the mountains.

Version II

I
T IS SAID that there was once a great town in a certain place, which had many people living in it. They lived upon grain only. One year there was a great famine. There was in that town a poor man, by name Masilo, and his wife. One day they went to dig in their garden, and they continued digging the whole day long. In the evening, when

the digging companies returned home, they returned also. Then there came a bird and stood upon the house, which was beside the garden, and began to whistle, and said:

"Masilo's cultivated ground, mix together."

The ground did as the bird said. After that was done the bird went away.

In the morning, when Masilo and his wife went to the garden, they were in doubt, and said:

"Is it really the place we were digging yesterday?"

They saw that it was the place by the people working on each side. The people began to laugh at them, and mocked them, and said, "It is because you are very lazy."

They continued to dig again that day, and in the evening they went home with the others.

Then the bird came and did the same thing.

When they went back next morning, they found their ground altogether undug. Then they believed that they were bewitched by some others.

They continued digging that day again. But in the evening when the companies returned, Masilo said to his wife:

"Go home; I will stay behind to watch and find the thing which eats our work."

Then he went and laid himself down by the head of the garden, under the same house which the bird used always to stand upon.

While he was thinking, the bird came. It was a very beautiful bird. He was looking at it and admiring it, when it began to speak.

It said:

"Masilo's cultivated ground, mix together."

Then he caught it, and said: "Ah! is it you who eat the work of our hands?"

He took out his knife from the sheath, and was going to cut the head of the bird off.

Then the bird said: "Please don't kill me, and I will make some milk for you to eat."

Masilo answered: "You must bring back the work of my hands first."

The bird said: "Masilo's cultivated ground, appear," and it appeared.

Then Masilo said: "Make the milk now," and, behold, it immediately made thick milk, which Masilo began to eat. When he was satisfied, he took the bird home. As he approached his house, he put the bird in his bag.

When he entered his house, he said to his wife, "Wash all the largest beer pots which are in the house," but his wife was angry on account of her hunger, and she answered: "What have you to put in such large pots?"

Masilo said to her: "Just hear me, and do as I command you, then you will see."

When she was ready with the pots, Masilo took his bird out of his bag, and said: "Make milk for my children to eat."

Then the bird filled all the beer pots with milk.

They commenced to eat, and when they were finished, Masilo charged his children, saying: "Beware that you do not tell anybody of this, not one of your companions."

They swore by him that they would not tell anybody.

Masilo and his family then lived upon this bird. The people were surprised when they saw him and his family. They said: "Why are the people at Masilo's house so fat? He is so poor, but now since his garden has appeared he and his children are so fat!"

They tried to watch and to see what he was eating, but they never could find out at all.

One morning Masilo and his wife went to work in their garden, and about the middle of the same day the children of that town met together to play. They met just before Masilo's house. While they were playing the others said to Masilo's children: "Why are you so fat while we remain so thin?"

They answered: "Are we then fat? We thought we were thin just as you are."

They would not tell them the cause. The others continued to press them, and said: "We won't tell anybody."

Then the children of Masilo said: "There is a bird in our father's house which makes milk."

The others said: "Please show us the bird."

They went into the house and took it out of the secret place where their father had placed it. They ordered it as their father used to order it, and it made milk, which their companions drank, for they were very hungry.

After drinking they said: "Let it dance for us," and they loosened it from the place where it was tied.

The bird began to dance in the house, but one said: "This place is too confined," so they took it outside of the house. While they were enjoying themselves and laughing, the bird flew away, leaving them in great dismay.

Masilo's children said: "Our father will this day kill us, therefore we must go after the bird."

So they followed it, and continued going after it the whole day long, for when they were at a distance it would sit still for a little while, and when they approached it would fly away.

When the digging companies returned from digging, the people of that town cried for their children, for they did not know what had become of them. But when Masilo went into the house and could not find his bird, he knew where the children were, but he did not tell any of their parents. He was very sorry for his bird, for he knew that he had lost his food.

When evening set in, the children determined to return to their home, but there came a storm of rain with heavy thunder, and they were very much afraid. Among them was a brave boy, named Mosemanyanamatong, who encouraged them, and said: "Do not be afraid; I can command a house to build itself."

They said: "Please command it."

He said: "House appear," and it appeared, and also wood for fire. Then the children entered the house and made a large fire, and began to roast some wild roots which they dug out of the ground.

While they were roasting the roots and were merry, there came a big cannibal, and they heard his voice saying: "Mosemanyanamatong, give me some of the wild roots you have."

They were afraid, and the brave boy said to the girls and to the other boys: "Give me some of yours."

They gave to him, and he threw the roots outside. While the cannibal was still eating, they went out and fled. He finished eating the roots, and then pursued them. When he approached they scattered some more roots upon the ground, and while he was picking them up and eating, they fled.

At length they came among mountains, where trees were growing. The girls were already very tired, so they all climbed up a tall tree. The cannibal came there, and tried to cut the tree down with his sharp and long nail.

Then the brave boy said to the girls: "While I am singing you must continue saying, 'Tree be stronger, tree be strong!'"

He sang this song:

> *"It is foolish,*
> *It is foolish to be a traveller,*
> *And to go on a journey*
> *With the blood of girls upon one!*
> *While we were roasting wild roots*
> *A great darkness fell upon us.*
> *It was not darkness,*
> *It was awful gloom!"*

While he was singing, there came a great bird and hovered over them, and said: "Hold fast to me."

The children held fast to the bird, and it flew away with them, and took them to their own town.

It was midnight when it arrived there, and it sat down at the gate of Mosemanyanamatong's mother's house.

In the morning, when that woman came out of her house, she took ashes and cast upon the bird, for she said: "This bird knows where our children are."

At midday the bird sent word to the chief, saying, "Command all your people to spread mats on all the paths."

The chief commanded them to do so. Then the bird brought all the children out, and the people were greatly delighted.

The Story of Five Heads
(From the Xhosa people, South Africa)

THERE WAS ONCE A MAN living in a certain place, who had two daughters big enough to be married.

One day the man went over the river to another village, which was the residence of a great chief. The people asked him to tell them the news. He replied that there was no news in the place that he came from. Then the man inquired about the news of their place. They said the news of their place was that the chief wanted a wife.

The man went home and said to his two daughters: "Which of you wishes to be the wife of a chief?"

The eldest replied: "I wish to be the wife of a chief, my father." The name of that girl was Mpunzikazi.

The man said: "At that village which I visited, the chief wishes for a wife; you, my daughter, shall go."

The man called all his friends, and assembled a large company to go with his daughter to the village of the chief. But the girl would not consent that those people should go with her.

She said: "I will go alone to be the wife of the chief."

Her father replied: "How can you, my daughter, say such a thing? Is it not so that when a girl goes to present herself to her husband she should be accompanied by others? Be not foolish, my daughter."

The girl still said: "I will go alone to be the wife of the chief."

Then the man allowed his daughter to do as she chose. She went alone, no bridal party accompanying her, to present herself at the village of the chief who wanted a wife.

As Mpunzikazi was on the path, she met a mouse.

The mouse said: "Shall I show you the way?"

The girl replied: "Just get away from before my eyes."

The mouse answered: "If you do like this, you will not succeed."

Then she met a frog.

The frog said: "Shall I show you the way?"

Mpunzikazi replied: "You are not worthy to speak to me, as I am to be the wife of a chief."

The frog said: "Go on then; you will see afterwards what will happen."

When the girl got tired, she sat down under a tree to rest. A boy who was herding goats in that place came to her, he being very hungry.

The boy said: "Where are you going to, my eldest sister?"

Mpunzikazi replied in an angry voice: "Who are you that you should speak to me? Just get away from before me."

The boy said: "I am very hungry; will you not give me of your food?"

She answered: "Get away quickly."

The boy said: "You will not return if you do this."

She went on her way again, and met with an old woman sitting by a big stone.

The old woman said: "I will give you advice. You will meet with trees that will laugh at you: you must not laugh in return. You will see a bag of thick milk: you must not eat of it. You will meet a man whose head is under his arm: you must not take water from him."

Mpunzikazi answered: "You ugly thing! Who are you that you should advise me?"

The old woman continued in saying those words.

The girl went on. She came to a place where were many trees. The trees laughed at her, and she laughed at them in return. She saw a bag of thick milk, and she ate of it. She met a man carrying his head under his arm, and she took water to drink from him.

She came to the river of the village of the chief. She saw a girl there dipping water from the river. The girl said: "Where are you going to, my sister?"

Mpunzikazi replied: "Who are you that you should call me sister? I am going to be the wife of a chief."

The girl drawing water was the sister of the chief. She said: "Wait, I will give you advice. Do not enter the village by this side."

Mpunzikazi did not stand to listen, but just went on.

She reached the village of the chief. The people asked her where she came from and what she wanted.

She answered: "I have come to be the wife of the chief."

They said: "Who ever saw a girl go without a retinue to be a bride?"

They said also: "The chief is not at home; you must prepare food for him, that when he comes in the evening he may eat."

They gave her millet to grind. She ground it very coarse, and made bread that was not nice to eat.

In the evening she heard the sound of a great wind. That wind was the coming of the chief. He was a big snake with five heads and large eyes. Mpunzikazi was very much frightened when she saw him. He sat down before the door and told her to bring his food. She brought the bread which she had made. Makanda Mahlanu [Five Heads] was not satisfied with that bread. He said: "You shall not be my wife," and he struck her with his tail and killed her.

Afterwards the sister of Mpunzikazi said to her father: "I also wish to be the wife of a chief."

Her father replied: "It is well, my daughter; it is right that you should wish to be a bride."

The man called all his friends, and a great retinue prepared to accompany the bride. The name of the girl was Mpunzanyana.

In the way they met a mouse.

The mouse said: "Shall I show you the road?"

Mpunzanyana replied: "If you will show me the way I shall be glad."

Then the mouse pointed out the way.

She came into a valley, where she saw an old woman standing by a tree.

The old woman said to her: "You will come to a place where two paths branch off. You must take the little one, because if you take the big one you will not be fortunate."

Mpunzanyana replied: "I will take the little path, my mother." She went on.

Afterwards she met a cony.

The cony said: "The village of the chief is close by. You will meet a girl by the river: you must speak nicely to her. They will give you millet to grind; you must grind it well. When you see your husband, you must not be afraid."

She said: "I will do as you say, cony."

In the river she met the chief's sister carrying water.

The chief's sister said: "Where are you going to?"

Mpunzanyana replied: "This is the end of my journey."

The chief's sister said: "What is the object of your coming to this place?"

Mpunzanyana replied: "I am with a bridal party."

The chief's sister said: "That is right, but will you not be afraid when you see your husband?"

Mpunzanyana answered: "I will not be afraid."

The chief's sister pointed out the hut in which she should stay. Food was given to the bridal party. The mother of the chief took millet and gave to the bride, saying: "You must prepare food for your husband. He is not here now, but he will come in the evening."

In the evening she heard a very strong wind, which made the hut shake. The poles fell, but she did not run out. Then she saw the chief Makanda Mahlanu coming. He asked for food. Mpunzanyana took the bread which she had made, and gave it to him. He was very much pleased with that food, and said: "You shall be my wife." He gave her very many ornaments.

Afterwards Makanda Mahlanu became a man, and Mpunzanyana continued to be the wife he loved best.

The Story of Tangalimlibo
(From the Xhosa people, South Africa)

THERE WAS ONCE A MAN who had two wives, one of whom had no children. She grieved much about that, till one day a bird came to her and gave her some little pellets. The bird said she must eat of these always before she partook of food, and then she would bear a child. She was very glad, and offered the bird some millet.

But the bird said: "No, I do not want millet."

The woman then offered an isidanga [an ornamental breast-band which women wear], but the bird said it had no use for that. Then she got some very fine gravel and placed before the bird, which it received at her hands.

After this the woman had a daughter. Her husband knew nothing of what had happened, because he never went to her house. He did not love her at all, for the reason that she bore no children. So she said:

"I will keep my daughter in the house till my husband comes; he will surely love me when he sees I have such a beautiful child."

The name given to the girl was Tangalimlibo.

The man went always to the house of the other wife, and so it happened that Tangalimlibo was grown to be a young woman when her father first saw her. He was very much pleased, and said:

"My dear wife, you should have told me of this before."

The girl had never been out of the house in the daytime. Only in the nighttime she had gone out, when people could not see her.

The man said to his wife:

"You must make much beer, and invite many people to come and rejoice with me over this that has happened."

The woman did so. There was a big tree in front of the kraal, and the mats were spread under it. It was a fine sunny day, and very many men came. Among them was the son of a certain chief, who fell in love with Tangalimlibo as soon as he saw her.

When the young chief went home he sent a message to the father of the girl that he must send her to him to be married. The man told all his friends about that. He told them also to be ready at a certain time to conduct his daughter to the chief. So they came and took her, and the marriage feast was very great. The oxen were many which were killed that day. Tangalimlibo had a large and beautiful ox given to her by her father. That ox was called by her own name. She took off a piece of her clothing and gave it to the ox, which ate it.

After she had been married some time, this woman had a son. She was loved very much by her husband, because she was pretty and industrious; only this thing was observed of her, that she never went out in the daytime. Therefore she received the name of Sihamba Ngenyanga [the walker by moonlight].

One day her husband went to a distant place to hunt with other men. There were left at his home with this woman only her father-in-law, her mother-in-law and a girl who nursed the little child.

The father-in-law said: "Why does she not work during the day?

He pretended to become thirsty, and sent the girl to Tangalimlibo to ask for water, saying: "I die with thirst."

The woman sent water to her father-in-law, but he threw it on the ground, saying: "It is water from the river I desire."

She said: "I never go to the river in the daytime."

He continued to ask, saying again: "I die with thirst."

Then she took a milk basket and a calabash ladle, and went weeping to the river. She dipped the ladle in the water, and it was drawn out of her hand. She dipped the milk basket in the water, and it was drawn away from her. Then she tried to take some water in her mantle, and she was drawn under the surface. After a little time the girl was sent to look for her, but she came back, saying: "I found her not who is accustomed to draw water only in the night."

Her father-in-law drove oxen quickly to the river. He took the big ox that was called by her name and killed it. He put all the flesh and everything else that was of that ox into the river, saying: "Let this be instead of my child."

A voice was heard saying: "Go to my father and my mother and say to them that I am taken by the river."

That evening the little child of Tangalimlibo, was crying very bitterly. Its father was not yet home. Its grandmother tried by every means to keep it from crying, but in vain. Then she gave it to the nurse, who fastened it on her back. Still the child continued to cry. In the middle of the night the nurse went down to the river with the child, singing this song:

> *"It is crying, it is crying,*
> *The child of Sihamba Ngenyanga;*
> *It is crying, it will not be pacified."*

Then the mother of the child came out of the river, and wailed this song:

> *"It is crying, it is crying,*
> *The child of the walker by moonlight.*
> *It was done intentionally by people whose names are unmentionable.*
> *They sent her for water during the day.*
> *She tried to dip with the milk basket, and then it sank.*
> *Tried to dip with the ladle, and then it sank.*
> *Tried to dip with the mantle, and then it sank."*

With the name as a chorus at the end of each line.

Then she took her child and put it to her breast to suck. When the child had finished suckling, she gave it back to the nurse, telling her to take it home. She commanded the nurse never to say to anyone that she came out of the water, and told her that when people asked where the child got food she must say she gave it berries to eat.

This continued for some days. Every night the nurse took the child to the river, when its mother came out and suckled it. She always looked round to see that no one was present, and always put the same command on the girl.

After a time the father of the child returned from hunting. They told him of Tangalimlibo's going to the river and not returning. Then the nurse brought the child to him. He inquired what it ate, and was told that berries were given to it.

He said: "That cannot be so; go and get some berries, and let me see my child eat them."

The girl went and brought some berries, but they were not eaten by the child. Then the father of the child beat the girl until she told the truth. She said she went at night to the river, when the mother came out and caressed her child and gave it of her milk.

Then they made a plan that the husband of Tangalimlibo should hide himself in the reeds and try and catch his wife when she came out of the water. He took the skin of an ox and cut it into a long riem, one end of which he fastened round his waist. The other end he gave to the men of that village, telling them to hold it fast and to pull hard when they felt it being drawn from them.

At night the man hid himself in the reeds. Tangalimlibo came out of the water and looked all round while she was singing her song. She asked the girl if anyone was there, and when the girl replied that there was no one she took her child. Then her husband sprang upon her, clasping her very tight. She tried to pull back, but the men at the village drew upon the riem. She was drawn away, but the river followed her, and its water turned into blood. When it came close to the village, the men who were pulling at the riem saw it, and became frightened. They let the riem go, when the river at once went back, taking Tangalimlibo with it.

After that her husband was told of the voice which came from the water, saying: "Go to my father and my mother and tell them I am taken by the river."

He called his racing ox, and said: "Will you, my ox, take this message to the father and mother of Tangalimlibo?"

The ox only bellowed.

He called his dog and said: "Will you, my dog, take this message to the father and mother of Tangalimlibo?"

The dog only barked.

Last of all he called the cock.

He said: "Will you, my cock, take this message to the father and mother of Tangalimlibo?"

The cock answered: "I will do so, my master."

He said: "Let me hear what you will say."

The cock answered: "I will sing:

"I am a cock that ought not to be killed – Cock-a-doodledoo!
I have come to intimate about Tangalimlibo – Cock-adoodle-doo!

Tangalimlibo is dead – Cock-a-doodle-doo!
She dipped water for a person that cannot
be named-- Cock-a-doodle-doo!
It was tried to send an ox; it bellowed – Cock-a-doodle-doo!
It was tried to send a dog; it barked – Cock-a-doodle-doo!"

The chief said: "That is good, my cock, go now."

As the cock was going on his way, some boys who were tending calves saw him.

One of them said to the others: "Come here, come here, boys; there is a cock for us to kill."

Then the cock stood up, and sang his song.

The boys said: "Sing again, we did not hear you plainly."

So he sang again:

"I am a cock that ought not to be killed – Cock-a-doodledoo!
I have come to intimate about Tangalimlibo – Cock-a-doodle-doo!
Tangalimlibo is dead – Cock-a-doodle-doo!
She dipped water for a person that cannot be named – Cock-a-doodle-doo!
It was tried to send an ox; it bellowed – Cock-a-doodle-doo!
It was tried to send a dog; it barked – Cock-a-doodle-doo!"

Then the boys let him go on his way.

He travelled far from that place and came to a village, where the men were sitting in the kraal. He flew up on the back of the kraal to rest himself, and the men saw him.

They said: "Where does this cock come from? We thought all the cocks here were killed. Make haste, boys, and kill him."

The cock began to sing his song.

Then the men said: "Wait, boys, we wish to hear what he says."

They said to him: "Begin again, we did not hear you."

The cock said: "Give me some food, for I am very hungry."

The men sent a boy for some millet, and gave it to him. When he had eaten, he sang his song.

The men said: "Let him go;" and he went on his way.

Then he came to the village of the father of Tangalimlibo, to the house of those he was seeking. He told the message he was sent to carry. The mother of Tangalimlibo was a woman skilful in the use of medicines.

She said to her husband: "Get a fat ox to go with us."

They arrived at the river, and killed the ox.

Then that woman worked with her medicines while they put the meat in the water. There was a great shaking and a rising up of the river, and Tangalimlibo came out. There was great joy among those people when they took her home to her husband.

The Story of the Girl Who Disregarded the Custom of Ntonjane
(From the Xhosa people, South Africa)

THERE WAS ONCE A CHIEF'S DAUGHTER who had reached the age when it was necessary for her to observe the ntonjane. She was therefore placed in a hut, in which she was to remain during the period of the ceremony.

One day her companions persuaded her to go and bathe in a stream near at hand, though this was against the custom of the ntonjane. When they came out of the water, they saw a snake with black blotches, called the Isinyobolokondwana, near their clothes. They were very much afraid, and did not know what to do at first. But by and by one of them commenced to sing these words:

> *"Sinyobolokondwana,*
> *Sinyobolokondwana,*
> *Bring my mantle!"*

The snake replied:

> *"Take it,*
> *And pass on."*

The companions of the chief's daughter, one after the other, asked the snake for their mantles in this manner, and obtained permission to take them. Last of all was the chief's daughter. But instead of speaking to the snake respectfully as the others had done, she said mockingly, "Ngcingcingci, ngcingcingci." [Words without meaning, but used to express contempt, being merely a repetition of the sound *ngci*] So the snake became very angry, and bit her, when she immediately became of the same hideous colour as it was. Her companions were so frightened that they left her and ran away home. They put another girl in the hut, and pretended that she was the chief's daughter. The girl, thus left alone, went to a forest close by, and climbed up a tree to hide herself.

About this time the chief was killing an ox on account of his daughter, and so he sent a young man to the forest to get pieces of wood with which to peg out the skin. The young man was cutting sticks, when he heard someone crying: "Man cutting sticks, tell my father and mother that the sinyobolokondwana bit me." He heard this repeated twice, and, without looking to see what was crying, he ran home and told the chief. Two young men were then sent back with him to see what it was, one of these happening to be the girl's brother. These two were told to hide themselves and listen while the other cut the sticks. They did so, and heard the voice crying as before. Then the brother of the girl knew the voice of his sister, and they all went to the tree where she was, and took her home with them.

The chief was very much surprised to see his daughter in that state, and was so angry with her companions for taking her to the river, and then for substituting another girl so as to deceive him, that he caused them all to be killed.

Then he sent some of his men with forty cattle to take his daughter to a distant country, where she was to remain far away from him. They did as they were told, and built huts in that place to live in. After they had been there a long time, they found that the cows which the chief sent with them were giving more milk than they could consume, so they poured what was left in a hole in the ground. To their amazement, the milk rose, and rose, and rose, higher and still higher, till at last it stood up out of the ground like a great overhanging rock. They called the girl to see this wonderful thing that was happening. In her curiosity she went close to the precipice, when it fell down on her, and, as the milk ran over her, all her ugly blotched skin disappeared, and she was again beautiful as at first.

Soon afterwards a young chief who was passing by saw the girl, and fell in love with her. He thought she was the daughter of one of the men who were there to protect her, but when he made inquiries they told him she was the daughter of their chief. Then he went to her father, and some of the men went also to tell how the milk had cured the girl. The young chief had very many cattle, which he offered to her father. So the old chief agreed to let him marry the girl, and she became his great wife, and was loved by him very dearly.

The Story of Simbukumbukwana
(From the Xhosa people, South Africa)

THERE WAS A MAN WHOSE WIFE had no children, so that he was much dissatisfied. At last he went to a wise woman [Igqirakazi] and asked her to help him in this matter. She said: "You must bring me a fat calf that I may get its tallow to use with my medicine" [or charms – the Xhosa word is Imifizi]. The man went home and selected a calf without horns or tail, which he took to the wise woman. She said: "Your wife will have a son who will have no arms and no legs, as this calf has no horns and no tail." She told him, further, that he was not to inform anyone of this.

The man returned to his home and told his friends what was to happen. Not long after this his wife bore a child, but it was a daughter and had arms and legs. The man would not own that child, he said it was not his. He beat his wife, and commanded her to take the child away and leave it to perish. Then he went to the wise woman, and told her what had taken place. The wise woman said: "It was because you did not obey my command about keeping this matter to yourself, but your wife will yet have a son without arms and without legs."

It was so. His wife bore another child, which was a boy without arms and without legs, therefore he was called Simbukumbukwana. He began to speak on the day of his birth. During this time the girl that was first born was growing up in the valley where her mother left her; she lived in a hole in an ant-heap, and ate honey, and 'nongwes' and gum.

One day the mother of Simbukumbukwana went to work in her garden, and left the boy at home with the door fastened. While she was away the girl came; she stood at a distance and said: "Where are the people?"

There came a voice from inside which said: "Here am I."

She said: "Who are you?

The voice replied: "I am Simbukumbukwana."

She said: "Open for me."

He answered: "How can I open? I have no legs and no arms."

She said: "My mother's Simbukumbukwana, have legs and arms."

Then legs and arms came on the boy, and he arose and opened for his sister. She went in and swept the floor; then she took millet and ground it and made bread. She told her brother when his parents asked him who did these things to say that he did them himself, and if they should ask him to do them again to reply, "I have done it already." Then she said: "My mother's Simbukumbukwana, sink legs and sink arms." Then his legs and arms shrunk up, and his sister went away.

After a time his father and his mother came home; they went in and saw the clean floor and bread ready for eating. They were surprised, and said to Simbukumbukwana, "Who did this?"

He replied: "I did."

They said: "Do so again that we may see you."

He answered: "I have done it already."

The next day the woman went again to work in her garden, but the man hid himself to watch what would happen. After a time came the sister of Simbukumbukwana and said: "Where are the people?" [Exactly the same conversation as before.] She went in and began to smear the floor; water was wanting, so she sent Simbukumbukwana to the river for some. His joy in walking was great, so that he did not stop at the river, but put the pot down there and continued to go forward. The girl thought he ought not to be so long absent, for the river was close by, so she went to look for him. She saw him walking up a hill far away, and she called to him to return. He would not. Then she sang, *Simbukumbukwana sikama, tshona milenze, tshona mikono*, and immediately his legs shrank up. Then she was going away, but her father came out and caught her; he kissed her, and said she must remain with him.

Her mother was coming home, when she saw something moving on the hillside. She went to see what it was, and found her son. She said: "How did you come here?"

He replied: "I came by myself."

She said: "Let me see you go further."

He answered: "I have done it already."

Then she put him on her back and went home. She found her daughter there, and her husband much pleased. The girl said: *Simbukumbukwana sikama, yiba nemilenze nemikono*, and legs and arms came on him.

One day his sister and some other girls went to get red clay, and he followed them. When they looked behind they saw him, and his sister got angry. She said to him: "What do you want here?"

He replied: "I am going for red clay for my mother."

His sister compelled him to sit down; but as soon as they went on, he followed; then his sister beat him, and left him on the path. After that there was a heavy storm of rain, but none fell where the little boy was. When the rain was over, the other girls said to the one who had beaten her brother: "Let us go and look after the little boy." They went and saw he was quite dry. He called to his sister: "You have beaten me," but she asked him to forgive her.

Then he said: "I want my father's house to be here," and immediately it came.

He said: "I want the fire of my father to be here," and there was a fire.

He said to them: "Now go in; although you have beaten me, there is a house and fire for you."

He said afterwards: "I want the cattle of my father to be here," and at once they were all there.

That was a nice place, so they remained there ever after.

The Story of Sikulume
(From the Xhosa people, South Africa)

THERE WAS ONCE IN A CERTAIN VILLAGE an old man who was very poor. He had no children, and only a few cattle. One day, when the sky was clear and the sun was bright, he sat down by the cattle fold. While he was sitting there, he noticed some birds close by which were singing very joyfully. He listened for a while, and then he stood up to observe them better.

They were very beautiful to look upon, and they sang differently from other birds. They had all long tails and topknots on their heads. Then the old man went to the chief and told him what he had seen.

The chief said: "How many were they?"

The old man replied: "There were seven."

The chief said: "You have acted wisely in coming to tell me; you shall have seven of the fattest of my cows. I have lost seven sons in battle, and these beautiful birds shall be in the place of my seven sons. You must not sleep tonight, you must watch them, and tomorrow I will choose seven boys to catch them. Do not let them out of your sight by any means."

In the morning the chief ordered all the boys of the village to be assembled at the cattle fold, when he spoke to them of the birds. He said: "I will choose six of you, and set my son who is dumb, over you, that will make seven in all. You must catch those birds. Wherever they go, you must follow, and you must not see my face again without them." He gave them weapons, and instructed them that if anyone opposed them they were to fight till the last of them died.

The boys set off to follow those beautiful birds. They chased them for several days, till at last the birds were exhausted, when each of the boys caught one. At the place where they caught the birds they remained that night.

On the morning of the next day they set out on their return home. That evening, they came to a hut in which they saw a fire burning, but no one was there. They went in, and lay down to sleep. In the middle of the night one of those boys was awake. He heard someone saying: "There is nice meat here. I will begin with this one, and take this one next, and that one after, and the one with small feet the last." The one with the small feet was the son of the chief. His name was Sikulume, for he had never been able to speak till he caught the bird. Then he began to talk at once.

After saying those words the voice was still. Then the boy awakened his companions, and told them what he had heard.

They said: "You have been dreaming; there is no one here, how can such a thing be?"

He replied: "I did not dream; I spoke the truth."

Then they made a plan that one should remain awake, and if anything happened, he should pinch the one next him, and that one should pinch the next, till all were awake.

After a while the boy who was listening heard someone come in quietly. That was a cannibal. He said the same words again, and then went out for the purpose of calling his friends to come to the feast. The boy awakened his companions according to the plan agreed upon, so that they all heard what was said. Therefore, as soon as the cannibal went out, they arose and fled from that place. The cannibal came back with his friends, and when the others saw there was no one in the hut, they killed and ate him.

As they were going on, Sikulume saw that he had left his bird behind. He stood, and said: "I must return for my bird, my beautiful bird with the long tail and topknot on its head. My father commanded that I must not see his face again unless I bring the bird."

The boys said: "Take one of ours. Why should you go where cannibals are?"

He replied: "I must have the one that is my own."

He stuck his assagai in the ground, and told them to look at it. He said: "If it stands still, you will know I am safe; if it shakes, you will know I am running; if it falls down, you will know I am dead." Then he left them to return to the hut of the cannibals.

On the way he saw an old woman sitting by a big stone. She said: "Where are you going to?" He told her he was going for his bird. The old woman gave him some fat, and said: "If the cannibals pursue you, put some of this on a stone."

He came to the hut and got his bird. The cannibals were sitting outside, a little way back. They had just finished eating the owner of the hut. When Sikulume came out with his bird they saw him and ran after him. They were close to him, when he took some of the fat and threw it on a stone. The cannibals came to the stone, and began to fight with each other.

One said: "The stone is mine."

Another said: "It is mine."

One of them swallowed the stone. When the others saw that, they killed him and ate him. Then they pursued again after Sikulume. They came close to him again, when he threw the remainder of the fat on another stone. The cannibals fought for this also. One swallowed it, and was killed by the others.

They followed still, and Sikulume was almost in their hands, when he threw off his mantle. The mantle commenced to run another way, and the cannibals ran after it. It was so long before they caught it that the young chief had time to reach his companions.

They all went on their way, but very soon they saw the cannibals coming after them. Then they observed a little man sitting by a big stone.

He said to them: "I can turn this stone into a hut."

They replied: "Do so."

He turned the stone into a hut, and they all went inside, the little man with them. They played the 'iceya' there. The cannibals came to the place and smelt. They thought the hut was still a stone, for it looked like a stone to them. They began to bite it, and bit till all their teeth were broken, when they returned to their own village.

After this, the boys and the little man came out.

The boys went on. When they reached their own home they saw no people, till at length an old woman crept out of a heap of ashes. She was very much frightened, and said to them: "I thought there were no people left."

Sikulume said: "Where is my father?"

She replied: "All the people have been swallowed by the inabulele" [a fabulous monster].

He said: "Where did it go to?

The old woman replied: "It went to the river."

So those boys went to the river, and Sikulume said to them: "I will go into the water, and take an assagai with me. If the water moves much, you will know I am in the stomach of the inabulele; if the water is red, you will know I have killed it." Then he threw himself into the water and went down.

The inabulele swallowed him without tearing him or hurting him. He saw his father and his mother and many people and cattle. Then he took his assagai and pierced the inabulele from inside. The water moved till the inabulele was dead, then it became red. When the young men saw that, they cut a big hole in the side of the inabulele, and all the people and the cattle were delivered.

One day Sikulume said to another boy: "I am going to the doctor's; tell my sister to cook food for me, nice food that I may eat." This was done.

He said to his sister: "Bring me of the skin of the inabulele which I killed, to make a mantle." She called her companions, and they went to the side of the river. She sang this song:

> "Inabulele,
> Inabulele,
> I am sent for you
> By Sikulume,
> Inabulele."

The body of the inabulele then came out. She cut two little pieces of the skin for sandals, and a large piece to make a mantle for her brother.

When he was a young man, Sikulume said to his friends: "I am going to marry the daughter of Mangangezulu."

They replied: "You must not go there, for at Mangangezulu's you will be killed."

He said: "I will go."

Then he called those young men who were his chosen friends to accompany him. On the way they came to a place where the grass was long. A mouse came out of the grass, and asked Sikulume where he was going to.

He replied: "I am going to the place of Mangangezulu."

The mouse sang this song:

> "Turn back, turn back, Sikulume.
> No one ever leaves the place of Mangangezulu.
> Turn back, turn back, O chief."

Sikulume replied: "I shall not turn back."

The mouse then said: "As it is so, you must kill me and throw my skin up in the air."

He did so.

The skin said: "You must not enter by the front of the village; you must not eat off a new mat; you must not sleep in a hut which has nothing in it."

They arrived at the village of Mangangezulu. They entered it from the wrong side, so that all the people said: "Why is this?"

They replied: "It is our custom."

Food was brought to them on a new mat, but they said, "It is our custom to eat off old mats only."

An empty hut was given to them to sleep in, but they said: "It is our custom only to sleep in a hut that has things in it."

The next day the chief said to Sikulume and his companions: "You must go and tend the cattle."

They went. A storm of rain fell, when Sikulume spread out his mantle and it became a hut as hard as stone, into which they all went. In the evening they returned with the cattle. The daughter of Mangangezulu came to them. Her mother pressed her foot in the footprint of Sikulume, and he became an eland.

The girl loved the young chief very much. When she saw he was turned into an eland, she made a great fire and drove him into it. Then he was burned, and became a little coal. She took the coal out and put it in a pot of water, when it became a young man again.

Afterwards they left that place. The girl took with her an egg, a milk sack, a pot and a smooth stone. The father of the girl pursued them.

The girl threw down the egg, and it became mist. Her father wandered about in the mist a long time, till at length it cleared away. Then he pursued again.

She threw down the milk sack, and it became a sheet of water. Her father tried to get rid of the water by dipping it up with a calabash, but he could not succeed, so he was compelled to wait till it dried up. He followed still.

The girl threw down the pot, and it became thick darkness. He waited a long time till light came again, when he followed them. He could travel very quickly.

He came close to them, and then the girl threw down the smooth stone. It became a rock, a big rock with one side steep like a wall. He could not climb up that rock, and so he returned to his own village.

Then Sikulume went home with his wife. He said to the people: "This is the daughter of Mangangezulu. You advised me not to go there, lest I should be killed. Here is my wife."

After that he became a great chief. All the people said: "There is no chief that can do such things as Sikulume."

The Story of Hlakanyana
(From the Xhosa people, South Africa)

ONCE UPON A TIME there was a village with many women in it. All the women had children at the same time except the wife of the chief. The children grew, and again all the women gave birth to others. Only the wife of the chief had no child. Then the people said: "Let us kill an ox, perhaps the wife of the chief will then bear a child."

While they were killing the ox, the woman heard a voice saying: "Bear me, mother, before the meat of my father is all finished."

The woman did not pay any attention to that, thinking it was a ringing in her ears. The voice said again: "Bear me, mother, before the meat of my father is all finished."

The woman took a small piece of wood and cleaned her ears. She heard that voice again. Then she became excited. She said: "There is something in my ears; I would like to know what it is. I have just now cleaned my ears."

The voice said again: "Make haste and bear me, mother, before the meat of my father is all finished."

The woman said: "What is this? There was never a child that could speak before it was born."

The voice said again: "Bear me, mother, as all my father's cattle are being finished, and I have not yet eaten anything of them." Then the woman gave birth to that child.

When she saw that to which she had given birth, she was very much astonished. It was a boy, but in size very little, and with a face that looked like that of an old person.

He said to his mother: "Mother, give me a skin robe." His mother gave him a robe. Then he went at once to the kraal where the ox was being killed.

He asked for some meat, saying: "Father, father, give me a piece of meat."

The chief was astonished to hear this child calling him father. He said: "Oh, men, what thing is this that calls me father?" So he continued with the skinning of the ox. But Hlakanyana continued also in asking meat from him. The chief became very angry, and pushed him, and said: "Get away from this place."

Hlakanyana answered: "I am your child, give me meat."

The chief took a little stick, and said: "If you trouble me again, I will strike you with this."

Hlakanyana replied: "Give me meat first, and I will go away;" but the chief would not answer, because he was very angry.

Hlakanyana continued asking. Then the chief threw him outside the kraal, and went on with his work. After a little time, the child returned, still asking.

So the chief said to the men that were with him: "What strange thing is this?"

The men replied: "We don't know him at all."

The chief asked of them also advice, saying: "What shall I do?"

The men replied: "Give him a piece of meat."

So the chief cut off a piece of meat and gave it to him. Hlakanyana ran to his mother and gave the meat to her to be cooked.

Then he returned to his father, and said again: "Father, give me some meat."

The chief just took him and trampled upon him, and threw him outside of the kraal, thinking that he was dead.

But he rose again and returned to his father, still saying: "Father, give me some meat."

Then the chief thought to get rid of him by giving him meat again. The chief gave him a piece of liver. Hlakanyana threw it away. Fat was then given to him. He put it down on one side. Flesh was then given to him, and a bone with much marrow in it.

Hlakanyana said: "I am a man today." He said. "This is the beginning of my father's cattle."

At this time the men were saying to each other: "Who will carry the meat to our huts?"

Hlakanyana answered: "I will do it."

They said: "How can such a thing as you are carry meat?"

Hlakanyana replied: "I am stronger than you; just see if you can lift this piece of meat."

The men tried, but could not lift it. Then Hlakanyana took the piece of meat and carried it out of the kraal. The men said, "That will do now, carry our meat for us."

Hlakanyana took the meat and carried it to the house of his mother. He took blood and put it on the eating mats at the houses of the men. The men went to their houses, and said: "Where is our meat?" They called Hlakanyana, and asked him what he had done with the meat.

He replied: "Surely I put it here where the blood is. It must have been taken by the dogs. Surely the dogs have eaten it."

Then those men beat the women and children because they did not watch that the dogs did not take the meat. As for Hlakanyana, he only delighted in this trick of his. He was more cunning than any of the old men.

Hlakanyana said to his mother, that she must put the meat in the pot to cook, but that it must not be eaten before the next morning It was done. In the night this cunning little fellow rose and went to the pot. His mother heard something at the pot, and struck with a stick. Hlakanyana cried like a dog. His mother said: "Surely a dog is eating the meat." Hlakanyana returned afterwards, and left nothing but bones in the pot. In the morning he asked his mother for meat. His mother went to the pot, and found nothing but bones. The cunning little fellow pretended to be astonished.

He said: "Where is the meat, mother?

His mother replied: "It has been eaten by a dog."

Hlakanyana said: "As that is so, give me the bones, for you who are the wife of the chief will not eat from the same pot with a dog."

His mother gave him the bones.

Hlakanyana went to sleep in the same house with the boys. The boys were unwilling to let him sleep with them. They laughed at him.

They said: "Who are you? You are just a child of a few days."

Hlakanyana answered, "I am older than you."

He slept there that night. When the boys were asleep, he got up and went to the cattle kraal. He killed two cows and ate all their insides. He took blood and smeared it on one of the boys who was sleeping. In the morning the men found those two dead cows.

They said: "Who has done this thing?"

They found the boy with blood upon him, and killed him, because they thought he was the robber.

Hlakanyana said within himself: "I told them that I was older than they are; today it is seen who is a child and who is a man."

Another day the father of Hlakanyana killed an ox. The head was put in a pot to be cooked. Then Hlakanyana considered in his mind how he could get that meat. So he drove all the cattle of the village into a forest, a very thick forest, and tied them by their tails to the trees. After that he cut his arms, and legs and breast, with a sharp stone, and stood on a hill, and cried out with a loud voice: "The enemy has taken our cattle; the cattle are being driven away. Come up, come up; there is an army going away with the cattle."

The men ran quickly to him.

He said to them: "Why are you eating meat while the enemy is going away with the cattle?

"I was fighting with them; just look at my body."

They saw he was covered with blood, and they believed it was as he said. So the men took their assagais and ran after the cattle, but they took the wrong way. Only one old man and Hlakanyana were left behind.

Then Hlakanyana said to the old man: "I am very tired with fighting; just go to the river, grandfather, and get some water."

The old man went; and as soon as he was alone, Hlakanyana ate the meat which was in the pot. When the old man returned with the water he was very tired, for the river was far for an old man to go to, therefore he fell asleep. When he was sleeping, Hlakanyana took a bone and put it beside the old man. He also took some fat and put it on the mouth of the old man. Then he ran to the forest and loosened the cattle that were tied by the tails.

At this, time the men were returning from seeking the enemy. Hlakanyana was coming also from the other side with the cattle.

He shouted: "I have conquered the enemy." He also said: "The meat must be eaten now."

When they opened the pot they found no meat. They found only dung, for Hlakanyana had filled the pot with dung.

Then the men said: "Who has done this?

Hlakanyana answered: "It must be the old man who is sleeping there."

They looked, and saw the bone by the side of the old man, and the fat on his mouth. Then they said: "This is the thief." They were intending to kill the old man because he had stolen the meat of the chief.

When the children saw that the old man was to be killed, they said that he did not eat the meat of the chief.

The men said: "We saw fat on his mouth and a bone beside him."

The children replied: "He did not do it."

The men said: "Tell us who did it."

The children answered: "Hlakanyana ate the meat and put dung in the pot. We were concealed, and we saw him do it."

Hlakanyana denied. He said: "Let me go and ask the women; perhaps they saw who ate the meat of the chief."

The men sent a young man with him to the women; but when they were a short distance away, Hlakanyana escaped.

The chief sent an army after him. The army pursued, and saw Hlakanyana sitting by a bush. They ran to catch him. When they came to the bush, only an old woman was sitting there.

They said to her: "Where is Hlakanyana?"

The old woman replied: "He just went across that river. See, you must make haste to follow him, for the river is rising."

The army passed over the river quickly. Then that old woman turned into Hlakanyana again. He said in himself: "I will now go on a journey, for I am wiser than the councillors of my father, I being older than they."

The little cunning fellow went to a village, where he saw an old woman sitting beside her house.

He said to her: "Would you like to be made young, grandmother?"

The old woman replied: "Yes, my grandchild; if you could make me young, I would be very glad."

Hlakanyana said: "Take that pot, grandmother, and go for some water."

The old woman replied: "I cannot walk."

Hlakanyana said: "Just try, grandmother; the river is close by, and perhaps you will be able to reach it."

The old woman limped along and got the water.

Then Hlakanyana took a large pot and set it on the fire, and poured the water into it.

He said to the old woman: "You must cook me a little first, and then I will cook you a little."

The old woman agreed to that. Hlakanyana was the first to be put in the pot. When the water began to get hot, he said: "Take me out, grandmother; I am in long enough."

The old woman took him out, and went in the pot for her turn. Soon she said: "Take me out now, my grandchild; I am in long enough."

Hlakanyana replied, "Not yet, grandmother; it is not yet time."

So the old woman died in the pot.

Hlakanyana took all the bones of the old woman and threw them away. He left only the toes and the fingers. Then he took the clothing of the old woman and put it on. The two sons of this old woman came from hunting.

They went into the hut, and said, "Whose meat is this in the pot?"

Hlakanyana was lying down. He said in a voice like that of their mother: "It is yours, my sons."

While they were eating, the younger one said: "Look at this, it is like the toe of mother."

The elder one said: "How can you say such a thing? Did not mother give us this meat to eat?"

Again the younger one said: "Look at this, it is like the finger of mother."

Hlakanyana said: "You are speaking evil of me, my son."

Hlakanyana said in himself: "I shall be discovered; it is time for me to flee." So he slipped quietly out of the house and went on his way. When he got a little way off, he called out: "You are eating your mother. Did anyone ever see people eating their mother before?"

The two young men took their assagais and ran after him with their dogs. They came to the river; it was full.

The cunning fellow changed himself into a little round stone. One of the young men picked up this stone, saying: "If I could see him, I would just throw this stone at him." The young man threw the stone over the river, and it turned into Hlakanyana again. He just laughed at those young men.

Hlakanyana went on his way. He was singing this song:

> *"I met with Nonothloya.*
> *We cooked each other,*
> *I was half cooked,*
> *She was well cooked."*

Hlakanyana met a boy tending some goats. The boy had a digging stick with him.

Hlakanyana proposed that they should pursue after birds, and the boy agreed. They pursued birds the whole day.

In the evening, when the sun set, Hlakanyana said: "It is time now to roast our birds."

The place was on the bank of a river.

Hlakanyana said: "We must go under the water and see who will come out last."

They went under the water, and Hlakanyana came out last.

The cunning fellow said: "Let us try again."

The boy agreed to that. They went under the water. Hlakanyana came out quickly and ate all the birds. He left the heads only. Then he went under the water again. The boy came out while he was still under the water.

When Hlakanyana came out he said: "Let us go now and eat our birds."

They found all the birds eaten.

Hlakanyana said: "You have eaten them, because you came out of the water first, and you have left me the heads only."

The boy denied having done so, but Hlakanyana said: "You must pay for my birds with that digging stick."

The boy gave the digging stick, and Hlakanyana went on his way.

He saw some people making pots of clay. He said to them: "Why do you not ask me to lend you this digging stick, instead of digging with your hands?"

They said: "Lend it to us."

Hlakanyana lent them the digging stick. Just the first time they stuck it in the clay it broke.

He said: "You have broken my digging stick, the digging stick that I received from my companion, my companion who ate my birds and left me with the heads."

They gave him a pot.

Hlakanyana carried the pot till he came to some boys who were herding goats. He said to them: "You foolish boys, you only suck the goats, you don't milk them in any vessel; why don't you ask me to lend you this pot?

The boys said: "Lend it to us."

Hlakanyana lent them the pot. While the boys were milking, the pot broke. Hlakanyana said: "You have broken my pot, the pot that I received from the people who make pots, the people who broke my digging stick, the digging stick that I received from my companion, my companion who ate my birds and left me with the heads."

The boys gave him a goat.

Hlakanyana came to the keepers of calves.

He said to them: "You foolish fellows, you only sit here and eat nothing. Why don't you ask me to let you suck this goat?"

The keepers of calves said: "Allow us to suck this goat."

Hlakanyana gave the goat into their hands. While they were sucking, the goat died.

Hlakanyana said: "You have killed my goat, the goat that I received from the boys that were tending goats, the boys that broke my pot, the pot that I received from the people who make pots, the people who broke my digging stick, the digging stick that I received from my companion, my companion who ate my birds and left me with the heads."

They gave him a calf.

Hlakanyana came to the keepers of cows.

He said to them: "You only suck the cows without letting the calf suck first. Why don't you ask me to lend you this calf, that the cows may be induced to give their milk freely?"

They said: "Lend us the calf."

Hlakanyana permitted them to take the calf. While the calf was in their hands it died.

Hlakanyana said: "You have killed my calf, the calf that I received from the keepers of calves, the keepers of calves that killed my oat, the goat that I received from the boys that were tending goats, the boys that broke my pot, the pot that I received from the people who make pots, the people who broke my digging stick, the digging stick that I received from my companion, my companion who ate my birds and left me with the heads."

They gave him a cow.

Hlakanyana continued on his journey. He saw a young man going the same way.

He said: "Let us be companions and travel together."

The young, man agreed to that. They came to a forest.

Hlakanyana said: "This is the place for picking up kerries [a traditional southern African tribal walking stick]."

They picked up kerries there.

Then they reached another place, and Hlakanyana said: "This is the place for throwing away kerries."

They threw the kerries away.

Again they came to another place, and Hlakanyana said: "This is the place for throwing away spoons."

The companion of Hlakanyana threw his spoon away, but the cunning little fellow only pretended to throw his away. In fact, he concealed his spoon. They went on.

They came to another place, and Hlakanyana said: "This is the place for throwing knives away."

It happened again as with the spoons. Hlakanyana concealed his knife, when his companion threw his away.

They came to a certain place, and Hlakanyana said, "This is the place for throwing away izilanda [awls used to make holes in skins when they are sewed together, and also for taking thorns out of the bare feet and legs of pedestrians]."

His companion threw his izilanda away, but Hlakanyana kept his. They went on and reached a place where they had to walk on thorns. Afterwards they looked at their feet, and saw many thorns in them.

Hlakanyana said: "Let us sit down and take out the thorns."

His companion replied, "I cannot do so, because I have no izilanda."

Then Hlakanyana took the thorns out of his feet, and the other was obliged to walk lame. They came to a village.

The people said to them: "Tell us the news."

Hlakanyana replied: "Just give us something to eat first; look at our stomachs and behold the pinchings of hunger."

The people of that village brought meat.

Hlakanyana said to his companion: "Now let us eat."

The companion of Hlakanyana answered: "I have no knife."

Hlakanyana said: "You are just a child; I shall not lend you my knife.'

The people of that village brought millet and put before them.

Hlakanyana said to his companion: "Why do you not eat?"

He answered: "I have no spoon."

Hlakanyana said: "You are just a child; I shall not lend you my spoon."

So Hlakanyana had all the meat and the millet to himself.

Hlakanyana met a girl herding some goats.

He said: "Where are the boys of your village, that the goats are herded by a girl?"

The girl answered: "There are no boys in the village."

He went to the father of the girl and said: "You must give me your daughter to be my concubine, and I will herd the goats."

The father of the girl agreed to that. Then Hlakanyana went with the goats, and every day he killed one and ate it till all were done. He scratched his body with thorns.

The father of the girl said: "Where are all the goats?"

Hlakanyana replied: "Can you not see how I have been fighting with the wild dogs? The wild dogs have eaten the goats. As for me, I will stay here no longer."

So he went on his way.

As he was going on, he saw a trap for catching birds. There were some birds in it. Hlakanyana took the birds out and ate them. The owners of the trap were cannibals. They saw the footprints of Hlakanyana, and said: "This is a little boy that is stealing our birds." They watched for him. Hlakanyana came again to the trap and saw a bird caught in it. He was just going to take the bird out when the cannibals caught him. They made a big fire and put a pot on for the purpose of cooking him. Hlakanyana saw two oxen. One was white, the other was red.

He said to the cannibals: "You can take which one of these oxen you like instead of me."

The cannibals said: "We will take the white one, because it is white inside also."

Then Hlakanyana went away with the red ox. The cannibals ate the white ox, and then pursued after Hlakanyana. They came up to him by a big stone. He jumped on the stone, and sang this song:

> *"I went to hear the news,*
> *About rain from the girls."*

The cannibals began to dance when they heard him sing. Then he ran away, and the stone continued to sing that song.

As he was journeying, Hlakanyana came to a place where some baboons were feasting. He asked them for some food.

The baboons replied: "If you will go for some water for us, we will give you food."

He agreed to that. When he returned with the water, the baboons refused to give him food. Then Hlakanyana shouted loudly and said: "At my village there is a marriage of baboons today."

When the baboons heard that they fled, old and young. So Hlakanyana remained there, and ate all the food.

As he was going along, he saw a hyena building a house, having cooked some meat.

Hlakanyana asked the hyena to give him some.

The hyena said: "No, I will not give you any; it is too little even for me."

Hlakanyana said: "Will you not have me to assist in building?"

The hyena replied: "I would have you without delay if you are intending to help me."

While they were fastening the thatch, Hlakanyana sewed the hair of the tail of the hyena fast. Then he took the pot and sat down.

The hyena said: "Let that pot alone, Hlakanyana."

He replied: "I am going to eat now."

The hyena wanted to come down, but he found his tail was fast, Hlakanyana ate all the meat, and threw the bones at the hyena. The hyena tried to frighten him by saying there were many hyenas coming quickly to devour him. He just answered: "That is false;" and continued eating till the meat was finished. Then he went on his way.

Hlakanyana came to a river. He saw an iguana that was playing on an ugwali [a simple musical instrument].

Hlakanyana said to the iguana: "Lend me your ugwali for a little, please."

The iguana said: "No, you will run away with my ugwali."

Hlakanyana replied: "How can I run away with a thing that is not mine?"

So the iguana lent him the ugwali. When Hlakanyana saw that he could play upon the instrument nicely, he ran away with it. The iguana pursued him. Then Hlakanyana changed himself into a rush. The iguana took that rush and threw it across the river, saying: "If I could only see him, I would throw him like this." Then the rush turned to be Hlakanyana again, and he went on his way playing on the ugwali of the iguana.

Hlakanyana came to the house of a leopardess. He proposed to take care of her children while the leopardess went to hunt animals. The leopardess agreed to that. There were four cubs. After the leopardess had gone to hunt, Hlakanyana took one of the cubs and ate it.

At the time for giving food, the leopardess came back and said: "Give me my children that I may suckle them."

Hlakanyana gave one.

The mother said: "Give all at once."

Hlakanyana replied: "It is better that one should drink and then another."

The leopardess agreed to that. After three had drunk he gave the first one back the second time. Then the leopardess went to hunt again.

Hlakanyana took another of the cubs and ate it. He also made the door of the house very small so that the mother of the cubs could not come in, and then he made a little hole in the ground at the back so that he could go out. The next day the leopardess came to give her children suck. There were only two left now. Hlakanyana gave them both back the second time. After that the leopardess went away as before.

Hlakanyana ate another of the cubs, so that only one was left. When the mother came, he gave this one four times. When he gave it the last time the leopardess said: "Why does my child not drink today?" It was already full, and did not want to drink more.

Hlakanyana replied: "I think this one is sick."

The mother said: "You must take good care of it."

Hlakanyana promised to do so, but when the leopardess was gone he ate that one also.

The next day when the leopardess came there was no cub left to give her. She tried to get in the house, but the door was too small. She sat down in front to watch. Then Hlakanyana went out through the hole he had made in the ground behind. The leopardess saw him and ran after him. He went under a big rock, and cried out loudly for help, saying the rock was falling.

The leopardess said: "What is that you are saying?"

Hlakanyana replied: "Do you not see that this rock is falling? Just hold it up while I get a prop and put under it."

The leopardess went to hold the rock up, and Hlakanyana did not return. He just ran away from that place.

Hlakanyana came to the village of the animals. The animals had trees that bore fruit. There was one tree that belonged to the chief of the animals only. This tree was a very good one, bearing much fruit on it. One day when all the animals were assembled, Hlakanyana asked them the name of the tree of the chief. They did not know the name of that tree. Then Hlakanyana sent a monkey to the chief to ask the name of the tree. The chief told the monkey. As the monkey was returning he struck his foot against a stone and fell down, which caused him to forget the name of the tree.

In the night when all were sleeping, Hlakanyana went up the tree of the chief and ate all the fruit of it. He took a branch of the tree and fastened it to one of the monkeys. In the morning when the animals awoke and found that the tree of the chief was finished in the night, they asked each other: "What became of the fruit of the chief's tree? What became of the fruit of the tree of the chief?"

Hlakanyana looked at the monkey with the branch on him, and said: "It is eaten by the monkey, it is eaten by the monkey; look at the branch on him."

The monkey denied, and said I don't know anything about it. I never ate the fruit of the tree of the chief."

Hlakanyana said: "Let us make a plan to find out who ate the fruit of the tree of the chief."

All the animals agreed to this.

Hlakanyana said: "Let us put a rope from one rock to another, and let all go over it. He that has eaten the fruit of the tree will fall down from that rope."

One of the monkeys went over first. The next was Hlakanyana himself. He went over carefully and avoided falling. It came to the turn of that monkey with the branch on. He tried to go, but when he was in the middle he fell down.

Hlakanyana said: "Therefore I have told you that it is this monkey."

After that he went on his way.

Hlakanyana came to the house of a jackal. He asked for food, but the jackal said there was none. Then he made a plan.

He said to the jackal: "You must climb up on the house and cry out with a loud voice, 'We are, going to be fat today because Hlakanyana is dead.'"

The jackal did so. All the animals came running to hear that news. They went inside the house, because the door was open. Then Hlakanyana shut the door, and the animals were caught. After that Hlakanyana killed the animals and ate.

Hlakanyana returned to the home of his father again. He was told that his sister was gone away for some red clay. When she was returning he shouted: "Let all the black cattle which have white teeth be killed. The daughter of my father is coming who has white teeth."

The chief said: "What is the matter with you, Hlakanyana?"

He just repeated the same thing.

The chief said: "Let a black ox be killed, but you must not break any of its bones, because it belongs to the daughter of a chief."

So Hlakanyana got fat meat to eat that day.

Hlakanyana went one day to tend the calves of his father. He met a tortoise.

He said: "Where are you going to, tortoise?"

The tortoise answered: "To that big stone."

Hlakanyana said: "Are you not tired?"

The tortoise replied: "No, I am not tired."

Hlakanyana took it and put it on his back. Then he went to the house of his mother.

His mother said: "What have you got there, my son?"

Hlakanyana answered: "Just take it off my back, mother."

The tortoise held fast to Hlakanyana, and would not be pulled off. His mother then heated some fat and poured on the tortoise. The tortoise let go quickly, and the fat fell on Hlakanyana and burnt him, so that he died. That is the end of this cunning little fellow.

The Story of Demane and Demazana
(From the Xhosa people, South Africa)

ONCE UPON A TIME a brother and sister, who were twins and orphans, were obliged on account of ill-usage, to run away from their relatives. The boy's name was Demane, the girl's Demazana.

They went to live in a cave that had two holes to let in air and light, the entrance to which was protected by a very strong door, with a fastening inside. Demane went out hunting by day, and told his sister that she was not to roast any meat while he was absent, lest the cannibals should discover their retreat by the smell. The girl would have been quite safe if she had done as her brother commanded. But she was wayward, and one day she took some buffalo meat and put it on a fire to roast.

A cannibal smelt the flesh cooking, and went to the cave, but found the door fastened. So he tried to imitate Demane's voice, and asked to be admitted, singing this song:

> *"Demazana, Demazana,*
> *Child of my mother,*
> *Open this cave to me.*
> *The swallows can enter it.*
> *It has two apertures."*

Demazana said: "No. You are not my brother; your voice is not like his."

The cannibal went away, but after a little time came back again, and spoke in another tone of voice: "Do let me in, my sister."

The girl answered: "Go away, you cannibal; your voice is hoarse, you are not my brother."

So he went away and consulted with another cannibal. He said: "What must I do to obtain what I desire?"

He was afraid to tell what his desire was, lest the other cannibal should want a share of the girl.

His friend said: "You must burn your throat with a hot iron."

He did so, and then no longer spoke hoarse. Again he presented himself before the door of the cave, and sang,

> *"Demazana, Demazana,*
> *Child of my mother,*
> *Open this cave to me.*
> *The swallows can enter it.*
> *It has two apertures."*

The girl was deceived. She believed him to be her brother come back from hunting, so she opened the door. The cannibal went in and seized her.

As she was being carried away, she dropped some ashes here and there along the path. Soon after this, Demane, who had taken nothing that day but a swarm of bees, returned and found his sister gone. He guessed what had happened, and followed the path by means of the ashes until he came to Zim's dwelling. The cannibal's family were out gathering firewood, but he was at home, and had just put Demazana in a big bag, where he intended to keep her till the fire was made.

Demane said: "Give me water to drink, father."

Zim replied: "I will, if you will promise not to touch my bag."

Demane promised. Then Zim went to get some water; and while he was away, Demane took his sister out of the bag, and put the bees in it, after which they both concealed themselves.

When Zim came with the water, his wife and son and daughter came also with firewood.

He said to his daughter: "There is something nice in the bag; go, bring it."

She went, but the bees stung her hand, and she called out: "It is biting."

He sent his son, and afterwards his wife, but the result was the same. Then he became angry, and drove them outside, and having put a block of wood in the doorway, he opened the bag himself. The bees swarmed out and stung his head, particularly his eyes, so that he could not see.

There was a little hole in the thatch, and through this he forced his way. He jumped about, howling with pain. Then he ran and fell headlong into a pond, where his head stuck fast in the mud, and he became a block of wood like the stump of a tree. The bees made their home in the stump, but no one could get their honey, because, when anyone tried, his hand stuck fast.

Demane and Demazana then took all Zim's possessions, which were very great, and they became wealthy people.

The Runaway Children; or, the Wonderful Feather
(From the Xhosa people, South Africa)

ONCE IN A TIME OF FAMINE a woman left her home and went to live in a distant village, where she became a cannibal.

She had one son, whose name was Magoda. She ate all the people in that village, until only herself and Magoda remained. Then she was compelled to hunt animals, but she caught people still when she could. In hunting she learned to be very swift of foot, and could run so fast that nothing she pursued could escape from her.

Her brother, who remained at home when she left, had two daughters, whom he did not treat very kindly. One day he sent them to the river for water, which they were to carry in two pots. These pots were made of clay, and were the nicest and most valuable in the village. One of the girls fell down on a rock and broke the pot she was carrying. Then she did not know what to do, because she was afraid to go back to her father. She sat down and cried, but that did not help, the pot would not be whole again.

Then she said to her sister: "Let us go away to another place, where our father will not be able to find us."

She was the younger and the cleverer of the two, and so she persuaded her sister. They walked away in the opposite direction from their home, and for two days had nothing but gum to eat. Then they saw a fire at a distance, and went to it, where they saw a house. It was the house of their aunt, but they did not know it. They were afraid to go in, but Magoda came out and talked to them. When he heard who they were, he was sorry for them, and told them their aunt was a cannibal, giving them advice not to stay there. But just then they heard her coming, so they went into Magoda's house and hid themselves, for he lived in one house and his mother in another.

The woman came and said: "I smell something nice; what is it, my son?"

Magoda said there was nothing.

She replied: "Surely I smell fat children."

But as she did not go in, they remained concealed that night.

The next morning, Nomagoda [so called because she was the mother of Magoda] went out to hunt, but she did not go far, so the children could not get away. They went into her house, where they saw a person with only one arm, one side and one leg.

The person said to them: "See, the cannibal has eaten the rest of me; take care of yourselves."

When it was nearly dark, Nomagoda came home again, bringing some animals which she had killed. She smelt that children had been in the house, so she went to her son's house and looked in.

She said to Magoda: "Why do you not give me some? Do I not catch animals for you?"

Then she saw the children, and was very glad. She took them to her house, and told them to sleep. They lay down, but were too frightened to close their eyes. They heard their aunt say, "Axe, be sharp; axe, be sharp;" and to let her know that they were awake, they spoke of vermin biting them.

After a while the cannibal went to sleep, when they crept out, first putting two blocks of wood in their places, and ran away as fast as they could. When Nomagoda awoke, she took the axe and went to kill them, but the axe fell on the blocks of wood.

As soon as it was day, the cannibal pursued the children. They looked behind, and saw clouds of dust which she made as she ran. There was a tall tree just in front of them, so they hastened to climb up it, and sat down among the branches. Nomagoda came to the tree and commenced to cut it down; but when a chip fell out, a bird [Ntengu, larger than a swallow and of a bright bluish-black colour. It may often be seen on the backs of cattle, seeking for insects on which it feeds] sang:

> *"Ntengu, ntengu,*
> *Chips, return to your places,*
> *Chips, return to your places,*
> *Chips, be fast."*

The chip then went back to its place and was fast again. This happened three times; but Nomagoda, who was very angry, caught the bird and swallowed it. When she put it in her mouth, one of the feathers dropped to the ground. Then she began to chop at the tree again; but as soon as a chip was loose the feather sang:

> *"Ntengu, ntengu,*
> *Chips, return to your places,*
> *Chips, return to your places,*
> *Chips, be fast."*

The chip then stuck fast again. The cannibal chopped till she was tired, but the feather continued to keep the tree from receiving harm. Then she tried to catch the feather, but it flew about too quickly for her, until she sank down exhausted on the ground at the foot of the tree.

The children, up in the branches, could see a long way off; and as they strained their eyes, they observed three dogs as big as calves, and they knew these dogs belonged to their father, who was seeking for them. So they called them by name, and the dogs came running to the tree and ate up the cannibal, who was too tired to make her escape.

Thus the children were delivered, and their father was so glad to get them back again that he forgave them for breaking the pot and running away.

The Story of Ironside and His Sister
(From the Xhosa people, South Africa)

A LONG TIME AGO a woman who went to cultivate her garden took her little daughter with her, and before she began to hoe the ground she laid the child down in the shade of a tree. About midday there came two birds and flew away with the girl. They carried her across a great river, and laid her gently down in a pumpkin field on a plain.

As the birds were carrying her away, she called to her mother, who took no notice of her cries, because she could not imagine her child was being carried away. In the afternoon the girl was missing, and her mother searched for her without success. She made inquiries of the neighbours, and some of them told her they had heard the child crying, "I am going away with the birds."

The plain on which the little girl was put down was near a town in which lived a nation of cannibals who had one leg much longer than the other. There she remained alone till the next day.

That night the chief of the cannibals dreamed that he saw a very pretty girl in that place; so in the morning he sent a party of men to look for her. When the girl saw them coming she was afraid, and hid herself among the pumpkins. But the men had already noticed where she was, so they easily found her, and took her home with them.

The chief was very much pleased with her appearance. He gave her to his mother to take care of, and when she grew up he took her to be his wife.

Afterwards she had two children, one very pretty, and with two legs like her own; the other ugly, and like its father, with one leg longer than the other. The cannibals saw the advantage of having two legs of equal length, and they became jealous of the woman and her child. They told the chief it would be dangerous to allow the child to grow up, because then a nation stronger than themselves might arise. They persuaded him to consent to her being put to death, and then they rejoiced greatly, because she was very fat, and they intended to eat her; but one of them, who had more compassion than the others, told the woman what they were about to do.

After the little girl had been taken away by the birds, her mother had a son, one of whose sides was flesh like other people's, and the other side was iron. His mother told him of his sister who was lost, and when he became a man he determined to go in search of her.

In his journey he came to a great river full of water. He had an iron rod in his hand, with which he struck the water, and at the same time he called out with a loud voice: "River, I have no sister. Be empty."

Then the river dried up, and he went safely across.

After this he came to the stream where the cannibals drew their water, and concealed himself among the reeds which grew on its banks. While there, his sister came to get water, and he at once knew who she was. She, of course, did not know him, but he told her he was her brother. Then she said the cannibals would eat him if he went to their town without an introduction. So they arranged that he should smear himself with mud and go to the top of a high hill, and when he was coming down she would tell the cannibals who he was.

Ironside went on the hill, and as soon as he came in sight of the town, his sister said: "There is the servant of the wife of the chief of the cannibals." These words she repeated twice.

When Ironside reached the town, a mat was brought to him and spread in front of his sister's house; but after a time he was allowed to go inside, still covered with mud.

The next day they all went to hunt, and Ironside killed more game than the others, upon which they became envious of him. This was shortly before the cannibals agreed to kill and eat the daughter of their chief. When the one who had compassion made known what was about to be done, Ironside was present and heard what was told. He said to his sister that she must pluck the hair from her head and scatter it about in different directions. This she did, after which Ironside and his sister and her child left the town in haste.

The cannibals came, and when they could not find the child they called her loudly by name. Then the tufts of hair all answered in her voice, and the seekers became confused.

Ironside and his companions, having two legs, could walk much quicker than the cannibals, and soon they were on the other side of the large river. The child trembled, and was very much frightened; but Ironside told her not to fear at all. After they had crossed, Ironside struck the river with his iron rod, and said: "River, I have found my sister. Be full." Then the water rose very high, quite to the top of the banks.

A party of cannibals who were in pursuit came to the river after it was full, and Ironside made a long rope, and threw the end over to them. They caught hold of it, thinking that he would pull them across; but when they were in the middle of the river he let go the rope, and they were all drowned. Another party then came and asked where their companions were. Ironside said they had gone to a ford further down; but they knew that was not true, so they returned home. Afterwards they discovered who it was that gave warning of their intentions, and they killed and ate that one.

Ironside took his sister home to her mother, who received her with the greatest joy, never having forgotten her during that long time.

The Story of the Cannibal Mother and Her Children
(From the Xhosa people, South Africa)

THERE WAS ONCE A MAN and a woman who had two children, a son and a daughter. These children lived with their grandfather. Their mother was a cannibal, but not their father.

One day they said to their grandfather: "We have been long with you, we should like very much to go and see our parents."

Their grandfather said: "Ho! will you be able to come back? Don't you know your mother is a cannibal?"

After a time he consented. He said: "You must leave at such a time that you may arrive there in the evening, so that your mother may not see you, only your father."

The boy's name was Hinazinci. He said: "Let us go now, my sister."

They started when the sun was set. When they arrived at their father's house, they listened outside to find out if their mother was there. They heard the voice of their father only, so they called to him. He came out, and when he saw them he was sorry, and said: "Why did you come here, my dear children? Don't you know your mother is a cannibal?"

Just then they heard a noise like thunder. It was the coming of their mother. Their father took them inside and put them in a dark corner, where he covered them with skins. Their mother came in with an animal and the body of a man. She stood and said: "There's something here. What a nice smell it has!"

She said to her husband: "Sohinazinci, what have you to tell me about this nice smell that is in my house? You must tell me whether my children are here."

Her husband answered: "What are you dreaming about? They are not here."

She went to the corner where they were, and took the skins away. When she saw them, she said: "My children, I am very sorry that you are here, because I must eat people."

She cooked for them and their father the animal she had brought home, and the dead man for herself. After they had eaten, she went out.

Then their father said to them: "When we lie down to sleep, you must be watchful. You will hear a dancing of people, a roaring of wild beasts, and a barking of dogs in your mother's stomach. You will know by that she is sleeping, and you must then rise at once and get away."

They lay down, but the man and the children only pretended to go to sleep. They were listening for those sounds. After a while they heard a dancing of people, a roaring of wild beasts and a barking of dogs. Then their father shook them, and said they must go while their mother was sleeping. They bade their father farewell, and crept out quietly, that their mother might not hear them.

At midnight the woman woke up, and when she found the children were gone, she took her axe and went after them. They were already a long way on their journey, when they saw her following them. They were so tired that they could not run.

When she was near them, the boy said to the girl: "My sister, sing your melodious song; perhaps when she hears it she will be sorry, and go home without hurting us."

The girl replied: "She will not listen to anything now, because she is in want of meat."

Hinazinci said: "Try, my sister; it may not be in vain."

So she sang her song, and when the cannibal heard it, she ran backwards to her own house. There she fell upon her husband, and wanted to cut him with the axe. Her husband caught hold of her arm, and said: "Ho! if you put me to death who will be your husband?"

Then she left him, and ran after the children again.

They were near their grandfather's village, and were very weak when their mother overtook them. The girl fell down, and the cannibal caught her and swallowed her. She then ran after the boy. He fell just at the entrance of his grandfather's house, and she picked him up and swallowed him also. She found only the old people and the children of the village at home, all the others being at work in the gardens. She ate all the people that were at home and also all the cattle that were there.

Towards evening she left to go to her own home. There was a deep valley in the way, and when she came to it she saw a very beautiful bird. As she approached it, the bird got bigger and bigger, until at last when she was very near it, it was as big as a house [i.e., a native hut].

Then the bird began to sing its song. The woman looked at it, and said to herself: "I shall take this bird home to my husband."

The bird continued its song, and sang:

> *"I am a pretty bird of the valley,*
> *You come to make a disturbance at my place."*

The bird came slowly towards her, still singing its song. When they met, the bird took the axe from the woman, and still sang the same song.

The cannibal began to be afraid.

She said to the bird: "Give me my axe; I do not wish for your flesh now."

The bird tore one of her arms off.

She said: "I am going away now; give me what is mine."

The bird would not listen to her, but continued its song.

She said again: "Give me my axe and let me go. My husband at home is very hungry; I want to go and cook food for him."

The bird sang more loudly than before, and tore one of her legs off.

She fell down and cried out: "My master, I am in a hurry to go home. I do not want anything that is yours."

She saw that she was in danger. She said to the bird again: "You don't know how to sing your song nicely; let me go, and I will sing it for you."

The bird opened its wings wide, and tore open her stomach. Many people came forth, most of them alive, but some were dead. As they came forth she caught them and swallowed them again. The two children were alive, and they ran away. At last the woman died.

There was great rejoicing in that country. The children returned to their grandfather, and the people came there and made them rulers of the country, because it was through them the cannibal was brought to death.

The girl was afterwards married to a son of the great chief, and Hinazinci had for his wife the daughter of that great one.

The Story of the Girl and the Mbulu
(From the Xhosa people, South Africa)

THERE WAS ONCE A WIDOW WOMAN who had one son and two daughters. On a certain day she went to her garden, taking with her one of the girls. While she was away the boy quarrelled with his sister and killed her.

In the course of the day the woman sent the girl that was with her to the hut, and when she came there a fly told her what had happened. She did not believe it.

Then a mouse told her the same thing, but still she did not believe it was true.

Afterwards the fly told her to look in a certain place, and there she saw the head and the bones of her sister.

When the woman came home and found out what had happened, she killed her son. Then she gave the girl a stick, and told her to go to her uncle's house, saying that when she got there she must strike the ground with the stick, and all the clothes and other things that belonged to her would then rise up out of the earth. The woman said she was now all alone, and therefore intended to kill herself.

The girl was very sorry, but she did as her mother told her. When she was a little way off, she looked back and saw smoke coming out of the hut, from which she knew that her mother had burned herself and was no longer a person under the sun.

After this she met an old woman, who called to her, but she took no heed and walked on. Next she met a mbulu [a creature that can assume the human form but cannot part with its tail; it never speaks the truth when it is possible to tell a falsehood.] at a place close by a river. The mbulu said, whoever wetted any part of their body in crossing the river must go in and bathe. The girl was standing on the bank, and the mbulu struck the water with its tail and splashed it in her face, so that she had to go in and bathe. Then the mbulu took her clothes and put them on.

When the girl came out of the water she asked for her clothes, but the mbulu said: "I will give them when you are dry."

So they went on together. After a while the girl asked again, and the mbulu said: "I will give them when we get to the village."

But when they arrived there the mbulu said: "You must tell the people here that you are my servant, and that I am the daughter of a chief."

The poor girl was so afraid that she promised to do so. They were well received at the village, because the people believed that the mbulu was a great person. They wondered at her voice, but she told them she had been ill and her throat was not well yet.

After a time one of the men of that kraal married the mbulu, and the real girl was sent to the gardens to drive the birds away from the corn. While engaged in this occupation she used to sing about the mbulu taking her clothes and passing itself off for a person, until the women who worked in the gardens took notice of this song of hers.

Then they made a plan to find out if what the girl was singing was the truth. They said: "The tail of a mbulu will want mice and fat," so they set snares to catch the mice. In the night the tail was pursuing mice, and itself got fast in a snare. The mbulu then asked the man who was married to her to go and get some medicine, as she was sick, and when the man went she took off the snare.

After this they made another plan. They said: "The tail of a mbulu will seek milk," so they dug a hole in the ground, put milk in it, and required everyone in the village to jump over the hole. The mbulu was unwilling at first, but they urged her. She tried to jump quickly, but the tail could not pass the milk. When it went down the people saw that this was a mbulu, so they killed it and buried it in that hole.

After this the same man who had married the mbulu took the girl to be his wife. She had a child, and one day, when it was playing, a square pumpkin came out of the ground where the mbulu was buried, and tried to kill the infant. But the people chopped the pumpkin in pieces, and burned it. They afterwards threw the ashes into a river, so that nothing more could come of that mbulu.

The Story of Mbulukazi
(From the Xhosa people, South Africa)

THERE WAS ONCE A MAN who had two wives, one of whom had no children, and for that reason she was not loved by her husband. Her name was Numbakatali. The other wife had one daughter who was very black, and several children besides, but they were all crows. The one who had no offspring was very downcast on that account, and used to go about weeping all day.

Once when she was working in her garden, and crying as usual, two doves came and perched near her. One of them said to the other: "Dove, ask the woman why she is crying." So the dove questioned her.

She replied: "It is because I have no children, and my husband does not love me. His other wife's children are crows, which come and eat my corn, and she laughs at me."

The dove said: "Go home and get two earthen jars, and bring them here."

Numbakatali went and got them. Then the doves scratched her knees till the blood flowed, and put the blood in the jars. The woman gave the doves some corn to eat, after which she took the jars home to her hut, and set them carefully down in a corner. Every day the two doves came to be fed, and always told the woman to look at what was in the jars.

At last, when she looked one day, she saw two children, one a boy, the other a girl, and both very handsome. She was very much delighted at the sight, but she did not tell anyone.

When the children grew a little she made a snug place for them in the hut, where they were to sit all day, because she did not wish them to be seen. Always before she went to her work she charged them not to go out, and as her husband never came to see her, no one knew of the existence of these children except herself and a servant girl.

But one day, when they were big, she went out, and after she was away some time, the boy said to his sister: "Come, let us help our mother by bringing water from the river."

So they went for water; but they had not reached the river when they met a company of young men with a chief's son, who was looking for a pretty girl to be his wife. The young chief was called Broad Breast, because his chest was very wide, and it was also made of a glittering metal that shone in the sun. These men asked for water to drink. The boy gave them all some water, but the young chief would only take it from the girl. He was very much smitten with her beauty, and watched her when she left, so as to find out where she lived.

As soon as the young chief saw the hut that the girl went to, he returned home with his party and asked his father for cattle with which to marry her. The chief, who was very rich, gave his son many fine cattle, with which the young man went to the girl's mother's husband, and said: "I want to marry your daughter."

So the girl who was very black was told to come, but the young chief said: "That is not the one I want; the one I saw was lighter in colour and much prettier."

The father replied: "I have no other children but crows."

But Broad Breast persisted, so the man called his wives, both of whom denied that there was such a girl. However, the servant girl went to the man and privately told him the truth. In the evening he went to his wife's hut, and to his great joy saw the boy and his sister. He was so delighted that he remained there that night, and after talking it over with his wife, he agreed to let Broad Breast marry the girl.

In the morning a mat was spread in the yard, and the young chief was asked to sit down. The two children and the servant girl who told their father about them were also called, and they all sat down on the mat.

The young chief, as soon as he saw her, said: "This is the girl I meant."

He stayed part of the day, and then with his attendants went to his father for more cattle, which, having obtained, he brought them to the father of the girl.

The mother of the very black girl and the crows was very jealous when she saw such a fine young chief coming with so many cattle. She wanted her daughter to be the one that was to be married; so she dressed her as finely as she could, but she had no such pretty clothes as the other girl had. Her name was Mahlunguluza, for she was called after the crows, who were the other children of her mother. The pretty girl's name was Mbulukazi, which name was given to her because her handsome dress was made of the skin of a mbulu.

The mother of Mahlunguluza spoke to the young chief about her daughter, and so he married both the girls. Their father gave to each an ox, with which they went to their new home. Mbulukazi's ox was a pretty young one, and Mahlunguluza's ox was an old and poor one. When they arrived, Broad Breast gave to Mbulukazi a very nice new house to live in, but to Mahlunguluza was given an old one quite in ruins.

Then the very black one saw she was not loved, and she became jealous, so she made a plan to kill her sister. One day she told her she heard their father was sick, and proposed that they should go to see him. Mbulukazi consented, and as soon as they obtained leave from their husband they left. Their road led them along the edge of a cliff, below which was a deep pool of water.

Mahlunguluza lay down on the rock, and said: "Come, see what is here in the water."

Her sister lay down with her head over the edge of the rock, when Mahlunguluza jumped up quickly and pushed her over. Mbulukazi sank in the water and was drowned. Then the very black one returned home, and when her husband asked where Mbulukazi was, she said that she was still with their father.

The next day the ox of the drowned one came running to the village and walked about lowing for a while, after which it tore down the old ruined house of Mahlunguluza with its horns. Its actions attracted the notice of the men, and they said: "Surely this ox means something, why is it doing this?"

Then it went to the deep pool of water, the men following it; it smelt all over the rock, and then jumped into the water and brought out the body of Mbulukazi. The ox licked her till her life came back, and as soon as she was strong once more, she told what had happened.

They all went home rejoicing greatly, and informed Broad Breast. When the young chief heard the story he was angry with Mahlunguluza, and said to her: "Go home to your father; I never wanted you at all; it was your mother who brought you to me."

So she had to go away in sorrow, and Mbulukazi remained the great wife of the chief.

The Story of Long Snake
(From the Xhosa people, South Africa)

ONCE UPON A TIME a certain girl left her father's place, and went to the village of Long Snake. Having arrived at the village of Long Snake she remained there, but the owner of the place was absent. The only person present was the mother of the owner of the place.

Then in the evening the mother of Long Snake gave that girl some millet, and told her to grind it. After it was ground she made bread. When it was ready the mother of Long Snake said: "Carry this bread into the house of Long Snake."

A short time after that girl went into the house, the owner of the place arrived. Then she gave him bread and fermented milk, and he ate. When they had finished the food they went to sleep. Then early in the morning Long Snake went away, because in the daytime he lived in the open country.

The girl went to the house of the parents of Long Snake. The mother of Long Snake clothed her with a very beautiful robe. After she was dressed she called for an axe, and went to cut firewood. Having arrived in the open fields she did not cut the firewood, but she threw away the axe and ran to her father's place.

When she arrived at her father's place, her sister asked for where she had got that beautiful robe. She told her, and her sister said: "I am going to that village too."

The girl said: "Just listen, and I will tell you the custom of that village."

But her sister said in reply: "I do not want you to tell me anything, because you yourself were not warned before you went."

Then she set off at once, and went on till she arrived in the evening at the village of Long Snake. When she sat down the mother of Long Snake gave her millet, telling her to grind it and make bread. When it was ready she took it into the house of Long Snake. Then in the evening the owner of the place arrived, and the girl gave him bread and fermented milk. When they had finished eating they went to sleep, and early in the morning Long Snake went away.

Then the girl went to the house of Long Snake's parents. His mother clothed that girl also in the same manner as she had dressed the elder one. Then she borrowed an axe and went to cut fuel. In doing so she made an excuse to run away.

On this day, however, the man went after his wives, and arrived at his father-in-law's place as the sun was setting.

They went out of the house that the bridegroom might sleep in it. While he was eating, the people of the village piled up bundles of grass, and the bridegroom was burned in the house. In this manner he died.

The Story of Kenkebe
(From the Xhosa people, South Africa)

THERE WAS ONCE a great famine in a certain country, and the people were obliged to eat wild plants to keep themselves alive. Their principal food during this time was nongwes, which they dug out of the ground.

There was living at that place a man called Kenkebe, and one day his wife said to him, "My husband, go to my father and ask him to give us some corn."

The man said, "Yes, I will go."

So he rose up early in the morning, and went on till he arrived at his father-in-law's village, where he was received with every mark of kindness. A very large ox was killed for his entertainment. It was so large that it was six days before it was all eaten. His father-in-law asked of him the news.

He said: "There is no news to tell to friends. All the news is this, that at my home there is not a grain to be eaten. Famine is over our heads. Will you give us some corn, for we are dying?"

His father-in-law gave him seven bags [i.e., skins of animals dressed entire] full of millet, and his wife's sisters went with him to carry them. When they came to a valley close by his home, he told his sisters-in-law that they could now go back to their father.

They said: "How will you manage to carry all those bags alone?"

He replied: "I shall be able to carry them all now, because we are not far from my home."

So those girls went back to their father.

Then he carried the bags one by one, and hid them in a cave under a great rock that was there. Afterwards he took some of the millet and ground it. When it was ground very fine he made it into cakes just like nongwes. Then he dug some real nongwes out of the ground, and went home to his wife.

He said to her: "There is a great famine at your father's also. I found the people there eating themselves."

He told his wife to make a fire. Then he pretended to cut a piece of meat out of his thigh, and said: "So are they doing at your father's village. Now, my wife, let us do the same."

His wife cut a piece from her leg and roasted it. The piece that Kenkebe put on the fire was some that he had brought home with him.

Then Kenkebe's little boy said: "Why does my father's meat smell nice in roasting, and my mother's meat does not smell nice?"

Kenkebe answered: "It is because it is taken from the leg of a man."

After this he gave his wife some nongwes to roast. He took for himself some of those he had made of corn.

The little boy said: "Why do my father's nongwes smell nice in roasting and my mother's do not smell nice?"

Kenkebe said: "It is because they were dug by a man."

After eating, he went outside, but he had dropped one of his nongwes by the fire. When he went out the boy found the nongwe. He broke it in two and gave half to his mother.

He said: "There is a difference between our nongwes and those of father's."

His mother said: "Yes, my child, this one is made of corn."

The next morning, just at the first beginning of dawn, Kenkebe got up and went away with a pot in his hand. The boy was awake, and saw his father go out. So he called to his mother, and said: "Mother, mother, wake, my father is going away with the pot in his hand."

So she got up, and they followed after Kenkebe. They saw him go to the cave where he took some corn out of one of the bags and began to grind it. Then they went on top of the rock, and rolled a big stone over.

When Kenkebe saw the stone coming he ran away, but it followed close behind him. He ran down the valley, the stone kept running too. He jumped into a deep hole in the river, down went the stone too. He ran up the hill, up went the stone also. He ran over the plain, but whenever he turned to look, the stone was there just behind him, So it continued all that day. At night he reached his own house, and then the stone stopped. His wife had already come home, and had brought with her one of the bags of corn.

Kenkebe came in crying.

His wife said to him: "Why do you cry as if you were a child?"

He said: "Because I am very tired and very hungry."

She said: "Where are your clothes and your bag?"

He replied, "I was crossing a river, and I fell down. The stream carried away my mantle, and my bag, and my kerries and everything that was mine."

Then his wife gave him his mantle, which she had picked up when he was running away, and she said to him: "You are foolish to do such things. There is no food for you tonight."

The next morning Kenkebe rose early and went out to hunt with his two dogs. The name of the one was Tumtumse, and the name of the other was Mbambozozele. He found an eland with a young calf, which he drove to his place. He cut an ear off the calf and roasted it in the fire. It was fat, and he liked it so much that he cut the other ear off and cooked it also. Then he wished to kill the calf, but he said to himself: "If I kill this calf I shall not be able to get milk from the eland."

So he called his two dogs, and said to the one: "Tumtumse, my dog, if I kill this calf, will you imitate it and suck the eland for me?"

The dog said: "No, I will bark like a dog."

Kenkebe said: "Get out of my sight and never come near me again you ugly, useless animal."

He said to the other, "Mbambozozele, my dog, if I kill this calf, will you imitate it and suck the eland for me?"

The dog said: "I will do so."

Then he killed the calf and ate it. He took the skin and put it upon Mbambozozele, so that the eland thought it was her calf that sucked before Kenkebe milked her. But one day the dog was sucking too long, and Kenkebe wanted him to leave off. He tried to drink just a few drops more, when his master got angry and struck him with a stick. Thereupon the dog began to howl, and the eland saw how she had been deceived. At once she ran after Kenkebe and tried to stick him with her horns. He ran one way and the eland ran after him, then he ran another way, and still the eland chased him.

His wife came out and saw him running. She cried out to him: "Jump up quickly on the big stone." He did so, and the eland ran with such fury against that stone that it broke its head and fell down dead.

They then cut the eland up and wanted to cook it, but there was no fire. Kenkebe said to his son: "Go to the village of the cannibals that is on that hill over the valley, and ask for some fire; but do not take any meat with you, lest they should smell it."

The boy went, but he hid a piece of meat and took it with him. When he got to the first house he asked for fire, but they sent him to the next. At the next they sent him farther, and so he had to go to the house that was farthest away. An old woman lived there. The boy gave her a little piece of meat, and said: "Do not cook it till I am far away with the fire."

But as soon as the boy was gone, she put it on the coals. The smell came to the noses of the cannibals, and they ran to the place and swallowed the old woman, and the meat, and the fire and even the ashes.

Then they ran after the boy. When he came near his own house, he cried out: "Hide yourselves, you that are at home."

His father said: "My son is saying, we must gather wood that will make coals."

His mother said: "No, he is saying we must hide ourselves."

The boy cried again: "Hide yourselves."

Then his mother hid herself in a bush: an old woman that was there covered herself with ashes, and Kenkebe climbed up into a tree, with the breast of the eland in his hand. The boy slipped into a hole that was by the side of the path.

The cannibals came to the place. First they ate the eland. Then one of them said: "Search under the ashes."

There they found the old woman, and they ate her. Then they said: "Search in the tree."

There they found Kenkebe. He cried very much, but they would not spare him. They ate him and the breast of the eland. Then the wise one said: "Look in the bush."

They looked there and found the wife of Kenkebe. They said: "We will eat her another time," and so they took her home with them. They did not look for the boy.

The woman made a plan to escape. She made beer for the cannibals, and they all came to drink. They sat together in a big house, and drank very much beer. Then she said: "Can I go out?"

They said: "You can go, but come back quickly."

She said: "Shall I close the entrance?"

They said: "Close it."

Then she took fire and put it on the house and all those cannibals were burnt to death. So the woman escaped, and afterwards lived happily with her son.

The Story of the Wonderful Horns
(From the Xhosa people, South Africa)

THERE WAS ONCE A BOY whose mother that bore him was dead, and he was ill-treated by his other mothers. On this account he determined to go away from his father's place. One morning he

went riding on an ox which was given to him by his father. As he was travelling, he came to a herd of cattle with a bull.

His ox said: "I will fight and overcome that bull."

The boy got off his ox's back. The fight took place, and the bull was defeated. The boy then mounted his ox again.

About midday, feeling hungry, he struck the right horn of his ox, and food came out. After satisfying his hunger, he struck the left horn, and the rest of the food went in again.

The boy saw another herd of dun-coloured cattle. His ox said: "I will fight and die there. You must break off my horns and take them with you. When you are hungry, speak to them, and they will supply you with food."

In the fight the ox was killed, as he had said. The boy took his horns, and went on walking till he came to a village where he found the people cooking a weed [called tyutu], having no other food to eat.

He entered one of the houses. He spoke to his horn, and food came out, enough to satisfy the owner of the house and himself. After they had eaten, they both fell asleep. The owner of the house got up and took away the horns. He concealed them, and put two others in their place.

The boy started next morning with the horns, thinking they were the right ones. When he felt hungry, he spoke to the horns, but nothing came out. He therefore went back to the place where he had slept the night before. As he drew near, he heard the owner of the place speaking to the horns, but without getting anything out of them.

The boy took his horns from the thief, and went on his way. He came to a house, and asked to be entertained. The owner refused, and sent him away, because his clothes were in tatters, and his body soiled with travel.

After that he came to a river and sat down on the bank. He spoke to his horns, and a new mantle and handsome ornaments came out. He dressed himself, and went on. He came to a house where there was a very beautiful girl. He was received by the girl's father, and stayed there. His horns provided food and clothing food for them all.

After a time he married the girl. He then returned home with his wife, and was welcomed by his father. He spoke to his horns, and a fine house came out, in which he lived with his wife.

The Story of the Great Chief of the Animals
(From the Xhosa people, South Africa)

T HERE WAS ONCE A WOMAN who had occasion to leave her home for a short time, and who left her children in charge of a hare. The place where they lived was close to a path, along which droves of wild animals were accustomed to pass.

Soon after the woman left, the animals appeared, and the hare at sight of them became frightened. So she ran away to a distance, and stood to watch. Among the animals was one terrible monster, which called to the hare, and demanded to know what children those were. The hare told their names, upon which the animal swallowed them entire.

When the woman returned, the hare told her what had happened. Then the woman gathered some dry wood, and sharpened two pieces of iron, which she took with her and went along the path.

Now this was the chief of the animals; therefore, when she came on a hill over against him, the woman began to call out that she was looking for her children. The animal replied: "Come nearer, I cannot hear you."

When she went, he swallowed her also. The woman found her children alive, and also many other people, and oxen and dogs. The children were hungry, so the woman with her pieces of iron cut some pieces of flesh from the animal's ribs. She then made a fire and cooked the meat, and the children ate.

The other people said: "We also are hungry, give us to eat."

Then she cut and cooked for them also.

The animal felt uncomfortable under this treatment, and called his councillors together for advice, but they could suggest no remedy. He lay down and rolled in the mud, but that did not help him, and at last he went and put his head in the kraal fence, and died.

His councillors were standing at a distance, afraid to approach him, so they sent a monkey to see how he was. The monkey returned and said: "Those whose home is on the mountains must hasten to the mountains;

those whose home is on the plains must hasten to the plains; as for me, I go to the rocks."

Then the animals all dispersed.

By this time the woman had succeeded in cutting a hole through the chief's side, and came forth, followed by her children.

Then an ox came out, and said: "Bo! bo! who helped me?"

Then a dogy who said: "Ho! ho! who helped me?

Then a man, who said: "Zo! zo! who helped me?"

Afterwards all the people and cattle came out. They agreed that the woman who helped them should be their chief.

When her children became men, they were out hunting one day, and saw a monstrous cannibal, who was sticking fast in a mud hole. They killed him, and then returned to tell the men of their tribe what they had done. The men went and skinned the cannibal, when a great number of people came out of him also. These joined their deliverers, and so that people became a great nation.